THE
PRINCESS PIRATE

BLADES
AND
BETRAYAL

THE PRINCESS PIRATE

BLADES AND BETRAYAL

STEVE CLENNEY

TATE PUBLISHING
AND ENTERPRISES, LLC

The Princess Pirate: Blades and Betrayal
Copyright © 2015 by Steve Clenney. All rights reserved.

No part of this publication may be reproduced, stored in a retrieval system or transmitted in any way by any means, electronic, mechanical, photocopy, recording or otherwise without the prior permission of the author except as provided by USA copyright law.

This novel is a work of fiction. Names, descriptions, entities, and incidents included in the story are products of the author's imagination. Any resemblance to actual persons, events, and entities is entirely coincidental.

The opinions expressed by the author are not necessarily those of Tate Publishing, LLC.

Published by Tate Publishing & Enterprises, LLC
127 E. Trade Center Terrace | Mustang, Oklahoma 73064 USA
1.888.361.9473 | www.tatepublishing.com

Tate Publishing is committed to excellence in the publishing industry. The company reflects the philosophy established by the founders, based on Psalm 68:11,

"The Lord gave the word and great was the company of those who published it."

Book design copyright © 2015 by Tate Publishing, LLC. All rights reserved.
Cover design by Joshua Rafols
Interior design by Manolito Bastasa

Published in the United States of America

ISBN: 978-1-68187-293-3
Fiction / Romance / Action & Adventure
15.10.05

To Caitlyn Dresser

Acknowledgments

Thanks to David Clenney, Charlene Stillman, Karen Barks, and God for making it all possible!

Contents

Part I

1. Jason Wells 17
2. Not My Friend Wells 20
3. That Was My Brother 23
4. Jack's Guilt Decision 26
5. You're Going to Die, Jack 30
6. That Was My Brother Jimmy 33
7. Making His Way Back to Pirates Cove 35
8. Going Back to the Castle and Being a Real Princess 37

Part II

9. Shandell Lee 43
10. The Runaway 45
11. Wise Prisoner 47
12. Bleeding Hands 51
13. Best First Mate I Ever Had 53
14. Like to Hurt Little Girls 56
15. The New Captain of the Ship 59
16. One Last Pirate to Find 61
17. The Dead Ship 63
18. Troy's Past 67
19. You Have to Do What You Have to Do ... 70
20. The Best Captain I've Ever Served 75
21. We Learn By Doing 80
22. Shandell Who? 82

23. Princess Who?..84
24. Meet a Fellow Swordswoman............................86
25. The Last Pirate...88

PART III

26. Shandell Lee Story (Continued).........................95
27. Rebekah and Shandell Meet...............................97
28. Troy Set Up for the Kill....................................101
29. You're a Coward, Shandell 104
30. Shandell, It's Finished.......................................107
31. The Sea Overrun by Women Pirate Raiders....110
32. Friends for Life..113
33. Pants a Little Snug..116

PART IV

34. A Taste of Love..121
35. No One's to Blame..123
36. Carlena, Rebekah's Sister, Falls in Love 125
37. The Betrayal...129
38. A Change of Plans..132
39. The **Black Rose** Out to Sea Again 134
40. Sam's Mutiny...137
41. The **Black Rose** Anchored at Freedom Port.......140
42. Getting a Message Back to Morgan.................143
43. Rebekah, You Will Stay....................................146
44. With a Mind like Morgan's..............................150
45. Look at You, Rebekah, Look at Your Dress ...153
46. Yea, Yea, Yea..158
47. There'll Be a Day...161
48. Flent's Life Ruined..162

Part V

49. Maddie 165
50. Terrible and Terrifying 167
51. The Princess Pirate Again 171
52. Tricked! 174
53. You Fool 176
54. There Is More to Life 178
55. Searching for Something? 180
56. Surprise! 183
57. You Killed My Sister 185
58. This Is Your New Home 189
59. Just Enough, Mr. Reese 192
60. The Search for the Princess and Jack 195
61. We Won't Hurt You, Princess 197
62. It Must Be the *Black Rose* 199
63. Thanked Them for What? 202
64. Micky the Doctor 204

Part VI

65. Love's Tightrope 209
66. First Spanish Ship 211
67. Death Knocks 215
68. Dr. Jack 218
69. The Letter 221
70. Courtney Grey Is My Name, Sir 229
71. Things Are Never What They Seem 234
72. I Ought to Kill You Where You Stand .. 236
73. Falling in Love 239
74. Joe Suspects Trouble 242
75. Out for Good Behavior 246
76. Returning Nightmare 249
77. Good-Bye, Angela 251

PART VII

78. The Patriot 255
79. A Day of Reckoning for Jack..................257
80. The Truth, Jack! 260
81. Not Getting Off That Easy 262
82. Rough Days Ahead on the *Black Rose* ...264
83. Drew Wilson Is the Name........................267
84. You're Not Him..271
85. Being Shadowed at Sea............................274
86. Has to Be a Reason...................................276
87. Very Observant 279
88. I'm a Patriot...282
89. All That Matters Now 285
90. Don't Push It 287

PART VIII

91. Morgan's Revenge 291
92. Death's Door Is Always Open.................294
93. The *Death Ship* at Sea 298
94. I'm Princess Ardola...................................302
95. Why Don't You Show Now?...................305
96. Oh, Jack..307
97. The Bigger They Are 309
98. The Pirate Plan..313
99. Good-Bye, Rebekah..................................316
100. Did You Love Her?...................................319
101. The Celebration..322

PART IX

102. One Evil and One Lazy 327
103. A Woman Scorned! 330
104. Licking Her Wounds................................332
105. Worthless Snake..336
106. A New Plan in the Works........................339

107. The *Drake* at the Cove 343
108. The Decision 347
109. The Princess Is on Her Way 349
110. A Leopard Doesn't Change His Spots 351
111. Double Betrayal 355
112. Ms. Stewart, We Could've Saved Him 358

PART X

113. Jack Returns Home 367
114. Rebekah Regains Her Self-Confidence 369
115. Not Always Smooth Sailing 374
116. Stealing, Killing, and Breaking the Law 377
117. Two Hangings Too Many 384
118. The Boot on the Other Foot 392

PART I

1
Jason Wells
1673

The short winter had passed on the high seas. Rebekah and her crew were eager to get back to sea and raid ships. While at sea, Jack was in Rebekah's cabin; they were discussing the cargo ship called the *Charlotte*.

"All right, Jack, you've explained to me that this ship is well manned and we should take extra caution with the captain and its crew."

"Yes, Princess, I sailed with this captain Pierce once, and he is no pushover. I'd like to pass this ship up because of the uncertainty of the outcome." (Unknown to Jack at this time, the *Charlotte* was under command of a new captain.)

Rebekah, with a smirk, said to Jack, "You're getting soft in your old age, Jack, and maybe you should retire from pirating."

"This is serious, Princess, and it's against my better judgment, but you're giving the orders."

"How many days before we intercept the *Charlotte*, Jack?"

"According to this chart Jake sold us, about four days if we don't run into rough weather."

"Jack, you keep things in order on my ship, and I'll take care of the rest."

Leaving Rebekah's cabin, Jack had an uneasy feeling about raiding the *Charlotte*.

Maybe the princess was right, Jack thought, *maybe I'm getting too old for pirating.*

As days passed, the men were feeling a little uneasy as though something bad was going to happen. Joe was mending another sail when Randy walked over and asked, "Are you having uneasy feelings about this trip, Joe?"

"What kind of uneasy feeling, Randy?"

"You know, Joe, that pirate feeling of something bad is going to happen but you don't know where or when."

Joe laid his tool down, giving Randy a stare. "Look, Randy, I've been pirating for over twenty years and have seen a lot of things, some strange and some not so strange. And no, I don't have that feeling."

"Why do I feel like this, Joe, and also the other men?"

"Listen, Randy, I'm not superstitious or believe in all of those pirate tales that have spread across the seas, so I really don't care. Randy, one thing I do fear is the princess getting upset when a job isn't finished when it is supposed to be. So leave me alone, Randy, and let me finish repairing this sail."

Later, Randy and all of Rebekah's men except Joe were at the other end of the ship talking about the strange feeling that has come over the ship's crew. Randy was doing most of the talking. "I don't know about all of you men, but I think we should tell the princess to turn back."

Curt gazed over at Pete and asked, "What do you think, Pete?"

"I'm not sure about all of this myself, Curt."

Jack, seeing the men all gathered together, asked, "What's going on here, a knitting party? Or are you men planning a mutiny?"

Randy told Jack what they were discussing and wanted him to ask the princess to turn back. Jack couldn't deny what he felt, but he couldn't let this fear continue. So he had to put a stop to it now before the men become unhinged and start to imagine things.

"Now you men listen to me. Things are getting out of hand over all of this talk of fear. The more you continue to talk about these things, the more fear it builds."

Louie spoke up, "There's something wrong, Jack, and I can see it in your face also."

Jack let out a deep breath. "So why doesn't Joe feel it?"

"We don't know about Joe, but we do feel uncomfortable about this next raid."

Jack stood there and couldn't believe this talk coming from men who have faced all dangers and never showed an ounce of fear until now.

"What's gotten into you men, are you pirates or not?" Jack looked at the fear in their faces.

The men looked at each other and said, "What has gotten into us?"

Jack, building their confidence, said, "We're pirates and are afraid of nothing. I hope you men don't let this fear grab a hold onto you again. The princess needs fighters, not women."

"We get the message, Jack. We won't buckle under superstition talk again. When we take that ship, the princess will be proud of us as always."

Even after feeling better about the men, Jack couldn't shake the uneasy feeling he had; it wasn't superstition that bothered him. It was as though he were going to meet his destiny.

The final day came, and the *Black Rose* was locked up to the *Charlotte*. Rebekah's men were magnificent as always with their swords. Rebekah never missed a beat with her sword as she cut the sailors down one by one. Jack was doing well also until he got into a sword fight with the captain of the ship—a different man, not Pierce who Jack was expecting, but the captain of the ship *Charlotte* was a man Jack once knew, a Tom Wells, an old friend who once saved his brother Chad's life.

NOT MY FRIEND WELLS
1673

WHILE THEY WERE fighting, Jack yelled out to Tom, "It's me, Jack Reese, you're sword fighting against, please stop." Tom didn't recognize Jack and kept on swinging and was doing his best on trying to kill Jack.

Jack was between a rock and a hard place while defending himself and trying not to hurt Tom, but Tom just didn't recognize Jack, and as far as Tom was concerned, Jack was just another pirate. Jack kept on backing up until he was against a wall and was trapped. Tom took a swing at Jack, but Jack, by reflex, came back with his sword and cut Tom down. Jack stood there in total disbelief; he killed his friend, the man who saved his brother's life.

All the fighting was over when Jack went back to where Rebekah was standing. Rebekah noticed the look in Jack's face as though he killed his best friend. Rebekah, observing Jack, said, "What's wrong, Jack? Are you sick?"

Jack lowered his head and said, "I just killed an old friend and didn't mean to."

Rebekah, feeling sorry for Jack, told him, "Go back to the ship, Jack, and when all of the gold is loaded, I'll meet you there later."

Thirty minutes later, all the gold was loaded onto the *Black Rose* and she was back out to sea. Rebekah rushed to Jack's cabin to see about him. Rebekah knocked, but there was no answer.

She knocked again. Still no answer. She opened the door and saw Jack sitting at his desk with his hands up against his face. Feeling Jack's sorrow, Rebekah said, "Please, Jack, look at me and say something."

Jack slowly raised his head and said, "I killed a friend, Rebekah, a close friend, a friend who saved my brother Chad's life at one time. I killed him Rebekah. I just run him through with my sword."

"Did he know it was you, Jack, that he was fighting with?"

"I tried to tell him who I was, Rebekah, but he just kept coming at me with his sword as though he didn't recognize me." Jack put his hands back up against his face and said nothing else.

Rebekah said, "Jack, Jack."

Jack just sat there. Rebekah didn't even go to an island to bury the gold. If possible, she'd give it all back if it would change what had happened. She ordered the ship to Pirates Cove from there.

The next few days, Jack just stayed in his cabin; he didn't eat or drink anything the whole trip back to Pirates Cove. The third day, Rebekah asked Joe, "Has Jack eaten anything today?"

"Jack just sits there at his desk and stares and says nothing, Princess."

Rebekah, having enough, said, "Joe, if Jack is trying to starve himself to death because of guilt, he's mistaken. We'll force-feed him if necessary."

Rebekah walked into Jack's cabin and stood in front of him. "You listen to me, Jack. I'm not going to let you starve to death over this grief you feel. Are you listening to me, Jack? Or am I going to have the men force-feed you? You better speak to me, Jack, or I'm going to get the men down here."

Jack, showing a soft grin, said, "I'll eat something now, Princess, and you won't have to force-feed me."

Rebekah was relieved. "I'm glad of that, Jack, and I'll have Micky fix a good hot meal for you."

One day later, the *Black Rose* was sitting back in the cove and Rebekah was over at the post telling Jake all that happened.

"Do you think Jack will be all right, Princess?"

"I don't know, Jake, he has started eating again. He does his duties around the ship, but Jack isn't the same as before by any means."

Jake, taking a drink, said, "I once had a friend that this sort of thing happened to, and in time, he did get over it. He finally accepted the fact all of the grieving in the world couldn't change what had happened."

"I hope Jack gets over this in time, Jake. I need him at his best before I even try to raid another ship."

During this time, Rebekah had her men make what needed repairs on the *Black Rose*. She told them to enjoy their free time at the post until Jack was ready, and then they'd get back to business as usual.

After a couple of days of rest, Jack said to Rebekah, "I'm feeling much better, Princess, and I'm ready to get back out to sea and raid our next ship."

Rebekah thought, *Jack, after the way he was feeling, was better too soon.* She had her men keep an eye on Jack at least for now.

Rebekah was in Jake's office purchasing another chart. The *Cargo Queen* was delivering bullion to a nearby country.

THAT WAS MY BROTHER
1673

BACK IN OLD England, Morgan was going over the last report on the *Charlotte* that the princess just raided and took all the gold bullion. This time, there was something else in the report that gave Morgan indigestion: the captain was killed on this raid. Morgan knew if he didn't change jobs, he was going to get ulcers from this one. One relief to Morgan was Hendrexson was busy with the Brits and France helping with their new laws. That kept Hendrexson off Morgan's back. Morgan sat down to sign the report when one of the other council members walked in with a man whose name was Jason Wells.

"Sir Morgan, I'd like for you to meet Jason Wells. His brother was captain of the *Charlotte*, and he is here to get more information on what happened on that ship."

"What can I tell him, Sir Thomas, that hasn't been written in the report already?"

"Well, Morgan, you've had more experience with the Princess Pirate than anyone else. Just maybe you can give Mr. Wells here some information that will help in his quest to bring in the pirate that killed his brother."

"What can I tell you that you don't already know, Mr. Wells?"

"It's very simple, Sir Morgan. Give me all of the information on the princess and her men that you have."

An hour passed when Morgan was finished. "That's all there is, Mr. Wells." Morgan laid the papers on his desk. "I don't know if there's anything there that can help you."

With a confident look, Wells said, "The information I just received tells me the pirate who killed my brother."

Morgan was totally in the dark himself and asked, "How do you know who and how?"

"It says here the first mate on the *Charlotte* heard the man's name called who killed my brother. It was the princess who called him by the name Jack!"

"Wells, wait a minute. I may have something else that might confirm what you've said." Morgan went through some more old folders when he came across a paper that goes back one year. "Here it is, Mr. Wells. A Jack Reese is his name, and he's the princess's first mate."

While reading the paper, Wells repeated to himself, "Reese, Jack Reese."

"One question, Mr. Wells."

"What's that, Sir Morgan?"

"You'll be going against the princess and her sword if you try going after her first mate. I hear they have a little love affair going on between them.

"If you think she'll give him up without a fight, you're dead wrong, Wells. She'll run her blade through you before giving him up."

"That was my brother Jack Reese killed, Sir Morgan, and I'll risk my life bringing in Jack or kill him for killing my brother. He'll die one way or the other, Sir Morgan. It's just a matter of time. Good day to you, Sir Morgan."

Morgan thought this was a good time to have a drink. *If this Jason Wells is successful,* Morgan thought, *he just might get the princess as a bonus.* Morgan took two drinks and said to himself, "Probably not," but it was a nice thought at the time.

Jason went to the room where he was staying and did a lot of thinking before going after this Jack Reese. Jason would stay around parliament for a while just to clear his mind for now.

The *Black Rose* was back out to sea, and Jack convinced Rebekah he was doing fine. But Rebekah still had her men keep an eye on Jack. One day, Jack was trying to be by himself when he noticed Troy following him everywhere he went on the ship. Jack walked around the standing cabin and waited for Troy to follow him around.

Jack stood there, and as Troy came around the corner, Jack grabbed Troy by the collar, threw him up against the wall, and yelled out, "Why are you following me, Troy?"

Troy, caught off guard, answered, "I'm not following you, Jack."

Jack was furious. "If you don't tell me the truth, Troy, I'm going to ram your head up against this wall until your brains fall out."

Rebekah, now standing behind Jack, ordered, "Jack, let Troy down. I gave him orders to follow you. Now release him."

Troy, rubbing his throat and coughing, said, "I'm sorry, Princess."

"Don't worry about it Troy, I'll take care of things from here."

Jack asked, "All right, Rebekah, why do you have the men watching me and my every move?"

"Jack, I'm concerned about you."

"What is it, Rebekah? You think I'm going to jump over the railing and drown myself?" he said. "Well, Rebekah, tell me!"

Rebekah stood there, surprised that Jack would've ever spoken to her that way. "I'm sorry, Jack," she said. "I'll tell the men to stop and for you to go about your business." Rebekah, with hurt and despair showing on her face, went back to her cabin.

JACK'S GUILT DECISION
1673

THE NEXT DAY, the *Black Rose* anchored outside the port of Jamestown. Jack and two of the men were rowing to the dock. He said to them, "I'm going to turn myself into the authorities, and when you return to the ship, you tell Rebekah to leave and forget about me."

Pete and Curt told him, "We can't let you do that, Jack."

Jack raised his pistol. "Pete, you and Curt have no choice. Curt, you row this boat up to the dock if you don't want a bullet in your brother's heart."

Curt did what Jack told him to do. Curt knew Jack would never shoot him or his brother, but in Jack's state of mind, Jack doesn't know what he's doing at this time.

Jack, now standing on the dock, said, "Thanks for not making me shoot you both. Tell the princess I have to do this for my own peace of mind. Also, tell her to forgive me, and tell her I'll always love her."

Jack walked away, and Pete and Curt rowed back to the ship.

When Jack entered the constable's office, the man behind the desk asked, "Yes, what can I do for you, mister?"

"My name is Jack Reese, and I'm here to give myself up for being charged for murder at the port of Emerson four years ago." Standing there, Jack let them put locks on his wrists as they took him and put him in a cell.

When Pete and Curt returned to the ship, they told Rebekah what Jack had done. Rebekah said to her men, "You men and I are going after Jack."

Pete blocked Rebekah's way and replied, "It won't work, Princess, if we try to bring Jack back."

Rebekah drew her sword and said, "Pete, get out of my way if you don't want to be run through."

Pete, still blocking Rebekah's way, said, "You, Princess, can kill me if you like, but it's too late for Jack. If we try to break him out and he won't leave, then we stand the chance of being caught and arrested."

Rebekah lowered her sword and said, "You're right Pete, and I'm sorry for threatening you."

"I understand, Princess, and I'm sorry for you losing Jack."

Rebekah just couldn't leave Jack but knew that in his frame of mind, he wouldn't return with them. Feeling like she lost her father all over again, Rebekah ordered the *Black Rose* back to Pirates Cove.

Back in Jack's cell, they removed the locks and asked Jack more questions.

"It reads in this report, Mr. Reese, you killed a Frenchman named Marcel Brit. Do you admit it now, because you claimed it was in self-defense before?"

"I still claim it was in self-defense, but now I'll face a trial and accept what punishment they decide to give me."

"All right, Mr. Reese. Just for your information, your turning yourself in could help you get life in prison instead of a death sentence." At this time, Jack didn't care which.

Back in England, Jason Wells, just after a few days, learned of Jack giving himself up to the authorities at Jamestown. Wells knew he had to act fast if he was to get to Jamestown first and get Jack and complete his plans. Jason hired a ship to take him straight to Jamestown and told the crew not to make any stops on the way. It would be four days to reach Jamestown.

Jason's timing was good; the prisoner ship from England that was sent by parliament to go and get Jack and to bring him back to England for trial was a day late in leaving. Four days later, Jason was at Jamestown.

Jason also purchased a small boat called a skipper boat, which can carry four men and sail hundreds of miles. Jason had plenty of time to go and change into his guard's uniform. With the forged papers he had with him, he would go and get Jack and they'd leave using the small skipper ship.

While Jack was waiting, Jason walked into the constable's office.

"Yes, what can I do for you, guard?" the constable asked.

"These are my papers, and I'm here to take Mr. Reese back to England for his trial."

"You by yourself, guard? This Reese is a pretty good-size man."

"No, the other guard that is with me is waiting at the ship."

"Let's see here. Your papers are well in order. Let's get your prisoner." The constable opened the door, put locks on Jack's wrists, and said, "The guard is here from England, and he is taking you back, Mr. Reese."

"I won't make any trouble. I'll go with the guard peaceably."

Not taking any chances on losing Jack, Jason held a pistol on Jack all the way back to the boat. When they arrived, Jason told Jack to get into the small skipper boat at the end of the dock. Jack turned and asked, "Where is the ship that is supposed to take us back to England?"

"That ship is a few miles out at sea waiting for us, Mr. Reese. This skipper boat will take us to where the ship is waiting."

Jason, pointing a pistol at Jack, told him, "Take this key and unlock the lock on your left wrist." Jack did what he was told.

"Now, Mr. Reese, wrap the chain of your bracelet around the steel bar inside the boat."

Jack wrapped the chain around the bar and latched the lock back onto his left wrist. Now Jason said, "I don't think you can break free from that steel bar."

Jason rowed the boat out to sea, and when an hour passed, Jack realized that there was no ship waiting for them. Jack looked out at the sea and said, "I know now you aren't a guard from England. Who are you?"

"That's easy, Mr. Reese. My name is Wells. Jason Wells, do you know the name?"

"Wait a minute, you have a brother?"

"A dead brother thanks to you, Mr. Reese."

"So it was your brother I accidentally killed on the *Charlotte*?"

"Yes, Mr. Reese, that was my brother you murdered with your sword."

"Jason, I know you won't believe me, but your brother was a close friend to me and my brother, Chad."

"You're right. I don't believe you, Reese, and you're going to pay for killing my brother. That's funny, Mr. Reese. If you and my brother were friends, why did you run your sword through him and kill him?"

"When we were fighting, I tried to tell him who I was, but for some strange reason, he didn't recognize me. And before I knew it, my sword was through his body and he was dead."

5
YOU'RE GOING TO DIE, JACK
1673

Jason looked down on Jack with hatred and said, "You're going to die, Jack, but it's going to be my way, and it's not going to be a pleasant way to die."

"Where are we sailing to, Jason?"

"There is a little rock island that is just fifty miles or so, and it's the worst of all islands—very little water and nothing but dust and dirt. Oh yes, I forgot. It gets around a hundred degrees in the shade. We're going to have fun when we get there, Jack, at least I will—you may not when you get thirsty."

Before nightfall, Jason and Jack arrived at the island. "Now listen to me very carefully, Jack, any trouble and I'll shoot you in the knee. Then instead of walking, I'll make you crawl to where we're going, understand? Now take this key and loosen your locks." Jason, being careful, was now standing outside the boat. Jack loosen the locks and stepped out of the boat.

"Now what, Jason?"

"Lock the bracelet back around your wrists, Jack."

Jack did what he was told, and then Jason pulled another chain from inside the boat. He wrapped that chain around the chain that was between the locks on Jack's wrists.

Taking no chances, Jason told Jack to back up five steps. Jason reached into the boat and brought out a water bag and a bag filled with food. Jason, staring off into the distance, said, "That way," as he pointed south. While they were walking, Jason had a hold of Jack's chains and kept a reasonable distance behind Jack all the way.

"You might as well kill me now, Jason, and get it over with."

"Oh no, Jack, you don't get off that easy. By the time I'm finished with you, you'll be begging me to put a bullet between your eyes."

"You know something, Jason. Your brother never told me he had another brother."

"Well, he did, Jack, and this brother is going to kill you when he's ready."

Jack felt he needed punishment to make up for his guilt, but this wasn't the way.

When it grew dark, they stopped. Jason looked around said, "Jack, this place is as good as any to make camp. Jack, you see that tree? Walk over to it."

Jack did as he was told. Jason, holding a pistol on Jack with his left hand, threw the long chain he was holding around the tree with his right. He then locked the chain together with another lock. He gave Jack the key to his locks and said, "Unlock your right wrist, Jack."

Jack, unlocking the lock, said, "Now what?"

"Lock your right bracelet to the chain that's around the tree."

Jack did as he was told.

"Very good, Jack, now give me back the key."

Jack handed it back and just sat down under the tree. Jason checked the chain and made sure Jack was held tight.

Jason put everything down and fixed himself something to eat. Jason ate and drank while Jack sat there and watched. "What about me?"

"What about you, Jack?"

"Do I get any water or food?"

"Just enough to keep you alive, Mr. Reese, just enough!"

The night was cold, and Jack almost froze while Jason was covered up in a warm blanket by the fire.

The next day, with the heat reaching a hundred degrees, Jack thawed real quick. Jason did give Jack just enough water to barely stay alive. Jack had to figure a way to break away from Jason before he weakens. They stopped to rest that afternoon.

THAT WAS MY BROTHER JIMMY
1673

WHILE THEY SAT. Jack tried to reason with Jason.

"Jason, I don't think you'll listen, but your brother, Tom, I killed saved my brother's life at one time. Why would I've killed him on purpose?"

"No, Jack, the brother you killed was Jimmy, Tom's twin."

Now it all makes sense, Jack thought to himself, but Jack was still Jason's prisoner. Jack had to make a move now!

"You know something, Jason? You're right. I killed your brother because he was like you—a coward and a rat."

Jason stood up, saying, "That's not true, Reese, and you take that back."

"No," Jack continued, "I won't, Jason, and you don't have the guts to shoot me with that pistol. You're just as gutless as your brother."

"Stop saying that, stop it, I said!"

"You know something, Jason? If you're half the man your brother was, you'd come over here and shoot me while staring me in the face."

Jason yelled out, "I told you to shut up, shut up!" Coming closer to Jack, he cocked the hammer of the pistol.

"Shoot me, Jason, if you got the guts."

Standing within inches of Jack, Jason shouted out again, "Shut up, Reese, or I'll pull the trigger."

Jack lurched forward for the pistol, and while they struggled, Jack turned the pistol inward toward Jason. The pistol went off. Jason backed up and held his hands over his stomach. He saw the blood flowing between his fingers and, as he looked back toward Jack, fell to the ground dead.

Jack reached over, got the keys, and unlocked the locks and went over to the water bag and took a huge drink. After eating something and getting some strength back, Jack buried Jason under some rocks and put up some kind of marker with his name scratched into it.

7
Making His Way Back to Pirates Cove
1673

Jack wondered how old Jason was and thought it was a shame he had to kill him, but it was either Jason or him. Jack knew someday he would have to face Tom Wells and tell him all this tragedy. That was something Jack was dreading to do.

When Jack was gathering things together, he noticed a piece of paper lying on the ground; it must have fallen from Jason's shirt pocket during the struggle.

It read, "Tom Wells died yesterday, June the tenth, on the naval warship *Montgomery* after a furious fight with war pirates; he will be given a medal of honor."

Jack now was spared the ordeal of facing Tom about what happened today and on the cargo ship. Jack put the paper inside the rocks of Jason's grave. Jack headed back to the skipperboat and hoped it was still there.

The next day, Jack arrived back to where the skipper boat was tied. Jack checked what supplies he had left. There was a good amount of supplies in the bag, and he did find extra water bags in the boat. Whatever Jason was planning, he was prepared to be on this island for a while.

Jack had to wait until night to get his position by the stars. Then he would know in what direction to sail back to Pirates Cove. Jack did accept the fact that sailing in this small skipper boat was going to be risky and he might not make it back to Pirates Cove. He could be lost in a storm or picked up by pirates.

Either way, he had no choice. When the stars came out that night, Jack got his position. Jack knew which direction he was headed but couldn't figure the exact distance. He figured the best he could, and if the journey was longer than five days, then he'd die at sea from the lack of resources.

Jack knew that by ship, it would take two days from Pirates Cove to Jamestown, so from his position now, it couldn't be more than four days with this small skipper boat. Jack rowed the boat out to sea, and when he was far enough out, he let down the sails and let the wind do the rest. The wind was stirring well that night, and if it continued, Jack would make it back to Pirates Cove alive.

Back at Pirates Cove that evening on board the *Black Rose*, Rebekah's men were standing around talking. Joe asked the first question, "Pete, you're the last one to see the princess this evening. How is she doing?"

"Not good, Joe," he said. "The last two days, the princess has done nothing but sit in front of her cabin windows and stare out at the waterfall."

"Well, Pete, has she said anything at all?" Randy asked.

"No, she just tells me to leave her cabin and for no one to bother her."

Pete suggested, "Look, all of us can't do anything at this time, so you men might as well go over to the post. If the princess needs us, I'll send Curt over and tell you men to come back to the ship."

Joe said, "I'm staying right here on board ship until the princess tells me otherwise, Pete."

Rebekah's loyal men stayed on board the ship doing their duties until the princess said otherwise.

Going Back to the Castle and Being a Real Princess
1673

Four days at sea and Jack was doing fine. Navigating by the stars at night let Jack know exactly where his position was at all times. Jack wasn't far from the cove at this time.

Back at the cove, in Rebekah's cabin, she was telling Pete, "Have the men line up on deck, Pete. I've something important to tell them."

"Yes, Princess, I'll do as ordered."

Rebekah, now walking on deck, saw her men lined up straight and were giving her their complete attention. At this time, Jack's small boat was sailing into the cove.

Standing before her men, Rebekah started by telling them, "I have the best fighting pirates on the high seas. No captain could be prouder of his or her men than I am of you. I'm returning to my father's castle to help my sister Carlena rule the kingdom."

"Princess," Joe spoke up, "what about Henry Morgan? He knows who you are and will send his men for you."

"I've thought about that, Joe, and if he does, I'll fight his men to the death as my father died. One more thing before I leave you men, I'll make out the maps to where all the treasures are buried, and you'll divide it amongst yourselves as I had promised."

"But why, Princess? You've so much to do."

"I can't go on pirating anymore without Jack. He was my strength and, and…" Rebekah lowered her head.

Jack was now on board the *Black Rose* and heard most of what Rebekah had said. The men, now seeing Jack walk up behind Rebekah, started grinning. Rebekah's back was to Jack.

"Princess."

"Yes, Joe."

"What if Jack returns and you're gone, what shall we tell him?"

"He's not returning, Joe," she said. "I've made my decision, and why are all of you men grinning?"

"Don't you think you should consult with me first, Princess, before leaving?"

With a huge smile shining on Rebekah's face, she turned around and yelled, "You're alive, Jack!" Then she jumped into his arms and kissed him. Jack, with a huge grin, told Rebekah, "Not in front of the men, Princess." The men started laughing as Rebekah kissed Jack again and said, "They're not looking, Jack." Rebekah, showing a sigh of relief, said to her men, "What are you men standing around for? You do have work to do, and we've another English ship to raid."

Before the men started back to work, Marty asked Joe, "What about all of that treasure the princess was going to divide up with us?"

Joe stared at Marty with a somber look and told him, "If you can't figure it out, Marty, I'm sure not going to explain it to you."

Sam said, "Jack's back, and things are back to normal, get it?"

Marty said, "Oh yeah, I do." And with a grin, he went back to work.

Joe said, "Marty reminds me of somebody I once knew."

Sam replied, "He does, doesn't he?"

After Jack shaved and washed up, he talked with the Rebekah in the galley while eating a good ole hot meal Micky prepared special.

"Well, how is it, Jack?" Rebekah asked.

"You know, Princess, Micky's food never tasted so good."

"Jack, tell me what happened, and why you changed your mind about things?"

While the hour passed, Jack explained everything to Rebekah. Rebekah was glad all this trouble was over and Jack was back. They talked about the next English ship that was on her list, and in a few days, they would be on their way to raid the ship *Star Dust*.

PART II

Shandell Lee
1673

In 1668, on the other side of the world, in the country of China, there was a young girl being sent by her father to a sword-fencing school for girls and boys of mixed ages.

The girl's name is Shandell Lee, and she was opposed to going and leaving her family, but her father wanted her to be able to defend and take care of herself in the troubled land around them. Shandell was half English and half Chinese.

Her hair was long and black that shined a tinted blue under the sun or moon; she was a girl of much beauty and desirability. Her father was Chinese, and her mother was of an English descent. Shandell has a sister named Christy, who was four years younger. Christy was very pretty as well.

Shandell was sought after for marriage by many wealthy suitors. A prince or king, when visiting the Orient to do business and trade, would see Shandell and offer great trade in jewels and gold to her parents for her, but her father was a businessman of fair wealth and would turn down the huge offers.

Before Shandell was taken to the sword-fencing school, she and her father were having one last argument about her going.

"But, Father, please don't send me away. I don't want to go and leave my home and family."

Shandell's father, Chon Lee, insisted and said to her, "Don't disgrace me and your mother Melissa, my daughter."

"But, Father," she cried again, "I don't desire to learn the art of sword fighting."

"What must I do, my daughter, to convince you we're living in very terrible times? There are the China raiders of homes, renegade pirates that sail the sea, and many more vicious and ruthless men and women that kill and maim without mercy. This is for your own good, and your sister will follow in time when she is of age."

When Shandell's mother, Melissa, came into the room, Shandell pleaded with her to change her father's mind. Melissa, holding back her tears, didn't want Shandell to go either, but when she married her husband who she loves very much, she took on his laws and way of life. She expressed strongly to Shandell, "This is for your good, my daughter, as well as the family." Shandell had a strong spirit and also had a stubborn streak in her, and she planned on leaving the school and running away.

Shandell was telling her sister good-bye before she left.

"I'll miss you, Shandell," Christy said as they hugged each other before Shandell left.

"I won't stay gone long, Christy."

"What do you mean, Shandell?" Christy asked with a strange look on her face.

"Soon as I get to that school, I'll sneak away and come back home, and if I do this enough times, then father will soon let me stay home."

"I don't know, Shandell. He has given us the strap several times when we've disobeyed him."

"I don't care, Christy, he can beat me until I bleed to death. I won't stay at that school, and father can't make me. I'm eighteen, Christy, and father hasn't the right to do this to me." Shandell's father walks in. "It's time to leave, Shandell. The carriage is waiting to take you to the village of Tibet."

THE RUNAWAY
1673

TIBET IS WHERE trainers of great samurai fighters dwelled. These men are known as the greatest swordsmen of the Eastern world. Being fearless and deadly men that they are, even the renegades and pirates fear these great men.

This is where Shandell is going to learn swordsmanship. These men of the sword trained women as well as men and were very diligent in their techniques. You'd never leave until all the tests they give you were passed. Some students have been there for years and are still under training, but soon, even they will pass all the tests and leave.

The first thing Shandell did when she arrived was run away through the woods and head back for home. Her father would send her back, but she'd do the very same thing again and again. After three beatings, her father knew he'd eventually kill her, and that would defeat the purpose of sending her to the school.

This time, when Shandell returned home, her father relented and let her stay but was down in spirits because of her disobedience. Shandell won, but, in a way, she lost. Shandell now was going to a higher school of learning; she wanted to be a teacher of language because she was fascinated with other cultures.

Her mother was of an English descent, and since Shandell was half Chinese and half English, she wanted to know more about her other side of history. Shandell was happy and content with what she wanted to do with her life.

A year passed, but her father was still feeling down over his daughter's disgrace to the family. One day, Shandell entered into her father's office and asked, "Why aren't you the same as before, Father? You used to be so happy and gay?"

"I was excited at the time when I was sending you to learn the art of sword fencing, Shandell, and for you to be able to take care of yourself."

"Father, I love you and mother with all of my heart, but times and things change, and doesn't what I want matter?"

Chon gazed upon Shandell with tears and said to her, "All I wanted was the best for you."

Shandell hugged Chon and said, "I do understand, Father, but I have to do what I think is best for me, and I have to live my life the way I want."

Chon was glad his daughter was strong willed, but that wouldn't protect her against evil men and these evil times, but he was letting her do what she wanted, and if she was happy, he was happy for her. After all, he loved both his daughters more than life itself.

At this time, there were pirate ships sailing from the Caribbean toward China to steal their jade statues. Then they would take them back across the Atlantic and sell them to people who would break them up, turn them into jewelry, and get rich. These were more than just one group of pirates; they were a band of fifty or more. One pirate ship sailing to China, called the *Renegade*, raided a prison ship sailing to France. The prisoners on board were being sent to France to be hung.

11
WISE PRISONER
1673

AFTER FINDING NOTHING valuable to take from the French ship, Pirate Captain Alex Fairbanks did find some prisoners locked in the brig below deck. He released them, and the men who followed him lived. The others who didn't were killed. There was a young man by the name of Troy Bowers who was one of the prisoners.

Troy, being a smart young man, followed Fairbanks. Having no choice, Troy traveled with the renegade pirate raiders that went to China seeking to steal jade statues under the command of Captain Fairbanks. Troy just learned the ropes and only killed in self-defense and would spare a man's life if he was down and helpless. Captain Fairbanks would never leave a survivor; his orders were to kill them dead!

During a raid on villages and homes searching for these jade pieces, they came upon Shandell's home one day when she was at school. Fairbanks and his men raided her home and killed her parents. Christy was hiding in an underground hole Chon had prepared in case of something like this would happen.

Fairbank's men found Christy, and of course, it was fun time as they were kissing her and passing her around like a bottle of cheap whiskey. Troy with other pirates just arrived from bringing up the rear. Troy saw what was happening to Christy and tried to stop her from being hurt. Christy saw Troy's face but didn't know he was trying to help her.

Troy was hit from behind with a pistol barrel and fell to the ground in a daze. Troy pulled his pistol and shot one of the pirates in helping Christy, and when he did, Christy got away and ran for help. Fairbanks kicked Troy in his side with his boot and told him, "When we return to the ship, you'll be getting twenty-five lashes with the whip for what you have done."

Christy ran and ran, but she was caught by the pirates. When she clawed one pirate named Val Dalton down his face, the pirate went into a rage. By pirate instinct, Dalton stabbed Christy again and again until he thought he killed her. Dalton looked down, spat, and said, "Animal," as Christy lay there dying. Fairbanks and his men took all the jade they could carry and went back to the *Renegade*.

When Shandell arrived home that evening, she found her parents dead and her home ransacked. After getting over the shock, she didn't see Christy in the house, so she went searching for her. When Shandell found Christy, she was still alive. She then went to get help.

For several days, Christy was doing fine and was sitting up in bed. Christy was a talented artist in drawing lifelike pictures. She was feeling better that day when she asked for some paper and something to draw with.

Christy remembered the faces of five of the pirates that attacked her and Val Dalton's face. She could never forget. She drew with exact detail their faces on paper: Fairbanks, Dalton, and three others. Unfortunately for Troy, his face was one of the five.

That evening when Shandell came to visit, Christy gave the drawings to her to give to the law officials. Later that evening, Christy started bleeding from her stomach again. The doctors weren't able to stop the bleeding. They told Shandell the stitches weren't holding and she might be bleeding from the inside. Christy was dying in front of Shandell's very eyes, and there was nothing she could do. Christy, as she was dying, asked

Shandell to come closer, and when Shandell leaned over to listen, Christy, with her last breath, told Shandell, "Now I know why father wanted us to learn the art of the sword." The last breath went out of Christy, her hand on Shandell's face dropped to her side. Shandell yelled out with a sorrowful grief, "Christy, come back, I need you," but there was no response. A day later after Christy was buried, Shandell went home to mourn.

During this time, Fairbanks was back on the *Renegade* and sailing out to sea toward the Atlantic. On board the ship, Fairbanks was keeping his promise to Troy and was going to give him twenty-five lashes, but during their travel back, Troy got away when Fairbanks and his men got into a battle with a small group of Chinese soldiers. Troy made his way back to a China port. He stowed away on different cargo ships until he was closer to the ports he came from originally.

The trip took several weeks, but when Troy was back to a familiar port, he hired back onto another pirate ship. This was all Troy knew how to do, so he accepted it.

Weeks passed for Shandell, and she was going to take Christy's drawings to the officials, but she forgot. With all that had happened, that was the last thing on Shandell's mind. Shandell was leaving with the drawings when her aunt stopped by to see how she was doing.

Shandell and her aunt talked a while. Then her aunt asked, "What are you holding in your hand, Shandell?"

"These are drawings Christy drew of the pirates that molested and killed her."

Her aunt looked at them and said, "Shandell, it's a shame about Christy because her drawings of these pirates are so lifelike. And the terrible thing is I don't think these pirates will ever be punished. They arrived by ship and got away on ship. Well, I'll be around if you need me, Shandell." Her aunt then left. Shandell thought of what her aunt had said about the pirates never being found or punished.

Shandell just lowered her head and cried. She cried for days until she finally stopped. The last words of Christy to Shandell were "Now, I know why father wanted us to learn the art of the sword." Shandell thought about what her sister had said. It was so embedded into her mind, and she couldn't rid her mind of the words no matter how hard she tried.

The drawings were still there. Shandell never took them to the law officials when another thought came to mind. The only rest Shandell was ever going to have is when these pirates were punished for what they did to her family. Shandell sold all her father's property and went to the school she fought so hard against in the beginning.

Things were different now for Shandell. She had no family to go back to, so her only home now was the school of the deadliest art of sword fighting. Shandell had now a cause—vengeance, cold vengeance! Shandell never took the drawings into the law officials; she would need them to identify each pirate that took her family away from her. Yes, Shandell was interested in swords now as she was planning her revenge against every man in those drawings.

The year Shandell started this very difficult work was in 1669. She would live here and train here. Shandell was determined to be the best student in the art of the sword that this school had ever put out. Shandell worked hard day in and day out. She was stubborn to the very core. Every day, she studied the drawings and implanted the faces in her memory so she would never forget.

Bleeding Hands
1673

Shandell would work with her sword from sunup until sundown. She'd practice until her hands would bleed from the blisters that would form. She was getting so used to the pain in her hands she got to the point where she couldn't feel the pain anymore.

The months passed, then a year, Shandell was very skilled with the sword by this time and was getting as good as her teachers. Shandell passed all her skill tests with the sword, pistol, and knife but stayed for one more year. Her goal was to be better than her teachers. The other students at the school told Shandell she'd never be as great with the sword as their teachers. After the second year, Shandell proved them all wrong.

At this point in her training, even the great teachers couldn't teach Shandell any more about the art of the sword. Shandell was now ready to go after the pirates who murdered her family. To complete her mission, she'd join a pirate ship and travel with them, and her hope was to eventually find the pirates she'd be searching for.

Shandell found a pirate ship needing to replace a crew member lost at sea and offered herself as a replacement. All the men laughed and rejected her. The captain, not caring about gender, gave her a try. All Shandell had to do was prove to the captain her sword ability on their next ship raid; that would tell the captain what he wanted to know. If she lived, she was accepted;

if she died, oh well. After Shandell's first ship raid, she proved herself to be worthy and was now part of the crew. The captain was so impressed with Shandell's sword abilities he made her his first mate.

The ship Shandell sailed on was the *Thunder Bay*. The captain's name was Miles Trent. His main concern was staying alive. Whoever was the best swordsman on his ship was first mate, and their job was to watch his backside and make sure he didn't get knifed in the back or run through with a sword. Shandell's job was to keep Miles Trent alive.

13
BEST FIRST MATE I EVER HAD
1673

A YEAR ON the *Thunder Bay* had passed, and so far, Shandell hadn't seen one of the pirates that were responsible for her family's death. The *Thunder Bay* traveled to many places, and Captain Trent and his pirates raided many ships during that time.

After one successful raid, Miles said to Shandell, "Your quickness with the sword today saved my life." On the last ship they raided, Captain Miles was down for the count when Shandell just removed her sword from a sailor and took another sailor down who was about to kill Captain Miles. Shandell was deadly with a sword, and Captain Miles respected her ability, and his men learned to do so as well.

A year earlier, when Shandell was on her first voyage with Captain Miles, his men tried to see what she was made of. One evening, Shandell was minding her own business when one pirate named Flint Monroe, who was one of the best with the sword Captain Miles had, decided to try Shandell. He walked up and grabbed Shandell manhandling her. He started kissing her and wouldn't let her go.

Shandell wore black leather boots that came up past her knees. She carried two knives, one in each boot, and could use them very skillfully. Flint had his arms around Shandell while the other men were laughing, saying, "When you're finished with her, Flint, don't be greedy, pass her around."

Just then, Flint felt something sharp slice into his gut. Flint looked down, and Shandell had part of her knife blade sticking in him and told him, "Let me go, Flint, or the rest of my knife blade will be going through your gut."

Flint backed up, holding his left hand over his bleeding stomach, saying, "You're going to die for that, Shandell."

Shandell inserted her knife back into her boot and replied, "Back away, Flint. This time, it was my knife. The next time, it'll be my sword."

Flint drew his sword on Shandell, and now the sword fight was in play. "I'm going to cut you into pieces, Shandell, and feed your remains to the sharks."

Shandell ignored Flint's threats and kept her mind on her sword fighting. The swords clanged against each other while the men took bets on who was going to win. Flint nicked Shandell's shoulder drawing first blood.

Not liking her blood spilled, Shandell decided to spill Flint's. With a swing to Flint's right, Shandell scraped his ribs. Flint wasn't hurt bad but was bleeding somewhat and still was able to use his sword. He planned on killing Shandell. Flint made some great moves, but was helpless against Shandell's ability. Flint was now buckling under her swings of deadly force. Flint was being hammered back toward the railing of the ship when he collapsed down to his knees. He looked up, and with the tip of Shandell's sword pointing directly at his chest, knew he had been beaten.

"Lay your sword down, Flint," she told him.

Flint was no fool and knew he was taken by a better swordsman and relented to Shandell.

From that day forward, not one man would ever try Shandell again. In his cabin, Miles was telling Shandell, "You're the best first mate, I've ever had Shandell, and I hope you stick with me."

"I can't, Miles," she said. "When I find the men I'm searching for and avenge my family, I'm going back to my home in the Orient."

Miles smiled while saying, "Shandell, I hope you forgive me, but I hope you never find them so you'll always stay with me."

"I'll find them, Miles. It's just a matter of time."

The years continued to pass, and still not one pirate responsible for her family's death has been found. It was the year of 1673 when the *Thunder Bay* anchored off a port one thousand sea miles from Pirates Cove. The Port of Little Rivers is what it is called.

14
LIKE TO HURT LITTLE GIRLS
1673

FLINT MONROE, WHO first challenged Shandell three years ago, knocked on the captain's cabin door.

"Yes, who is it?" Miles asked.

Flint entered and said, "It's Flint Monroe, Captain, and the men are ready. Sir, are there any last orders?"

"Shandell will instruct you and give you your orders."

Flint saw Shandell on deck and asked, "What are your orders?"

"No fighting, no stealing, and stay out of the way of any law authorities. We're here for relaxation and supplies, not to raid or steal, understand, Mr. Monroe?"

"Yes, your orders are very clear."

In this Port of Little Rivers, a man takes care of his own battles. There's not much in law enforcement here—even the owners have weapons of sorts to protect themselves. You cause trouble or get caught stealing, you would face the consequences of your actions. The owner had his choice of punishment, shooting you, stabbing you, or having you hung. Any trouble between you and someone else was a different matter altogether. If you lost a fight with another person and was killed, they just buried you behind the place or building you were killed at, very simple and tidy.

There was a tavern in the town called the Queen of Whales, you'd find just about the worst of the worst in this place. Miles had some business with the owner there, and afterward, he was taking Shandell to a nicer establishment so they would have a nice dinner together.

Miles was forty years of age, and Shandell was twenty-three. With the time he has spent with Shandell, Miles had fallen in love with her and wanted to marry her. He was going to ask her at dinner.

There was another pirate under Miles Trent's command; his name is Glenn Austin. He had been with the ship for a year now and was also in love with Shandell. Glenn always showed respect to Shandell and would always obey her orders without question. Glenn was great with the sword next to Shandell—not as good, but could hold his own. Shandell liked Glenn, but she had only one goal at this time.

While Shandell waited for Miles to complete his business with the owner of the tavern, eight men walked in, and they were ornery looking and bold. They weren't your average customers; they were pirates. Shandell was having a drink, a little rum with lots of water. This would settle her down a little from a long voyage. Shandell was just sitting and minding her own business when one of the pirates yelled, "Bartender, set up eight rounds of the best whiskey you have and don't be slow about it."

Shandell looked at the pirate making all the noise with his loud mouth. He was Val Dalton. Shandell recognized his face from the picture her sister drew. Shandell's heart raced. Finally, one of the pirates she had been searching for was standing within several feet of her. Shandell didn't know which pirate did the actual stabbing, but as far as she was concerned, she was getting them all for it.

Then Captain Alex Fairbanks walked in and told his men to bring him a whole bottle to the table. Shandell recognized Dalton, Fairbanks, and two other men from Christy's drawings. The pirate missing was Troy, but Shandell would deal with these four and worry about Troy later.

Shandell approached the bar, turned, leaned her back up against it, and faced Fairbanks and his men sitting at their table drinking it up and having a good time. Shandell spoke up, "There are those who like to hurt little defenseless girls."

Dalton looked up and told Fairbanks, "What do we have here, Captain?"

Fairbanks gazed up at Shandell and said, "You talking to us, you pretty little thing?"

"Yes, I'm talking to you, you filthy murdering vermin."

With a snarly laugh, Dalton replied, "I've been called a snake and a lowdown monster but never a vermin."

Shandell's hand was resting on her sword handle as she was getting ready to put four miserable pirates out of their misery. Fairbanks spoke up again, "Before we have our fun with you, who are you, and why the poison against us?"

"You killed my mother, father, and my dear sister while in China stealing jade statues, and now I'm going to kill you for revenge."

Fairbanks took a sip from his bottle, and with a little whisky dripping from his beard, he asked, "So what's your name? I want to know before you die."

"It's Shandell Lee, and my sword is the last thing you'll remember in this lifetime."

15
The New Captain of the Ship
1673

DURING THE CONFRONTATION between Shandell and Fairbanks, Miles Trent walked out of the back room and saw what Shandell was getting herself into and tried to stop her. Glenn, now entering the tavern, also saw what was happening. With sword in hand, Shandell said to Miles and Glenn, "This is my fight, so don't interfere. I have a job to do."

Fairbanks was as ruthless as they come and wasn't a fair fighter. He and his eight men stood up to face Shandell. Miles and Glenn were not letting Shandell face these nine pirates alone. With swords drawn, the fighting was going full blast and furious as Shandell was taking her liberties. With just a few swings, Shandell sliced two pirates across their stomachs, spilling their guts onto the floor. Miles and Glenn were doing very well in taking two pirates each. Shandell wanted Fairbanks and Dalton for herself, and she got what she wanted. Fairbanks shouted out to Shandell that she couldn't take him and Dalton as they both were swinging their swords toward Shandell with glazed fear in their eyes.

Shandell, with a twist of her sword, slung Dalton's sword from his hand. Fairbanks tried to strike Shandell down with a wide swing of his sword. Shandell, with the swiftness of her blade, came back around and blocked Fairbanks's sword blade, and then she sliced him across his throat. Fairbanks died instantly.

Dalton retrieved his sword, and now Shandell faced him and another pirate. With swords swinging back and forth, Dalton told Shandell how soft her sister was and how he enjoyed kissing her before she died and laughed about what he had said. Shandell sliced Dalton and the other pirate across their chests with deep cuts through to the bone.

Dalton and the other pirate fell to their death. Shandell told them as they hit the tavern floor, "Laugh that off." Dalton, before he died, knew who Shandell was by looking at her; Even though they were several years apart, Christy and Shandell looked identical.

The fighting was over, and Fairbanks and his men lost, and lost bad. Miles was walking toward Shandell when one pirate that was still alive pulled his knife and threw it at Miles and got him right in the middle of his back. Miles fell to the floor. Shandell pulled her knife and threw it and stuck the pirate through his heart with pinpoint accuracy.

Shandell knelt down by Miles. He looked up and said, "You're supposed to guard my backside, Shandell, but you're still the best first mate I ever had." He laid his head back and died. Shandell looked up at Glenn with tears in her eyes, then she looked back down at Miles, and lowered her head in sadness.

The next day on the ship, Shandell was taking Miles's body out to sea for his burial. After they buried Miles at sea, it was time to pick a new captain. Flint spoke up first. Of course, Glenn thought he wanted the captain's position for himself. Flint stood before the men and said, "I propose Shandell for the captain's seat on *Thunder Bay*."

All the men agreed because while she was first mate, Miles Trent always let her give most of the orders.

Shandell accepted because she needed a ship and its crew to find that one last man.

16
ONE LAST PIRATE TO FIND
1673

NOW THAT SHANDELL was the captain, she gave the first-mate job to Glenn in appreciation for his help back at the tavern. Shandell had the men to remove Miles's things from his cabin since she was going to occupy it from here on.

A few days later, Miles Trent's old cabin was now Shandell's. Glenn was in Shandell's cabin asking her what her orders were now. "Glenn, I'm taking the captain's position until I find that last pirate, then I'm sailing back home to the Orient."

Glenn wanted so much to tell Shandell he was in love with her but was afraid she would reject him.

"Glenn."

"Yes, Captain."

"We need a ship to raid for whatever wealth she carries to pay for supplies and things so we can continue on our voyage to wherever we need to sail to."

Glenn, carrying out his orders, told a crewman named Cody, "Cody."

"Yes, sir."

"Be on the lookout up in the crow's nest for a ship to raid. We need gold and silver to purchase supplies."

"Aye, sir."

Back in her cabin, Shandell was looking out the cabin windows. Shandell was taught right from wrong in life and knew what she was doing—raiding ships for their gold or silver—was wrong. But this was the only way she knew in finding the men who did this awful injustice to her and her family.

Shandell was planning to give up this pirating after the last man fell from her sword. Shandell lowered her head in shame from the blood she had already spilt during her three-year travel with Miles Trent. But how else was she going to get her revenge and for her family to rest in peace?

Shandell knew it took three years just to find these men she just killed and it could take three more. But one thing is for sure. If these men and their captain were this far from her home of China, then the last man she was seeking has got to be here on this side of the world as well. When Fairbanks's crew learned of his death, plus eight more of his men, they pulled up anchor, and moved on. Shandell couldn't even search that ship for the other man she was looking for. The information she did get was Fairbanks's ship was called the *Renegade*, and that gave her something to go on. Shandell would keep searching for that ship in hopes of finding her last man, and then her search would be over.

Meanwhile at sea, several hundred miles from where this all took place, the *Black Rose* sat anchored offshore of a pretty little island just several days sail from Pirates Cove.

Rebekah's men had just buried a chest full of gold that her and her men had taken three days earlier. Rebekah just loved this island because of its beautiful waterfalls. Rebekah and her men have buried valuable bullion here once before.

Jack and Rebekah were taking a stroll around the island, looking at the different waterfalls. Jack was always using these waterfalls and other beautiful sights he and Rebekah would come across during their travels to persuade her to give up the war with England and marry him. While Jack and Rebekah were standing below a waterfall, they watched the water flow over the rocks as it gave off a rainbow from the sun shining down upon them.

Rebekah commented, "Isn't it beautiful, Jack?"

17
THE DEAD SHIP
1673

JACK SAW THE look on Rebekah's face asking him to kiss her, and Jack did. Jack and Rebekah kissed for several minutes when Jack had to come up for air. Sighing deeply, Rebekah opened her eyes and told Jack, "I wish this moment would never end. It makes me feel so relaxed and free."

Here is my opportunity, Jack thought to himself. "We can make this happen every day, Rebekah, and all you have to do is say the word."

"What word is that, Jack?" Rebekah said, raising her right eyebrow.

Jack stopped there; he knew this conversation would lead into an argument and thought it best to enjoy the time here with Rebekah.

"What word, Jack?" Rebekah asked again.

Jack, thinking fast, said the magic words, "Rebekah, you remember when we were children? We would wish for these things even though we knew they weren't going to come true."

Jack grinned and hoped he diverted an argument.

Rebekah smiled at Jack, and then she reached up and kissed him again. Jack and Rebekah were at this waterfall for quite a while before returning to the ship.

Back on the *Rose*, Sam was complaining as always about something. "How long are we going to wait on the princess and

Jack? I'm ready to get back to the cove and down several bottles of my favorite fire water."

Troy told Sam, "If you'll stop complaining, Sam, I'll go and find the princess and Jack and let them know you want to leave and get back to Pirates Cove."

"Just ask them, Troy. No need to get the princess upset."

Troy rowed back over to the island; he was also concerned about Jack and the princess.

Jack, after kissing Rebekah, said, "We should start back to the ship, Princess. The men must be wondering what has happened to us."

Taking in a breath of the island's sweet air, Rebekah said, "Yes, Jack, we best be getting back before the men decide on a mutiny and leave us here to stay."

Jack wanted to stay here on this beautiful island with Rebekah and never leave, but things don't last forever, and the time he spent here with her was something for him to always remember. Halfway back to the ship, Troy met up with Jack and Rebekah. "Troy, what are you doing here?" Rebekah asked.

"The men and I were getting concerned about you and Jack, Princess, and Sam was complaining, so I volunteered to come ashore and look for you two."

Jack said, "I'm glad you're here, Troy. You can take the princess back to the ship while I gather up some bamboo poles for Pete and Curt."

"I can help you do that, Jack," Troy uttered.

"We only need a few, Troy. Take Rebekah back to the ship, and I'll be along shortly."

While Rebekah and Troy were following the trail back, Troy was talking to Rebekah, and they both weren't paying attention and took the wrong path back to the ship. After ten minutes of walking down the wrong path, Rebekah stopped. "I don't think this is the right path, Troy. We should've been at the shore by now."

"I think you're right, Princess. Let's go back the way we came and try and find the right path." When Rebekah and Troy came to another path, Troy said, "I think this is the way, Princess." Rebekah wasn't sure but agreed.

Troy, being taller than Rebekah, saw the shore ahead, and with much relief, he said, "The shore is straight ahead, Princess."

When Troy and Rebekah got to the shore, there was no rowboat and no ship sitting offshore. "I think we're lost, Troy," Rebekah told him with a touch of despair in her voice.

"We better go back the way we came, Princess."

"No, I've a better idea, Troy. We'll walk along the shoreline, and hopefully, it'll take us around the island and we might meet up with the *Rose* sitting offshore not too far from here."

While Rebekah and Troy were walking the shoreline, they came upon a derelict ship that was stuck in the muddy sand just offshore.

Rebekah, of course, was curious and wanted to get a closer look. Rebekah noticed the ground leading up to the derelict was soft but dry. "Let's go aboard, Troy, and get a closer look."

"I don't think we should, Princess."

"Where's your sense of adventure, Troy?"

"It's all in one ship, Princess, the *Black Rose*, and we better get going."

"I'm going aboard, Troy. You wait here."

"I'm going with you, Princess. If I let something happen to you, Jack will have me flogged and then make me walk the plank."

After Rebekah and Troy climbed to the top of the ship's deck, Rebekah said, "I'll go first, Troy."

Rebekah stomped her boot down on the wooden planks and saw how solid they were. After a few stomps, Rebekah relayed to Troy, "It sounds pretty solid to me." Then she and Troy proceeded to walk across the deck of the ship. "We better go, Princess. Jack and the others might be looking for us."

"Just a few minutes more, Troy. I'd like to go to the captain's cabin and find out what pirate owned this ship."

Troy knew how stubborn Rebekah was but agreed to go with her down below deck.

Rebekah pulled her sword from her sheath and laid it on the deck.

Troy asked, "Why are you leaving your sword here, Princess?"

"Just in case something unforeseen should happen, Troy, not that it's going too. Leaving my sword here, will let Jack know where we are."

When they started down the steps that led to the lower deck, Troy saw two lanterns hanging on a wall. He picked them up and shook them. "These lanterns are still full of oil, Princess." He struck a match and lit the wick in the first lantern and then lit the other lantern, which Rebekah was holding. "We'll need the light going below, Princess." Troy led the way, knocking down cobwebs.

They approached the last cabin at the end of the ship. Troy opened the door. This cabin was much larger than the others. Rebekah, being excited, said, "This has to be the captain's quarters, Troy."

18
Troy's Past
1673

Rebekah walked over to a desk that was covered in dust and tried to pull the drawer open but couldn't. "It's stuck, Troy," she said. "See if you can get it open." Troy was tall and very strong as he gave the drawer handle a mighty pull. Slowly but surely, he opened the drawer.

"Princess."

"Yes, Troy."

"Before searching the drawer with your hand, let me use my knife and feel around inside the drawer and make sure there isn't any spiders are something else creepy inside."

"That's a good idea, Troy. You have my permission."

With his knife blade, Troy felt around inside the drawer and said, "Princess, it looks safe to me." Then Troy brought the lantern closer, so Rebekah could see inside the drawer.

Rebekah pulled some papers from the drawer, and after reading a few lines, she said, "Do you know who sailed this ship at one time, Troy?"

"Who, Princess?"

"This ship, at one time, was under the command of Sir Frances Drake." (Frances Drake had been dead for many years before Rebekah came onto the scene.)

Rebekah also found a pistol in the drawer as well. "Look at this, Troy, a pistol. It had to be the captain's. I'm taking this back to the ship as a souvenir."

"I don't know, Princess. The stories I heard from other pirates when I was on other ships said it was bad luck to take a pirate's belongings when he was dead."

"Troy, you don't believe in that old folklore, do you?" Just then, the old ship moved and slid in the soft, sandy mud just hard enough to cause Rebekah and Troy to lose their balance and fall to the floor of the ship.

Then the old ship creaked and cracked, and heavy boards fell in front of the cabin door, blocking their way out. Troy helped Rebekah to her feet and then proceeded to the cabin door. Troy tried to remove the heavy wooden beams that blocked the cabin doorway but was unable to. Rebekah and Troy couldn't get out.

"Troy, can you move those boards?"

"I'm trying, Princess, but they're too large and heavy." Troy tried again, but they wouldn't budge.

"Maybe we can get out through a back window, Troy." Rebekah took her lantern to the back of the cabin. There were no windows in the back of the ship as Rebekah looked and looked. "What kind of pirate was he, Troy? He didn't have any windows to look out of."

"I don't know, Princess, but what I do know is we're trapped until help arrives."

Troy made a suggestion, "It'll be best if we have only one lantern lit, Princess. Then when one goes out, we'll have another one for later."

"Good thinking, Troy." Rebekah raised the lantern glass and blew hers out; at least they would have light for a day or two. Rebekah sat on the old, dusty floor, and so did Troy. They waited for help to arrive.

By this time, Jack had already organized a search party for Rebekah and Troy. Jack did arrive to the *Rose* first, and since

Rebekah and Troy weren't back, he knew something was wrong and wasted no time in getting some men together and searching for Rebekah and Troy.

Before leaving, Jack gave these orders: "Brad, if the princess and Troy return, fire off several shots and we'll return."

It was still early in the day. Jack had at least several hours before the sun went down.

Back at the derelict ship, the princess said, "Troy."

"Yes, Princess."

"I'm very sorry for getting you in all of this mess."

"Princess, I was just as curious about this old ship as you were. It took a little of a push to get me to explore it too."

"Yes, but if it wasn't for me, Troy, you would've went on to the ship and not be waiting to die."

"Nobody's going to die, Princess. Jack will find us. Remember you left your sword lying on the deck of the ship? And when they see it, they'll know where we are."

"I hope so, Troy," Rebekah said, showing signs of doubt. Rebekah wasn't afraid for herself; she was feeling bad for Troy because she pushed him into this, and if he died, she would feel she was responsible—that's if she lived and he didn't. Rebekah has been in worse spots than this, so she decided to take her mind off it.

"Troy."

"Yes, Princess."

"How long have you been a pirate, and how did you get started?"

"Princess, I didn't plan on being a pirate. It just happened. I guess it started, well, when I was fourteen years old. My parents and I were starving, and there were no jobs for my father. Whatever food would come our way they gave to me to eat."

19
YOU HAVE TO DO WHAT YOU HAVE TO DO
1673

"This went on for several months, and my parents would give me the food to eat when that was all there was. I couldn't take this any longer, so I left my mother and father in search for any work I could find and hoped I could bring my mother and father back food to eat. The little cabin I left was so hard to leave. I was born and raised there, but I had to look for some kind of job, or my parents were going to starve.

"I was big and tall for my age and could do the work of two men. Someone out there would have to hire me for the double work they could get out of me. I did get some work, but the pay was so little it barely bought enough food for me to live on, but I'd save as much money as I could. I'd eat very little food just enough to keep up my strength.

"During the weeks I'd worked, I lost several pounds and would get very weak, but I'd stay strong in hopes of helping my mother and father. After three months, the place I worked had finished the building or project. They told the men to come back in two weeks for more work. I went back home to bring food to my parents and prayed they were still alive.

"One week later, I was back home carrying a small bag of food and taking it to my parents. I knocked on the door, but there was no answer. I knocked again. Still no answer. I walked inside the house fearing the worst, and the worst had happened. I called for my mother and father, but no answer. I went to the back room, and no one was there either. Then there was a knock on the front door. I went to see who it was. It was the farmer who lived just across the way.

"The farmer said, 'Troy, I have bad news, son. Your parents, Joan and Matt, died last week from a fever, and I had to bury them in the back of the house. I'm sorry.'

"I went to the back of the house to cry over their grave and ask them to forgive me for being late in returning. Before I left to go to who knows where, I gave the old farmer, whose name was Ben, some of the food I brought back in payment for what he did for my parents."

Rebekah, now having tears in her eyes, lowered her head so Troy couldn't see them. Troy asked, "You all right, Princess?"

Rebekah cleared her throat and said, "Troy, continue, and that's an order."

Troy continued where he left off. "Well, Princess, I left there and went back to the place I worked before. They told me that the people who were hiring for the next job decided to put off the next building project until next year. I went on from there, Princess, and worked odd jobs for very little pay.

"I did this for years until I was nineteen years old, and one day, I was in the wrong place at the wrong time. I was minding my own business, waiting to see a man about a job on a naval ship, when the port I was at was attacked by pirates. I tried to help the people in the building but was knocked unconscious from a blow to the back of my head.

"When I awoke, I was considered part of the band of pirates that looted the port and killed the people there."

"You told them who you were, didn't you, Troy?"

"Yes, I did, Princess, but the man who could answer in my behalf was killed in the pirate raid, so they put me on a ship sailing to France for hanging."

"Apparently, you escaped, Troy! You're here with me now."

"That was a stroke of luck but a curse in a way, Princess."

Rebekah was so deep into Troy's life story she forgot all about their situation and kept listening, wanting to know the end of the story.

Troy continued, "The ship I was on was attacked by a pirate ship that was captained by a man named Alex Fairbanks, and he was a very vicious man, Princess. You followed him, or he'd kill you then and there.

"His men found us below deck in a cell, and the men who followed Alex Fairbanks lived, and the ones who said no were run through with a sword."

"So you followed him, Troy, and lived."

"A man has to do what a man has to do, Princess."

"The first pirate raid I was on was a horrifying experience, Princess." For a moment, Troy hesitated.

"You all right, Troy?"

"I'm all right, Princess. It was just something I thought one human wouldn't do to another. I heard of pirates being ruthless but never dreamed how ruthless they could be. Captain Fairbanks heard in the Orient in the country of China you could get very wealthy from taking their rare jade statues and bringing them back to this side of the world and selling them for great wealth."

"I've never heard of that type of gemstone before, Troy."

"Yes, Princess, there is also belief of whoever wears this stone will be cured of certain sicknesses. As I was saying before, Princess, these pirates I was with were nothing but a deadly disease themselves. I was one of fifty pirates that were in this raid of the China territory, and we were fighting the Chinese army as we were confronted from time to time.

"Captain Fairbanks was able to keep ahead of the army, but sometimes we'd be in a fight with a small group here and there. Fairbanks was brutal, and the pirates also, who followed him. His orders were to every man we run through with a sword not to leave him alive. I couldn't obey those orders, and when possible, I'd spare a man his life.

"I knew if Fairbanks ever found out, he'd have no second thoughts in killing me. Fairbanks and half the men that were with him already came to one home several miles from one village. He and his men raided it and killed the man and woman who lived there and ransacked their home for any jade or any other valuables.

"The pirates I was with arrived a little while later. Soon as I arrived, Fairbanks men had found a young Chinese girl hiding in a hole in the ground. I thought she was Chinese, but she looked half English or French. I was close to her when Fairbanks's men started hurting her and passing her around like she was a bottle of whiskey being drank.

"They were taking turns kissing her as she screamed and struggled in fear but couldn't get free. I tried to help her but was knocked in the back of my head and was laying on the ground in a daze. I was still conscious and pulled the pistol from my belt, and as the young girl was still screaming for help, I pointed the pistol at one man and shot him.

"The girl was able to escape, but I don't know if she got away as Fairbanks kicked me in my side with his boot and told me when we get back to the ship, I was getting twenty-five lashes with the whip for what I had done.

"During a small battle with some Chinese army soldiers on the way back to the ship, I was able to slip away from Fairbanks and his pirates. I barely made it back to the port in China alive. I had to steal food from people's gardens and anywhere else I could find it to survive the trip back to a Chinese port.

"When I did finally make it back there, I stowed away on their cargo ships until I reached ports that were closer to this side of the world."

"How did you survive on those cargo ships, Troy?"

"It wasn't easy, Princess. At night, I would sneak around the ship and steal food from the food galley. Sometimes there were grain sacks in the hold of the ship, and that would be nourishing, plus there was always plenty of fruit."

"What about water, Troy? Where did you get your water from?"

"When I got food from the galley, I would fill a wooden bucket with water, and that would be enough for a five-day trip if I drank very little.

"Over the years, I was afraid the authorities were still searching for me, so I hired onto more pirate ships."

20
THE BEST CAPTAIN I'VE EVER SERVED
1673

JACK AND HIS men returned to the spot where he left Troy and Rebekah. Looking down at Rebekah's and Troy's footprints, Jack saw which direction they went.

"What do you think, Jack? Is it their footprints?" Randy asked.

Marty knew right away Troy's footprint when he made the statement. "I never knew Troy had such a big foot."

Jack looked at Randy and said, "And we know the smaller boot print belongs to the princess and they go down that path toward the right and not the left which goes toward the ship."

A while later, Jack and his men came to where the tracks stopped. Randy saw right away that the tracks started back the way they came. "It looks like they knew they were going the wrong way, Jack, and backtracked the way they came."

Then Jack, Randy, and Marty started back the way they came. Then the tracks went toward a different direction, toward some trees that when they passed them, they came to the same shore Rebekah and Troy came to where they found themselves lost.

Jack, Marty, and Randy weren't too far from finding the old, derelict ship. Jack looked down on the sandy shore and saw large boot prints and small boot prints, and he and the men followed those tracks to the place where the derelict ship was sitting in the mud right offshore.

Marty, after seeing the old, derelict ship, said, "They're in that old ship, Jack, I just know it!" Marty started toward the old ship. Then Jack ordered Marty to *stop*. "But, Jack, they must be in there, or they might be trapped. We must help them." Marty proceeded toward the old ship again. Jack yelled out at Marty again, "Stop, and that's a direct order."

Marty got upset and shouted, "Jack, what if the princess is hurt? We must help her."

"If she's in there, Marty, we will. But if you walk on that ship's deck and the planks give way under your weight, you could be killed, and then how will you be able to help the princess if you're dead?"

"Oh yeah, Jack. I never thought of that." Marty lowered his head, feeling stupid.

Jack put his hand on Marty's shoulder and said, "Marty, plenty of men have made the same mistake, so don't worry about it."

Jack, Randy, and Marty climbed up the side of the ship and stood on the ship's edge. Jack stomped on the planks to see if they were strong enough to hold their weight.

Jack proceeded with care when he noticed Rebekah's sword lying on the deck of the ship. He started to yell Rebekah's and Troy's names.

Troy finished with his story, saying, "That's my story, Princess. The last captain I served under was Captain Rance Morgan, and now you."

Rebekah, thinking she heard something, said, "Troy, I heard a voice, didn't you?"

"I didn't hear anything, Princess."

Rebekah listened again and, with her keen ears, heard Jack's voice, and yelled back, "We're in here, Jack, down below."

Jack approached a little closer to the cabin wall that went below deck.

Jack yelled out again, "Rebekah, Troy, do you hear my voice?" Then Jack listened to hear if anyone yelled back.

Rebekah yelled again, "We're down here, Jack, below deck. Please hurry!"

Jack thought he heard Rebekah's voice and said to Randy and Marty, "Stay put where you are. I don't want any more weight on the old planks as possible."

Jack went below deck and noticed a dim light toward the end of the hallway and called out again, "Rebekah, Troy, you down here?"

Troy heard Jack this time and yelled, "In here, Jack. We're behind all of the wood blocking the cabin door."

Jack hurried to the end of the hall and said to Troy, "Between me and you, we should be able to remove these boards."

After a hard try, they couldn't. Jack went back to get Marty and Randy.

Jack had them walk softly down the steps toward the cabin. Jack said to Troy, "Work from your end, and Marty, Randy, and I will work from this end."

The men pulled with all their strength while Troy pushed his hardest from the other side. The heavy wooden beam started to move as they struggled to remove it from the doorway.

Marty, with a real strong tug with his strong muscles, helped pull the beam completely away as they pushed it aside and the doorway was clear. Rebekah ran out to Jack and said, "I'm so glad to see your faces."

Jack said to Rebekah, "I don't want to spoil the reunion, Princess, but we should all leave—and leave now."

When they were crossing the ship's deck, the old ship started creaking and cracking loudly, making all kinds of scary noises. Jack yelled out, "Off the ship now even if you have to jump!"

Randy, Marty, and Troy jumped. Rebekah started to but froze. Marty yelled up at Rebekah, "I'll catch you, Princess. Jump!"

There was no time, so Jack pushed Rebekah off the ship and knew Marty would catch her on the way down. Then Jack jumped. Marty caught Rebekah with ease as Rebekah fell into his arms like a soft pillow. Marty put Rebekah down, saying, "You're not as heavy as you look, Princess." Before she responded to what Marty said, Jack had everybody move away from the derelict as it was still making popping noises.

Rebekah was already upset from being pushed off the old ship and asked Jack, "Why were you risking every ones neck getting them off of that ship, Jack?"

"Watch the old ship for a minute, Princess." The old, derelict ship broke in half and started to sink deeper into the soft, sandy mud.

Rebekah and her men watched it sink more than half of its height down into the mud. Rebekah stared back at Jack with a thankful look in her eyes. Jack wasn't saying a thing because Rebekah learns fast, and from now on, she'll never venture onto an old, derelict ship again.

Rebekah turned to Marty and said, "What did you mean, Marty, by you thought I was heavier then I looked?"

Marty knew he was in trouble. "Please, Princess, don't be too upset with me. I only meant—"

"Don't worry about it, Marty. I know what you meant, and I forgive you."

"Thanks, Princess."

Jack said, "Let's get back to the *Rose*. The rest of the men are worried about you, Princess."

Before they headed toward the ship, Troy said to Rebekah, "One more thing I forgot to tell you, Princess."

"Make it quick, Troy, or we'll be left behind, and I don't want to go through what we just been through again."

"You've been the best captain I've ever served under, Princess."

"Well, thank you, Troy. That was very nice to say, but let's go."

"Oh, before I forget, one more thing, Princess."

"What now, Troy?"

"Where's Captain Drake's pistol? You had it in your hand before we left the old ship."

"I must've dropped it on the way out, Troy, so let's forget it."

"You weren't afraid of the curse of owning a dead pirate's belongings, were you, Princess?"

"I said forget it, Troy, unless you want guard duty for a whole week."

"Yes, Princess, let's forget about that pistol and the curse that went with it. Who believes in that stuff? We don't, do we, Princess?"

"That way, Troy, and keep walking."

"Yes, Princess, I'll do that."

Everything was as it should be now on the *Black Rose*. The ship was sailing back to Pirates Cove, and Rebekah had learned something new.

That evening, Jack and Rebekah were at the railing of the *Rose* talking, at least Jack was.

"What's wrong, Princess? You haven't said one word while we've been standing here."

"Jack, Troy, and I could've drowned in that old ship today because of my lack of knowledge of such things."

"Princess, plenty of well-seasoned pirates and ship captains have made the same mistake."

"You knew, Jack, and I didn't. How can I continue to captain this ship with lack of such knowledge?"

21
WE LEARN BY DOING
1673

"Not only that, Jack, but how do I protect my men from the lack of knowledge on my part?"

"Rebekah, I didn't know these things either before I sailed on my brother's ship. It took me five years to learn what you've learned in just two years."

"You're not just saying that, Jack? You're telling me the truth?"

"Rebekah, I've never lied to you—and never will. You're a better captain than most that have sailed the seas for many years, and we learn by doing, Rebekah. Never forget that."

Rebekah always trusted Jack, and always will. She always has confidence in what Jack tells her, and that continues to add to her strength. No, Rebekah wouldn't have given up. She was too stubborn for that. She would've found new strength in herself. It was the strength she got from Jack that made things easier for her to accept.

In three days, the *Rose* would be at the cove and the men would be enjoying their relief time while Jack and Rebekah would be making plans on the next ship they were going to raid. As for Shandell, she with her ship was sailing closer and closer to Pirates Cove.

Several hundred sea miles from Pirates Cove, Shandell's ship, the *Thunder Bay*, was anchored off a port known as Sailor's Warf.

Glenn and two other men from the *Thunder Bay* went ashore to purchase some supplies while Shandell and some of her other men would be along later.

Two hours passed, the supplies were taken back to the *Thunder Bay*. Glenn told Mike, one of the pirates under his command, to tell Shandell he'd wait for her in the tavern called the Coral Reef.

Shandell Who?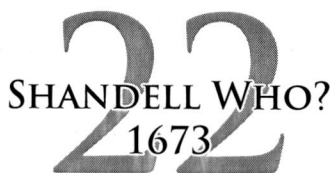
1673

Shandell with three of her men, Mike, Rodger, and Coleman, walked in the Coral Reef as several men in the tavern stared. A man named Johnson leaned over and asked the man who he was sitting with. "Jim, that girl standing by the bar, is she the one they call the Princess Pirate?"

"I don't know, Johnson. There's something different about this girl."

"She has to be the Princess, Jim. She carries a sword and is giving orders to the men."

"Let's listen, Johnson, and hear what they are saying."

Glenn, motioning with his hand, said, "Over here, Shandell."

Johnson and Jim, being puzzled, said, "Shandell who?"

During the time Shandell and her men were sitting and minding their own business, ten pirates entered the tavern.

The tavern owner yelled out, "Pete, the Pirate Merchant, how is my old and closest friend?"

With a gravelly voice, he replied, "I'm the best I've ever been. I've sunk a Spanish war ship." He chuckled.

"How many drinks, Pete?"

"Nine, Ryley, and five for me." Pete chuckled again. Pete looked around the room searching for trouble and saw Shandell sitting a few tables down from where he and his men were standing.

"Ryley," Pete yelled out. "What's going on here? Last year, Jake lets this girl who thinks she's a pirate into his post. Now I see one in your tavern."

Setting down the drinks, Ryley said, "Look, Pete, there are women pirates and men pirates, and their money all spends the same, so let it go."

Determined to make trouble, Pete continued to throw more fuel onto the fire. "You can't sail anywhere without seeing a woman there. You give women an inch, and they'll take the whole sea." Pete stared at Shandell, daring her to say something.

Shandell looked over but ignored Pete because to her, he wasn't worth the effort of removing her sword from her sheath. Pete was going to get a fight started even if it killed him.

"Ryley," Pete said, "I know of one other girl who calls herself the Princess Pirate, and she thinks she's good enough to sit and drink with us men." With drink in hand, Pete approached Shandell, daring her to make a move.

Shandell had finished a long trip on the ship and wanted to be left alone and drink her rum and water, but Pete kept needling her. Glenn spoke up, "Go back to the bar, mister, and please leave us alone."

With a wild look in his eyes, Pete yelled out, "Please! What kind of pirates are you who say please?"

After taking all she could, Shandell stood up with this warning to Pete: "Listen, you old derelict, I'm not in the mood to listen to an old man's ramblings that has one foot in the grave and is ready to have the other one to follow make noise, so shut up and leave us alone!"

Getting what he wanted, Pete said, "You have a sword hanging on your side, little girl. Use it if you have the guts."

Shandell pulled her sword from her sheath at the same time Pete and his men pulled theirs. Shandell's men had their swords drawn as well, and then it really got exciting as the swords were clanging against one another with a tremendous sound!

 Princess Who?
1673

Pete was doing his best to take down Shandell but wasn't succeeding. He gave it all he had. He hated women to his very core, and he was planning to have one less in the world. Shandell, swinging her sword from left to right, said to Pete, "If you want to see the sun come up tomorrow, old man, lay down your sword."

Pete got that much more infuriated as he answered, "You talk just like that princess I hate." Pete thrust his sword toward Shandell's' left side but missed. Shandell could've run her sword straight through Pete's chest with ease but cut him in his left side just enough to bring him to his knees.

Glenn and Shandell's men had everything else under control with several of Pete's men lying on the tavern floor dead and some sliced open like watermelons. Pete looked around and knew he was at the mercy of a woman when he spoke out, "Kill me and get it over with. I'll never submit to a woman."

Shandell slid her sword back into her sheath after wiping the blood from the long, shiny blade. Then she removed her knife from her left boot, putting the blade under Pete's chin; and as she raised his head with her knife blade, she asked, "Who's this girl they call the Princess Pirate?" Pete, having eyes of bloody hate, grunted and said, "Go ahead and kill me because I'm not talking."

"I'll spare you your life, Pete, if you tell me what I want to know."

Pete laughed crazily and told Shandell, "Go ahead and run me through, you vixen, because if you don't, I'll find you someday and run my sword straight through your bloody heart!"

Ryley approached Shandell and said, "Don't kill, Pete, and I'll tell you what you want to know about the Princess Pirate. But one question first. Why do you want to know about the princess? You after her and going to try and kill her?"

Lowering her knife, Shandell said, "I'm curious about her and why she's called Princess Pirate."

"A warning first to you, miss."

"Call me Shandell if you would."

"All right, Shandell, the warning is if you do meet the princess, don't engage her into a sword fight because you'll be the loser."

"I'm not looking to fight with her, just to meet her. Now tell me where I can find her."

Pete and his men were picking themselves up off the floor while Ryley told Shandell and Glenn where to find the Princess and also revealed the code signals that would give them permission to enter the cove. Then Ryley took Pete and his surviving men in the back room to patch their wounds.

The pirates that were not hurt took the dead pirates to the back of the tavern building and dug several six-foot holes and just threw their bodies in like sacks of grain. When Pete's men were finished, they entered back into the tavern as though it was a normal thing to do.

24
Meet a Fellow Swordswoman
1673

The *Thunder Bay* pulled up anchor, let down her sails, and sailed toward Pirates Cove. Glenn was in Shandell's cabin, telling her the ship was set on course and they should be at Pirates Cove in four or five days, depending on the weather and sea conditions. Before Glenn left, Shandell asked Glenn to wait; she wanted to ask him something. Glenn stood there in the cabin doorway and waited as Shandell confronted him.

Shandell couldn't contain her feelings toward Glenn any longer and asked, "Do you love me, Glenn?"

"Why do you ask me that question, Shandell?"

"I see it in your eyes, Glenn, whenever you talk to me and stare me in the face."

Glenn knew this was the time when he pulled Shandell close to him and leaned over to kiss her on her lips.

Shandell, who has never been kissed like this before, felt a beautiful, sensational feeling in herself she has never felt before or experienced. Shandell returned his kisses with greater and more emotion. Stopping to gather herself, Shandell's face glowed as she said, "I'm also in love with you too, Glenn."

Mike, one of Shandell's men passing by the cabin, saw her door was still open. He interrupted Shandell's and Glenn's conversation. "Pardon me, Captain, I didn't mean to interrupt, but the men would like to know about this Pirates Cove we are sailing too."

Glenn, still gazing into Shandell's eyes, said, "I'll be on deck within a few minutes and will give the helmsmen the code signals."

"Aye, sir." Glenn kissed Shandell again and said, "I better get top side and take command Shandell if we're to get to Pirates Cove on time." Shandell leaned up against the doorpost, watching Glenn while he walked away.

The men on the *Thunder Bay* have never been this far into England territorial seas before. The men on these pirate ships sailed the Caribbean seas most of their lives. They stayed to the south of the Atlantic seas and never have heard of Pirates Cove.

Later, on board the *Thunder Bay*, Shandell and Glenn met again and were alone on the other side of the ship taking up where they left off earlier. Shandell was hyped up now and was enjoying this new experience.

Glenn, being curious, asked, "Why do you want to meet this princess when it'll take time away from you searching for the last pirate that you haven't found yet?"

"I'd like to meet a fellow swordswoman, Glenn. It would be exciting to me to meet another woman that can use a sword and find out how good she really is."

Not feeling right about this, Glenn said, "Shandell, let's sail away from Pirates Cove and continue the search for that last pirate."

"What's wrong with you, Glenn? You act as if I were wanting to have a personal sword duel with this princess."

"I just have a bad feeling about this, Shandell."

"Relax, Glenn. I'm going to introduce myself and hope we can become friends, and then we'll leave." Glenn was hoping that was all it was going to be, but he had a bad feeling down deep that there was going to be trouble, and when he got those feelings, he hated them.

25

THE LAST PIRATE
1673

BACK AT THE cove, Rebekah was looking for Troy; he was nowhere to be found on the *Rose*. Bret and Rex were putting up some wood alongside the cabin wall that led below deck. The wood they were replacing rotted from the salty seawater that raked havoc on wooden ships.

"Hi, Princess," Bret said, "Can we be of help to you?"

"Yes, Bret, I'm looking for Troy, and he's nowhere to be found on the ship."

"I saw Troy walking along the dock going toward the jungle, Princess," Rex told her.

"Thank you, Rex, and the wood work is beautiful." Rebekah climbed over the railing going down to a long boat that sat alongside the *Black Rose*.

Rebekah arrived at the dock, climbed onto the dock, and headed toward the jungle-like area looking for Troy. The cove was surrounded by caverns of rock ledges, and in the center of the island was the jungle where the sun comes shining through.

Rebekah was always amazed how the cove was so warm during wintertime, and the jungle never did freeze, and the plants and trees always stayed fairly green during that time. Jack explained to her it has something to do with the hot-water springs that flow underground. The warmth coming up from below kept the cove and jungle at certain temperatures all year round.

Rebekah just loved it here at the cove and was glad she had a warm place to be when the weather changed. Seeing Troy's boot prints in the sand, Rebekah followed them. Rebekah came upon Troy sitting under a palm tree looking out toward a stream that flowed through the island.

Rebekah cleared her throat while walking up; she didn't want to surprise Troy. Troy acknowledged Rebekah and said, "Princess, what are you doing here?"

"I wanted to talk with you, Troy, but you weren't on the ship. Rex told me he saw you go into the jungle, so I followed you here."

"What can I do for you, Princess?"

"I just wanted you to know, Troy, how sorry I am about almost getting you drowned in that old ship last week."

"Princess, I was just as curious about that old ship as you were. I was too scared to go in. You just gave me the courage to do so, Princess."

"I still want to say I'm sorry, Troy. Before I leave, Troy, may I ask why you're here all by yourself?"

"I come here to think, Princess, about the girl I tried to help six years ago and always wondered if she got away safe. After telling you the story about my first raid as a pirate, the memory of her came back to me."

Understanding his concern, Rebekah said, "You did all you could possibly do, Troy. You were overpowered, but at least you tried."

"I guess, Princess, I'm not sure. After all of these years, I always thought maybe I was a coward and let the girl down."

"Troy, you're no coward! I see you on those raids and watch you fight with your sword and never see fear in your face. You're a very brave man, and I wish I had more men like you to fight by my side."

"You mean that, Princess?"

"Yes, I do, Troy, and remember princesses don't lie!"

Troy smiled at Rebekah and said, "I best get back to the ship, Princess, and get back to work before Joe comes looking for me."

"I'll walk back with you, Troy."

Back out at sea, the *Thunder Bay* wasn't far from Pirates Cove. On board Shandell's ship, there was a fight between some of her men, and it was getting bloody. Flint and another pirate named Cody were exchanging blows and were about to kill each other when Glenn broke it up.

Glenn got struck by some fists during the struggle. Glenn was a patient man, but to stop the fight, he returned back those blows with his fists and knocked both men down and implanted their rears in the deck of the ship. Standing over the two men, Glenn asked, "What started the fight?"

Flint, who served four years with Shandell and became loyal to her, said, "I threw the first punch, sir."

"Why, Flint?"

"Cody said some things about Shandell I didn't like, and the other men didn't either, so I hit him, Glenn."

"What do you have to say about this, Cody?" Glenn asked.

"I said what I said, Glenn, and meant it. If you want to run a sword through me, go ahead."

"What did you say about Shandell that got this fight started, Cody?"

"I told Flint and the other men I wanted Shandell and desired her for myself, and I still do."

Glenn ordered the two men, "Get to your feet, the both of you." Standing firm, Glenn said, "Let me put all of you men straight. Shandell makes her own decisions. She's a grown woman, and whoever she chooses for her man, well, Cody, you'll just have to live with her decision like the rest of the men on this ship."

Every man on that ship knew who Shandell picked for her man, and that was Glenn Austin.

That very night, the *Thunder Bay* was just outside the Pirates Cove entrance giving the code signals for permission to enter.

Rebekah and all her men were in the post, relaxing. Jack was talking to Rebekah, "You know, Princess, things have been a little too quiet around the post these last several days."

"What do you mean quiet, Jack?"

"I mean no pirates coming in the post and starting trouble."

"It has been quiet, hasn't it, Jack?" Rebekah said, now taking a drink of her hot chocolate.

The *Thunder Bay* was now sailing into the cove. Glenn went below deck to inform Shandell. "We're sailing into Pirates Cove Shandell. They gave us permission to enter. How many men do you want to row over to the trading post with us?"

"I'll leave that decision up to you, Glenn."

"Very well, I'll pick four of our best."

Back in the post, Troy decided to sit with Jack and Rebekah. "You all right, Troy?" Rebekah asked.

"I'm not doing too well at poker tonight, Princess. Pete and his brother, Curt, are on a lucky streak tonight and are winning all the hands."

"I'll give you some money towards your next pay if you need it, Troy."

"No, thank you, Princess, my mother always told me to quit when you're ahead."

Jack laughed and said, "My brother would tell me the same thing when I was losing with the men on my brother's ship."

The *Thunder Bay* settling into the cove lifted her sails and let down the anchor. Seeing the *Black Rose* sitting by the waterfall, Shandell was anxious to meet the princess. After the long boats were lowered, Glenn gave orders.

"Flint, Cody, Mike, and Patrick, you four will accompany Shandell and me over to the trading post."

"Aye, sir."

PART III

Shandell Lee Story (Continued) 1673

Last time, you remember, Shandell and five of her crew were rowing over to the trading post at Pirates Cove in a longboat. Shandell had already caught up with four of the pirates that murdered her family and had one man left to find. Then her journey would be over. The last man unfortunately was Troy Bowers, a man under the princess's command. When the boat Shandell and her men are in arrive at Jake's post, things should get interesting when Shandell enters into the post and sees Troy.

At the same time, Shandell and her men were climbing onto the dock. Jake was over at Rebekah's table where she and Jack always sat.

"Troy."

"Yes, Jake."

"I need you and Marty to help me move some gunpowder barrels in the back room." "Sure, Jake. I'll get Marty, and we both will be in the back room waiting for you."

Soon as Troy and Marty entered in the back room with Jake, Shandell and her men just entered through the doors at the post.

Rebekah, observing Shandell and her men entering into the post, asked Jack, "Why couldn't Jake ask some of the pirates that hang out at the post here to do some of the work in the back instead of using Troy and Marty?"

"Jake probably doesn't trust them in handling such explosive material. Besides, some of that gunpowder is ours, Rebekah." Before taking another drink of her hot chocolate, Rebekah said, "That makes sense."

Coming from the back room, Jake noticed he has several new customers at the bar and welcomes them. "Welcome to Pirates Cove. They call me Jake. What can I do for you?"

"Shandell is my name, and my first mate standing next to me is Glenn Austin, and the other men are some of my ship's crew."

Rebekah listened with great curiosity to find out who this young girl was and where she was from. Jack was staring at Shandell with a glow shining in his face.

Rebekah noticed Jack's stare at Shandell and told him, "Your face might freeze in that position if you stare at that girl too long, Jack."

Jack grinned, and after taking another drink from his mug, said, "Yeah."

Rebekah, observing Shandell closely, noticed she wasn't an ordinary girl commanding a crew of pirates with a sword hanging on her right side and a huge knife in each boot. This Shandell could mean trouble. Glenn laid a sack of gold on the bar, telling Jake, "This should pay for any supplies we'll need plus our drinks."

Jake picked up the sack, shuck it, and while listening to the gold coins jingle, he replied, "Your credit sounds good to me." Then Jake started serving them their drinks.

27
Rebekah and Shandell Meet
1673

Shandell noticed Rebekah and Jack, she approached their table with Glenn by her side, and introduced herself. "My name is Shandell Lee, and this is my first mate Glenn Austin."

Rebekah stared at Glenn with a glow in her eye and uttered loud enough for Jack to hear: "He can sail on my ship anytime."

Jack, hearing what Rebekah said, just took another drink knowing he had it coming.

"Please sit, Shandell, you and Glenn. We have something in common."

"What might that be?"

"My name is Rebekah Martin, and I have my own ship and crew as well, but I go by my title the Princess Pirate."

"I've been wanting to meet you Rebekah, a fellow swordswoman."

"Maybe you and I can exchange war stories later, Rebekah, or should I call you princess?"

"Either one is fine, Shandell, or maybe tomorrow we can talk again."

"Excuse Glenn and me, Rebekah. I still have some business with Jake."

Shandell, getting more acquainted with Jake, went back to the bar. Jake stared at Shandell and gave her the once-over and then asked, "Yes, Shandell, what will you have?"

"I'll have rum with lots of water, Jake."

Jake poured and asked, "I never have heard of you before, Shandell, where are you and your men from?"

"From the Orient, Jake, the country of China."

"What brings you here, Shandell, and how did you learn about Pirates Cove?"

"When we were at Sailor's Warf, the tavern owner their told us about Pirates Cove and about your trading post for supplies, and I also heard about the princess and wished to meet her."

"Now that you have your supplies and have met the princess, planning on staying long?"

"We'll be sailing on, Jake. I have one more job to attend to before sailing back to the Orient."

Taking her last drink, Shandell looked up above the rim of her mug and saw Troy and Marty come out of the back room. Troy, wiping the sweat from his brow, said, "The work is all finished, Jake, and could Marty and I have a drink of brandy to quench our thirst?"

"Why, sure, Troy, have two if you want." Jake poured two mugs full with brandy.

Shandell stood within a few feet of Troy and knew from the drawings he was the other man. Shandell, with her hand gripping tightly around her sword handle, started to pull her sword from the sheath when Glenn stopped her by grabbing hold onto her hand. Shandell looked up at Glenn and said, "It's him, Glenn. Don't stop me. I want to see his blood spilled all over the tavern floor."

"Don't be foolish, Shandell. Look around the room. We don't know how many of these pirates are under the princess' command, and he might be too."

Gritting her teeth and keeping control, Shandell nodded and slid her sword back into the sheath.

Rebekah noticed something was wrong by the way Shandell and Glenn were exchanging words quietly to each other and asked, "Something wrong, Shandell?"

With a glazed look in her eyes, Shandell said, "Everything is fine, Rebekah, my men and I are going back to the ship. It's been a long day."

Walking out of the post with her men, Shandell just stood there, staring out at the waterfall. She was beside herself. There was Troy, the last man she was searching for, and she had to put off killing him until the time was right.

Glenn put his hand on Shandell's shoulder and said, "You did the wise thing in there, Shandell. This princess and her men look well trained and experienced in sword fighting. You'll have to wait for the right time in killing this man."

"I know, Glenn. It has been so long, and he was standing right there within inches of my sword blade.

"My hand itched to pull my sword, Glenn, and run him through."

"I understand, Shandell, but this is not the time."

"Let's get back to the ship, Glenn. I want to be away from here right now so I can think."

Back inside the post, Troy notice something strange about Shandell standing there. It's like he met her before but couldn't place where or when. Shrugging it off, he and Marty went back to drinking their brandy. Rebekah watched Troy down his brandy and asked, "I didn't know you drank strong drinks, Troy?"

"I don't, Princess, but moving all of those barrels makes a man thirsty."

Rebekah thought she knew all there was to know about Troy, but he continued to surprise her.

"Princess."

"Yes, Troy."

"Who's the girl you were talking to at the bar a few minutes ago?"

"Her name is Shandell Lee. She came all the way from China."

Troy stood there for a moment, thinking.

"You all right, Troy?"

"I guess so, Princess. There's something about that girl, but I can't put my finger on it. Maybe if I see her again, it'll come to me."

Back on the *Black Rose*, standing by the railing, Rebekah and Jack were talking, least Jack was talking.

"Princess, Princess."

"Yes, Jack, I'm sorry. My mind was somewhere else at the moment."

"Somewhere else, as in Shandell Lee?"

"I can't believe she's just here at the cove to meet me and get supplies."

"I do, Rebekah. You have made quite a name for yourself and have a reputation with that sword of yours."

"So you believe her, Jack?"

"In a way, Princess. She and her men are a long way from home."

"That's why I'm suspicious, Jack. She's come this far for a reason other than what she told us, and I'd like to know why. There are plenty of ships for her and her men to raid in the Orient, Jack. Why come here?"

"One thing is for sure, Rebekah. She didn't have to tell us she and her men were pirates. You would have to be blind not to see that. Something else I was wondering about, Rebekah."

"What's that, Jack?"

"How good is Shandell with that sword she carries?"

"I don't know, Jack, but I hope what she said it true. She wanted to meet me and pick up supplies. Good night, Jack." Rebekah kissed Jack and went to her cabin.

28
Troy Set Up for the Kill
1673

Over at the *Thunder Bay*, Glenn and Shandell were by the railing of her ship, having a discussion of their own.

"I know how bad you want to kill this man, Shandell, but I think it'd be in your best interest and the crew if you forget about him."

"I ought to run you through with my sword, Glenn, for saying that."

"I'm serious, Shandell. This princess is no pushover. I can see it in her eyes, and if this is one of her men, she isn't giving him up without a fight."

"Troy...Jake called him Troy."

"What was that, Shandell?"

"Jake called his name, Troy."

"Please, Shandell, think this over. You could be getting in over your head with this princess and her men."

"If this Troy is one of her men, Glenn, and she gets in the way, then I'll have to kill her as well."

"That doesn't sound like you came here to be friends with the princess, Shandell?"

"I'll be her friend, Glenn, as long as she stays out of my way. I'm getting a headache from all of this talk, Glenn. I'm going to my cabin and will see you in the morning."

Glenn knew the bad feeling he had was coming true. Shandell was willing to fight against Rebekah to kill the last man she has been searching for. It seemed to Glenn that the search for these men had put a bloodthirsty taste in Shandell's mouth, and it was eating away at her good side. This worried Glenn because this type of emotion could destroy her permanently.

The next morning, Shandell was up bright and early when she saw Troy over at the post and walking down the dock toward the jungle-like area. This was her chance, and she was taking it while nobody else was around. Shandell took a rowboat over to the post side, and when she got there, she climbed onto the dock and followed Troy toward the jungle.

Not long after Jack saw Glenn on the *Thunder Bay*, he decided to row over and have a talk with Glenn.

Rebekah was up and in the galley. She just had black coffee this morning instead of her hot chocolate. Rebekah noticed her pants were getting a little snug around the waist and was getting worried she was putting on weight.

While over at the *Thunder Bay*, Jack and Glenn were having a talk.

"Tell me this, Glenn, man to man, what's Shandell's motive for being here? Does she want to try her sword skills against Rebekah's?"

Glenn stood there and said nothing.

"What's wrong, Glenn? Why don't you answer me?"

Glenn, with his jaw muscles twitching, answered, "No, that's not why she's here, Jack. She did tell Rebekah the truth about wanting to meet her, but it's Troy she's after."

After Glenn told Jack the story, Jack went and got Rebekah so Glenn could repeat the story to her.

At the same time Glenn was telling Rebekah why Shandell was here, Shandell caught up with Troy by the water stream that he always sits by when thinking.

"Hello, Troy," Shandell said when she approached him.

Troy stood up and asked, "How do you know my name?"

"Remember last night when Rebekah and I were talking in Jake's post?"

Troy replied, "Yes, I do remember you a little, and I told the Princess there was something about you that was familiar, but I couldn't remember."

"I'm going to fill in the blanks for you, Troy."

29
YOU'RE A COWARD, SHANDELL
1673

"It was six years ago in the country of China. There were these pirates who came to our land to steal our precious jade that our people have worked so hard to find and even risked their lives for. Are you following me so far, Troy?" Shandell's left hand was resting on her sword handle while she continued the story.

"I think so, but who are you?"

"I'm getting around to that, Troy. Back to what I was saying, these pirates weren't satisfied with taking the jade statues—they also found an innocent little girl hiding for her life in a hole in the ground."

Things were now coming back to Troy, and he thought he knew who Shandell was. "I'm the man who helped you escape, don't you remember? I fired a shot from my pistol and killed one of the pirates that was hurting you, and you got away."

"What do you mean I got away?" Shandell staring at Troy strangely.

"I tried to help you escape, and after all of these years, I've wondered if you had gotten away, and now I know you did."

Not believing Troy, Shandell told him, "That was my sister, Christy, you're mistaking me for, and no, she didn't get away. The pirates that molested and stabbed her to death got away until now. I've gotten revenge on them all, and you're the last one, Troy."

Shandell pulled her sword from her sheath. "Pull your sword, Troy, or I'll just run you through as you stand there."

Putting two and two together, Troy tried to explain to Shandell he was innocent. "I'm sorry about your sister, but I did try to help her."

"I don't believe you, Troy. Now pull your sword—at least you'll have a fighting chance. That's more than my sister had." Shandell wheeled her sword around toward Troy.

Then Shandell heard Rebekah's voice boldly say, "Put your sword down, Shandell. You aren't killing Troy!"

"You think not, Rebekah." Shandell turned to stare at Rebekah with defiance and saw Jack and Glenn standing there also.

"Why did you tell them, Glenn? You were supposed to be on my side, but I see you're against me."

"That's not true, Shandell. I believe Troy is innocent, and if you kill him, it'll be murder just like the men who killed your sister. Do you want that on your hands?"

"He's just as guilty for murdering my sister as the rest, Glenn."

Shandell started swinging her sword toward Troy. Troy tried to defend himself but was no match against Shandell as she took him down and was about to run him through. Rebekah shouted out, "You're a coward, Shandell."

Rebekah approached Shandell, holding her sword in hand. Shandell stopped and turned and said to Rebekah, "I'm no coward, but Troy is going to die for the death of my sister."

"Yes, you're a coward, Shandell. Troy wouldn't have a chance coming up against you with your sword abilities, and you know it. I'll fight in his place, Shandell, if you aren't a coward to face me."

"Rebekah, I don't want to hurt you or kill you, so stay out of this—it's not your concern."

"That's where you're wrong, Shandell. Troy is under my command, and his safety is my concern, and if you continue and run him through, I'll avenge his death by killing you."

"To prove to you, Rebekah, I'm no coward, you can fight in Troy's place, but I warn you this—if you fail and I run you through, I'm still going to kill Troy."

"That sounds fair enough, Shandell. Troy."

"Yes, Princess."

"Go over and stand with Glenn and Jack."

Shandell, It's Finished
1673

Before this fight got started, all of Shandell's men and Rebekah's men were present. This was going to be a fight to remember, they all said to each other.

"Shandell, you can back out now. There's no shame in letting a man live for trying to help your sister."

"He was there, Rebekah—that makes him just as guilty."

Shandell started swinging her sword toward Rebekah. Rebekah blocked Shandell's first move and came back with killing swings of her own, but Shandell was no amateur as Rebekah learned real quickly. Shandell blocked Rebekah's sword blade and came back swinging toward Rebekah with such deadly slicing. Rebekah had to block and block as she was being forced backward so not to be cut in half by Shandell's deadly blade. Rebekah hasn't faced anyone so deadly with a sword since the sword fight with Wayne Murphy.

Rebekah was defending herself, barely keeping out of range of Shandell's devilish blade. Observing Shandell's every move, Rebekah waited for an opening. Now it was time for Rebekah to show Shandell some great moves of her own. Having to use some of the techniques Ike showed her when she got into a situation such as this, Rebekah started making her moves on Shandell.

Rebekah was faster in her maneuvers than Shandell was, and when Rebekah figured her enemies' moves, then they were big in trouble. With her sword abilities, Rebekah came swinging back toward Shandell and was now backing her down. Shandell was no pushover by any means as she, with a straight slice of her sword, cut Rebekah across her left arm. Rebekah screamed out in pain, and blood started dripping from her deep wound.

With adrenaline and anger rushing through Rebekah's body, she came after Shandell with deadly cutting slices! With two swings of her sword, Rebekah cut Shandell deep in her left side and sliced her right wrist that caused her to drop her sword. Gritting her teeth, Rebekah forced Shandell up against a tree, and with the tip of her sword blade up against Shandell's throat, Rebekah yelled out to her, "It's finished, Shandell. It's finished!"

Coming to herself, Shandell lowered her head and said, "Yes, Rebekah, it's finished."

Rebekah lowered her sword and backed away. Troy picked up Shandell's sword and handed it to her, saying, "I did try to help your sister, Shandell, and I'm very sorry to have let her down." Troy lowered his head and walked away.

Standing next to Rebekah, Jack wrapped her arm with some cloth he tore from his shirtsleeve. Glenn, doing the same for Shandell, took his shirt and tied it around Shandell's ribs. Flint tore off his shirtsleeve and wrapped it around Shandell's wrist. Shandell, weakened from bloodloss, asked Rebekah, "Why did you spare me my life, Rebekah? From the sword abilities I witnessed from you, you could've run me through. Why did you let me live?"

"I saw no reason in killing you, Shandell. I lost my father to a man who run him through with his sword and showed no mercy. I wasn't going to kill you, Shandell. I knew you're hurt and all you wanted was vengeance for your family so they can rest in peace. And maybe someday my father will rest in peace."

"I'm sorry to hear that, Rebekah. I didn't know about your father."

"Let's go back to our ships, Shandell, and after we're bandaged up properly by old Jake and Micky, we can talk and patch up our differences."

THE SEA OVERRUN BY WOMEN PIRATE RAIDERS 1673

WHILE REBEKAH AND Shandell were being doctored up by Jake and Micky, Jake, who missed the sword fight of the century, complained the whole time he was cleaning and bandaging their wounds.

Later, when Rebekah and Shandell went back to their ships to get the rest they needed, Jake asked Jack, "Why didn't somebody come and get me, Jack? I would've loved to see the sword battle between Rebekah and Shandell."

Jack stood there, telling Jake, "All of the years you've been running this post, Jake, haven't you seen enough bloodshed and guts spilled?"

"I have, Jack, but the princess and Shandell? Come on, Jack, that'll probably never happen again in my lifetime."

Jack walked away, turned, and said, "Yes, and I hope it never will again."

Back in good Old England, Morgan is going over the last two ships that were raided in three weeks. One, of course, was by the princess herself, but the other one was raided by Shandell and her ship, the *Thunder Bay*.

Morgan read the report and talked to the captains of the two ships. They were both in his office getting the boom lowered on them by Morgan. As Morgan was marching back and forth in his office, he said, "Captain Thomas."

"Yes, Sir Morgan."

"Your ship was raided by the Princess Pirate?"

"Yes, sir, it was."

"Captain Sims."

"Yes, Sir Morgan."

"Your ship was raided by a young girl who calls herself Shandell Lee?"

"Yes, Sir Morgan, and I thought she was the Princess Pirate herself the way she used that sword of hers like the devil himself."

"You men may leave and go back to your ships," Morgan said while thinking out loud. "We now have a new female pirate who calls herself Shandell Lee in our waters raiding ships." Morgan poured a drink and sat down to think this one out. Morgan read the reports again, thinking that the princess was now raiding ships under a different name.

No, that can't be, Morgan thought. One ship was raided five hundred sea miles from the other, and on the same day, even the princess's ship couldn't travel that fast. Morgan believed now that there were two different women raiding England ships and these two women can use the sword like the devil himself according to the reports.

Morgan had to do something before the seas became overrun by women pirate raiders. Morgan sat and contemplated about this. Even when he went home to his mansion, he still thought about how he was going to stop the princess and these other pirates.

The days passed back at Pirates Cove while Rebekah and Shandell were letting their bodies heal. Shandell was letting her mind heal as well.

Three days after the sword duel, Glenn was in Shandell's cabin talking with her.

"Glenn, I've been thinking."

"Yes, Shandell, I'm listening."

"I was wrong in trying to kill Troy. I knew he was telling the truth from the beginning. I was so bent on getting all of those men in Christy's drawings. I let my emotions dictate my judgment, and I could've killed an innocent man who risked his life in trying to help Christy."

"When did you come to the conclusion that Troy was telling you the truth?"

"When Troy picked up my sword and handed it to me. A guilty man would've fled before the fight between me and Rebekah was over."

32
FRIENDS FOR LIFE
1673

"So you're satisfied with things now, Shandell?"

"Yes, Glenn," she said. "When we killed the first four pirates, that's when my family started resting in peace."

"I'm so glad of that, Shandell. Now we can get back to business?"

"What business is that, Glenn?"

"Back out to sea, raiding ships for their treasure."

"I'm going home, Glenn, back to the Orient, and hanging up my sword."

Glenn, not being able to live without Shandell, kneeled before her. "Marry me, Shandell, and we both will settle down together."

Shandell started to give Glenn an answer when somebody knocked on Shandell's cabin door. Shandell said, "Come in."

Opening the door, Rebekah entered and said, "I just come over to see how you were doing, Shandell."

"Glenn, would you please excuse Rebekah and me for a little while?" Glenn asked Rebekah to excuse him as he walked out and closed the cabin door behind him.

"Please sit, Rebekah, while we talk."

Rebekah sat while Shandell started with the conversation.

"I wanted to thank you, Rebekah, for all that you did for me."

"I didn't do anything, Shandell, really!"

"Yes, you did, Rebekah. I was so eaten up inside on killing every man that was on that paper my sister drew. I never thought of one of them being innocent."

"What about the other four men you caught up with several weeks ago, Shandell?"

"If you were there, Rebekah, and heard their words and saw their actions that admitted to their guilt, you, Rebekah, would've known too they were the ones who murdered my family and probably other families before they left China.

"The last man I saw fall from my sword told me my sister was soft and kissed real good. Then he laughed about what he had said. Soon after he said those words, he fell from my sword. I'm not regretting those men who I killed, Rebekah, but you've saved me from future grief if I would've learned later Troy was innocent."

"I know my men, Shandell, and Troy is a good man. He was just in the wrong place at the wrong time."

"I know that now, Rebekah, and you can be assured—and Troy also. You two have a friend in me forever, and if you ever need my help, I'll be there."

"Thank you, Shandell for saying that, and I know we are friends for life."

"One more thing, Rebekah, before you leave."

"Yes, Shandell, what is it?"

"I was trained by the best sword fighters in the Eastern world. Why did I lose against you? Not that I'm glad I didn't, but what was I doing wrong?"

"You did everything right, Shandell. There was only one man I ever come up against with a sword that I almost lost against, and you're next to him in his abilities."

"So what did I do wrong, Rebekah?"

"It wasn't your sword fighting that was off—it was your emotions that betrayed you."

"Emotions, Rebekah?"

"Yes, Shandell, if you would've concentrated more on your fighting than wanting to run your enemy through, I might not have beaten you."

"I'll remember that in the future, Rebekah. Thank you."

"Just don't challenge me to another sword fight, Shandell," Rebekah expressed with a firm look on her face.

"Rebekah, I want to do something." Shandell stood up and walked over to Rebekah. "Give me your hand, Rebekah."

Rebekah handed Shandell her hand. Shandell took her knife and pricked her own thumb and then Rebekah's thumb. Shandell then put their two thumbs together and squeezed. "Now our blood runs through each of our bodies, Rebekah. We're now blood sisters, and sisters don't fight each other with swords."

Rebekah hugged Shandell, telling her, "I now have two sisters, you and Carlena."

"Yes, Rebekah, and you're now my new sister."

A few more days passed when Shandell and her ship, the *Thunder Bay*, was leaving the cove. Shandell stood in the rear of her ship with Glenn by her side waving to Rebekah goodbye. With a deep sigh, Rebekah told Jack, "I now have two close friends I'll miss, Shandell and Gabriella.

That evening in the trading post, Rebekah and Jack were at their table while her men were playing pirate poker. Jack sat there and thought he smelled coffee and asked, "Is that coffee you're drinking, Princess?"

"Yes, Jack, I thought I'd give coffee a try for a while. I was getting tired of hot chocolate." Then she smiled.

Jack thought for a minute and said, "I was sure, Princess, you told me one time your favorite drink is hot chocolate and you couldn't stand the smell of coffee."

"Things change, Jack. I, all of a sudden, had a desire for coffee."

33
PANTS A LITTLE SNUG
1673

JACK KEPT THINKING about what Rebekah said when he asked her, "It isn't because your pants are starting to feel a little snug around your waist, is it, Princess?"

"Why do you ask that, Jack?" Rebekah blushed. "I always thought, Princess, if you kept drinking that hot chocolate, it would catch up with you sooner or later."

"You know something, Jack?"

"What, Princess?" Jack grinned.

"Don't ever challenge me to a sword fight. My sword might accidentally slip, and you won't have to worry about growing old." With that said, Rebekah retired for the evening and went back to the ship.

Troy came over and asked Jack, "Is the princess all right? She left as though she was upset?"

"She's fine, Troy. Soon as she gets back out to sea and raids another ship or two, she'll be fit as a fiddle."

"I hope so, Jack. I don't like seeing the princess upset."

"I know the princess, Troy. She has been cooped up here at the cove too long, and she starts getting restless." Jack got up and went back to the *Black Rose* also.

That night, Rebekah was looking at her father's picture before bed. "Father," she was saying to the picture.

At that very same moment, Jack was standing in front of Rebekah's cabin door. He wanted to apologize to her for what he had said, but before he knocked on her cabin door, he heard her talking and listened.

"Father, I wish you could've met Jack, my first mate. He is such a help to me, and I depend on him so much. I love Jack with all of my heart and couldn't live without him."

Jack was smiling when he heard those words.

"Something else, Father, Jack loves me, I'm sure, but he sometimes gets me upset. I guess that's one of Jack's faults, but I still love him."

Jack, of course, frowned when he heard that. *But Rebekah is right*, he thought to himself.

Rebekah told her father good night as she put his picture back under her pillow, and she went to bed. Jack, entering his cabin, thought about Rebekah and how much he loved her. He loved her so much, and he made a promise to watch over her safety no matter the cost.

Back in Old England, Morgan was thinking about the princess and this new pirate girl that was raiding their ships and something had to be done. The next day, Morgan was drinking a little wine to help him think.

John Hendrexson entered Morgan's office. That's what Morgan didn't need while he was trying to think. "Morgan, I guess you've already read the report on this pirate girl who raided one of our ships the same day the Princess Pirate raided one?"

"Yes, Sir Hendrexson, I have, and I'm working on a plan to put a stop to both of these women pirates as we speak."

"You've told me this before, Morgan, and still no princess."

"I know, sir, but it's just a matter of time."

PART IV

34
A TASTE OF LOVE
1673

A FEW DAYS after Shandell's ship left the cove, Rebekah was thinking about Carlena. Rebekah would stare out of her back ship windows and remember the good times they had together as young girls. Rebekah had been home only once in four years to see Carlena. Being homesick, Rebekah was going back home to see Carlena and visit her father's grave. Tomorrow morning, she'd have Jack set the *Black Rose* on course to her father's island, Freedom Port. Rebekah laid her head back on her pillow, thinking of Carlena while her eyes closed to sleep. The following morning, Rebekah and Jack were having breakfast together.

"Jack, I want to go home and see my sister, Carlena, at Freedom Port."

Before taking a bite of food, Jack said, "That's not going to be possible, Princess."

Rebekah sat her cup of hot chocolate down and asked, "Why not?"

"Pete and Randy were in the hold of the ship inspecting for damage, and there was water slowly, but surely, leaking in from a five-foot crack on the left side of the ship."

Rebekah said, raising her voice, "Five-foot crack! How did this happen?"

"Things of this nature just happen to old ships, Princess. There are no explanations. Maybe it was stress from that explosion last year from the *Hogan*, and that's just a guess." Jack could see the disappointment in Rebekah's face.

"I'll be in my cabin, Jack. Find out how long it'll take to make the repairs."

Rebekah was leaving the galley while some of her men were coming in. "Good morning, Princess," they said.

"Don't say good morning to me. You get my ship fixed, and I mean soon as possible."

Louie asked Jack, "What's wrong with the princess this morning?"

"She's upset about the damage in the hold of the ship. She wanted to visit her sister, but now she has to wait a little longer."

Joe, staring at Micky with a hangover, said, "I need some hot coffee and make it strong. I had too much to drink last night and need something to get me motivated this morning." Micky shook his head, mumbling, "Not only am I the cook—I have to play doctor to a bunch of pirates."

After breakfast, Jack consulted Pete about the damage. "How long will it take to repair the crack in the ship's side, Pete?"

"At least two weeks, Jack. I've got to make sure the ship is watertight."

"I dread going to tell the princess the bad news, but somebody has to. Wish me luck, Pete."

Jack tapped on Rebekah's cabin door.

"Come in," Rebekah said.

Jack entered through the door, hoping Rebekah was in a better mood.

"Yes, what is it, Jack?"

"I know you're anxious to go and visit your sister, Princess, but if we sail thirty miles out, the *Black Rose* could possibly sink."

Rebekah, looking to blame someone, said, "Why didn't Pete and Curt find this crack last week when we didn't have anywhere to sail to?"

"Don't blame them, Rebekah," Jack growled back, putting Rebekah in her place.

35
NO ONE'S TO BLAME
1673

"Then who should I blame? Should I blame you, Jack? You're the first mate and are responsible for things on this ship."

"Nobody's to blame, Rebekah, and you ought to be very thankful this didn't happen out at sea a hundred sea miles from the cove."

"Jack, please leave. I'm getting a headache from all of this arguing."

"One more thing, Rebekah, you better think about—you have the best fighting pirate crew on the high seas, and they've given their total loyalty to you. Something I thought I'd never live to witness."

"You can leave now, Jack."

"Not just yet, Rebekah. I'm not finished." Jack now confronted her face-to-face. "Another thing you better think about before blaming your men for something that can happen to any ship: they'd all die for you."

Having a hard time dealing with her growing pains, Rebekah slapped Jack's face and said, "Jack, leave my cabin now, or I'll find someone else to take your place as first mate. Now get out!" Rebekah turned her back on Jack saying nothing else.

Jack turned and walked out knowing Rebekah didn't mean the hurtful words she spoke. Jack left to give Rebekah time to think about what she had said. After a few minutes, Rebekah turned to face Jack with tears in her eyes. She wanted to tell Jack she was sorry for the hurtful words she had spoken to him, but he was gone. Rebekah sat at her desk, laid her head into her hands, and wept.

That evening after Rebekah thought things out, and feeling better, she left her cabin and went top side. Standing on the deck of the ship, Rebekah saw Joe.

"Joe."

"Yes, Princess."

"Line all of the men up. I've something to say to them and Jack."

Marty was always excited when the princess had them line up for a talk. Rebekah was facing her men, and before she spoke, she saw Marty's smiling face and got all choked up and almost couldn't speak. Pulling herself together, Rebekah hesitated for a second and then said to her men, "I owe every man here an apology for my actions this morning. I know I have the best fighting pirates on the high seas and wouldn't trade you men for all the gold in China. Is there someone here who'd like to speak?"

Joe spoke up, "Princess, your men have a lot of work to do on the *Black Rose*. The sooner we get the repairs finished, the sooner you'll visit your sister."

Rebekah choked up a bit and said, "All right, you men get back to work, and that's an order."

"Yes, Princess!" her men yelled as they went back to work.

Carlena, Rebekah's Sister, Falls in Love
1673

Jack went over and gave Rebekah a great big grin and said to her, "You're not only a captain, Rebekah, but a good one as well."

"I'm sorry for what I said to you earlier, Jack. I'd never replace you as first mate. You're like my right arm."

Jack put the palm of his hand up against Rebekah's cheek, speaking these words, "Rebekah, I never believed you would, and if you did, I'd find a reason to stay on the ship. That's how much I love you."

Rebekah wasn't going to show any weakness in front of her men. She smiled at Jack then went back to her cabin. Marty, concerned about Rebekah, asked Jack a question. "Is the princess all right, Jack? I thought I saw a sad look on her face."

"Marty, as long as you're always there and fighting by her side, the princess will always be happy."

With that childlike grin, Marty went back over to Joe and told him, "You know, Joe, I think the princess likes me."

Joe never grins much but cracked just a small one after hearing what Marty had told him.

Later that evening, Jack and Rebekah were by the railing of the ship.

"Princess."

"Yes, Jack."

"Pete told me today it'd be less than two weeks repairing the crack in the side of the ship."

"That's great, Jack." Rebekah then gave Jack that beautiful smile of hers.

"You've never met my sister, Jack, but you'll like her. I'm sure." Rebekah reached up and kissed Jack good night, then went to her cabin.

Back at Freedom Port, Rebekah's sister, Carlena, had fallen in love with a man named Flent Kindel. Flent was one of Rebekah's suitor's when she turned eighteen, and her father thought it was time for her to marry, but Rebekah turned him down. Carlena, on the other hand, wanted Flent from the first day she saw him. Their meeting again all came about one day a few months ago when Flent, now working for his father, was delivering cargo from one of his father's ships. Flent, not knowing of Rebekah's war against England, thought she was still living at the castle.

Flent noticed a girl standing out on the balcony from the castle on the hill one evening while he was standing on the docks. Flent got his spyglass, and while staring through it, he thought he saw Rebekah standing there out on the balcony. Flent put another man in charge of things while he went to the castle to say hello to Rebekah.

Flent knocked on the huge door. The door opened, and the manservant asked, "Yes, may I help you, sir?"

"Yes, my name is Flent Kindel. May I speak with Miss Rebekah, please?"

"I'm sorry, sir, Miss Rebekah doesn't reside here anymore, and she's on an adventure, so I'm told."

"I saw her standing on the balcony moments ago."

"Oh, that's her sister, Carlena, sir. Several men who have visited here in the past have mistaken Carlena for Miss Rebekah."

Flent, remembering Carlena, asked, "May I then see Miss Carlena?"

The manservant let Flent in through the castle door, telling him, "Wait in the guest room, sir, while I summon Miss Carlena."

As Carlena entered into the guest room, seeing Flent, her heart started to beat a little faster as she approached and handed him her hand. Flent kissed her hand as they sat. Flent was totally taken away how Carlena resembled Rebekah in every way.

"Flent," Carlena spoke, "what brings you back to Freedom Port?"

"Deliveries for my father brought me back, Carlena, but if I would've known about you and how you've grown, I'd been back sooner."

"I'm so flattered, Flent."

"Carlena."

"Yes, Flent."

"I do have to get back to my ship. It sails in thirty minutes. May I come back and call on you again?"

Carlena's heart didn't want Flent to leave.

"Yes, you may, Flent, anytime and please make it soon."

The more time Flent spent visiting Carlena, the more their love grew for each other. Carlena was nineteen years of age now and was ready for marriage. Flent, after spending so much time with Carlena, learned of Rebekah being the Princess Pirate. That wasn't going to discourage him from asking Carlena for her hand in marriage.

Unfortunately, Flent's father's businesses were in trouble financially. If his father couldn't pay off their growing debts, then both businesses would go under. Flent, not wanting this to happen, was thinking of a way to help save his father's businesses. A wild thought came to Flent's mind: *Turn Rebekah into the authorities*. Flent remembered what he read several months ago about her reward, and it was five gold crowns for her capture. That'd be enough money to stabilize his father's businesses and make them solvent once again. Flent visited Carlena once again, and while they sat after dinner, they kissed.

"I've missed you so much, Flent, and I'm glad to have you back."

"I've missed you too, Carlena."

They kissed again.

"Carlena, when's the last time you spoke with Rebekah?"

"I haven't spoken with her since the day she came to visit me, and that was a year after she left to go see an old friend named Ike Taylor."

"She hasn't contacted you since?"

"Why, no, Flent. Why do you ask?"

"I'd like to see her, Carlena, and wish her well."

Carlena was disappointed; she was hoping Flent would ask her to marry him. *Maybe next time,* she thought.

The Betrayal
1673

Flent sailed back to England in hopes of seeing Sir Henry Morgan. After four days, Flent finally got permission to go and talk with Morgan. While Flent was standing in Morgan's office, he waited until Morgan was through signing some papers before Morgan would speak to him. Morgan was very rude in the way he did things.

When Morgan finally stopped what he was doing, he looked up at Flent and said, "I'm a very busy man, Mr. Kindel, but your letter sounded urgent. That's why I'm granting you this interview."

"Thank you very much, Sir Morgan."

"Now, Mr. Kindel, what's so urgent you have to interrupt my day?" Morgan said, being his impolite self.

"I need money, Sir Morgan—"

Morgan interrupted, "This isn't a bank, Mr. Kindel. You need to go down the street for that."

"I didn't come here for a loan, Sir Morgan, but a trade."

"Tell me something, Mr. Kindel. I know your father and he owns several successful businesses. Why come to me?"

"My father's businesses are failing, Sir Morgan, because of the new tax laws and people don't have the extra money to spend."

"You blaming parliament and the queen for that, Mr. Kindel?"

"Oh no, Sir Morgan, I'd never do that, sir."

"So why are you here, Mr. Kindel? I'm a busy man."

"I have a plan to trap the Princess Pirate and turn her over to you."

That interested Morgan. "Mr. Kindel, not that I think your plan will work after so many have failed, but if you can do that, your father wouldn't have any more financial worries." Morgan poured himself a drink of wine and asked Kindel, "Would you care for some?"

"I don't drink, sir."

Morgan, sitting behind his desk asked, "Now, Mr. Kindel, what's your plan?"

"I'm planning to marry the princess's sister, Carlena Martin. If I can somehow get the princess to show up at her sister's wedding and beforehand know when she is coming, I'll get a message back to you. Then you'll send a ship full of men to capture her."

Morgan set his wineglass down and thought a minute. "You know, Mr. Kindel, the plan sounds so simple, and it might just work. That's if you can get her there." Morgan made something else clear. "Better remember this, Mr. Kindel, no princess, no reward money, understand?"

Flent returned to Freedom Port to see Carlena once again. Flent knows Carlena would never marry him if she knew what he was planning to do. He'd make sure after Rebekah was captured that she'd never know it was he who betrayed her and her sister. Flent was very much in love with Carlena but would betray a hundred Rebekahs for his father's welfare. After the proposal, he and Carlena planned about their wedding. Flent was now going to put his plan into action.

"Carlena, my love."

"Yes, Flent."

"Is it possible to contact your sister, Rebekah, and invite her to the wedding?"

"I don't know how to contact her, Flent, because I don't where she is."

"Surely, Carlena, now that we're going to be married, you can confide in me about your sister."

"I'm telling you the truth, Flent, and why would I lie to you?" Carlena leaned over and kissed him to let him know she was telling him the truth.

A Change of Plans
1673

Flent sailed back to England to let Morgan know how things were progressing. While in Morgan's office, you could hear Morgan speaking: "So you believe this Carlena is telling you the truth about her not knowing where to contact her sister, the princess?"

"Yes, Sir Morgan, I am. We've been very intimate with each other, and she wouldn't lie to me."

Taking a sip of wine, Morgan replied, "Yea, I thought that once about a woman I was intimate with. She took me for three gold crowns."

"Beg your pardon, sir."

"Forget it, Flent. You just figure out a way to get the princess to that island, and I'll have enough men waiting for her and her pirates. The princess and her men will either die in fighting or surrender/ I care not which."

Several days later, Flent was back at Freedom Port where the wedding will be held. Flent's father, Mel, was coming, his mother, Kathy, as well. Flent figured that, sooner or later, Rebekah would have to visit her sister, Carlena, and then he'd keep her there long enough for Morgan and his men to arrive.

For now, Flent was getting ready for the wedding that would take place on Rebekah's birthday, June fifth.

It had been two weeks now back at the cove, and the *Black Rose* was ready to set sail. At this time, Jack was getting things ready for Rebekah's birthday, in eleven days. They would be back from Freedom Port by that time. The celebration would take place here at the cove when they return from visiting her sister. One thing Jack was making sure of when he was speaking to Rebekah's men was the presents they present to the Princess better not be stolen.

The *Black Rose* Out to Sea Again
1673

"Would we do that, Jack?" Sam was saying, being his sarcastic self.

"Just remember what I said, Sam, the present you give to the princess better be purchased. Jake has a lot of miscellaneous items in his post that are present worthy for the princess."

"All right, Joe, put the men back to work."

"You men heard the first mate, back to work. We want this ship ready so she can sail out tomorrow morning."

Sam was doing his usual complaining: "Why all of this nonsense of a birthday celebration for the princess? Are we pirates or women?"

Joe, wanting to get under Sam's skin, said, "Sam, you don't have to come to the princess's celebration. In fact, it would be pleasant not to have you and your attitude there to ruin it for the princess."

Pulling his knife on Joe, Sam said, "I'll show you my attitude, Joe. I'm going to cut your heart out."

Before Joe could take action against Sam, Marty grabbed Sam by his wrist, saying, "You drop that knife Sam, or I'll break your arm."

Squinting his eyes from Marty's strong grip, Sam yelled out, "Okay, Marty, I'll drop it, just release my wrist."

Sam dropped the knife, then Marty released his wrist.

Joe confronted Sam, saying, "Look, Sam, we're all in this together with the princess. I gave her my loyalty, and so did every man here, so why can't you?"

"She's a little princess who wants to play pirate, and I just can't accept it, Joe." Sam walked away, rubbing his wrist.

Bret spoke up, "What are we going to do about Sam, Joe?"

"I'll talk to Jack about Sam's lack of loyalty to the princess. I would've thought by now he'd be giving his support to the princess like the rest of us, but it seems Sam will never adjust."

The next day, the *Black Rose* was out to sea sailing to Freedom Port that was only four days away. Joe met with Jack in his cabin to discuss Sam's attitude against the princess. "It's simple, Jack. Sam's hostility against the Princess can no longer be tolerated on this ship. He must go."

"I understand what you're saying, Joe, but the princess has to make that decision, and she wants Sam to stay."

"You're second in command, Jack. I'm only a crew member, but you know as well as I Sam's attitude could get one of us killed— or maybe the princess."

"I'll talk with the princess, Joe, and see what can be done about Sam."

Jack relayed this to Rebekah: "I think we should remove Sam from the ship, Princess."

"No, Jack, he has been with this ship from the beginning. It wouldn't be fair to him."

"Fair, Rebekah, what's fair? It could mean your life. I just got through telling you how Sam feels about you and the power of authority you have and being a captain of a ship."

Rebekah didn't want to argue any more about Sam. She went over and stood by the back windows of her ship, folding her arms while looking out toward the sea.

"Princess, don't turn your mind off from this. Sam has been sailing with this ship now going on three years, and he still has resentment toward you."

"But, Jack, he has performed magnificently with the sword in every raid we're on. I can't believe he's against me."

"Rebekah, I'd never would've believed these pirates under your command would've been so loyal, but there comes a time when there's just that one that won't go along with the rest, and I think Sam is that one."

"I'm the captain, right, Jack?"

"Yes, Rebekah, you're the captain."

"I make the decision that Sam stays. I believe he'll come around. It's just a matter of time."

Sam's Mutiny
1673

Four days later, the *Black Rose* was nearing Freedom Port. Sam, who hasn't given his full support to the princess, was talking with Marty. Marty was saying, "I don't know, Sam. I like the princess, and I think she likes me."

"Are you a fool, Marty? And can't see with your own eyes that the princess, and Jack are lovers?"

"Oh, that's not true, Sam. The princess likes all of us."

"She's using us, Marty, and she doesn't like you, and if you don't believe me, just ask her."

Joe passed by and asked, "What's going on here, Sam?"

Marty spoke up, "You know, Joe, Sam told me that the princess doesn't really like us."

"Sam's a liar, Marty, don't believe him."

Jack walked up and asked, "Why are all of you men standing around doing nothing while there's plenty of work to do?"

"The princess doesn't like us, Jack."

"Who told you that, Marty?"

"Sam said the princess is using us and doesn't like us."

Jack let out a deep breath. "Enough of this nonsense, Marty. Now get back to work."

Marty, being defiant, said, "No!"

"I said get back to work, Marty, and I mean now!"

Marty was a large, muscular man, and Jack didn't want to tangle with him but had to maintain discipline or things would definitely get out of hand.

"I told you to get back to work, Marty, and I said now. That's an order."

Marty punched Jack in outrage and knocked him backward to the deck of the ship. Joe tried to stop Marty, but Marty punched Joe and knocked him down as well. Jack wasn't letting Marty get away with this as the other men come running to assist.

"Stand back," Jack ordered. "This is between Marty and me."

Marty, still defying Jack's orders, said, "I'm not taking your orders anymore, Jack!"

"Yes, you are, Marty." Jack told him with a strong, commanding voice. Marty lunged at Jack again and tried to hit him with his fist. Jack ducked, and with all of his strength, he punched Marty so hard in his left ribs. It knocked the breath out of Marty. While Marty was leaning over to catch his breath, Jack gathered the last of his strength and, with his fist, hit Marty downward against his left jaw. Marty went down face-first. Marty was shaking his head and was getting back to his knees when Jack, with his left fist, came down and struck Marty on his right jaw. That knocked Marty down to the floor once again. Marty was in a little bit of a daze, and Jack surely didn't want Marty to get back up.

Joe, trying to calm Marty down, said, "Listen to me, Marty. You have to stop before someone gets hurt."

Jack, waiting to punch Marty again, didn't know if he had the strength and almost broke both hands the first time. Marty stood up and realized he did wrong and walked away to think. Jack let out a big sigh while asking Sam, "What do you think you're doing inciting a mutiny that could've gotten someone killed?"

Sam, knowing Jack was ready to throw him overboard, said nothing and just gave Jack a blank stare.

Rebekah was now on deck finding out what all the commotion was about. "What's going on here, Jack? Rex came to my cabin telling me to get on deck fast—you and Marty were in a fight."

"It's all over, Princess, and I don't know where Marty went off to. The real problem is Sam. He got Marty all upset, and Marty went on a rebellious streak and didn't want to go back to work, and I had to show Marty otherwise."

THE *BLACK ROSE* ANCHORED AT FREEDOM PORT 1673

"You got into a fight with Marty, Jack?" Rebekah expressed her fear.

"Everything is fine, Princess. It's a good thing Marty is a brawler than a fighter, or I'd be dead by now. The issue here, Princess, is Sam. He's determined to make trouble."

Sam stood there, saying nothing. Rebekah confronted Sam face-to-face and asked, "Why, Sam?"

Sam wouldn't speak; he just stood there in silence.

"Sam, you've a choice—either come to my cabin and have a private talk or be a cast away set out to sea in a longboat. You better make a quick decision. You've just exhausted my patience."

Sam, making no more trouble, went with Rebekah to her cabin. When Rebekah and Sam were in her cabin, Rebekah turned and asked, "Why, Sam?"

"I think you're a young girl who plays pirate, Princess, and I can't serve under you anymore."

"Why stir up trouble among the men, Sam? Just tell me you want out, and I'll give you the twenty-five gold crowns, and you can be on your way."

Scratching his beard, Sam said, "I want out, Princess."

Rebekah put her hands on her hips and said, "You're out, Sam, but I'm very disappointed with your decision because you're such an asset to the crew and the *Rose*. One more thing, Sam." Rebekah was making things clear to him. "When we get back to the cove, you'll receive your twenty-five crowns, and you can stay at the post with Jake until you find a pirate ship you can serve with. But if you try one more mutiny on my ship, you'll have two choices. One choice is Jack will throw you overboard. The second choice, you'll face me with your sword in hand, understand, mister?" Rebekah, not thinking she got through to Sam, said again, "I said do you understand, mister?"

"Yea," Sam grunted.

"Get out, Sam!" Sam turned, leaving out the door, while Jack entered in.

"How long have you been standing outside my door, Jack?"

"Long enough, Princess, to make sure Sam wasn't causing any more trouble."

"I was so sure, Jack, Sam would adjust, but I see I was wrong."

"Princess, don't feel to upset. Twelve out of thirteen pirates isn't a bad average."

"I want Sam with this crew, Jack. He's great with the sword and completes the circle."

"You'll find a replacement, Princess. You replaced Max and Lonnie."

"I've known Sam longer Jack and will miss him."

What Jack and Rebekah didn't know was Sam hadn't left yet; he was still standing outside her cabin door listening to what they were saying. Sam, showing a different expression on his face, was going top side when he met Marty coming down the stairs. "Where're you going, Marty?"

"I ought to punch you out, Sam, for trying to get me against the princess."

Sam looked on, and kept walking.

Jack and Rebekah had just finished talking when there was a knock on Rebekah's cabin door. Rebekah said, "Yes, come in."

Marty came in with his head pointed down staring at the floor.

"What is it, Marty?"

"I want to say I'm sorry, Princess, for the trouble I caused and to you too, Jack."

Rebekah approached Marty. "Go back to work, Marty, and pretend it never happened."

"I'm ready for my punishment, Princess."

"No punishment, Marty, just don't do it again, all right?" Rebekah said with a smile.

Marty stared at Rebekah with that childlike grin and said, "It's a deal." Marty turned and left as a happy child.

"Now that this is out of the way, Princess, through my glass, I spotted what looks like your father's island straight ahead."

Rebekah said with a happy face, "We're here, Jack!"

"Yes, and I'll anchor the ship a few miles from the docks for safety precautions. Then we'll row a small boat over, and we'll go and visit your sister."

Before leaving, Jack gave these orders to Joe. "If an unfriendly ship approaches the island, move the ship out a ways a few miles or so just for precautions, but if there's a real danger you suspect, send two men over to get me and Rebekah, and we'll return."

"Got it, Jack."

Flent Kindel, Carlena's fiancée, was staying at the castle until the wedding before returning to England.

Getting a Message Back to Morgan
1673

Flent has one of his father's ships docked there in the port just in case Rebekah does show up to see Carlena. Jack and Rebekah rowed a small boat over to the dock. Later when they were on the road that led up to the castle, Jack was looking up toward the castle and said, "You've been telling the truth, Princess, about living in a castle."

"Did you think I was lying to you all of this time, Jack?"

"No, Princess, it's something you just have to see to believe. That's all. I never doubted you, Princess."

Rebekah and Jack arrived at the front door of the castle, and Jack, with the doorknocker, knocked. Carlena's manservant opened the door. The manservant recognized Rebekah and said with a cheerful smile, "Welcome home, Miss Rebekah, please come in."

Jack, following in behind Rebekah, had never been inside a castle before and looked around in amazement.

"Is Carlena here, Maxwell?"

"Yes, Miss Rebekah. She's with a man friend. I'll go and get her, and she'll be so happy to see you."

Carlena, upon entering the castle's ballroom and seeing Rebekah, went running to her and hugged her tight. "Oh, Rebekah." Carlena said excitedly. "I've missed you so. I hope you're home to stay."

"I'm here for a short visit, Carlena. I can't stay long."

"You just can't leave right this moment, Rebekah."

Flent entered the room, and when he saw Rebekah, he gasped.

Rebekah, remembering Flent, asked, "Carlena, isn't that Flent Kindel?"

"Yes, Rebekah, it is, and we're getting married on your birthday, so you must stay."

Jack, wanting not to be left out, cleared his throat.

"I almost forgot, Carlena, with all the excitement. This is Jack Reese, my first mate on my ship, and you never got to meet him the first time I was here."

Carlena gave Jack her hand to kiss, and while Jack kissed her hand, she said, "You're so handsome, sir."

Staring over at Rebekah, Jack replied, "I thank you very much, Miss Carlena, for the complement. I rarely get to hear those words."

Rebekah gave Jack a strong stare that was telling him to turn it off. Rebekah then turned her attention to Flent. "Well, Flent, how have you been?"

Flent was surprised at Rebekah being there. He replied, "Fine, Rebekah, just fine, and I'm looking forward to marrying Carlena."

Carlena, being hospitable, said, "Rebekah, you and Jack, please sit and dine with Flent and me. Maxwell is getting ready to set the table."

"I must wash up first, Carlena. Is my old room still available?"

"It was as you left it, Rebekah, four years ago."

Jack and Flent talked while Rebekah went to her old room. Rebekah, opening her bedroom door, entered as though she had never left. She went over to her closet and opened the doors. Those pretty dresses she once wore were still hanging the way she left them.

There was water in the basin. Carlena always made sure it was filled with fresh water in case of Rebekah's return. Rebekah had to see if her dresses still fit while she undressed to try one on. Rebekah washed up and put on her blue dress and shoes. Everything fit just as well as it did when she was nineteen years old.

Rebekah walked down the beautiful staircase and back into the dining room. Jack was about to take a sip of soup, but when he saw Rebekah, he wasn't hungry anymore as he put the spoon back into the bowl.

"Rebekah, you look so ravishing in that blue dress."

"Thank you, Jack." Rebekah sat down at the table.

Flent stared at Rebekah and then stared at Carlena. With both girls wearing blue dresses, they almost looked like identical twins. Rebekah said, "Let's eat. I'm starved." She started sipping her soup eloquently.

Flent, being with Rebekah once again, didn't want to betray her, but it was Rebekah or his father's businesses. Flent's concern and love for his father was more important than his love for Rebekah. While they sat and ate, Jack really enjoyed it. He liked good food. Flent sat there picking at his food and was quiet during the dinner. He was wondering how long he could keep Rebekah here at the castle so Morgan's men would have enough time to come and capture her.

Carlena noticed Flent wasn't eating and asked, "Aren't you feeling well, Flent? You haven't eaten a bite of your steak."

"Yes, Carlena, I'm fine. I'm just not that hungry. That's all." Flent smiled then took a drink of his water.

43
REBEKAH, YOU WILL STAY
1673

BEFORE TAKING ANOTHER bite of food, Rebekah said, "Carlena, Jack and I'll be leaving in the morning. We can't stay, and you know the reason why."

Flent stood up and said, "You must stay, Rebekah, please. This is Carlena's wedding, and you'll regret it later if you leave."

Carlena, feeling a little embarrassed by Flent's outburst, said, "Flent, don't get upset. I'm sure Rebekah will stay."

"Yes, I'm sorry, Carlena. It's so important to you. I got carried away."

After dinner, Carlene and Rebekah sat in the guest room. Carlena spoke up first, "You'll stay, Rebekah. I'll not hear of you leaving."

Jack, while finishing his steak, got to thinking about Flent being so upset about Rebekah's leaving. Flent was now in the guest room, hoping Carlena could convince Rebekah to stay for the wedding. Jack walked in and said, "We better leave tomorrow as planned, Rebekah. It'd be safer that way."

Seeing the sad look on Carlena's face and not knowing when she'd see her again, Rebekah said, "I've made up my mind, Jack. We're staying until after the wedding."

Not wanting to argue with Rebekah in front of her sister, Jack would discuss this with her later in private.

Carlena, happy Rebekah was staying, said, "Jack, Maxwell will show you to your room."

That night, Jack wasn't getting much sleep while thinking about Rebekah's decision to stay for the wedding. The clock was now striking midnight. Flent, thinking everyone was in bed and asleep, went to his father's ship that was sitting at the dock.

Flent knocked on the captain's cabin door.

"Yes, who is it?"

"It's me, Flent Kindel, Captain."

The captain opened the door, and while he was in the middle of putting on his pants, he asked, "Yes, Mr. Kindel, what can I do for you at this hour, sir?"

"Take this message I'm giving you and sail back to England. You personally give it to Sir Henry Morgan at the courthouse. He'll know what to do from there."

"You'll be all right here, Mr. Kindel?"

"You just get that message to Morgan as soon as possible, Captain."

Not long after Flent was back in the castle and safely in his room. He hoped he could keep Rebekah here long enough so Morgan's men could capture her.

While on board the *Black Rose*, Rebekah's men were playing a few pirate games. These games weren't the same games played at the post. Sam was watching the men having what they call a good time, but being stubborn, he was just watching and not participating.

As far as Sam was concerned, the princess had turned her men that were once hardcore pirates into soft women. Marty and Rex approached Sam and said, "Come and join us, Sam. Things are a lot more fun when you're playing."

"Get away from me, you two. I'm a pirate, not a woman."

Rex, who was against the princess at first, told Sam, "I like this new way of pirating, Sam. I don't have to watch my back all the time waiting for some pirate to stick a knife in it." Rex went back to the games. It was his turn now as the men started yelling, "Yes, Rex, yes Rex."

Back at the castle the following morning, Jack was waiting to speak with Rebekah after breakfast. Rebekah was going into her father's garden when Jack stopped her to talk to her.

Rebekah said, "Yes, Jack, what is it?"

"I'd like to talk to you, Rebekah, about you deciding to stay for Carlena's wedding."

"Can't it wait, Jack? I'd like to visit my father's grave first."

Jack walked with Rebekah out into the garden. Rebekah stood by her father's grave and bowed her head in silence. A few minutes passed. Looking down, Rebekah spoke these words, "I've returned, Father, but I haven't as yet found the man who was responsible for your death." Rebekah wept just a little.

Jack went over to comfort Rebekah while putting his arm around her. Jack now understood why Rebekah named her ship the *Black Rose* after seeing the black rosebush her father was buried by. Rebekah and Jack went back into the castle, and Rebekah made things clear to Jack. "There's no changing my mind, Jack. I'm staying for my sister's wedding, and that's final." Jack gave out a sigh, turned, and went back to his room.

Three days later, Flent's father's ship was back home in England. The captain was in Morgan's office.

"Sir Morgan, this message is from Flent Kindel."

After reading the message, Morgan asked, "Did Flent say how long the princess will be staying at Freedom Port?"

"All he said sir was for me to hurry. He didn't know how long he could keep the princess there."

Morgan stepped outside his door. "Guard."

"Yes, Sir Morgan."

"Go and get the captain of the cargo ship the *SS Bold*. I've a job for him."

Later that evening, the captain was in Morgan's office.

"Captain Chambers."

"Yes, Sir Morgan."

"You're taking the *SS Bold* and sailing to Freedom Port."

"May I ask why, sir?"

"The Princess Pirate is staying at the castle there, and I want her brought back to England to hang, understand? And to make sure she doesn't get away, take what fighting sailors you need with you."

"What if she and her men put up a fight and it's not possible to bring her back alive, Sir Morgan?"

"Listen, Captain Chambers, that's why the extra men. If she puts up a fight, then kill her and her pirate crew."

"Why a cargo ship, sir? Why not a naval warship with fighting men?"

"I'm sending you and your cargo ship instead. If her men see a warship, they'll alert the princess and she could get away. I want her caught off guard so she'll be easier to capture and without a fight."

"I see why you're head commander and oversee the safety of ships, Sir Morgan. You have a military mind."

"You bring the princess back to England, Chambers, and keep your kissing rear comments to yourself."

"Yes, sir, leaving right now, sir."

WITH A MIND LIKE MORGAN'S
1673

WITHIN THE HOUR, the cargo ship *SS Bold* was sailing toward Freedom Port at full speed and would be there in two days instead of three.

Back at the castle, Carlena and Rebekah were eating lunch and talking about their childhood. "We sure had some good times, Rebekah," Carlena was telling her.

"Yes, there were those good times, but there was some not so good, Carlena."

"Oh, I remember when Father took a small leather strap to you, Rebekah. It was when we got into the field of old man Kerber's watermelon patch and we gorged ourselves on his watermelons. You, Rebekah, took the blame for me because you didn't want to see me get the strap."

"After all, Carlena, I was your big sister, and I had to watch out for you. And don't forget, Carlena, God punished us for stealing. We both had bellyaches for two days afterwards."

Carlena stopped laughing with a sad look on her face. "What's wrong, Carlena?"

"Why do you steal from England, Rebekah, when you know it's wrong?"

Rebekah stood up and went over to the castle window looking out toward the courtyard.

"Why, Rebekah?"

"You know why, Carlena, to avenge Father's death."

"But do two wrongs make a right, Rebekah?"

Rebekah sat back down, saying, "Someday this'll all be over and things will be right again, Carlena, and I do hope someday you'll understand."

"No matter what you do, Rebekah, you'll still be my big sister, and I'll always love you."

Back on the cargo ship the *SS Bold*, the captain was talking to his first officer, Cramer. "We'll be sailing into Freedom Port tomorrow afternoon, Cramer, and when we arrive, I don't want to arouse suspicion. If the princess's ship is close by, we don't want to get into a fight with her men unless we have too. We'll dock and send the sailors to the castle. If things go well, we can arrest the princess and be on our way back to England."

"This is Morgan's plan, and we better make sure we're successful."

"With a mind like Sir Morgan's, he should be giving orders to the naval fleet instead of sitting in that cushion office of his," Cramer said.

"He was fleet commander at one time, Cramer. That's why he has the cushion office job he has now."

The next day back on the *Black Rose*, Marty was in the crow's nest with his spyglass when he spotted the cargo ship *SS Bold* sailing into Freedom Port and docked. Marty rushed down from the crow's nest to tell Joe. Joe stood at the bow of the ship and observed the cargo ship through his spyglass. Thirty minutes passed, and no activity stirred from the cargo ship, which looked very suspicious to Joe.

"I don't like the looks of things," Joe told the men.

"It's just another cargo ship, Joe," Pete said.

"I don't agree, Pete. All cargo ships I've seen start delivering their cargo soon as possible and pick up a new load to take back. They don't wait this long to start unloading. I don't see that, and that's why I'm suspicious."

"What do you propose, Joe?" the men asked.

"Lower the sails and move the *Rose* in closer, but don't arouse their suspicion."

The *Black Rose* was slowly sailing toward the dock of Freedom Port with an English sail showing and an English flag waving in the wind. Back on the cargo ship, the captain was getting fifteen of the sailors together and leaving the rest to guard the ship

"All right men, let's go up to the castle, and if the princess is still here, we'll capture her and bring her back to the ship."

The *Black Rose* was easing its way closer to the dock. Joe, with his spyglass, was looking toward the cargo ship when he observed fifteen sailors and the captain walk off the ship and head toward the castle. Joe's suspicions were confirmed—the princess was in trouble. Joe ordered the men to get their pistols and swords.

"The princess in trouble, Joe?" Marty asked.

"Yes, Marty, and we're going to her rescue as soon as the *Black Rose* docks."

It would be several minutes before they could tie up to the docks. At this time, the captain and his men were halfway to the castle when Rebekah was looking out of her room upstairs and saw that history was going to repeat itself once again. Just like it happened four years ago when England sent its fighting men to the island and murdered her father.

Look at You, Rebekah, Look at Your Dress
1673

Rebekah didn't have time to change her clothes as she ran out of her room and yelled for Jack.

"What's wrong, Rebekah?"

"There are sailors coming to the castle, and we better go out the back way. They could be here looking for me."

The *Black Rose* was now docked. Rebekah's men, including Sam, were now on their way to rescue her and Jack. The other sailors on the cargo ship jumped down to try and stop Rebekah's men after they realized they were pirates.

It wasn't much of a fight. Rebekah's men took the sailors down—one, two, and three—while the rest fled back to the ship. Sam struck down two sailors and watched the others run off. Sam, putting his sword back into his sheath, said, "Sailors, hum!"

Joe said, "Let's go—the princess and Jack, they're in trouble."

With a mighty pirate yell, they stormed toward the castle.

The captain knocked on the castle door. The manservant Maxwell opened the door and asked, "Yes, may I help you?"

The captain and his men forced their way in, and the captain said, "Where's the princess?"

Maxwell said, "But, sir, you can't come barging in here like this. Princess Carlena wouldn't approve."

The captain shoved Maxwell out of the way and said, "Get out of my way. We'll search the castle ourselves." The captain and his men walked further into the castle.

Carlena, entering from the sitting room with Flent, asked, "Who are you men, and why do you invade my castle?"

Rebekah and Jack were upstairs listening when they were about to go down the back stairs of the castle. Rebekah, with fear for Carlena, said, "Oh no, Carlena." Rebekah walked out onto the top of the staircase, yelling down to the captain, "You hurt my sister, Captain, I promise you before your men get me I'll run my sword straight through your heart."

"Princess, if you come quietly, there'll be no trouble. I promise you."

At that moment, you heard this loud screaming and yelling as Rebekah's men stormed through the castle door with their swords drawn. They started hacking away at the captain's men. Joe, seeing Carlena in danger, picked her up and carried her to safety. Rebekah saw what Joe did as she and Jack came running down the stairs to fight with her men.

Jack and Rebekah's men saw something different that day—the princess was sword fighting in a dress. The fighting was intense, and blood was being spilled all over the castle's white marble floor. It was mostly the captain's men and his that was being spilt. Rebekah sliced the captain across his right arm, and he fell backward toward the castle floor.

A sailor noticed Rebekah's back wasn't being guarded, so he thought he had a clear shot by running her through with his blade. Sam, thinking fast, put himself between the princess and the sailor's blade. Sam got run through his left shoulder and yelled out in pain. Rebekah turned, and, with her sword, she ran the sailor through his chest, and he died instantly.

Carlena was in total shock of what she was witnessing. Carlena put her hands over her mouth, saying, "Oh my lord."

Flent comforted Carlena and held her in his arms. The fighting continued. Marty was struck in his left arm but still ran three more men through before this was all over.

Bret, Brad, and Troy got their share of sailors, and that you can believe. The captain and his men were losing. Instead of losing more men, the captain pulled his pistol and shot up toward the castle ceiling. The sword fighting stopped as the men stood there waiting. The captain yelled out, "All right, Princess, you and your men win."

The captain, holding onto his bleeding arm, said, "All of you men, lay down your swords. We're surrendering to the princess." Randy, with his pistol, rounded the captain's men up that were still alive and could walk.

Rebekah approached the captain.

"I ought to run you through, Captain, for bringing more blood into my father's castle."

Jack said, calming Rebekah down, "Rebekah, it's over. There's no reason for more bloodshed."

Rebekah, giving the captain permission to leave, said, "Captain, you may leave with your wounded and your dead, but if you ever return to this castle, I'll hunt you down and won't spare you your life next time."

Rebekah stared up toward the top of the stairs and saw Carlena run to her bedroom with Flent following. Jack asked Pete, "Can you and the men help Maxwell clean the castle floor and put things back in order?"

"If there's the right powders and things in the castle, Jack, it'd be like none of this ever happened."

Jack followed Rebekah upstairs to see about her sister. Rebekah entered the room and saw Carlena crying on her bed, with Flent standing by her side.

Rebekah sat on Carlena's bed and asked, "Why are you so upset, Carlena?"

Carlena leaned up from her bed with tears flowing down her cheeks, saying, "Look at you, Rebekah. Look at your dress with those bloodstains covering it. Then you ask me what's wrong? It's you, Rebekah, that's wrong. You must stop this insane vengeance before more people are killed, and it might be you the next time, Rebekah."

"Carlena, I know you probably will never understand what I'm doing, but I can't rest until Father's death has been avenged or until parliament arrests Roy Jenson for our father's murder. I can't and won't stop until that day comes."

Jack was standing there in the doorway, observing Flent when he asked Rebekah, "How did they know you were here in the first place, Rebekah?"

Rebekah stood up from Carlena's bed and looked over at Flent. "The only ones who knew you were here, Rebekah, were me, Carlena, Maxwell, the servants, and Flent."

Flent knew he was under suspicion as he made a run toward the door in hopes of catching the captain before the cargo ship set sail. Flent was almost out the door when Jack's boot tripped him, and he fell to his face. Jack picked him up by his collar. Carlena got up from her bed to confront Flent face-to-face. Carlena, with a disoriented stare, asked, "Why, Flent?"

Flent stood there and didn't answer.

Carlena asked Flent again, and this time, she was screaming at him, "Why, Flent? Why did you do it? Rebekah is my sister!"

Flent yelled back in anger, "I had to—that's why! My father's businesses were at stake, and I needed the reward money. That's why, Carlena, that's why!"

"Is the blood spilt here today worth your father's businesses, Flent?" The tears were flowing down Carlena's face.

"You don't understand, Carlena. It wasn't your father that was in trouble."

"Understand, Flent? Understand? Don't stand there and tell me I don't understand! My father's blood was shed down in the throne room here four years ago, so don't tell me I don't understand." Carlena hauled off and slapped Flent as hard as she could.

"You get out of my castle and off my island Flent and never show your face here again."

Flent left the castle knowing the bloodshed here today was by his own hand. Flent made his way to the cargo ship and was on it and was sailing back to England.

The next day, Rebekah, and Carlene were having a talk before she left back to Pirates Cove.

"You going to be all right, Carlena?"

"I'll be fine, Rebekah. And the strangest thing about all of this is today is your birthday, Rebekah."

"It was a good birthday, Carlena."

"How, Rebekah? You and your men were almost killed."

"That's why, Carlena. I lived to see my twenty-second birthday."

YEA, YEA, YEA
1673

Jack was looking over things in the room where the fighting took place, and it looked as though it never happened. Jack was saying, "Well, Maxwell, it looks great, doesn't it?"

"Yes, sir, it sure does. Better than what I could've done, sir."

Jack said, "Sir, hum, that sounds nice."

Carlena asked Rebekah, "Are you going into the throne room and visit it before you leave, Rebekah?"

"No, Carlena, I'm not. It would bring back those bad memories, and after what happened yesterday, I don't' need the extra pain."

Carlena hugged Rebekah and handed her two more pictures of their father and said, "Here, Rebekah, just in case you lose one."

"Thank you, Carlena. I only have one picture of Father left, and it's under my pillow in my cabin."

"Carlena."

"Yes, Rebekah."

"I'm sorry about what happened between you and Flent. I know you loved him."

"Yes, Rebekah, for just a little while, I had a taste of love."

"When my men show, Carlena, I'll be on my way."

Jack was ready to go when he noticed one man was missing—it was Marty. "Louie, did you see Marty anywhere? We're ready to leave."

"Yes, Jack, I saw him in the galley."

"You mean the kitchen."

"What, Jack?"

"In civilized society, Louie, in homes on land, they call the galley the kitchen."

"I see the princess isn't the only one, Jack, that knows big fancy words—you do too."

Jack went toward the kitchen to tell Marty they were ready to leave. Entering the kitchen, Jack watched Marty eating some food that one of the servants had given him.

"Marty, it's time to go."

"Just a minute, Jack. I'd like to finish my cake."

Marty washed the cake down with water and told the female servant, "Thank you for the cake."

The young lady smiled and said, "Marty, you come back and see me again when you sail by this way."

Rebekah's men were heading back to the ship while she was giving Carlena her last good-bye and hug.

"Rebekah."

"Yes, Carlena."

"I do understand somewhat about what you're doing for Father. You be careful and come back home safe."

"There's no other way to come back home, Carlena." Rebekah smiled, turned, and headed back to her ship. Back on the *Rose*, everything was almost back to normal. Sam was back to work as though nothing had happened the week before.

Rex asked Sam," I thought you were finished working for the princess?"

The other men gathered around Sam. Sam replied, "I'm busy trying to fix this sail using my right hand. You know how the princess gets when things are left unrepaired."

Rebekah walked up. "Thanks for saving my life, Sam, and why are you working with your left shoulder in a sling?"

"It's just a flesh wound, Princess. It doesn't hurt."

"Just the same, Sam. I don't want you straining it and making it worse, or you'll not be able to work on another pirate ship when you leave."

"I'm not leaving, Princess. I'm staying on the *Black Rose* with your permission."

"Permission granted, Sam," Rebekah said with a great big grin.

"All right," Jack said, "you men get back to work and sail the *Black Rose* back toward home."

Rex and Randy told Sam, "You know, Sam, you saved the Princess's life back there at the castle."

"Yea, yea, yea, I know, so what?"

Rex and Randy padded Sam on his right shoulder and told him, "Welcome back."

Sam went back to work and mumbled to himself, "Pirates, they call themselves."

There'll Be a Day
1673

Back in Old England just three days later, the captain of the cargo ship the *SS Bold* was getting it down one end and up the other from Morgan.

"You coward, you fool, I gave you enough men to get the job done but still you failed."

"You wasn't there, Sir Morgan. Her men came out of nowhere and overpowered us."

"Overpowered my Aunt Margie! You were incompetent and a coward. You should've fought to the death, Captain Chambers. Now get out before I have you arrested for desertion of duty."

Morgan couldn't believe the princess got away again. Things were in his favor this time, and she still managed to escape. Morgan wasn't giving up. There'll be a day when the princess would slip up and come falling down and he'd be there with the hanging rope to catch her.

Flent's Life Ruined
1673

Flent went back home to his parents and wondered why they never showed up at Freedom Port. When Flent returned home, his mother greeted him at the front door and asked, "Shouldn't you be on your honeymoon, son?"

"My honeymoon, Mother, where were you and Father? You didn't come to the island, and I was worried about you two!"

"We've great news, son, a wealthy man named Bentley bought into your father's two businesses, and things will be fine from here on out. Isn't that great, son?"

Flent walked over to the window looking out toward the darkness and, now with his life ruined said, "Carlena."

PART V

MADDIE
1673

Out in the dark Atlantic sea, two ships were locked together. They were both pirate ships, and the strange thing was there were no sounds of cannon fire or pistol fire going on, which was unusual. Even pirates raid each other's ships for valuables.

In the captain's cabin of the ship called the *Sea Warrior*, a pirate captain and a rather hateful old woman were talking.

"So, Captain Micks, you know who was responsible for my sister's death and the sinking of her ship?"

"Yes, I do, Maddie."

"Well, just don't sit there like a wart on a frog's back. Tell me who!"

"You have the gold I requested, Maddie?"

"You'll get the gold when I have the information, Micks, and not until then." Spittle was dripping from Maddie's lips as she spoke.

"When I see the gold, Maddie, then I'll tell you what you want to know."

"All right, all right, you men are all the same. Monk."

"Yes, Maddie."

"Hand me that sack I gave you."

"Here it is, Micks. Now tell me what I want to know."

"Just a minute, Maddie, while I inspect the sack, it might contain rocks instead of gold."

Micks untied the string around the sack then poured twenty Spanish gold coins out onto the desk.

"Well, Micks, or you satisfied?" Maddie cried out.

"Yes, Maddie, they look good to me." Micks put the gold back into the sack and opened the desk drawer and set the sack inside.

"Now tell me what I want to know, Micks. I'm getting impatient."

50
Terrible and Terrifying
1673

"The person who killed your sister and sank her ship is a young girl they call the Princess Pirate, and her ship is the *Black Rose*."

Maddie leaned closer to Micks, and as spittle dribbled from her lips, she asked with vigor, "Where can I find her? And how do you know this for a fact she killed my sister?"

"Two of my men were in a French prison cell waiting to be hung. Maddie, you've known me long enough to know I'd never let this happen to any of my men."

"Well, get on with it, Micks, and tell me. I haven't got all day."

"When my men and I raided the small town outside of France, and broke them out, two of your sister's pirate crew were there also, so we took them with us. They served on my ship for a while and told me about this princess who was on your sister's ship and how her and her men killed your sister and sank her ship then delivered them to prison."

"You could've just told me that in the first place instead of going across the high seas, Micks."

"Now that you have what you came aboard for, Maddie, what's your plan?"

"I'm going to find this princess and make her suffer at my hand before she dies a terrible death."

"One more thing, Maddie."

"Well, what is it, Micks? I'm growing older by the minute waiting here on your ship."

"This princess has a first mate named Jack Reese."

"So what about him? The princess is the only one I'm interested in."

"From talk that has gathered from one ship to the next, the princess is very much in love with him."

"You don't say, Micks, very interesting." Maddie put her wrinkling old fingers to her chin while she thought of something more sinister in having the princess suffer.

"Yes, Maddie, I thought I'd throw that in as an added bonus."

"Yes, I'll add to her misery by killing her lover in front of her eyes before I run a knife though her heart." Maddie laughed with a joyful wickedness. Maddie and her men left the *Sea Warrior* and went back to her ship the *Crimson Tide*.

While on board the *Crimson Tide*, Maddie told her number 1 man, Monk, to set sail to Pirates Cove.

"Why Pirates Cove, Maddie?"

"There's a man there named Jake Spencer. I met him when he first opened his little getaway for pirates. He might be able to tell me where to find this little princess, so do as your told, Monk, and stop asking stupid questions!"

"Yes, Maddie, I'm going."

Maddie was a terrible and terrifying woman; she would threaten to kill a man just to hear him scream for mercy. She was so wicked. She had snake venom running through her veins instead of blood. This woman Maddie did every evil kind of trading on the high seas. Slavery of men and women, you name it, she has done it. She has no conscience or fear. Maddie was worse than her sister who was also into every wicked kind of dirty dealings. Now Maddie was searching for the princess to get her bitter revenge.

The princess was on her way at this time to raid another English ship, the *Star Lighter*, which she has raided before. Rebekah and Jack were discussing it in her cabin.

"This will be a surprise to England, Jack. They'd never expect us to raid the same ship twice."

"I have to admit it, Princess. England would be better off if you were on their side instead of you being against them."

"It's not that I like what I'm doing, Jack. My father taught me and my sister, Carlena, right from wrong. But until England admits their wrong, I'll continue to fight them until they surrender or they hang me."

"Don't say things like that, Princess."

"I'm sorry, Jack, but you once told me this isn't a game, remember?"

"Yes, Rebekah, I do, and I still live by what I had said, but please take things more serious than what you do."

"I will, Jack. From here on, I promise." Feeling very sensual today, Rebekah leaned up and kissed Jack passionately.

Jack took Rebekah into his arms and returned her passionate kiss, and when they stopped, Jack said, "I love you with all of my heart, Rebekah."

Rebekah was breathing heavier, her heart started to pound faster. She said, "It would be best for you to leave my cabin now, Jack."

Jack, being the man he is, would always respect Rebekah and never take advantage of her inexperienced youth. After Jack left her cabin, Rebekah cooled down and gathered herself.

The cargo ship *Star Lighter* at this time was a three-day sail from England and was still under the command of Captain Lee Brant. The captain's first mate, Johnson, was in his cabin discussing the ship's course to a port called Little Rivers.

"Yes, Captain, this little port has grown by leaps and bounds, sir. The population has grown from just twenty-five people to three hundred in the last year."

"I see, Johnson. That's why we're delivering all of this grain and other supplies to them."

"Yes, Captain, and they'll give us gold and silver in trade. From the report I received from Sir Morgan, this Little Rivers Island is loaded with rich mining caves."

"Very good, Johnson, and I thank you for the update."

"No problem, sir. I knew you would want to know since you just arrived back on ship and didn't have time to read Morgan's report."

Back on the *Black Rose*, Jack was giving orders to Joe. "Make sure the *Black Rose* will intercept the *Star Lighter* on the way back from Little Rivers Island, Joe. From Jake's report, the *Star Lighter* will be loaded with gold and silver bullion. It'll receive in payment from the port of Little Rivers."

"No problem, Jack. If the *Star Lighter* follows its original course back to England from which it came, we'll be waiting for her."

"According to the information we received from Jake, the *Star Lighter* was ordered to sail straight back to England and make no stops on the way, Joe."

"If the day and time Jake gave us is correct, Jack, we should be intercepting the ship in two days."

A few days later, the *Star Lighter* had delivered its cargo and was sailing back to England. Captain Brant was feeling confident about the trip back. Brant said to his first officer, "You know, Johnson, the *Star Lighter* has only been raided once since I've taken command."

"Yes, that's great isn't it, sir?"

"Well, Johnson, I'll be in my cabin if needed."

"Yes, Sir Captain."

Captain Brant was feeling good today but didn't have any idea that the princess was going to raid his ship again that very afternoon. Marty in the crow's nest spotted the *Star Lighter*. He climbed down to tell Jack.

51
THE PRINCESS PIRATE AGAIN
1673

Through his glass, Jack saw the *Star Lighter* just several sea miles ahead, and they were sailing toward her. Back on the *Star Lighter*, the man in their crow's nest spotted the *Black Rose* and reported to the first officer of the approaching ship. Johnson, through his, glass saw that the approaching ship was waving a French flag and had a French sail.

"Should I alert the captain, Mr. Johnson?" the sailor asked.

"I don't see any danger here, Sailor Banks. Let the captain have some quiet time."

Observing the *Black Rose* again, Johnson noticed its course was directly toward the *Star Lighter*. First Officer Johnson was now getting concerned. He had one of the sailors go and get the captain.

"What's that French ship doing, sir?" Sailor Banks asked.

"I don't know myself, Banks, but have the helm turn the ship to her starboard because that French ship is closing in directly toward us." No matter how they tried to avoid the *Black Rose*, it was to no avail.

Captain Brant was now on deck as the *Black Rose* and the *Star Lighter* rammed up against each other with a hard jolt. The two ships were now locked up side by side. Captain Brant thought he was reliving a nightmare when he saw pirates jumping onto his ship once again.

When the princess jumped over onto his ship and was fighting with her men, Captain Brant saw her and thought he was in his bed dreaming. But this was no dream; the princess was attacking his ship again. And just like last time, his men were losing, and the princess was going to rob his ship all over again.

When the fighting was over, Rebekah's men rounded the captain's men up against a standing cabin on the ship. Rebekah remembered Captain Brant as she approached to greet him. "I see we meet again, Captain." Rebekah grinned.

"I don't see what's so humorous about it, Princess." Brant had a sour look on his face.

"Don't you get it, Captain? It was just three years ago. You were the first ship I raided, and my men and I are celebrating by raiding your ship again."

"You're no lady, Princess." Brant was so humiliated he spat in Rebekah's face.

Joe, standing there, struck the captain with his fists again and again and proceeded to beat the captain to death when Rebekah ordered him to stop. Joe just kept hitting the captain until Rebekah's men pulled him off. Joe yelled, "Don't stop me, Princess. Nobody's going to spit on you and live!"

"I order you to stop, Joe. The captain's life is more important than my dignity."

Rebekah with her sleeve, wiped her face, and told the captain, "You're a very fortunate man, Captain, that I'm not a pirate's pirate, or you would've felt my sword through your body and be dying at this moment."

"I'd kill you, Princess, if I had a sword in my hand," the captain said in outrage.

Louie, wanting the captain to get run through, handed him his sword and said, "Here, Captain, use my sword against the princess and die."

Rebekah gave the captain his wish and rested her left hand down on her sword handle, saying, "I'm waiting, Captain. You now have a sword in your hand while mine is still in its sheath."

Captain Brant hesitated. Rebekah said, raising her voice, "Well, Captain, what are you waiting for?" Brant threw the sword to the deck floor.

"Wise decision, Captain. I'm not raiding your ship to kill your sailors or you, Captain, just for its bullion."

TRICKED!
1673

Now that the bullion has been loaded onto the *Black Rose*, Rebekah and her men were back on board sailing away. Standing on the railing of her ship, Rebekah shouted over to the captain, "Don't try and fire your cannons, Captain. They've been disabled."

Captain Brant didn't only come close to losing his life but also had to face Morgan once again.

The *Black Rose* was about out of sight when the first mate Johnson went to Captain Brant's cabin to tell him, "We've been tricked by the princess again, Captain!"

"What do you mean, Johnson? We've been tricked?"

"The cannons, sir. They're functional and can be fired."

Brant exploded with anger, saying, "I've been humiliated twice by that woman, and she still hasn't been captured yet. Someday, Johnson, the Princess Pirate will get her just dues. It's just a matter of time."

Back on the *Rose*, Jack ordered Joe to set the ship's course toward an island called Paradise Island where they would bury the gold and silver, less Jake's payment.

Five hundred sea miles away and unknown to Rebekah, an old woman walked into a tavern at a port called Lockport. The old woman was Maddie, and she was searching for Rebekah. Maddie approached the bar, holding a whip in her right hand, and shouted out to the bartender, "Whiskey, and I want the whole bottle!"

The bartender stared at Maddie as though she was a beggar and said, "Do you have enough money to pay for this bottle, old woman?"

Maddie slammed her whip down onto the bar and ordered again, "Whiskey, a whole bottle, or I'll wrap this whip around your throat and squeeze what miserable life you have left out." Monk laid money down onto the bar and asked, "This enough?"

The bartender set a bottle of whiskey onto the bar and said, "Yea."

Maddie removed the cork from the bottle with her teeth and said to the bartender, "You're lucky, mister. My man laid that money on the bar, and you handed me the whisky, or I'd have showed you how this whip would've felt around your throat." Maddie went to sit and drank her whisky. The owner, hearing the disturbance at the bar, went to see what all the noise was about.

"What's going on out here, Mike? What's all of this talk about whips and things?" Mike the bartender pointed to Maddie who was downing a bottle of whiskey as though it was water. "I see, Mike, an old woman with a whip trying to cause trouble."

The owner, Todd Williams, checked under the bar to make sure the three pistols were still there.

Maddie, after finishing her whiskey, got up and walked over to the bar. "You the owner?" Maddie shrieked.

"Yes, miss, I am. What may I do for you?"

"Well, manners to an old woman, how sweet?" The man watched in disgust as spittle dripped from her lips. "All right, you sweet talker, let's get to the point." Maddie then slammed her whip down on top of the bar. "I want to know about this Princess Pirate. What do you know about her?" Maddie picked up her whip and slammed it back down onto the bar again.

Todd, with his hand resting on one of the pistols under the bar, said to Maddie, "I've only heard of the princess, and that's all I know about her."

53
You Fool
1673

MADDIE LOOKED AROUND the tavern and then looked back at the bar owner. Maddie was more dangerous than a wolf with a bleeding wound in its side but knew she didn't have enough men to win in a fight if she started something. Maddie—opening her mouth and showing her rotted teeth—said, "All right, mister. You win this time." Maddie and her men left the tavern and went back to her ship.

Back on the ship, Monk asked Maddie, "Why didn't you use your whip on the bar owner to make him talk?"

"You fool, didn't you see we were outnumbered, and besides, the bar owner was no fool—he had his hand resting on a pistol under the bar's ledge and would've shot me with it."

"What are your next orders, Maddie?"

"It seems nobody is willing to talk about the princess, so continue our course to Pirates Cove. Maybe old Jake will tell me what I want to know about this princess and where I can find her."

"We're sailing a long way, Maddie, just to ask one man."

"According to what Micks said, the princess is well-known in this part of the sea, so I figure she has to get her supplies some place. So why not from old Jake?"

"Yea, that makes sense, Maddie."

"Of course, it does, you idiot. Now get out and do as your told, Monk, if you don't want this whip on your backside."

"Yes, Maddie, I'm leaving."

Monk left Maddie's cabin with great fear running down his back.

Few days later on Paradise Island, Rebekah and her men have just buried the gold and silver bullion. Rebekah knew her men were tired and needed some relaxing time. She ordered them to take two days on this island and rest. Rebekah and Jack did what they normally do on these beautiful islands—go and seek out the waterfalls.

As usual, Sam was complaining, "What good is it resting on an island without my firewater?"

Rex told Sam, "You starting that again?" Rex and the men went in another direction to get away from Sam and his complaining.

Sam, watching them leave, said, "Pirates, they call themselves."

Sam just sat under a tree and fumed. That evening, Rebekah and Jack found a beautiful waterfall, and while they stood there watching it, Rebekah was waiting for Jack to kiss her. Jack loved to tease Rebekah and was waiting for her to make the first move.

"Isn't that waterfall beautiful, Jack?" Rebekah then leaned her back up against a tree.

"Yes, Princess, it is, but you're more beautiful." Jack's eyes were now fixed directly into Rebekah eyes with his right hand up against the tree.

Rebekah, being impatient, said to Jack, "Well, I'm waiting."

"Waiting, Princess?"

"Yes, Jack, for you to kiss me."

Jack leaned over to kiss Rebekah and said, "I thought you'd never ask."

54
THERE IS MORE TO LIFE
1673

JACK AND REBEKAH kissed for quite a while until Rebekah had to come up for air. "I love you, Jack, and like being here with you in paradise."

"Rebekah, we can get married and come back here to live if that's what you desire."

"Jack, why spoil this loving moment between us trying to use it by getting me to marry you and give up on Jenson?"

"There's more to life than vengeance, Rebekah."

"I'll see you back at the ship, Jack. This loving moment has just went south for the winter." Rebekah went back to the ship. Jack stood there, knowing he blew his big chance to spend two days with the most beautiful girl in his life. Jack let out a sigh of despair and went back to the ship as well.

The next day, everybody on the ship was ready to sail back to the cove. Rebekah was in a bad mood, and Sam wanted his firewater. The *Black Rose* was on her way home when Jack met Rebekah in the galley. Jack sat as Micky handed him his coffee. "Hi, Princess."

Rebekah sat there drinking her hot chocolate and didn't reply. When she was finished, she got up and left. Micky said to Jack, "Whatever you said to her this time must have really gotten under her skin, Jack."

"Yea, and I don't know what to do about it, Micky."

"I'd let her cool off for a day or two, Jack, and then bring her a gift with an apology attached to it."

Jack tried what Micky suggested that evening. Rebekah was standing by the railing when Jack came up. Rebekah stood with her face toward the sea and waited for Jack to speak.

"It's a nice night, Princess."

"Yes, it is, Jack, and the breeze is nice as always."

"Princess, I've something for you." Rebekah, loving gifts, turned, and then Jack handed an envelope to her. "Open it, Rebekah!"

Rebekah opened the envelope, and there was a note inside. Rebekah, as she was reading it, had tears in her eyes: "I'm sorry, Princess, that this is all I can give you. After all, there are no stores this far out at sea."

Rebekah, being emotional, said, "What you've written you can't buy in any store, Jack." Rebekah leaned up and kissed Jack passionately.

Jack, impressed with Rebekah's kiss, said, "We need to fight more often, Rebekah, because I enjoy it when we make up."

Rebekah returned to her cabin and put the note Jack wrote to her under her pillow with the picture of her father. Rebekah, looking at her father's picture, said, "You see, Father, Jack loves me with all of his heart." Rebekah put her father's picture back under her pillow with Jack's note and then laid her head back and closed her eyes.

55
SEARCHING FOR SOMETHING?
1673

THE *BLACK ROSE* was on course to Pirates Cove at the same time the *Crimson Tide* was. One evening on the *Crimson Tide*, one of Maddie's men was in Maddie's cabin searching for some gold she always has hidden for when she needs it. This pirate's name was Homer Clark, and he has stolen a lot of gold from Maddie's cabin before and has gotten away with it until tonight when Maddie walked in on him.

"What are you doing in my cabin, Mr. Clark?" Maddie asked, staring at Clark with a crazed look in her eye.

"I was searching for ah…"

"Well, does the cat have your tongue, Mr. Clark? Or are you looking for something to steal from me?"

"No, Maddie! I wouldn't do that."

"I'll cut your tongue out if you're lying to me, Mr. Clark, so you better tell me the truth." Maddie reached down and pulled her knife from her boot.

Clark, getting nervous, shouted, "All right, Maddie, I was looking for something to steal."

Maddie yelled out her cabin door, "Monk, you and Mort, get yourselves in here."

Rushing in, they asked, "What do you need, Maddie?"

"Take Mr. Clark to the top deck. I want to show the other men what's going to happen when someone steals from me."

"I didn't steal anything, Maddie, I give you my word." Clark pleading for his life.

"You didn't this time, Mr. Clark, but you have in the past."

"That wasn't me, Maddie."

"Oh, I think it was Mr. Clark. Your thinking I'm an old woman and wouldn't remember the gold I have hidden in my cabin, but you're wrong! Now I know who's been stealing my gold, all I had to do was wait, and what to my surprise, Mr. Clark, it was you."

"No, Maddie it wasn't."

"Shut up, you dirty lying dog." Maddie grabbed her whip from off the ship's wall. Maddie stood there and flung her whip toward Clark; he could hear the whip snap as it came close to his face.

Clark cried out, "Please, Maddie, don't kill me with your whip. I haven't been stealing your gold."

"Then who, Mr. Clark?" Maddie snapped her whip at Clark again, this time striking him on his hands that covered his face.

"Please, Maddie, don't kill me!"

"'Please don't kill me.'" Maddie said, mocking Clark as she snapped the whip again. "You're a sniveling, thieving coward, Mr. Clark." Not believing Clark, Maddie snapped her whip again, and this time, struck him across his face. Clark screamed and fell to his knees, begging for mercy.

"Please, Maddie, stop before you kill me!"

"Get him to his feet, Monk. So you want mercy, Mr. Clark, I'll show you mercy, take him to the top deck."

On deck with her crew, Maddie told Clark, "Take the knife Monk is handing you."

Clark took the knife and asked, "What are you going to do, Maddie?"

"I'm showing you mercy, Mr. Clark. You have a knife, and you now have a chance to defend yourself."

"But, Maddie, I can't win against your whip."

"Discussing time is over with, Mr. Clark. Use the knife, or just stand there while I whip you to death with my whip."

Maddie snapped her whip toward Clark again and again. Clark, trying to guard his face, was no match against Maddie's whip as he came at her with his knife. The lashes Maddie gave Clark soon beat him down until he laid on the deck of the ship bleeding to death. Clark's body looked as though he had been dragged through a thorn patch several times.

Maddie was satisfied and said, "Throw his dead carcass overboard, and let the fish have him."

Monk said, "Maddie, he's still alive. He isn't dead."

"Do as I say, Monk, unless you want what Clark got. Now do what you're told and shut up!" The men picked up Clark's body and threw him overboard, and Clark, still alive, screamed out as he hit the water below.

"I'll be in my cabin, and don't bother me unless it's important, understand?"

"Yes, Maddie, we understand."

Mort told Monk, "I don't know about you, Monk, but when I get the opportunity at the next port, I'm deserting this mad, crazy, insane old woman."

Monk agreed, "I'm with you, Mort. We'll leave together when the opportunity comes."

Back at the cove two days later, the princess and her men were there in the post. Jack entered just minutes after the princess. "Where were you, Jack?" Rebekah asked. Then Rebekah's men walked out of the post.

"Now where are they going, Jack?"

"To answer your questions, Princess, come with me. I'd like to show you something." Jack and Rebekah went down the docks ramp, which leads into the jungle. When they got to a certain place, Jack said, "Rebekah close her eyes."

"Why close my eyes, Jack?"

"Please, Rebekah, just do as I ask for once."

"All right, Jack, I'll play your little game." Rebekah closed her eyes.

SURPRISE! 1673

Jack walked with Rebekah a little ways farther and then said, "Rebekah, you can open your eyes now."

When Rebekah opened her eyes, she saw her men standing there as they yelled, "Surprise! Happy birthday, Princess."

Rebekah was really surprised at the party her men were giving her. Tables were set up and everything. "Blow out the candles on your cake," Marty shouted. Rebekah counted them first to make sure there were twenty-two candles and no more.

Then she blew, and all the candles went out. All her men brought her a gift and gave it to her. Jack assured her that the men purchased the gifts from Jake's post. After the presents were opened and the cake finished off by Marty, Rebekah told all her men, "Thanks!"

Later on the ship after Rebekah put her now-cherished presents away, she went back on deck to wait for Jack at the ship's railing.

Jack approached Rebekah, saying, "I haven't given you your birthday gift yet."

Rebekah closed her eyes, waiting for Jack to kiss her. When Jack didn't kiss her, she opened her eyes. Jack handed Rebekah a present.

Rebekah opened the present, and inside was her father's picture inside a golden frame. "I hope you don't mind, Princess. I took the liberty of taking your father's picture earlier this evening and putting it in this frame." Then Jack kissed Rebekah.

After the kiss, Rebekah told Jack, "I'm honored, Jack, for what you did with my father's picture."

"I was taking a chance, Princess. I know how close you are to something this personal, and all you could do was make me walk the plank."

"I love you too much for that, Jack." Rebekah leaned up to kiss Jack this time. "What a day!" Rebekah said going back to her cabin. The first thing Rebekah did was put her father's picture under her pillow and then got ready for bed. When Rebekah laid her head on the pillow, she said, "Oh my, this'll never do." She pulled her father's picture from under her pillow and put it under the other pillow on her bed. Rebekah, laying her head down this time, said, "This feels much better." Rebekah closed her eyes to sleep.

Back on the *Crimson Tide* Monk was in Maddie's cabin. "We'll be at Pirates Cove tomorrow evening, Maddie."

Maddie was eating her dinner and ripping some meat from its bone with her teeth. She said, "All right, Monk, you told me. Now get out."

The following morning, Jake was in his office with Rebekah and Jack selling her another chart. Jake rolling the chart out on his desk said, "Princess, this ship called *Sullivan* belongs to a very wealthy businessman who has big ties with parliament. She'll be carrying one million in gold ingots."

57
YOU KILLED MY SISTER
1673

Curt, entering the post, was looking for Jack. Curt knocked on Jake's office door.

Jack opened the door. "Yes, Curt."

"The ship is ready for sail anytime if the princess is ready."

"Jack."

"Yea, Jake."

"You'll have to give the *Sullivan* two days' sail from England, then she'll be in deep waters, which will make it easy for you to raid."

Jack liked the odds to be in their favor in every raid. Especially in the middle of the sea where from the crow's nest, you can spot a naval war ship for miles. That late evening, Rebekah and Jack were over at the post while all her men were on the ship. This was a little unusual. Jake set a cup of hot chocolate down over at Rebekah's table and asked, "Where are your men tonight, Princess?"

"Over at the ship, Jake. They must be exhausted from working all day on the ship."

The princess was right; her men were in their bunks early for a change. Marty, lying there in his bunk next to Joe's, asked, "Shouldn't we be over at the post guarding the princess in case something happens?"

"Nothing is going to happen, Marty, not at the post with Jake and his men there, so let me sleep. The princess has pushed me hard the last several days, and I am bushed."

Marty laid there thinking he should go back over to the post, but with Jack being there with the princess, she would fine. Marty closed his eyes and went to sleep. At this time at night, the *Crimson Tide* was sailing into the cove after she had permission to enter. Monk went to Maddie's cabin to tell her they just entered the cove.

Maddie and Monk were on deck as Maddie looked around the cove. "What's wrong, Maddie?"

"Look, you fool, that ship on the other side of the cove near the waterfall."

"It's just another pirate ship, Maddie."

"No, it isn't just another pirate ship. It's the *Black Rose*, the princess's ship. The ship Micks told me to look out for."

"I see, Maddie. There's a big black rose on her main sail."

"Yes, you idiot. Now go and get ten more of the men. I'll need them when we go over to the post."

"You thinking she might be there, Maddie?"

"Let's hope, Monk. I want to catch her off guard and take her by surprise."

Maddie and her eleven men rowed over to the post. Soon as they got out of the boat and onto the dock, Maddie told them, "Listen, you fools, we might only have one chance at this. I want that princess and want her alive, do you understand?"

"Yes, Maddie."

Maddie and her men slowly entered into the post, and then Maddie looked around, and low and behold, there was the princess sitting with Jack. Maddie was careful with her next move while she approached the bar. "Jake, it's Maddie, remember me?"

Jake wasn't thrilled, but business is business.

"Well, Maddie, it's been a long time."

"Yes, Jake, it has." Maddie kept staring at Rebekah and was making sure she was the princess before she and her men started something. Jake poured Maddie some whiskey. "I thank you, Jake." Maddie took a drink and then asked, "Who's that young girl sitting with that man?"

"That's the princess, Maddie. Go and introduce yourself to her."

Maddie took the rest of her drink down and then went to confront Rebekah. Maddie motioned for her men to have their pistols ready. Maddie's men went over to where Jake's men were sitting and stood behind them. Maddie walked over and stood before Rebekah.

Rebekah looked up and asked, "May I help you, miss?"

"Well, isn't that nice coming from a princess?" Maddie's sarcasm was so thick you could cut it with a knife.

Suspicious of Maddie, Rebekah said, "You seem to know me, but why the sarcasm?" Rebekah now noticed the whip in Maddie's right hand.

"I've heard many things about you, Princess."

Rebekah and Jack noticed Maddie dropping the tail of her whip to the floor like she was getting ready to use it. Jack wished he would've brought his French flintlock with him. Rebekah continued speaking while resting her hand on her sword handle.

"I hope the things said about me were all good."

"I'm tired of the talking game." Maddie came right out and said, "Stop with the princess act, you venomous little snake."

Rebekah stood with her sword in hand as well as Jack.

"So you want to come against me with your sword, huh, Princess?" Maddie backed up and snapped her whip into the air at Rebekah.

Rebekah stepped out from behind the table and told Maddie, "I don't know who you are and why you're starting something that'll get you hurt or killed, but you better leave now."

"I'll leave, Princess, but you and your boyfriend are coming with me." Maddie snapped her whip into the air at Rebekah again. Rebekah raised her sword toward Maddie, and then Maddie, with her whip, lashed out toward Rebekah's sword. The whip wrapped itself around Rebekah's sword blade, Maddie then, yanked the sword from Rebekah's hand. Rebekah's sword now lay on the floor in front of Maddie. Jack was coming around the table with his sword when one of Maddie's men told Jack to drop it. Jack, with a pistol barrel stuck in his back, had no choice as his sword dropped in front of him. Maddie told Mort to grab the princess. Mort tied Rebekah's hands and Jack's hands as well.

58
This Is Your New Home
1673

"Who are you? You old witch!" Rebekah shouted.

"My name is Maddie, and I've come searching for you, Princess," Maddie said, picking up Rebekah's sword. "You'll not need this anymore." Maddie laid Rebekah's sword down on the table behind her. Jake watched, but he and his men were powerless with pistols held on them.

"Maddie, who and why are you taking me and Jack with you?"

"You killed my sister, Tabby, and I'm going to kill you, Princess, after I've made you suffer."

Remembering Tabby Hawkens, Rebekah said, "So you're Tabby's sister?"

"Yes, I'm Maddie Hawkens, Tabby's sister, who you murdered. You and your boyfriend are going to die too when the time comes."

"Monk," Maddie yelled.

"Yes, Maddie."

"Take our little princess and Jack to the ship."

"Yes, Maddie." Monk hated Maddie but still followed orders.

"Another thing, Monk."

"Yes, Maddie."

"Be quiet about all of this. Tie cloths around the princess's mouth and her boyfriend's. We don't want them yelling for help and alerting her men on her ship. I want to leave without a fight, understand, Monk?"

"Yes, Maddie!" Her men gagged Rebekah and Jack.

Maddie had Jake and his men locked into the back room while she and her men went back to the *Crimson Tide*. When Jack and Rebekah were secured below deck, the ship lowered its sails and sailed out of the cove without making a sound.

Back on the *Crimson Tide*, Maddie came down to the lower deck where Rebekah and Jack were tied up all night, leaning up against the wall of the ship. "Did you two sleep well last night?" Maddie said, laughing with wicked pleasure.

"What are you going to do with us, you old viper?" Rebekah yelled out.

"I'd normally kill you for saying that to me princess, but then I wouldn't get to enjoy watching you scream and squirm begging me to kill you." Maddie gritted her brown rotted teeth at Rebekah.

"Why don't you just kill us and get it over with, Maddie?" Jack told her.

"Why are you two in such a hurry to die?"

"That's simple," Rebekah replied, "because if we get the chance, we're going to run our swords straight through your heart if you have one."

"You not only killed my sister, Princess, but you have an arrogant mouth, which I shall close in time."

"Monk!" Maddie yelled.

Monk came a running just like a dog being whistled for. "Yes, Maddie."

Mort was standing there, holding a pistol on Jack and Rebekah.

"Monk, open those wooden cages and show our guests their new home."

After untying their hands, Mort escorted Rebekah and Jack toward two small wooden cages where you couldn't stand up in, only crawl into. Monk opened the cage door, telling Rebekah to crawl in. Rebekah crawled in and leaned her back up against the wooden bars. Jack crawled in on his knees, and as he sat up, he had to bend his knees some so the cage door would close. Monk locked the cage doors. Maddie wickedly said to Rebekah, "This is your new home until you die."

59
Just Enough, Mr. Reese
1673

Maddie walked over to Jack's cage, telling him, "You may be a big man, Jack Reese, but don't think you can kick your way out of this wooden cage. The wood is five inches thick and is solid oak." Maddie cackled wickedly.

Rebekah yelled out at Maddie, "I'll see a sword through your wicked heart before this is all over, you old viper!"

Maddie showed Rebekah who was in charge as she snapped her whip toward Rebekah's cage. Maddie's whip lashed Rebekah across her upper right thigh through the wooden bars. Rebekah screamed out while covering her thigh with her hand to stop the bleeding.

"You all right, Rebekah?" Jack yelled out.

"Yes, Jack."

"Now, Princess, unless you want some more of this whip, keep that little trap of yours shut." Maddie snapped her whip toward the wooden bars again.

Jack knew not to say anything at this point as it would make Maddie more furious and cause her to do something she's not ready for, like kill him and Rebekah. Another man of Maddie's came down. His name was Marvin Monroe. "Maddie!"

"Yes, what is it? I'm busy!"

"We need you on top deck, Willy is asking about course changes."

"Tell Willy I'll be up shortly, Mr. Monroe."

Before Monroe left, he got a good look at Rebekah. He thought he and Monk would come back and have some fun with her later.

"What are you looking at, Mr. Monroe? Do as you're told, now!" Maddie turned her attention back to Rebekah.

"If you don't bleed to death and die on me, Princess, I'd like to starve you to death first after a few more beatings." Maddie cackled again.

"No food, no water? That it, Maddie?" Jack exclaimed.

"Just enough, Mr. Reese, to keep you alive so you can beg for more."

Maddie left laughing with delight. Jack looked over toward Rebekah and saw her right thigh was bleeding.

"Rebekah."

"Yes, Jack."

"You have to stop the bleeding."

"Yes, Jack, I know." Rebekah started tearing her sleeves from her blouse.

"That's it, Princess," Jack told her.

"Now tie the ends together and then tie it around your thigh real tightly to stop the bleeding." Rebekah did as Jack instructed her, and when she tied the sleeves real tight around her thigh, Rebekah hollered out, "Wow, that hurts."

"That should stop the bleeding, Princess."

"I hope so, Jack. I have to live long enough to see that insane woman removed from this earth."

Back at Pirates Cove, Rebekah's men were searching for her and Jack.

"They're nowhere on this ship, Joe," the men told him.

"Let's go over to the post. Maybe they're there." When Joe, Marty, and Smitty entered the post, there was nobody around. Jake's men who stand watch on the mountaintop walked in the post.

"What's going on here, and where's Jake?" one man asked.

"We're looking for Jake too," Joe said.

Then there was a pounding on the back room door. Joe opened it.

"Why are you and your men locked in the back room, Jake?" Joe asked.

Jake explained all that happened there last night.

"What are we going to do now, Joe?" Smitty asked.

60
THE SEARCH FOR THE PRINCESS AND JACK
1673

JOE, ALWAYS KEEPING his head, sat down to think this out. Jake's men were now exchanging shifts on the mountaintop. Joe was watching Jake's men leave when he jumped up and went to talk with Jake's other men who just came back. "Make it fast, Joe. I've been sitting up all night, and I'm bushed."

"Kirby, how many ships came into this cove yesterday and last night?"

"There was only one ship that sailed into the cove last night."

Jake spoke up, "Joe, that was the *Crimson Tide*."

"When did that ship sail out of the cove, Kirby, and in what direction?"

"The moon was bright last night, Joe, and we could see well out toward the sea. The ship sailed south toward the Caribbean Sea, about midnight."

Joe ordered the men back to the ship. The *Black Rose* was out to sea and sailing in the same direction as the *Crimson Tide*.

Back on the *Crimson Tide*, Maddie was on deck talking with Monroe and Willy. "Let's keep our course directly toward the Caribbean Sea, Mr. Willy."

Willy went back to the helm to take it over.

"Do you think her men will follow, Maddie?" Monroe asked.

"Maybe, but I think not. If they're the pirates they should be, they'll take this opportunity and take the princess's ship and vote in a new captain."

"You think so, Maddie?"

"Of course, they will, you fool. They're pirates, and that's what pirates do. There's no loyalty and honor among pirates, Monroe, you know that. I'll be in my cabin if needed."

After Maddie went to her cabin, Monroe was finding Monk who had the key to Rebekah's cage. Monroe was planning to have some fun with Rebekah now that the opportunity came. Monroe had to be careful not to alert the other pirates, or they would want in on the same fun.

When Monroe found Monk on the other side of the ship, he asked him for the key to Rebekah's cage and asked him to come with him and share in the fun.

"You crazy, Monroe?" Monk told him.

"Listen, Monk, we may never have another opportunity like this again. The princess has had her fangs pulled—she is without her sword. We can do what we want. Come on and give me the keys, and if you want out, fine, I'll go without you, Monk."

Monk was tempted too and, liking beautiful women, couldn't resist the temptation, so he went with Monroe as a foolish man into a lion's den full of lions. Below deck, Jack was trying to kick the door open with his boots but was not having much luck. Jack would stop to rest and go again.

"Don't hurt yourself, Jack."

"Rebekah, every jail and cage has a weak point, and so does this cage, and I'm going to find it." Jack gave another solid kick with his boots. Again and again, Jack kicked at the cage door. Then a little crack appeared in the doorframe wood. Jack told Rebekah, "One more kick ought to do it, Princess." Right before Jack gave the door another kick, Monk and Monroe were heard coming down the stairs. Then Jack stopped.

61
We Won't Hurt You, Princess
1673

Monroe and Monk walked over to Rebekah's cage and stood there staring at her.

"What are you two animals staring at with drool all over your faces?" Rebekah asked, knowing something was on their minds, and it wasn't good.

"We'd just like to stare at you for a moment, Princess. That's all," Monk said.

Monroe said, licking his lips, "Give me the keys, Monk. I'll open the cage and go in and get her."

Monk handed Monroe the keys. Rebekah watched and was getting ready to put the heel of her boot into one of their faces. Jack was waiting for the right moment for the last kick that should break his cage door open.

Monroe unlocked the cage door and told Rebekah, "We won't hurt you, Princess. Just do what we say." Monroe reached in for Rebekah.

With her boot, Rebekah struck Monroe so hard in the face he fell backward to the floor with a bleeding, broken nose. Monroe lay there almost unconscious, holding his nose with his hand.

Monk pulled his knife, telling Rebekah, "I'll stab you if you try something like that again."

Monroe got up, and then he and Monk were going into the cage after Rebekah together.

"We don't want any trouble out of you, Princess," they said as they were trying to pull Rebekah out of the cage with her kicking them all over their body. Then Jack, with that last mighty kick, kicked the cage door open with broken wood flying everywhere. Jack was out of his cage and on top of Monroe and Monk, pulling them from Rebekah's cage. Jack yanked Monk backward to the floor while striking Monroe with his fist and knocking him down. Then Jack kicked Monroe in the face, knocking him out.

Monk got up and ran toward the stairs that went up to the top deck. Jack caught him by grabbing the collar of his shirt. Rebekah was out of her cage, limping toward Jack. Jack got his hands around Monk's throat and said, "I want to know how many men are on this ship?"

Afraid for his life, Monk spilled his guts and answered every one of Jack's questions. Jack checked the stairs to make sure no one else was coming down.

Monk pulled a knife he had hidden in his shirt. Rebekah, thinking quickly, knocked the knife from Monk's hand. Jack picked up Monk's knife, saying, "Pick up your friend and put him in the cage, and then you squeeze inside too."

Monroe was coming around when Monk helped him crawl into the cage. Monk squeezed himself inside as well. Jack closed and locked the cage door.

Standing by the cage, Rebekah asked, "Now how do you two like it?"

"We've gotten this far, Jack, but what do we do next?"

"Good question, Princess. We better think of something soon before Maddie comes back and checks on us." As soon as Jack spoke those words, an explosion rocked the ship. Rebekah fell against Jack.

Rebekah yelled out, "What's happening, Jack?"

"It sounds like cannon fire, Princess."

Maddie came out of her cabin and yelled at one of her men running up to the top deck, "What's all that noise?"

"I think we're being attacked by cannon fire, Maddie."

It Must Be the *Black Rose*
62
1673

More explosions rocked the ship. Maddie's men fired back at the attacking ship. Rebekah was excited and shouted out, "It must be the *Black Rose*."

"I don't think so, Princess. Joe wouldn't fire on this ship if it was going to endanger us, but this does give us a chance to escape if Maddie's ship is being attacked by other pirates."

Jack was taking this opportunity to escape. Rebekah looked back toward Monroe and Monk. She limped back toward them and threw the key into their cage so they could escape.

Jack yelled out, "Come on, Rebekah, we don't have much time."

"I'm giving those two a chance to escape."

"Go, Rebekah, up those stairs and wait on top for me."

Monroe and Monk did get out of their cage, but did they survive? Nobody knows.

Maddie was in her cabin gathering some personal belongings. She was planning to escape on a small boat, which two of her men were now lowering to the water below. Jack and Rebekah were on deck when Jack saw two of Maddie's men by the railing lowering a boat. Jack, having Monk's knife, said, "Wait here, Rebekah, I'm going to take care of those two."

With the explosions and cannons being fired that rocked the ship, Jack dodged flying wood and other debris while he ran up behind the two men. One man turned, and Jack stuck a knife in his gut. The other man grabbed Jack around his shoulders. Jack headbutted him, and when he was let loose, Jack, with both hands, clenched in a fist, struck the man so hard he went over the ship's railing down toward the sea. Jack motioned for Rebekah. She came limping over. Jack carefully helped her safely over the railing and down toward the small boat that was Maddie's way of escape.

Jack started over the railing when another cannon was fired from the attacking ship, which rocked the *Crimson Tide* so hard it caused Rebekah to lose her grip and she almost fell from the ship. Rebekah caught back her hold and continued down to the small boat. Jack started his climb down and noticed the attacking ship wasn't the *Black Rose* and the pirates jumping over onto the *Crimson Tide* weren't Rebekah's men. Jack proceeded down toward the small boat when the *Crimson Tide*'s gunpowder room exploded. Maddie's men and the invading pirates that were standing above the gunpowder room went flying into the air after the explosion and to their death. Rebekah was in the boat waiting for Jack when Maddie ran out and saw Jack climbing over the railing and down the side of the ship.

With spittle dripping from her lips, Maddie cried out, "Princess!" Maddie, with her pistol, ran over to the railing and looked over. Jack was halfway down when Maddie pointed her pistol at Jack and said, "Oh no you don't, Reese. That's my boat."

Maddie started to pull the trigger when a pirate from the attacking ship saw Maddie and, thinking she was escaping, pulled his pistol and shot Maddie in the back.

Maddie's arm jerked upward as her pistol went off, and the lead pellet went into the air. Jack looked up and saw Maddie leaning over the railing and her pistol falling into the water below.

Maddie, still alive, stared down at Rebekah and Jack while they were rowing away. She spoke out, "Tabby."

Jack, with strong arms, rowed the small boat out toward the sea and away from the sinking *Crimson Tide*. Rebekah looked back and saw the sail on the attacking ship; it was the *Blue Scarlet* captained by One-Eyed Jackson and Pegleg Wilson.

63
THANKED THEM FOR WHAT?
1673

"REBEKAH."

"Yes, Jack."

"You'll have to thank One-Eyed Jackson and Pegleg Wilson when you meet them again."

"Thank them for what?"

"If they wouldn't have attacked Maddie's ship, we'd still be there thinking of a way out."

"Jack, you're right. The next time we meet, I'll buy them a cup of hot chocolate."

Jack laughed while he continued to row.

An hour out to sea, Jack asked Rebekah about the wound she received from Maddie's whip. "Princess, how's the wound, and has the bleeding stopped?"

"It has stopped bleeding for now, Jack."

"We'll have to get you to a sea port, Rebekah, and make sure you get proper care for that leg so you don't lose it." Jack knew they were miles from any large port but kept up hope for a friendly ship or a small seaport.

Back on the *Rose*, Marty was in his favorite place, the crow's nest looking out toward the sea for the *Crimson Tide*. Marty, using his spyglass, spotted something out at sea about the size of a small longboat. Marty climbed down and reported it to Joe. Joe ran up toward the bow of the ship and looked through his glass.

Joe shouted out, "It's the princess and Jack. Bring the ship in a little closer, Randy."

When Rebekah and Jack were onboard, Jack picked Rebekah up and took her to her cabin and told Troy to go and get Micky. While Rebekah's men waited on deck, Micky was doctoring Rebekah.

 Micky the Doctor
1673

"Do you think Micky knows what he's doing, Jack?" Louie asked.

"Micky has doctored Rebekah several times before, Louie, and the princess has survived. I think we can trust Micky once more, Louie."

Micky said, "Now, Miss Rebekah, I have to take this knife and cut away your pants leg." Micky cut slowly and carefully until he removed the pants leg from Rebekah's thigh. "Those are deep slashes, Miss Rebekah, but the wound looks clean."

"Am I going to lose my leg, Micky?"

"You didn't lose your arm the time you were shot did you, Miss Rebekah?"

"No, Micky."

"I'm pretty sure you aren't going to lose your leg either."

Rebekah laid her head back with a sigh. Micky finished cleaning Rebekah's wound. Then there was a knock on Rebekah's cabin door. Micky opened the door.

"Here's the bottle of brandy you asked for, Micky."

"Thanks, Rex."

Rebekah, seeing the brandy, said, "I'm not thirsty for any brandy, Micky."

"This isn't for drinking, Miss Rebekah. I'm pouring this inside your wound."

Rebekah sat up and cried out, "You're going to do what?"

"I have to, Miss Rebekah. This is to ensure of no infection setting in."

"Here, Miss Rebekah, take this small wooden spoon and put it between your teeth. This is going to burn like fire for just a few minutes."

Rebekah put the spoon between her teeth. Micky told her, "Bite down hard."

Micky poured the brandy into the open cut wound. Rebekah bit down hard but couldn't help letting out a death scream when the brandy soaked into her skin.

Jack said, "I'm going in."

At the same time Jack was at the cabin door, Micky opened it and came out.

"Micky, is she?"

Micky put up his hand toward Jack and said, "She's fine, Jack, and is resting comfortably and doesn't need to be disturbed. Now all of you men go back to work, and I'll take care of Miss Rebekah."

"Thank you, Micky," Jack said.

"I have to wash up now, Jack. I have to fix some hot soup for Miss Rebekah to help build up her strength. Then cook for all of her men after that."

"Yes, Micky, Rebekah and I haven't eaten since we were abducted two days ago."

"I'll bring Miss Rebekah some hot soup first, Jack, and after you wash up, come to the galley, and I'll fix you some."

"You have a deal, Micky."

Later on deck after Jack had some hot soup, he was talking with Joe. Joe asked, "How did you and the Princess escape, Jack?"

Jack told Joe all that had happened, and Maddie was now dead, and her ship was sinking when they were rowing away.

"Joe."

"Yes, Jack."

"Thanks for coming after me and Rebekah."

Avoiding any emotion, Joe said, "We have more ships to raid, Jack, and we had to have our captain back." Joe cracked a small grin and went back to work. Jack looked out toward the huge sea and just stared at the water.

PART VI

LOVE'S TIGHTROPE
1673

IN A PORT called Donavan, there sat a man in a tavern looking at a young girl of twenty-one years of age serving drinks to the men. The owner of the tavern hired women to serve drinks to the men hoping it would bring in more business, which it did. It also caused more fighting over the women, but it was worth it in the long run. The man staring at the young girl not only stared at her but would look at a picture he was holding from time to time. When he was sure of what he was looking at, he asked the girl to come and sit while he asked her some questions.

Before she sat down, she said, "Mister, if this is social, you'll have to buy me a drink."

The man laid five pieces of silver on the table and said, "Will this buy ten minutes of your time?"

The girl sat, and after putting the silver inside her blouse, she said, "You just purchased ten minutes of my time, mister."

"What's your name?" he asked.

"If you must know, it's Courtney Grey."

Then the man showed her a picture. She looked at the picture then responded, "Where did you get this picture of me?"

"It's not you," the man answered back. "Of course, it is, but I don't remember wearing that pretty red dress."

Courtney continued staring at the picture, saying, "If not me, then it must be my twin sister I never knew I had."

Taking the picture back, the man said, "This picture was drawn nine years ago, and you don't have a twin sister."

"That's not possible, and how do you know so much about me?"

"I know all about you, Courtney, and your habits."

"But why?"

"You're the twin to this girl in the picture, and I need your help."

"Help for what?"

"Courtney, how would you like to be rich beyond your wildest dreams?"

The tavern owner approached the table telling Courtney, "I pay you to buy and serve drinks to these men, not to socialize all day."

Courtney stared at the man she was talking to then stared at her boss. "I quit."

"You can't quit, Courtney. I haven't anyone to take your place."

"Watch me, Devon." Courtney stood and said to the man she was talking to, "We can go back to my place and talk."

In Courtney's room, the man discussed his plans and told Courtney how she fitted in and all she had to do was follow his instructions to the letter. "Are you sure about this?" Courtney asked.

"It can't fail," he said.

Feeling strange about all this, Courtney said, "Here in my room, I'm talking to a total stranger, and I don't even know your name."

The man revealed his name and then gave Courtney two hundred English pounds to purchase the things she needed such as certain colored dresses and shoes, plus a ship's ticket to Key West Port.

First Spanish Ship
1673

"Where do we meet when I've finished my part in all of this?" Courtney asked.

"I'll contact you at the West Port Inn when you've accomplished what I've sent you there to do. Then I'll give you further instructions." The man grabbed Courtney and kissed her.

Courtney pulled back and said, "How did you know I wanted you to do that?"

"I know women, Courtney, and you're no different." Then he kissed her again before he left.

Courtney closed the door after he left and leaned up against it with a smile on her face. Courtney now has to get things ready and go to a port called Key West where she's supposed to wait and let herself be seen every day in the town.

That'd be the easy part, she thought, but when the man she is supposed to meet approaches her, she has to give the right impression to make the plan work. Even Courtney had doubts about the plan working but was willing to give it a try now that she quit her job.

Back Pirates Cove, the *Black Rose* was sailing out and was on her next raiding mission. Jack was in Rebekah's cabin going over the final plans.

"It looks good to me, Princess." Jack was confident.

"Yes, Jack, it does. This ship should make up for the one we missed last month when we were sidetracked by Maddie Hawkens."

"How is your leg healing, Princess?"

"After the last bandage was removed, I started rubbing that salve Jake gave me on the scars, and they're slowly fading away."

"I'm very glad of that, Princess."

"It's my leg, Jack, not yours. I should be the one saying that."

"Yes, Princess, I was just being happy for you. That's all."

Rebekah grinned. "Jack, you best make sure the *Rose* is ready for the next raid."

"Right away, Captain."

Sitting in front of her mirror, Rebekah put her hair up a bit to see how she looked. She had done this before and now thinking of putting her hair up more often as she stared and said, "Hmm, not bad."

Later that day, Jack was in his cabin staring at a picture of a girl named Angela who he once was going to marry. This girl, Angela, was Jack's whole world at one time until she was shot with a pistol from a renegade pirate and died. Jack kept the picture in memory of her even though he was now in love with Rebekah.

The years that Jack had been with Rebekah, not once had he mentioned Angela. Then there was a knock on Jack's cabin door. Jack quickly put the picture away inside his desk drawer and said, "Come in."

Rebekah entered and said, "Joe is waiting on deck for you, Jack, to give him the course change toward the Spanish ship *Marietta*."

"Yes, Princess. I was about to go up and do that before you knocked."

"Very well, Jack, I'll be in my cabin if needed."

On deck, Jack was giving Joe the course changes he needed to intercept the *Marietta*.

"This is the first ship from Spain we've ever raided, Jack. What's so special about it?"

"The information we got from Jake was she'll be delivering Spanish gold doubloons to England in payment for two warships. The princess wants this gold badly. It could possibly put a huge financial burden on England."

"Consider the course change done, Jack."

Back in England, Hendrexson was in Morgan's office laying down the situation to him. "This gold coming from Spain, Morgan, will be on your shoulders if it's lost to pirates."

"Yes, Sir Hendrexson, I know about it, sir, and will have a naval warship escort her to our harbor when she gets halfway here."

"Very well, Morgan, I see you're on your toes."

"Thank you, Sir Hendrexson."

Leaving Morgan's office, Hendrexson had a concerned look on his face instead of a confident one. Morgan was thinking that with an escort of the naval ship, the *Marietta* should get here safely.

It would be three days before the *Black Rose* and the ship from Spain meet.

Back at the port of Donavan, Courtney Grey was making her plans and buying her ship ticket to Key West Port. At the same time, the strange man who set this deal up with her was down at the docks making another deal with a ship captain.

The men talked for a while and then the captain was handed two envelopes. The captain opened one envelope and pulled out paper money then counted it. Afterward, the two men shook hands and then the captain went back to his ship.

When the captain returned to his ship, his first officer asked, "What was that all about Captain Miller?"

"Mr. Wilson."

"Yes, sir."

"Set a course to Pirates Cove."

"Did I hear you right, sir?"

"Yes, you did, Wilson, and do it now."

"One question, sir?"

"Yes, Wilson, what is it?"

"There are strict orders for no vessel to go into those waters."

"I know, Wilson, but I do know Jake Spencer who runs that little getaway for pirates and know the signals to enter."

"We're going into the cove, Captain?"

"No, Mr. Wilson. Not this time. When we sail within ten miles of the cove, you'll have one of your men send a signal of truce that will tell Jake we want to talk in peace."

"As you order, Captain, and I sure hope you know what you're doing."

"It'll be fine, Wilson. I have to deliver a letter to a Jack Reese who is the first mate on a pirate ship that makes its home there at the cove."

"Sir."

"Yes, Wilson."

"You could possibly lose your captaincy if the big brass finds out."

"Don't worry about the big brass, Wilson. I wouldn't be doing this if I didn't have the upper hand on some that big brass."

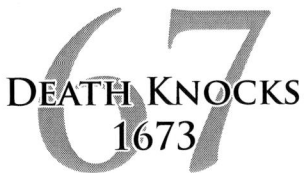

Death Knocks
1673

The days passed on the *Black Rose* when finally on the third day, she was locked up to the ship from Spain. You could hear swords clanging and pistols fired. Rebekah and her men were having a difficult time with the Spaniard sword fighters; they were great swordsmen.

Rebekah didn't know of their great swordsmen history and thought this ship would be taken easy as all the others, but she was wrong. Rebekah took two Spanish sailors down while Jack, Joe, Marty, and Sam took one each with great difficulty. Randy took a shot from a pistol in his left shoulder that took him down as he fell to the deck of the ship. Marty, with his wrath, rushed up behind the Spanish sailor who shot Randy, put his arm around his neck, and snapped it like a twig off a tree. Jack yelled to Rebekah that they had a man down. Rebekah had to retreat to save Randy's life, so she ordered her men back to the *Black Rose*.

The naval escort, not far away, was now firing her cannons at the *Black Rose*.

Marty picked up Randy and carried him back to the *Rose*. Rebekah's men back on the *Black Rose* unhooked the grappling hooks and sailed away from the Spanish ship. The cannon fire from the naval ship missed the *Rose* twice as she sailed farther out to sea. The captain of the Spanish ship was relieved when he saw the naval ship sailing closer to the *Marietta*. He was also thankful his men were able to fight off the pirates without losing more of his men.

Back on the *Rose*, Rebekah was asking Jack about Randy's condition.

"Micky has stopped the bleeding, but Randy's got a lead pellet lodged in his left shoulder, Princess."

"Will Randy make it back to the cove, Jack?"

"The lead pellet in his shoulder has to come out soon if Randy is to live."

"He should be all right until we reach the cove, Jack."

"We can't wait until we get back to the cove, Rebekah."

"Why not Jack?"

"If Randy doesn't bleed to death first, by the time we get back, the lead pellet possibly could set up an infection and Randy will die for sure."

"What are we going to do, Jack? We just can't let Randy die."

"Listen, Rebekah, death knocks on everybody's door sooner or later."

"We have to help Randy, Jack. There must be something we can do."

"One thing might work Rebekah, but I make no promises."

"Anything, Jack. What is it?"

"I can try and remove the lead pellet."

Rebekah thought about it and asked Jack, "Are you sure?"

"No, I'm not sure, but on my brother's ship, I watched many men getting shot by pistols from pirate raiders. The lead pellets were always removed with knives."

"Did they all live, Jack?"

"Not all, Rebekah, but more than half."

"Do it, Jack. This is Randy's only hope."

The thing that made this a death situation was the lead pellet was near Randy's heart. This will bring back terrible memories for Jack because Angela, the girl he loved, lost her life in the same situation.

There was a knock on Rebekah's cabin door. "Yes, come in." It was Marty. "Yes, Marty."

"I have the information on that naval ship, Jack."

"Go ahead, Marty."

"It was an English ship all right, and she sailed toward the Spanish ship after we retreated."

"That's good news, Marty. We now know that the naval ship won't be chasing us."

"Marty."

"Yes, Jack."

"Have the men take Randy to the small cabin in the back of the ship."

"Micky has already had us to do that, Jack."

"Tell Micky the princess and I'll be there shortly."

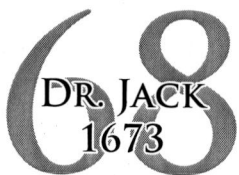

DR. JACK
1673

Brad, Randy's brother, was in the cabin sitting in a chair by Randy's bed. Jack, Micky, and Rebekah entered the cabin and told Brad that Jack was going to remove the lead pellet from Randy's shoulder. Rebekah put her hand on Brad's shoulder, giving him her support. Brad said to Rebekah, "He's my only brother, Princess, and I always looked up to him, but we're pirates, and this is a pirate's way of life."

"We all want Randy to live, Brad."

"Like I told you before, Princess, this is a pirate's life, and if my brother dies, then he died the way he lived."

Micky asked Jack, "What are you using for a probe, Jack?"

Jack pulled out his huge knife and said, "This is what the men on my brother's ship used, and it worked."

Micky exclaimed, "No, no, here, use this small sharp metal pick."

Jack shook his head and said to Micky, "I can't find that pellet with such a small thing as that."

"Yes, you can, Jack, and I'll guide you through it. I'd do it, Jack, but my eyes aren't as sharp as they once were, and I don't want to sever an artery."

Making sure things were sterile as possible and giving Randy more brandy to drink, they were ready. Troy, being the tallest, held two lanterns above the bed to give Micky and Jack plenty of light. Micky gave Randy most of the brandy that was on the ship to drink to help numb the pain as much as possible.

Micky said, "Here, Randy, take this wooden spoon and bite down."

Jack said, "Are you ready, Randy?" Randy, feeling sleepy from the brandy, shook his head yes.

Using the metal-like pick, Jack probed around inside Randy's shoulder trying to locate the lead pellet with Micky guiding him. Randy was breathing deeper when he felt the metal object moving around inside his shoulder. Randy was too much of a pirate to let out a yell, but the pain he felt was extreme as he did jerk a little back and forth from the pain. Rebekah watched and was turning a little white in her face at times but was determined to stick it out.

Micky warned Jack, "Be real careful. Don't damage an artery."

"I'm watching, Micky." Feeling around with the pick, Jack was watching very carefully not to get near an artery. Minutes were passing, and Jack was sweating as he kept probing. Randy jerked again. Jack removed the pick and took a rest.

"I don't know if I can do this, Micky. You may have to take over."

"Gather yourself, Jack, and go back in. You can do it. I know you can."

With the sweat wiped away, Jack took a deep breath and went back in with the probe and slowly felt around. Digging a little deeper, Jack felt the pick against something hard. Jack said, "I felt something solid, Micky."

"That's it, Jack. That's the pellet. Now can you see it?" Jack moved the metal pick a little, and there it was. Micky kept wiping the blood from around the shoulder wound so Jack could see. Jack, slowly with the curved part of the metal pick, brought the pellet to the surface. With a tweezer-like tool, Jack pulled the pellet from Randy's shoulder.

Micky told Troy to hold Randy down tight as he poured a little of the brandy into the wound to sterilize it from possible infection. Of course, Randy yelled out. Jack poured some brandy onto the blade of his knife and then put the blade inside a hot lantern over the flame. Micky instructed Jack, "The blade must be real hot to seal Randy's wound completely."

Laying there sweating and breathing heavy, Randy thought it was all over until Jack laid the hot blade of his knife onto the wound to seal it closed. Troy held Randy down tight as he yelled out again in agonizing pain. Jack removed the blade so Micky could get a closer look and see if the wound was completely closed.

"Well, Micky?"

"It looks good to me, Jack. But Jake will have to inspect our work when we return to the cove."

Micky bandaged Randy's shoulder and told him, "It's over, Randy. You can relax."

Randy was so worn-down from the experience he just closed his eyes and fell to sleep. Brad sat on a chair to be with his brother, and watched over him that night.

Micky gave orders, saying, "Everyone can leave now. Randy needs his rest, but you, Brad, can stay."

"Thanks, Micky."

THE LETTER
1673

JACK AND REBEKAH went to the galley while Rebekah's men went back to their duties.

"Princess, I'll make you some hot chocolate and me some coffee. Micky will be a while with Randy yet."

"Sure, Jack, that'd be nice of you."

After Jack sat, he handed Rebekah her hot chocolate, and he took a sip of his coffee.

"Not bad, Jack," Rebekah said, taking another sip of her hot chocolate.

"Yea, I do make a pretty good cup of coffee too."

"This'll be a day I won't forget, Jack, losing that gold shipment and almost losing one of my best men."

"It was close, Princess, and I hope we never have it that close again."

"Jack."

"Yes, Princess."

"Jake should've known about the naval ship escorting the Spanish ship."

"This could've been a last minute maneuver by parliament, Princess, and Jake never received that bit of information with the information he sold us."

"One thing Jake isn't going to like, Jack."

Taking another sip of coffee, Jack asked, "What's that, Princess?"

"His share of the gold. He won't get it."

"He'll have to wait for the next ship we raid for that, Princess."

They both chuckled while finishing their drinks.

Getting late, Jack escorted Rebekah to her cabin. Before they kissed good night, Rebekah asked, "Jack, how did you feel inside yourself taking Randy's life in your hands trying to take out that led pellet?"

"I was scared all the time, Rebekah. I was afraid of damaging an artery and killing Randy, especially in front of his brother, Brad."

"I can understand, Jack. I felt that way inside when we delivered Jody's baby that time."

Jack glad this day was over, kissed Rebekah good night, and then he went to his cabin.

The next several days, Randy was recovering and getting stronger. Things were going well until Sam made a remark to Louie about Randy yelling in pain. "You know, Louie, a real pirate wouldn't have yelled out so like Randy did when Jack removed that lead pellet."

"Maybe the next time, Sam, it'll be you Jack is removing a lead pellet from, and we'll see if you don't yell out in pain when he starts feeling around inside your body to remove it."

Brad, going to the galley, overheard Louie and Sam talking about Randy.

"Listen, Sam, when we were rescuing the princess several mouths ago, you got it in the shoulder, and I was next you and heard you yell out, so don't say my brother, Randy, isn't a real pirate."

"What do you know, Brad? You're still not even weaned yet. You need to stay home with your momma and get your milk nourishment before calling yourself a pirate."

Brad drew back his fist and struck Sam across his chin, knocking him down. Brad was standing over Sam, waiting to hit Sam again when he asked, "How did that feel, Sam, coming from a pirate not weaned yet?"

Sam standing back to his feet and said to Brad, "You want to try that again, boy?"

Brad took another swing as Sam ducked and struck Brad in his gut, knocking the wind out of him. Sam said while moving his fists around, "Come on, boy, you want some more?"

Brad came at Sam again, throwing a right punch, but Sam blocked it with his left hand and took his right fist and struck Brad again, knocking him to the deck of the ship. Sam said again, "Get up, boy, your lessons are just beginning."

Brad staggered to his feet; he wasn't giving up.

Louie grabbed Sam and told him, "That's enough, Sam. He's had enough."

Sam pulled himself loose from Louie, telling him, "Let me go, Louie, if you don't want what Brad got."

Joe ran up and gave orders for them all to stop. "All right, Sam, what's going on here?"

"Brad and I were settling a few differences, Joe, and Brad lost."

Wiping the blood from his lip, Brad said, "Yes, Joe, we're settling our differences."

"All right, these differences better be settled now. You two understand?" Knowing Sam started it, Joe poked his finger on Sam's chest several times, saying, "Understand, Sam?"

"Yes, Joe, I understand." Sam went back to what he was doing before all this got started.

"Brad."

"Yes. Joe."

"I don't want to know what started this, but you better be able to defend yourself better than that if you're going to get into fights, especially with someone like Sam."

Brad grinned and said, "Yea, I'll remember that, Joe."

"Get back to the cabin and keep Randy company, Brad."

"Thanks, Joe."

Joe confronted Sam, "Sam."

"Yes, Joe, what do you want? I'm busy."

"First, it was the princess, now Brad. When are you going to settle in and be a part of the group?"

Sam, who was tying several ropes together, stopped and confronted Joe. "Listen, Joe, my life was scrapped when I was a child. Nobody wanted me. My mother sent me away to a hellhole called a children's home where they starved and beat you every day. When I turned fifteen, I fought back and killed one of the butchers that ran that place and escaped. I became a pirate after that and have been fighting for survival ever since." Sam then stared out toward the sea.

Joe was shocked as Sam never discussed his life before. "Sam, I'll keep this between you and I, but remember you're among friends now. We have a cause with the princess, and we're not a ship load of savages."

Joe left Sam to be by himself to think. Later that evening, Sam went to the cabin Randy was in and knocked. Brad said, "Come in."

Entering, Sam asked Brad, "How's Randy feeling, Brad?"

Brad had to look twice to see if this was Sam asking about Randy. Letting what happened earlier go, Brad replied, "He's feeling better, Sam. Thanks for asking."

"I've to get back to work, Brad. You know how the Princess gets with work left undone."

Sam left with a feeling he hadn't felt before. But still down deep, Sam was still all pirate.

The next day, the *Black Rose* was back home at the cove. Jake was over at the *Rose* not too long after she sailed in checking on Randy. Micky was waiting patiently while Jake was bandaging Randy back up.

"Well, Jake?" Micky asked.

"It looks great, Micky, no infection and the shoulder is healing perfectly."

"Thanks, Jake, and you're invited to stay on the ship for dinner."

"I'll just do that, Micky."

Jake was standing on deck of the *Rose* when one of his men rowed over from the post to tell him about a ship outside the cove. "Is it a friendly ship?" Jake asked.

"They want to meet in peace, Jake. The captain of the ship is waving a white flag."

"All right, let's go out and talk."

Later as the two small boats met several hundred yards out, Jake recognized Captain Miller. The boats were tied together to hold them steady.

"It must be seven years since you saved my life, Jake, and we, at last, saw each other."

"I thought you were dead, Miller, when your boat came floating into the cove that day."

"It's Captain Miller now, Jake."

"Captain, not bad, not bad at all, Tim."

"The reason I'm here Jake is this letter." Captain Miller handed Jake the letter.

"You come all the way here to deliver one letter, Tim?"

"The man who sent this letter paid me rather handsomely to make sure a Jack Reese got this letter. Do you know him, Jake?"

"Yes, I know him well. He's first mate to the Princess Pirate. I'm sure you've heard of her."

"Every sea captain that sails from England knows about the Princes Pirate and hopes she never raids their ship."

Jake chuckled. "Can you stay, Tim?"

"I must be going, Jake. You know I'm not supposed to be here. Besides, my first officer is back at the ship having kittens thinking the cannons on the mountain could start firing and blow our ship out of the water."

"Not your ship, Tim, assure him of that."

"Good-bye, Jake, and take care of yourself and remember parliament hasn't forgotten about this little getaway for pirates of yours. They're always thinking of a plan to destroy this island, but they haven't figured away to get that close without being blown to kingdom come by your cannons."

"Thanks for the information, Tim, and sail safely."

Looking at the letter addressed to Jack, Jake was curious about it. Jake had his man row him over to the *Rose* so he could give Jack the letter. Jake also wanted to know what it read. Jake, now back on the *Rose*, went to Jack's cabin and delivered the letter. While in Jack's cabin, Jake waited while Jack opened the letter and read it.

Jack sat while reading the letter.

"Well, Jack."

"It's from my brother, Chad. He wants me to come to Key West Port."

"Is he all right, Jack?"

Jack started laughing and said, "My brother is getting married and wants me there for his wedding."

"How did he know where to find you, Jack?"

"After I was sure about the princess being serious about her war against England, I gave a letter to a tavern owner in a town of Port Vermont. My brother and I knew this man for years, and I knew when Chad returned to this certain tavern, this man, Tanner, would give the letter I wrote to Chad, telling him he could always reach me here at Pirates Cove."

"What are you going to do, Jack?"

"I'll need the princess's ship to sail to Key West Port. Excuse me, Jake, I've got to go and talk to the princess."

Later in Rebekah's cabin, the princess said, "Congra-tulations, Jack, on the news of your brother."

"Thank you, Princess, and would you like to come with me and meet my brother?"

"You can take the *Rose*, Jack, and go, but I need to stay here at the cove with Randy."

"Rebekah, Randy will be fine here at the cove. He doesn't need a nursemaid. Besides, how will it look to the other men? These are pirates, not little children who need a mother."

"Jack, you said it right the first time. They do act like children sometimes and need our wisdom and guidance to see them through. Another thing, Jack, I don't want Randy thinking I was running out on him."

"I'll go without you, Princess, but please don't smother Randy, or he'll be useless as a pirate, and Sam is always looking for something or somebody to complain about."

"I'll handle Sam and the other men who stay behind, Jack. You go to your brother's wedding and have a good time."

Jack leaned over to kiss Rebekah and told her, "I don't know of any first mate that gets to kiss their captain." Jack kissed her again.

Afterward, Rebekah asked Jack, "Do you know the men who should sail with you, Jack?"

"I'll make that decision later, Princess. Where will you sleep when the *Black Rose* is gone?"

"Jake told me whenever I needed a place to stay he has a nice room in the back of the post."

"I'll make sure half of the men stay, Princess, to keep you safe."

Later that day, Jack was sailing out of the cove and decided to take Joe, Pete, Smitty, Louie, Brett, Micky and Sam with him to Key West Port, especially Sam to keep him out of Rebekah's hair. That would be plenty of men to sail the *Black Rose* to Key West Port. Besides, this was a wedding, not a raid.

Joe was the most important man on this trip for his experience on the seas and being able to elude other pirate ships. While the *Black Rose* was sailing out of the cove, Rebekah watched and was thinking she should be on that ship as it was leaving. Jake saw the expression on Rebekah's face and asked, "You feeling homesick, Princess, without your ship?"

"Yes, Jake, I was homesick when I left my sister and my father's castle but never knew I'd feel that way about a piece of floating wood."

"Come on in the post, Princess, and I'll show you to your room."

Out at sea, Joe was discussing the time distance with Jack, saying, "We should be at Key West Port in three days, Jack."

70
Courtney Grey Is My Name, Sir
1673

Back at the post the next day, Randy was talking with Rebekah, "Why did you stay at the post, Princess, and not go with Jack?"

"You're under my command, Randy, and my responsibility. That's why I stayed."

Randy didn't like to be mothered by the princess; it made him feel less than a pirate. But on the other hand, it did give him a place of belongingness. That was something he and his brother, Brad, never had at the abusive home for boys that they both escaped from.

Marty went over to Randy and asked, "Can I get you a drink from Jake's bar?"

"I can do that myself, Marty, thanks." Randy, showing his independence, walked over to the bar without one bit of trouble.

"Jake," Randy called.

"Yes, Randy, what can I get you?"

"I'm feeling on top of the world today. Give me what I always have—rum in a tall mug."

Marty strolled up to the bar and stood next to Randy. Randy asked Marty, "What will you have to drink Marty if I buy?"

Marty, licking his own lips, said, "Two whiskies in tall mugs, Randy."

Jake poured the drinks, saying, "I'm putting this on the princess's tab because neither of you have one."

Randy laid a silver crown on the bar and said, "No need, Jake. The princess gave us our pay for the week. Now, pour my friend, Marty his two whiskies in tall mugs."

Marty drank both mugs down and then let out a belch. "Thanks, Randy, that should hold me over for a while."

"Thank you, Marty, for carrying me off that ship and saving my life."

"It was nothing, Randy. You would've done the same for me."

"Let's find the others and get a poker game going, Marty."

"Yea, that sounds great, Randy. Let's go."

Back on the *Black Rose*, Sam was asking Joe about this wedding Jack was going to.

"It's just his brother's wedding, Sam. That's all."

As usual, Sam walked off complaining, saying, "We're supposed to be pirates, not nursemaids to a wedding."

The days passed on the *Black Rose* when on the third day, the *Rose* was anchored outside Key West Port's harbor. Joe, impressed with the size of the harbor, expressed to Jack, "This is a big harbor. It reminds me of a town where they were going to hang me, Jack."

"They must have failed, Joe, or you wouldn't be here talking to me now."

"Yea, the stupid sailor who walked me up to the hangman forgot to tie my hands. I grabbed his pistol and shot him, jumped from the gallows, and got away."

Jack has known Joe for a few years now, and Joe doesn't lie, but some of his stories sound a little fishy. Jack, with his bag of extra clothes, left the *Black Rose* in Joe's hands while he went looking for his brother. Joe looked up at the ships sails. They were flying an English flag and sail. *Things looks good*, Joe thought. All they had to do now was wait for Jack's return. Jack got a room at the Sailor's Comfort Inn and asked about his brother, Chad, who was staying there also. This was where Jack was supposed to meet him according to what the letter read.

Signing his name on the registry, Jack asked the clerk, "Is there a man by the name of Chad Reese staying here? And if so, would you please give me his room number."

"I don't remember anyone by that name registering here, Mr. Reese."

"Maybe someone else was on duty when you were out."

"Let's look at the registry and see if anyone by that name has registered over the last week...no Chad Reese listed, Mr. Reese."

"My letter stated that my brother, Chad, would be staying here at this inn."

"I'm very sorry, sir. You might try the other inn down the street."

"I'll do that."

Jack took his bag to his room and then went searching for Chad. Jack searched and asked questions for two days, and no one had seen his brother Chad or heard of him. Jack just couldn't leave until he found out what happened to his brother, Chad.

Jack sat in a restaurant having lunch that afternoon, and while he was waiting for his sandwich, Jack took a drink of his water, and as he did, he saw a girl walk by the window that looked just like Angela, a girl he once loved. Jack hurried out of the restaurant door to catch up with her. Jack, catching up with the girl, grabbed her by the arm. Turning her around, he said, "Angela!"

The girl was startled for a moment and said, "My name is Courtney Grey, sir, and would you please let go of my arm."

"I'm very sorry, and would you forgive me?" Jack pleaded.

Courtney now knew she has made contact with the man who just now accosted her. Not giving herself away, she said, "You look very upset, sir. May I be of some help?"

Jack kept staring at Courtney knowing it was impossible for this girl to be Angela. But Courtney could pass as Angela's twin;

they were so identical in every way. Courtney expressed again, "Sir, can I be of help to you?"

Not wanting her to get away, Jack said, "Please sit and talk with me at the restaurant, and I'll buy you lunch."

With a pretty expression and a smile on her face, Courtney said, "How can I turn down such an offer as that and with such a handsome man?"

While Jack and Courtney went into the restaurant, a man was standing not too far distance watching. Then this man went into the same inn Jack was staying at and into a room. He poured a little whiskey into a small glass and lay upon his bed with a pillow under his head. He took a drink and said to himself, "Finally, Jack Reese, you got here. Now you, Reese, will pay me back for what you stole from me." The man took another drink while his memory returned to his past. "Yes, I remember you, Jack…"

Ten years ago in Jack's hometown of Regend, a man walked off a ship and made himself at home in Regend. Not knowing any one in Regend, he tried to get a job. This town of Regend was where Jack lived, and it was one year before he and Angela were to be married. Jack was teaching swordsmanship to his students when he saw a new man in town.

Jack, being curious, turned his class over to his best student and went and introduced himself to this stranger in town. The stranger just came out of a building after being turned down for a job. Jack approached and introduced himself, saying, "I see you're new here, mister. My name is Jack Reese. Can I help you in some way?"

The man put his hand out to Jack and said, "My name is Travis McGreevy, and I need a job but, so far, no luck."

After shaking Travis's hand, Jack said, "I do know of a man who needs a good hand in his warehouse. That's if you aren't afraid of hard work."

"Anything will do, Jack," Travis said with a grin. Jack, proud of his new friend, could hardly wait to introduce him to Angela.

At dinner, Jack was telling Angela about Travis, the man he met today.

"He must be special, Jack," Angela replied.

"I think so, Angela," Jack said, taking a bite of his steak.

The next day, Jack introduced Travis to Angela.

"I didn't know God let his angels roam the earth, Jack. Miss Angela is like manna from heaven." Travis then kissed her hand.

"You're such a gentleman, Mr. McGreevy."

Angela pulled her hand back and then put her arm around Jack, letting Travis know she was Jack's girl.

"How are things going at the warehouse, Travis?" Jack was asking.

71
THINGS ARE NEVER WHAT THEY SEEM
1673

"Mr. Pender took to me like a duck to water, Jack. He says if I continue working like I have been, he'll promote me in no time."

"That's great, Travis, and on your first day."

"Yes, and I owe it all to you, Jack." Travis grinned, but behind that grin, Travis knew something Jack didn't.

The days passed, and Jack and Travis had become better friends. Jack told Travis of his brother, Chad, and everything about him and knew he'd be back someday to see about him.

"You haven't seen your brother since he left, Jack?" Travis asked.

"No, I haven't, but I'll see Chad again someday," Jack said with assurance.

More days passed, and Travis was given more responsibility at the warehouse. Mr. Pender lost his son in a war and took Travis in like a son. A month had gone by now, and Travis was in charge of the pay to a contractor. The payment involved Mr. Pender's ten thousand in gold coins.

The transaction of the ten thousand was to be deposited in the bank in town. Monday came, and when Mr. Pender checked on the money, it was never deposited, and Travis was nowhere in town to be found.

When Jack found out what Travis had done, he went searching for Travis. Jack told Angela and his parents, "I might be gone for quite a while. I'll not return until I find Travis and bring him in to be punished and the money returned."

I Ought to Kill You Where You Stand
1673

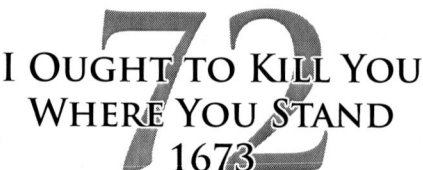

Jack got all the information on Travis that he could before leaving on the next ship. There was only one port Travis could go and exchange the gold he stole for cash money. A port just two days' sail, Port Monte. Two days later, Jack was there in Port Monte. Jack was being inconspicuous. He didn't want Travis to know he was there. If Travis found out, then he'd take another ship out and escape. Jack didn't have to wait long in finding Travis; he was at the next tavern he searched.

Coming in through the doors, Jack saw Travis sitting with a young girl on his lap, and they were laughing away. Jack walked over to Travis's table, and when Travis saw Jack standing there, he said, "Sit down, Jack, and have a drink. There are plenty of women to keep us company." Travis laughed while taking a drink.

"I'm not here to have a drink, Travis. I'm here to take you back to Regend for stealing."

"I don't think so, Jack," Travis said, taking another drink.

Travis pushed the girl from his lap and stood before Jack.

"I ought to kill you where you stand, Travis."

"Looks like that's what you're going to have to do, Jack." Travis pulled his knife on Jack.

Jack, being quicker, grabbed Travis's wrist and pounded his wrist against his knee until Travis let the knife loose from his hand.

Jack, with his fist hauled off, struck Travis across the face and knocked him across the table and onto the tavern floor. Jack picked Travis up by his collar, telling him, "I trusted you like a brother, and you stabbed me in the back."

Travis, not being strong enough to get loose from Jack, asked, "Now what, Jack?"

"I'll take you back, Travis, and then you'll face a trial, and I hope they put you away for a long, long time." Jack took Travis back to a ship and back to Regend.

At Travis's trial, he wasn't only convicted of that crime but also other crimes he committed from other ports and towns. (This was Travis's record: he was a conman, thief, and almost committed murder once, but the man lived. Travis was a loner and cared for no one, and no one cared for Travis.)

Two weeks after the trial was over, Jack was there when Travis was being taken to prison to serve ten years at hard labor. Travis, seeing Jack before he was taken away, made this threat. "You'll never know when I'm there hiding in the shadows, Jack, but you'll pay for me going to prison. I make this promise to you."

"Threats don't hurt anybody, Travis, and you ought to be thankful I didn't kill you when I found you." Travis gritted his teeth at Jack. "Another fact, Travis, you may never leave prison, so don't make threats you can't keep." Then they took Travis away.

Travis's memory returned back to the present. Taking another drink, Travis said to himself, "So far Jack, I've kept part of my promise to you. I'm here in the shadows, and you don't know it, plus you're working into my plan of revenge nicely." Travis lay on his bed laughing.

During this time in the restaurant, Jack was explaining to Courtney why he stopped her in the street. Courtney tricked Jack into her confidence, saying, "I'm very sorry for your loss, Jack."

Then Courtney put her hand on Jack's hand and stared deep into his eyes and said, "I feel in some way I know you, Jack." Then she leaned over and kissed him.

Letting his emotions take over, Jack returned her kiss and asked, "May I walk with you to where you're staying?"

Courtney accepted, and Jack escorted her back to the inn. Standing with Courtney in front of her room, Jack asked, "May I see you tomorrow?"

Courtney leaned up and kissed Jack again. Her kiss, this time, was really passionate. Courtney, not helping herself, fell in love with Jack. "Yes, Jack, I'd like for you to see me tomorrow."

Jack left, forgetting all about his brother and Rebekah. Jack was on a new high, and Courtney was on top of it.

That night in Jack's room, all he thought about was Courtney and what they could do together. They could run away together, and Jack would leave everything behind. Then Jack thought of Rebekah and his love for her—it was equal to the love he felt toward Courtney.

Jack was beside himself, leaving Rebekah for a girl whose Angela's twin down to her toenails. Let alone he didn't know anything about her, where she was from or if she was married or on the run. Jack was restless all night and couldn't wait to see Courtney in the morning.

The next day, Jack took Courtney to different places and was having the time of his life. Being with Courtney, talking with Courtney, and kissing Courtney, Jack forgot everything, his responsibility to Rebekah, the ship, the crew, and Chad. Jack was walking a tightrope with out of control emotion.

Back on the *Rose*, days passed, and Joe was thinking Jack should be back by now. Joe would wait one more day then go into town looking for Jack.

FALLING IN LOVE
1673

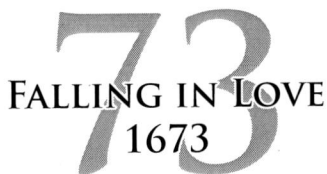

THAT NIGHT IN Courtney's room, there was a knock on her door. Courtney, who had fallen madly in love with Jack, ran to the door thinking it was him. When Courtney opened the door, it was Travis standing there. She said, "Oh, it's you!"

"You don't seem glad to see me, my little pet."

"I'm not your pet, and I think what we're doing is wrong."

Staring into Courtney's eyes, Travis said, "You've fallen in love with him, haven't you?"

Courtney turned her back toward Travis, telling him, "So what if I have? What business is it of yours?"

"Plenty, my dear. I need you to complete the job I sent you here for and not to fall in love."

"I do love, Jack, and can't help it, Travis, and I won't go on with this charade any longer."

"You will, Courtney, or you'll see your boyfriend dead with a knife in his back."

"You wouldn't, Travis, you wouldn't dare!"

"Oh, wouldn't I, my love? You cut out on me now and your lover boy won't see another tomorrow."

Courtney hung her head with tears, telling Travis, "All right, you despicable excuse for a man, I'll see this through, and when this is over, I don't want to see you ever again. Now get out!"

Travis, before he left, warned Courtney, "Now don't you go and do something stupid, Courtney, like tell Jack about this."

"Get out!" Courtney yelled!

Travis left laughing as he went out the door. Courtney slammed the door, leaned up against it, and started crying.

The next day, Jack and Courtney were in the park sitting on a wooden bench. After Courtney and Jack kissed, she asked, "Why haven't you ask me to marry you, Jack? I'm in love with you, and you know it."

Jack, being shocked, stood up from the bench and walked over to a tree and didn't answer. Jack thought of Rebekah and the tightrope he now walked between her and Courtney.

Courtney stood next to Jack, put her hand upon his shoulder, and asked, "You do love me, don't you, Jack?"

Jack turned around to face Courtney, and while staring her in the eyes, he put his arms around her and said, "I love you very much, Courtney, and yes, I'll marry you."

They kissed and sat back down.

Courtney's plan now was to get Jack to find some of the gold that the princess had buried to fulfill her part in all this. This was what Travis's plan was all about—finding some of the gold the princess had hidden. By using Courtney and Jack, this would set him up for life, and Jack would be paying him back for the years he spent in prison.

Courtney, now having Jack's full confidence, asked, "Jack, how can we live and be happy the way you talked about when we first met?"

Jack remembered where the last chest of gold Rebekah had buried and the island it was on. Jack would be betraying Rebekah, but he had served her well these four years and thought it was time to move on.

"Yes, Courtney, we can live and be happy together. I know where there's gold buried, and when we retrieve it, we can live happy together for the rest of our lives."

Jack's next problem was convincing Joe to take the ship where he wanted to go.

The next day, Jack and Courtney boarded the *Black Rose*. Jack gave Joe orders to set the ship's course toward Paradise Island where they had just recently buried a chest full of gold.

Joe Suspects Trouble
1673

The *Black Rose* was now sailing toward Paradise Island. Jack introduced Courtney to the crew.

"Courtney, I'd like for you to meet my crew."

Joe and the men were puzzled about Courtney being on the ship but nodded their heads at Courtney with respect. They were waiting for Jack to explain later.

Jack took Courtney to Rebekah's cabin.

"I think you'll find these accommodations satisfactory, Courtney. You're just borrowing this cabin for a few days, and then we'll be on our way to a life of our own."

"Are you sure, Jack? This does look like a woman's cabin, but I feel uncomfortable being here for some reason. And those men, they look like pirates."

"Trust me, Courtney. In a few days, you'll be Mrs. Reese, and we'll be sailing on another ship celebrating our new life together."

Jack kissed Courtney; then, she lowered her head.

"What's wrong, Courtney? You seem sad when you should be happy."

Wiping some tears and after a sniffle or two, Courtney said, "I'm happy, Jack, I just want to be on that ship with you and us living the life we talked about."

Jack left with a smile, assuring Courtney of their future.

Jack went to the galley for some coffee when Joe confronted him with a curious question: "Who's this Courtney, Jack? And why are we sailing to Paradise Island?"

"I'll explain when we get there, Joe, and not until then."

"I want to know now, Jack, and who's this young girl you brought aboard?"

"Are you disobeying my orders, Joe, and planning a mutiny?"

"I don't like that accusation, Jack, and something stinks about all of this."

Jack knew he wouldn't get Joe's cooperation under these circumstances, so he tried a different approach. "Trust me, Joe, and I'll explain when we get to the island."

Building up a liking for Jack over the years, Joe avoided a fight between them and decided to wait things out and give Jack the time he needed to explain all this later. Courtney settled down after a few days, especially when she got to be friends with Micky, the cook.

"I've been the cook on this ship for three years, Miss Courtney, and Miss Rebekah has been very good to me."

"Miss Rebekah, Micky, who's Rebekah?"

"Jack didn't tell you who captains this ship and that he's first mate to Miss Rebekah?"

"No, Micky, Jack never mentioned anything about her."

"Oh yes, they are quite close those two, and someday the crew expects them to marry."

Courtney left the galley with questions for Jack to answer when she sees him.

Later that evening, Courtney confronted Jack about Rebekah. Jack, almost speechless, explained everything. "I was going to tell you about Rebekah after we were married, Courtney."

"You love her, Jack?"

"Yes, Courtney, I do, but I'm still in love with you also."

Not liking this love triangle, Courtney said, "Since I resemble Angela in all your memories, Jack, you're marrying me instead."

"You don't understand, Courtney."

"I think I do, Jack. You're betraying Rebekah and marrying me."

Jack's head was spinning—how could he do this to Rebekah?—but when he looked at Courtney, his heart made his decision. "Yes, Courtney, I'm betraying Rebekah, but I can't go on living without you after we've met."

Courtney, not feeling right in her heart about betraying Jack, was torn inside with guilt. Courtney backed off arguing with Jack and hoped all of this would wash under the bridge and she and Jack could go away together. "Jack, I'm sorry. I do trust you and will go with you wherever you say." Jack kissed Courtney, saying, "It'll all work out, Courtney. I promise."

Unknown to Jack or his men, Travis was in a ship of his own following the *Black Rose*.

The *Black Rose* was now anchored offshore of Paradise Island. Jack was getting the men he wanted to go with him ready.

"I'm taking Smitty and Brett with me, Joe, while you, Sam, Louie, and Pete stay with the ship."

"I see you're taking shovels too, Jack. Any particular reason?" Joe asked suspiciously.

"I'll let you in on this when I'm ready, Joe, now follow my orders. You understand that, Joe?"

Not wanting to make trouble, Joe would later follow Jack and see what he was up to.

Travis's ship sailed to the other side of the island and let down anchor. Travis briefed his men. "I'm taking six men with me. After Jack and his men have dug up the gold, we'll take it from him."

"You're sure seven of us will be enough, Captain?"

"It shouldn't be any trouble, Ned. We'll wait behind rocks and trees, watching them, and when we're sure about the gold, we'll have a surprise for them."

After briefing his men, Travis and his men rowed a boat to shore. "This way men, over a few hills, and we shall meet up with Jack and our gold."

Joe, after giving Jack and the men time to be gone for a while, told Pete and Sam, "Stay with the ship. I'm following after Jack."

"Why, Joe?" Pete asked.

"Something is wrong, Pete, and I think Jack is headed for trouble."

"We better go too, Joe."

"Somebody has got to stay with the *Rose*, Pete."

"Aye, Joe, but if neither you nor Jack return by sundown, we're coming after you."

Two hours into the island, Jack found the correct spot where some of the gold was buried. Jack ordered Brett and Smitty, "Dig here where my boot prints sink into the soil."

"What are you doing, Jack?" they both asked with a surprised look on their faces.

Jack pulled his pistol and said, "I told you two to start digging."

75
Out for Good Behavior
1673

"You don't have to hold that pistol on us, Jack," Smitty told him. "We'll obey your orders."

While the shovels struck the dirt, Travis and his men were getting closer. Twenty minutes later, Smitty and Brett's shovels struck something hard. Jack yelled out, "That's it! Dig the rest of the dirt out from around the chest, Smitty."

After the dirt was cleared from around the chest, Jack helped Smitty and Brett to bring it up and set it on the ground. Jack took a steel bar and broke the lock and then, opening the lid, showed Courtney the gold inside.

Courtney let out a sigh. "Oh, Jack, I never knew there was that much gold in the whole world."

Joe, arriving there minutes earlier, was hiding behind some trees, watching all that was going on. Travis and his men were just arriving and, from a distance, saw Jack and Courtney leaning over the chest looking at the gold.

Travis and his men slowly sneaked up on Jack, Courtney, Smitty, and Brett.

Jack heard footsteps, looked up, saw Travis, and started to pull his pistol when Travis told him, "I don't think so, Jack, not with seven pistols pointing at you and your men."

Travis took Jack's pistol and said, "I told you, Jack, we'd meet again!"

"You should be in prison, Travis. They gave you ten years."

"They let me out for good behavior, Jack." Travis smirked.

"What's this all about, Travis?" Jack asked.

"This was part of my plan, Jack—you meeting Courtney and falling in love with her, but I didn't count on her falling in love with you, which almost spoiled everything."

Courtney put her hands over her face and started crying.

"Now, now, Courtney, you've done your part and did a good job. You should've been an actress."

Jack turned his attention to Courtney. "What's he talking about, Courtney?"

"I betrayed you, Jack. Don't you understand?" Courtney cried that much more.

Thinking all this being humorous, Travis said, "Don't you get it, Jack? Or do I have to explain further?"

Putting two and two together, Jack now knew why Courtney wanted him to find this gold.

With his insides twisted in knots, Jack asked, "Why, Courtney?"

"I'm sorry, Jack. I didn't want to go through with this after I fell in love with you, but Travis threatened to kill you if I didn't continue to go along."

"Question, Travis?"

"Make it fast, Jack, I want to get off this island with my gold."

"How did you know about my brother, Chad, and where to find me?"

"Jack, that took some time a year, in fact, to get all of the information on your brother. The part about you and the princess was easy. I learned about you turning pirate and serving on the princess's ship while in prison. The pirates there talked about the princess with the flaming sword. The more questions I asked, the more information I learned about you and where to send the letter. I did pretty good, don't you think, Jack?" Travis said, grinning from ear to ear.

"What about, Courtney? Where did you find her?"

"I was real lucky about her, Jack. I stole Angela's picture from her parents' home back in Regend and used it to find a girl that had a resemblance to Angela. I didn't have any idea I would find a girl that would pass for her twin. Now if you would excuse me, Jack, I must take my gold and leave."

Joe stepped out from behind the tree, holding his pistol on Travis, telling his men, "Stop where you are if you don't want to stop a lead pellet."

Travis's men fired their pistols at Joe but missed as he jumped toward the ground. With the pistols all fired except for Travis's, the fighting continued with swords. Jack and his men pulled their swords, and so did Travis and his men.

76
RETURNING NIGHTMARE
1673

It was Jack, Smitty, Joe, and Brett taking on Travis and his six men. Travis's men were no match for Smitty, Joe, and Brett. Smitty run one man through, and as soon as he removed his sword from the body, he ran another man through his chest. Joe hacked two men down, one getting his throat slit and the other one getting it through his gut. Brett, with his sword clanging, was taking the other two men while Jack and Travis were having their own private war. Cutting one of Travis's men down, Brett received a severe cut across his left arm while the other man ran away.

Travis, standing there all alone, pulled his pistol on Jack. "If you remember, Jack, I never fired my pistol and still have a shot left."

"You'll never make it, Travis. My men will cut you down before you step five feet."

"Maybe so, Jack, but I'm going to see you dead first." Travis started to pull the trigger when Courtney yelled out, "Jack!" Distracted for a second, Travis looked over at Courtney. Joe threw his knife at Travis, sticking him in his chest. Travis jerked backward, firing the pistol, and as the pistol was being swung upward, the lead pellet struck Courtney, and she fell to the ground.

Jack ran to Courtney's side. Jack picked her up into his arms and cried out, "Don't die on me, Courtney. I can't go through this again."

Courtney stared up at Jack and said with a soft voice, "You must have loved Angela very much, Jack." Courtney's eyes closed while dying in Jack's arms.

Jack sat on the ground next to Courtney's body, saying, "Oh no!" Not wanting to believe he was reliving a nightmare he suffered several years earlier. The scene grew distant with Jack's head lowered and him weeping bitter tears of sorrow.

Before Jack and his men left the island, they buried the dead pirates' bodies. Alone, Jack buried Courtney's body by a beautiful waterfall. Before Jack left, he said to Courtney, looking down at her grave, "Courtney, my love, I buried you where you can always be by a waterfall that flows bright shining water day and night."

Good-bye Courtney was in Jack's thoughts as he walked away not looking back. The gold was buried back to where it belonged while the *Black Rose* sailed back home.

GOOD-BYE, ANGELA
1673

JACK REGRETTING WHAT had happened knew Rebekah would find out sooner or later. He was willing to face the consequences and would honor any request or punishment Rebekah dished out to him. If Rebekah banned him from her ship, he'd leave without an argument. He would ask for forgiveness before leaving but would understand if she'd throw him off the ship.

Jack was walking toward the rear of the ship when Joe stopped him.

"Yes, Joe, what is it?"

"I was talking with the rest of the men, and we all agreed to stay silent about what happened at the island."

"No, Joe, that's not the way. There's going to be trust between the princess and I if I am to remain on the ship."

"You're going to tell the princess everything, Jack?"

"Yes, Joe, everything and something else too."

"What's that, Jack?"

"I'm telling her about Angela who she never knew about."

Joe was thinking they better start getting used to another first mate especially when this fat hits the fire. Jack left Joe as he proceeded to the rear of the ship. Jack stood there pulling Angela's picture from his shirt pocket.

Jack gazed upon her picture one last time and threw it into the wind, saying, "Good-bye, Angela, I can't love a dead girl!"

Angela's picture floated in the air and then downward toward the water and landed on the surface. While the *Black Rose* continued on, the picture of Angela continued floating in the opposite direction. Jack turned and walked away.

PART VII

78
THE PATRIOT
1673

BACK IN OLD England, Morgan was meeting with a man who prided himself on his bounty-hunting skills and was trying to sell himself to Morgan.

"So you're the best bounty hunter on this side of the high seas, you claim."

"Sir Morgan, there's probably only one man that equals my skills as a bounty hunter, and you don't have enough English gold to hire him."

"But I do have enough English gold for you. Is that right?"

"You can mock and criticize all you want, Sir Morgan, but if there isn't something done about this Princess Pirate of yours, you may be searching for another job."

"How dare you insult my authority with such criticism?" Morgan slammed his hands down on his desk as papers flew everywhere.

"Stop your raving, Sir Morgan, and stop denying it. You know I'm right, so why do you keep on believing you're going to catch the princess?"

"You inconsiderate bounty hunter, I ought to have you thrown in jail for your disrespectfulness to me and this office I hold with that barbaric attitude of yours."

"That's not true, Sir Morgan. I'm a patriot and love this great country of England. That's why I'm here."

Morgan settled down and poured himself some wine. Morgan took a big swallow and asked, "Why are you so interested in the princess? And what will it cost parliament if you succeed in your mission?"

"That's simple, Sir Morgan. I want her stopped for the good of my country that I love."

"All right, Mr. Patriot, what do you call *simple* in money terms?"

"I'll settle for five hundred English pounds, Sir Morgan, and that's a deal."

"All right," Morgan said. "I'll agree, but remember there are no almost, understand?"

"As an added bonus, Sir Morgan, I'll find her maps on all of the wealth she has taken and buried and bring them back to prove my patriotism. I have to go now, Sir Morgan. My ship is waiting."

"What about a contract?"

"I trust you, Sir Morgan. After all, you love this country too, correct?"

Morgan had to have another drink after that little conversation. The best thing about all this was until this bounty hunter brought in the princess, it wasn't costing parliament one red shilling.

Looking out his window toward the harbor and the sea, Morgan said to himself, "I don't believe Mr. Big Talk can bring in the princess alive, but I'll accept a death document on her." Morgan grinned and took another drink of his wine.

A Day of Reckoning for Jack
1673

TODAY, THE *BLACK Rose* sailed back into the cove and was at home once again. Of course, Jack would rather face a firing squad than confront Rebekah with his confession and his actions back at Key West Port. While the men rowed over to the post for their firewater, Joe gave Jack some advice: "You ought to reconsider telling the princess what happened, Jack."

"I have to be honest with her, Joe. It's the only way. I might not be in second command at this time tomorrow, so I'll tell you now. Thanks for being a support to me, and may I call you *friend*?"

Joe nodded his head, confirming their friendship. "When are you confronting the princess?"

"Later in the evening, Joe, when we're standing by the railing after dinner. Rebekah is more willing to listen and is more reasonable when she's comfortable." Jack was hoping.

Entering the post that afternoon, Jack was greeted by Rebekah with a hug and a kiss. "I've missed you, Jack. It seemed like you've been gone for an eternity."

Jack's guilt hit an all-time high after hearing Rebekah's words. Jack and Rebekah sat at their table while Rebekah wanted to know everything about Chad's wedding. "Well, Jack, how did Chad's wedding go? Did you give the bride away?"

"There wasn't any wedding, Princess."

"There wasn't?" Rebekah was disappointed.

Jack quickly changed the subject. "How were things here at the cove, Princess, while we were gone?"

"Everything has been fine and quiet here, Jack, but why was the wedding called off?"

"Chad didn't show, Princess. The wedding will be held at another time."

Rebekah knew down deep when Jack was avoiding the truth. "There's something you aren't telling me, Jack."

"Princess, I'll explain everything that happened at Key West Port after dinner."

Not being his usual self, Jack said, "Princess, I've had a long trip, and I'm going to my cabin for a rest. And please excuse me."

Rebekah gathered her things from Jake's room and had Troy row her back to the ship. "It'll be nice, Troy, to sleep in my big comfortable bed when I return to my cabin."

"Yes, Princess, I know how you feel. I've missed my old bunk and will be glad to see it again."

Returning to her cabin, Rebekah was glad to see it once again. While putting her stuff away, Rebekah noticed things have been moved around inside her cabin. *Maybe the ship run into some bad weather and things got knocked over and the men tried to put them back in their place*, she thought.

Rebekah stared at her bed and said to herself, "My bed looks so inviting. I'm taking a nap before dinner." Rebekah removed her boots and laid her head back on her nice, soft pillow.

Laying there, Rebekah got a whiff of perfume that wasn't hers. Rebekah sniffed the air again and then put her nose to her pillow. Smelling her pillow, Rebekah said, "That's not my perfume."

Suspicious about Jack's activities, Rebekah went to have a talk with Micky in the galley. Rebekah entered the galley and sat, staring at Micky.

Micky said, "Hi, Miss Rebekah, how have you been?"

Rebekah was sitting at the table with her arms folded. She kept staring at Micky.

Micky set a pan down and asked, "You upset about something, Miss Rebekah?"

"Micky."

"Yes, Miss Rebekah," Micky answered nervously.

"Who was in my cabin and sleeping in my bed when Jack was at Key West Port?"

THE TRUTH, JACK!
1673

"Miss Rebekah, I really have to get the men's meal fixed before they come back from the post, and you know how Sam gets when he's hungry."

"Answer the question, Micky, and tell me the truth."

Micky, showing yellow, told Rebekah about the young girl Courtney Grey.

"Micky, was there?"

"Oh no, Miss Rebekah. She stayed in your cabin alone, and I assure you of that."

"I believe you, Micky, but Jack is still in big trouble." Rebekah stormed out the door and back to her cabin to cool off.

Jack wanted some coffee, so he went to the galley. "Hi, Micky, I'd like some coffee, and what's for dinner this evening?"

"Trouble, Jack, that's what's on the dinner plate tonight."

Jack knew right then Micky told Rebekah about Courtney. "Is she in her cabin, Micky?" "Yes, Jack, I think that's where she went when she stormed out of the galley."

Jack, now standing in front of Rebekah's cabin door, tapped lightly.

"Come in," she said.

Jack took a deep breath, opened the cabin door, and entered with a smile. "Hello, Princess, I think it's time we talked."

Rebekah sat at her desk staring at Jack, saying nothing. Jack looked over at Rebekah's bed and said, "Your pillows are missing, Princess."

Rebekah, still staring at Jack with a blank look on her face, said, "I threw them into the cove."

"Why did you do that, Princess?"

"They smelled of perfume, Jack. That's why."

"Your perfume, Princess?"

"No, not my perfume, Jack. I think it was Courtney's. You know Courtney Grey, the girl that slept in my bed!"

"I was going to tell you everything about her princess but wanted to wait until we were standing by the railing."

Rebekah, now folding her arms, replied, "Tell me now, Jack. I want to know, now!"

Jack stumbled a little and hesitated. Rebekah, steamed and ready to boil over, said, "The truth, Jack, and I mean all of the truth."

Jack sat and told Rebekah everything from the beginning. Rebekah was not only shocked by what she heard but also stunned as well. Rebekah got up from her desk and went toward the back of her cabin and just stared out the ship windows.

Rebekah then turned to face Jack. "That gold wasn't only mine, Jack, but the men as well, and you were going to take it?"

"Rebekah," Jack said, trying to intervene.

"I'm not finished yet, Jack. I trusted you as my own father, and you betrayed that trust."

Jack was already feeling lower than a snake, but Rebekah's words were cutting him through like a sharp knife.

"I'm sorry, Rebekah, truly I am, but you weren't there. This girl looked like Angela's twin, and I lost myself."

Rebekah ignored the pleading for forgiveness. "I haven't any pity for you, Jack. You not only kept this secret about Angela from me but you would've left me for a total stranger who you knew nothing about."

81
NOT GETTING OFF THAT EASY
1673

"I'll no longer spoil your presence by me being here, Rebekah. I'll gather my things from my cabin and will be on my way out on the next pirate ship." Jack turned with grief showing in his face when Rebekah told him, "You're not getting off that easy, Jack!" Jack stood there like a whipped puppy and listened to what Rebekah had to say.

"You'll remain as my first mate and do your job, understand?" Rebekah wasn't asking; she was commanding.

"I don't see why I should stay, Rebekah. Is it so you can punish me every day and remind me of my mistake?"

Rebekah stood in front of Jack and asked, "You a man Jack or a coward?"

"Why would you ask such a question, Rebekah? I'd die for you."

"You'd die for me, Jack, but you wouldn't think twice about stealing my gold and run off with a girl you only knew for a few days? Answer my question, Jack." Rebekah shouted out again, "Are you a coward or not? Are you staying or running away?"

"All right, Rebekah, I'll play your game and stay on as your first mate, but don't expect me to come crawling like a dog for his bone. Let's make that perfectly clear."

"That's clear, Jack, but remember from now on, you're treated no different than the rest of my men. Do I make myself clear?"

"Yes, Captain, you do." Jack stormed out and slammed Rebekah's cabin door behind him. Then there was another knock on her cabin door.

"Yes, what is it?" Rebekah yelled.

Pete opened the door and walked in with her new pillows.

82
ROUGH DAYS AHEAD ON THE *BLACK ROSE* 1673

"I just brought you your new pillows, Princess."

"I'm sorry for acting hateful towards you. Pete, just lay them on my bed."

On deck, Jack was looking out toward the cove when Joe came walking up. "Are you leaving us, Jack? I heard from Micky what happened."

"No, Joe, I'm not. She wants me to stay on as first mate so she can rub salt into my wound."

"The men will still obey your orders, Jack. I told them some of what happened, but you'll have to explain the rest in your time."

"I'm explaining nothing, Joe. The men will obey my orders, or they'll be kicked off this ship. You make that perfectly clear to them."

"I understand, Jack, and the men will too."

In her cabin, Rebekah did a lot of thinking about Jack. She didn't like the way she treated Jack, but what he had done to her was inexcusable, and Jack had to be held accountable for his actions. Down, down deep in Rebekah's heart, she'd be totally lost without Jack, but the hurt she felt now overrode her love for him and her trust.

Even Rebekah doesn't know if this hurt is repairable. It was a wait-and-see thing. Rebekah pulled out her father's picture that was now in a beautiful gold frame that Jack gave her for her birthday, which made it that much harder for her. Rebekah looked at her father's picture and then asked, "What do I do now, Father?" Then she put the picture back under the pillow and went to bed. Feeling so hurt and abandoned by Jack, Rebekah never went to the galley for dinner. This night was going to be a rough one for Jack and Rebekah.

The next day, Jack was over at the post talking to Randy. "Are you ready for some hard work, Randy?"

"I'm fine, Jack. The princess took great care of me."

"That's good to hear, Randy. Joe will give you your orders when you return to the ship."

The following day, Jake sold Rebekah a chart on a ship that was just out of England and was carrying gold just for the taking. Jake was puzzled though. This was the only ship sailing out to sea over the next month, but sometimes that's the way it is—you take what you can get.

Rebekah ordered Jack, "Meet me in my cabin later, Jack, so we can we talk over the plans on raiding this ship."

A while later, Jack knocked on her cabin door. She said, "Come in."

"You want to talk to me about the next ship we're raiding, Captain?"

Jack was now addressing her as captain instead of princess.

"What happened to you calling me princess, Jack?"

"We're on a formal relationship remember, Captain? Your words."

"Fine, Jack, then that's the way things will be." Rebekah rolled out the chart, showing it to Jack. "Here's the English ship, the *McConner*. It's delivering gold and jewels to a port called Port Central. We, of course, will intercept the ship in the east part of the seas before she makes her delivery."

"I'll set the *Black Rose* on course after I leave your cabin, Captain," Jack said, showing no emotion toward Rebekah. "Is there anything else before I leave, Captain?"

"That'll be all for now, Jack."

After Jack left her cabin, Rebekah said to herself, "I must be dreaming, and this is a nightmare."

83
DREW WILSON IS THE NAME
1673

THE DAYS PASSED on the *Rose*, and the men could feel the tension between Jack and Rebekah. It was so strong you could cut it with knife. After dinner each night, Rebekah would be waiting at the railing of the ship, but there would be no Jack standing there waiting for her. Rebekah was hurt and upset with Jack at the same time, but what could she do in this type of situation? Rebekah couldn't sweep what Jack did under the rug; that would show weakness in front of her men, and Jack would lose his respect for her.

At night before bed, Rebekah always looked to her father's picture for answers. When she put her father's picture under her pillow this time, she made a captain's decision—after this next raid, she was letting Jack go. With them both being together on the same ship, the tension would continue to build between them. To keep the morale of the men up, Rebekah was going to tell Jack to leave the ship. Rebekah had no other choice.

The next day, Sam was talking to Louie and Randy about the fight between Jack and Rebekah. "Well, which one of us is taking Jack's place as first mate when he leaves?" Sam asked.

"It surely won't be you, Sam." Randy laughed.

"I guess you're thinking you'll get the first mate's job, huh, Randy?"

"Maybe, Sam, just maybe!"

"The princess must've taken real good care of you, Randy, while we were gone. Let me guess, she must have tucked you in your bunk at night and gave you some warm milk to help you sleep." Sam stood there laughing.

Randy hauled off and hit Sam, and then Sam came back with his fist and hit Randy. Both men were trading blows when Jack ran over and broke up the fight.

Jack pulled them apart and said, "I ought to throw you both over the railing for fighting. And you, Randy, shouldn't be fighting unless you what to break your shoulder wound open and start bleeding."

Randy wiped the blood from his lip and said, "I started the fight, Jack."

"I don't care who started the fight, Randy. Just keep your problems to yourself until we get back to the cove. Do you understand?"

Sam said to Jack, "Just like the problems you and the princess are having, huh, Jack?"

Jack would normally have punched Sam out for that but just walked away. Jack knew this wasn't going to work between him and Rebekah, so he made a decision: after this raid, he was packing his things and moving on.

The next day, Rebekah and her men were raiding the cargo ship *McConner*. When Rebekah and her men jumped over and boarded the ship, the sword fighting was in action and pistols were being fired. Rebekah, after cutting down a sailor, noticed the captain was at the back of the ship with several sailors. They were about to hang a man. Rebekah yelled to Marty and Rex, "Follow me to the back of the ship."

When Rebekah and her men arrived, the captain was telling the man he was hanging, "Nobody can help you now, Wilson."

The captain kicked the barrel the man was standing on out from under him. Rebekah, with her sword in hand, made a leap toward the rope that hung from the pole and cut it with her sword just as the man was falling to the deck of the ship. All the fighting on the ship was over, and Rebekah's men had things under control as usual.

The captain yelled out at Rebekah and said, "How dare you stop the hanging of this thieving pirate."

"I don't think hanging a man for stealing is a fair punishment, Captain," Rebekah conjectured.

"This is my justice. And who are you that came aboard my ship and attacked my men?"

"I'm here to take your gold and jewels, Captain. That's who I am."

The man that was to be hung gave Rebekah his thanks. "I don't know who you are, miss, but thank you for stopping them from hanging me."

Rex untied the ropes from his hands. "Do you want to come with us, mister?" Rebekah asked.

"What do you think?" The man then pulled his knife from his boot and faced the captain.

"What are you going to do with that knife?" Rebekah asked.

"I'm cutting the captain's throat to show him how death feels."

"I don't think so, mister," Rebekah said, pointing her pistol at his chest. "You hurt the captain, I'll shoot you with this pistol." The pistol went click as Rebekah cocked the hammer back.

"All right," he said. "You're holding all of the aces."

Jack reported to Rebekah, "The gold and jewels are on the *Rose*, Captain."

Rebekah and her men plus the new passenger were on the *Rose* and sailed away. The *Black Rose* was moving away fast. The first officer asked, "We just going to let her get away, sir?"

"Listen, Mathews, my instructions were if the princess raids this ship and takes the gold and jewels, do nothing and let her get away."

The first officer stood there, puzzled, and asked, "But why, Captain? That makes no sense, sir."

"That's what I was told, Mr. Mathews. Now get back to work so we can report this back to England."

Unknown to Rebekah or her crew at this time, an unknown ship was trailing the *Black Rose*.

On board the *Rose*, Rebekah was asking the new man his name, "Drew Wilson is the name, miss, and may I ask your name?"

"It's Rebekah Martin, and my men call me the princess."

"You the Princess Pirate I've heard so much about?"

"Yes and please don't believe the bad things you've heard about me. I'm sure they've been exaggerated."

"What are you going to do with me, princess?"

"Can you use a sword, Drew?"

"I was a fencing instructor in the navy."

"Would you like to join my crew, Drew?"

"You mean as in raiding ships and stealing gold, Princess?"

"I think you have the wrong picture, Drew. I'll explain things in more detail later, but do you want to join us for now?"

"Yes, Princess, it sounds exciting."

Rebekah announced to the crew Drew Wilson was joining the ship. Jack changed his mind and decided to delay his departure from the ship until he was sure about Drew. After the gold and jewels were buried and the *Black Rose* was on her way back to the cove, Rebekah was standing by the railing that evening.

Drew walked up behind Rebekah. Thinking it was Jack, Rebekah turned with a smile, but seeing Drew, her smile faded.

84
YOU'RE NOT HIM
1673

Drew asked Rebekah, "Did I startle you? And if I did, I apologize."

"No, you didn't startle me, Drew."

Drew leaned over and kissed Rebekah on the lips. Rebekah backed away, telling Drew, "There's only one man on this ship that has my permission to kiss me, and you're not him, Drew. You touch me again in that manner, and I'll take you down with a swing of my sword, or I'll shoot you with my pistol. Is that clear?"

Drew cleared his throat and said, "Very clear, Princess."

"Now why were they going to hang you, Drew?"

"Something about me being a pirate is what they told me." Drew grinned seductively but not a grin that would cause Rebekah to be suspicious of him.

"You're among pirates here, Drew, so feel at home but obey my rules."

Rebekah was going back to her cabin when she met Jack on the way. "Just the person I wanted to see, Jack. Come into my cabin. I want to talk to you."

Jack entered in through the cabin door behind Rebekah. Rebekah turned and said, "I was going to tell you to leave the ship Jack because of the tension that's between us, but I changed my mind."

This was a shock to Jack because he wasn't leaving until he was sure about Drew Wilson.

Jack, with his cool way of doing things, said to Rebekah, "Thank you, Princess. I want to stay and continue being your first mate."

Rebekah was so glad to hear him call her princess once again. "Jack, I'd like that also."

The sad part about this was Jack was only staying until he knew more about Drew Wilson, making sure he wasn't a danger to Rebekah. Then he would pack his things and leave. "I'll be available anytime you need me, Princess."

The men on the *Black Rose* were definitely discussing the new man, Drew Wilson. Sam, of course, was going to test the new man out and see how much pirate he really was by starting a fight with him.

Troy said to Sam, "Sam, you're going to get yourself killed one of these days starting fights with men you know nothing about."

"Listen, Troy, you may be tied to the princess's blouse strings, but I'm a pirate, and I'm going to find out if this Drew Wilson is pirate enough to serve on this ship."

Drew was mending a sail while all the men watched. Sam walked toward Drew, and as he went by, he tripped himself on Drew's boot.

"Hey, Wilson, what's the idea of you sticking your boot out and tripping me?"

"I didn't trip you, Sam. You tripped on your own stupid feet."

"You tripped me, Wilson, and if you call me a liar one more time, I'll cut your heart out with this knife."

Drew knew only one way to put a stop to this and the others from giving him trouble: to take Sam down hard and fast. Drew grabbed Sam's knife, and as they struggled, Drew turned the knife inward toward Sam, stabbing him in his own gut, and then threw Sam to the floor.

The men come running over as Sam lay there bleeding with his own knife sticking in him. Marty was outraged and hit Drew and knocked him to the ship's floor and was about to pick him up and do it again when Jack ordered him to stop.

Jack saw Sam and said, "Some of you men take Sam to the rear cabin of the ship and then go and get Micky." Jack turned his attention to Drew. "Why, Drew?"

"That's simple, Jack. It was either him or me. What would you do in a similar situation if a knife was pulled on you?"

Jack knew how Sam was, and he always started trouble first. Jack couldn't find fault concerning Drew's actions. "Very well, Drew, but for your sake, you better hope Sam lives."

After stitching Sam up a bit, Micky went to Rebekah's cabin to tell her about Sam. "Miss Rebekah, it was Sam who started the fight with Drew. Unfortunately for Sam, he was stabbed with his own knife."

"How bad is he, Micky?"

"The cut is deep, Miss Rebekah. I put in a several stitches."

"Will Sam live, Micky?"

"These old pirates, Miss Rebekah, you can't kill them with a little knife blade. It'd take a sword to do that. Excuse me, Miss Rebekah, I've to go and fix dinner for all your men."

Rebekah was glad of Sam living but was going to have a strong talk with him tomorrow, a real strong talk.

The next day, the *Black Rose* was back home at Pirates Cove. Rebekah's men except Sam were having their relaxation time as usual, playing poker and downing their firewater. Rebekah introduced Drew to Jake at the post.

Being Shadowed at Sea
1673

While Rebekah and Drew were talking at the table, Joe was talking to Jack, "Are you sure about what you've seen, Joe?"

"I'm very sure, Jack. We were being shadowed at sea by another ship. I've been a pirate for over twenty years, Jack, and I know how this is done. The pirate ships I've served under always used the same tricks to take the unsuspecting ships and raid them."

"If it was another pirate ship, Joe, why didn't they attack us? And try and take the gold we had just taken."

"That's a good question, Jack, and I don't have the answer to that question myself."

"Joe, let's keep this to ourselves at the moment. Don't tell the princess either, all right?"

"I'll play it your way, Jack, because I trust your judgment, but sooner or later, I'll have to tell the princess."

"I understand, Joe, and I know if anything ever happened to me, she'd be in good hands with you and the men protecting her."

Joe cracked a seldom grin and said, "I think the princess has been taking care of us, Jack."

Jack patted Joe on the shoulder, telling him, "Remember our secret for now, Joe."

Jack went back over to the ship to do some more thinking about Drew. Drew was good at taking care of himself and was a man of high intelligence, which Rebekah needed for her guidance in her youth. If Drew turned out to be what he said, he'd be a good replacement for Jack when he left the ship. Jack would make that suggestion to Rebekah before he left. Jack's other concern was that ship that was following them. Jack had Pete and Curt go with him as they rowed a small boat out toward the cove's entrance.

When the small boat they were in was about three miles out, Jack looked through his spyglass to see what he could see. Curt asked, "What are we searching for, Jack?"

"You two look through your glass and see if you spot a ship or something like a ship out at sea."

It was evening, but there was plenty of light left when Jack spotted a small object out at sea, and it was a ship. The ship started to move away as Jack was watching it until it was out of sight. "Did you see something out there, Jack?" Pete was asking.

Jack confided to Pete and Curt about the ship that had followed them back to the cove. Then he said, "Don't say anything to the princess or the other men."

"But why, Jack?"

"I don't what to alarm the princess unnecessarily, understand?"

Jack went back to the post but ordered Pete and Curt to go back outside the cove with their spyglasses in hopes of getting a better look at this ship if it returns. Jack wanted to know if it was a pirate ship or a naval ship before the *Black Rose* sets sail again. Jack was now sitting with Rebekah and Drew.

Being curious about Drew, Rebekah asked, "Where are you from, Drew? And why were you being hung on the ship we raided?"

"I told you, Princess, they accused me of pirating."

Jack intervened, "So you're innocent, Mr. Wilson?"

"I'm not a pirate, Mr. Reese, and have no plans of being one."

HAS TO BE A REASON
86
1673

"Pardon my suspicion, Mr. Wilson," Jack responded, "but ship captains don't hang men on their ships without a reason. There has to be a reason there was a rope around your neck when we came aboard."

Drew relented by saying, "I ran off with the captain's daughter and wanted to marry her, and she wanted to marry me, but the captain wouldn't give her permission to marry me. So we ran away together, but her father caught up with us, and he, being judge and jury, decided to hang me."

Rebekah asked, "What about the girl?"

"Her father took her back to England and brought me back out to sea for my execution. His charge against me was stealing his daughter."

Rebekah said, "I'm sorry for your troubles, Drew."

"By the way, Princess, I never thanked you properly for saving my life."

"You're welcome, Drew. What are your plans now?" Rebekah asked.

"I plan on going back for Kristen, and I'm still going to marry her when I find a way of sailing back to England."

"I can't help you there, Drew, but I wish you and Kristen luck." Rebekah finished drinking down her hot chocolate.

It was still early as Drew asked Rebekah's permission to go back to the *Black Rose* for some rest. Rebekah nodded. After Drew left, Rebekah saw that look on Jack's face and asked, "All right, Jack, out with it. What's on your mind? It's written all over your face."

"His story sounds a little fishy, Princess. Why would a respected captain just hang a man for wanting to marry his daughter? And then accuse him of being a pirate?"

"Look at it this way, Jack," Rebekah said, explaining a woman's view. "Drew stole his daughter away, and to him, that was an act of a pirate, and by hanging him, the captain wouldn't have to worry about Drew returning for his daughter."

Jack thought he would chew on that thought for a while before returning an answer. He got up, said nothing, and went back to the *Black Rose*. Rebekah was still hurting inside by Jack's actions, but she loved him so much she'd give time a chance for all this to heal and someday hoped it would be just a bad memory.

Jack was back on board the *Rose*, going to his cabin. Jack was about to open his cabin door when he heard a noise coming from Rebekah's cabin. Jack got his pistol from his cabin and then proceeded to Rebekah's cabin. Jack stood outside the door with his ear up against it and listened.

Jack heard things were being moved around and knew someone was in her cabin as he slowly opened the cabin door. Jack saw Drew rummaging through Rebekah's things. With his pistol in hand, he pointed it at Drew. He asked, "Searching for something, Drew?"

Being startled, Drew turned with a surprised look on his face and just stood there facing Jack.

"I'll ask you one more time, Drew. What are you looking for?"

"I'm a bounty hunter, Mr. Reese, and I'm here to put a stop to the princess and her pirating." Drew grinned.

"Why are you grinning, Drew? You may not leave this ship alive after what you've told me."

"I think I will, Mr. Reese," Drew spoke confidently.

"I'm taking you to the princess, Drew. Let's go!" Jack motioned with his pistol.

Drew and Jack were now on deck. Drew turned to face Jack. "You're a coward hiding behind the princess's sword, aren't you, Mr. Reese?" Drew was hoping to trick Jack into a sword fight.

Joe and Marty returned on board the ship and asked Jack why he was holding a pistol on Drew Wilson.

Jack said, "Marty, go and get my sword and bring one for Drew also."

"Why, Jack?" Marty asked.

"Just do it, Marty, and be quick about it," Jack demanded.

"I see you're no coward, Mr. Reese. That's good," Drew exclaimed.

"Your chances would be better with the princess, Drew. She likes you, where I don't."

"That's because women are more easer to fool, Mr. Reese."

"Maybe so, Drew, but before you die, two questions."

"Let me answer them both for you, Mr. Reese. May I?"

"Yes, Drew, you may."

"I was searching for the maps the princess has hidden. And after I made sure she was no longer a threat to England, I was planning on sailing out of the cove in a longboat!"

"Don't tell me, Drew. Let me guess, the ship that we've been keeping an eye on sitting miles out from the cove is your rescue ship?"

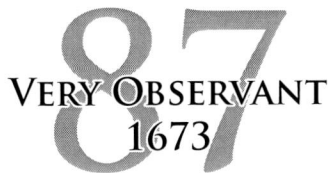 Very Observant
1673

"Very observant, Mr. Reese, how did you know?"

"Joe here, who's an expert sailing pirate ships, noticed on the way back from the last ship we raided that we were being shadowed all the way back."

"I take my hat off to you, Joe. You have great pirating skills, and you're very observant."

Marty was back with two swords. Jack handed Drew one of the swords Marty gave him.

"Another question, Drew?"

"Yes, Mr. Reese, what may that be?"

"Not that you're going too, but if you get lucky and win this sword fight, how are you planning your escape with Marty and Joe here?"

"Just like I got out of being hung, I do have a plan. But on guard, Mr. Reese." Drew thrust his sword toward Jack.

Jack, of course, was doing a great job of defending himself and striking back with forceful swings. The swords struck one another time after time while the fighting was getting intense.

"Not bad, Mr. Reese." Drew took more death swings at Jack.

"I see you've had some training yourself, Drew," Jack replied back as he cut Drew across his left shoulder, and it started to bleed. Drew looked at his shoulder but wasn't down as he started swinging at Jack once again.

At this time, Rebekah and her men climbed on board the *Rose* and watched what was happening. Jack took his best swing across Drew's middle in hopes of taking him down, but when his sword missed the target, Drew ran his sword toward Jack's ribs and struck him deep. Even Jack heard some of his ribs crack when the sword blade went through. Drew removed his sword, and Jack fell to the deck of the ship.

Rebekah yelled out, "Jack!" She ran over to his side. Joe pulled his pistol on Drew to make sure he wasn't going anywhere. Jack looked up at Rebekah, telling her with a weak voice, "I do love you, Princess." Then his eyes closed.

"No! No!" Rebekah cried.

Pete put his ear to Jack's chest. "He's still alive, Princess, but barely."

Gathering herself, Rebekah said, "Get Jake over here and take Jack to his cabin and hurry!" Rebekah said to Drew, "I want the truth. Why were you two sword fighting?"

Drew had nothing to hide now as he explained. "I'm a bounty hunter, Princess, and I'm here to put a stop to you and the raiding of England ships."

"That was a real convincing show you put on, Drew, back at the ship we raided," Rebekah said, raising her right eyebrow.

"Yes, I have to admit it, Princess. I was convincing, wasn't I?" Drew was standing there with a smile on his face.

"You should've been an actor, Drew. You might have lived longer."

"I might look into being an actor, Princess, after I leave this ship."

"You think so, Drew?"

"Yes, Princess, I do."

"Marty."

"Yes, Princess."

"Go and get my sword that's hanging in my cabin."

"Aye, Princess."

"If Jack dies, Drew, you'll never leave this ship alive. I'll run my sword straight through your heart. That, you can be assured."

Marty returned and handed Rebekah her sword. Rebekah told Joe, "Give Drew back the sword he used to fight Jack with."

Looking at Jack's blood staining the shiny sword blade, Drew said to Rebekah, "I'll mix your blood, Princess, with Mr. Reese's when I run you through."

I'm a Patriot
1673

"I don't think so, Drew." Rebekah whipped her sword around into the air. She said to Drew, "You're the one going to die."

"Maybe, Princess, just maybe, but I'm a patriot to my country. I knew the risks of not returning home when I took on this job."

Jake was already on board, and he and Micky were mending Jack as the sword play between Rebekah and Drew were in action. Drew tried this move and that move, but Rebekah was just toying with Drew for a few moments deciding to kill him or not. And if Jack did die, killing Drew wouldn't bring him back. Drew wasn't having any second thoughts about killing Rebekah as he was doing his best to run her through.

"Why are you so against me, Drew?" Rebekah said, defending herself with each clang of the swords.

"You're a murdering thief and a danger to my country. That's why I'm going to kill you, Princess." Drew thrust his sword toward Rebekah's left side.

Unfortunate for Drew, it didn't work against Rebekah as it did against Jack. Rebekah blocked his move and came back with a slice of her blade that cut Drew straight across the middle part of his body. Rebekah's sharp blade cut Drew deep. Drew, with a surprised look on his face, dropped his sword. Then he grabbed the middle part of his body with both hands as the blood was bleeding through his fingers. Looking down, Drew fell to the floor face first. Rebekah stood over Drew's body and said, "I hope what parliament offered you for you patriotism was worth it, Drew." Rebekah handed Marty her sword and went to see about Jack.

Joe had Marty take Drew's body to the small boat below. They were going to take Drew's body and bury it out at sea several miles from the cove entrance. Rebekah stood in Jack's cabin and watched while Jake finished bandaging Jack's ribs.

"Will he live, Jake?"

"The cut was deep, Princess, and cracked a few ribs, but Jack is strong and is in great health. I believe he'll live."

Rebekah sat in a chair next to Jack's bed and said, "I'm staying with Jack until he recovers."

Micky suggested, saying, "Miss Rebekah, he should be alone and have his rest."

"I'm staying, Micky, and if Jack dies, I want to be by his side, understand me?"

"Yes, Miss Rebekah, I do." Micky and Jake left Rebekah sitting right beside Jack's bed. Feeling guilty for treating Jack the way she did, Rebekah sat there trying to hold back the tears.

Out at sea several miles from the cove, Joe and Marty pushed Drew's body over the boat's edge and into the sea. Joe, knowing now the strange ship they observed earlier was Drew's rescue ship, made sure they saw Drew's body being buried here out at sea. The ship that was to rescue Drew sat several miles out at sea waiting for him to show after he completed his mission. The captain looking through his spyglass toward the cove entrance noticed a small boat and two men pushing an object about the size of a man wrapped in a blanket into the water.

The first officer asked, "Captain Spencer, can you make out what those two pirates are doing?"

"I'm not sure, Mr. Riley, but I'd guess it was a body being pushed overboard into the water."

"You thinking it could be Drew Wilson's body, sir?"

"I was thinking along those lines, Mr. Riley. We'll give Mr. Wilson two more days, and if he doesn't show, we'll have to assume the body was his."

"That doesn't make sense, captain, pirates having some kind of burying for their enemies?"

"I've heard some strange things about this Princess Pirate," the captain said, lighting his pipe. "She and her men are not the usual pirates you'd normally run into on a raid. She raids ships for whatever wealth it carries but only kills in self-defense."

"That doesn't make sense, Captain. All pirates kill their captives and sink their ships."

"The princess is different, Mr. Riley, and I don't understand her logic either," the captain said, puffing away on his pipe. The captain looked through his glass again and said, "We'll call it a night, Mr. Riley. If Wilson doesn't show, we'll set a course back to England."

"Aye, Captain."

Joe made sure they were seen and told Marty to row back to the cove.

Back on the *Black Rose*, Rebekah did a little praying on her own. Believing there was a God up there somewhere, Rebekah looked out of the windows of her ship, and while staring up toward the sky, she hoped he would spare Jack's life. Rebekah sat back down on her chair and started speaking to Jack while he lay there unconscious.

ALL THAT MATTERS NOW
1673

"Jack, I don't know if you can hear me, but I have to tell you how sorry I am about the way I treated you. No matter what you've done, I understand and forgive you. All that matters now, Jack, is you coming back to me."

Rebekah, while growing older, learned more wisdom each day. She had learned through this experience that Jack was of a greater importance to her then what he had done.

The night passed, and Rebekah was trying to stay awake, but as the night wore on, she just couldn't keep her eyes open any longer and went into a deep sleep. Rebekah dreamed of her father and mother and that she was back home in the castle. In her dream, she was so happy. It was great being home again. Then Rebekah was awakened by a hand on her face. Rebekah opened her eyes, and Jack was speaking to her.

Jack said in a soft voice, "Rebekah, wake up, wake up!"

Rebekah took Jack's hand into hers and said, "You're alive, Jack." Tears formed in her eyes.

"You look tired, Princess."

"Yes, Jack, but it's a good tired." Rebekah put her hand up against Jack's cheek, touching him ever so softly.

Then a knock was at the cabin door. "Come in," Rebekah said.

It was Jake, and seeing Jack awake, he said, "How's our patient this morning?"

"He's still alive, Jake, and that's all that matters."

"Princess, I'm checking Jack's ribs. You wouldn't mind stepping out for a moment, would you?"

"I'll be outside the door Jake if you need me." Rebekah closed the door behind her.

DON'T PUSH IT
1673

Rebekah waited outside the door while Jake looked over Jack's wound. Rebekah watched Micky go into Jack's cabin carrying a bottle of whisky. She knew what was coming next. Jack, seeing the whisky bottle, said, "I'm not thirsty for anything, Micky. All I want to do is sleep."

"This isn't for drinking, Jack," Jake said, removing the cork. "Jack, this is going to burn like coals of fire, but I have to make sure the wound is sterilized thoroughly as much as possible before I put on a fresh bandage."

Jake poured some of the whiskey onto Jack's wound. Jack yelled out. Oh boy, did he yell as the alcohol burned and burned until it stopped. Rebekah rushed in to see about Jack. Jack was completely exhausted after that go around. He laid back in bed and went to sleep.

"He'll be all right, Princess," Jake said. "He'll sleep comfortably now."

Exhausted herself, Rebekah sat in the chair and fell back to asleep. Micky had Marty take Rebekah to her cabin and lay her on her bed.

Marty pulled the bed cover up and laid it over Rebekah to keep her warm. Staring at Rebekah sleeping, Marty took a deep breath and let out a sigh and then left.

The days passed, and Jack was out of his cabin making his rounds on deck and resuming his place as first mate. Later that evening, Rebekah and Jack were back at the railing meeting like old times.

Rebekah was telling Jack after they kissed, "No matter what you've done, it's all forgotten, and you're forgiven, Jack."

"I thank you, Princess." Jack leaned over to give Rebekah another kiss.

After Jack kissed Rebekah, he told her, "You missed that, didn't you, Princess?"

Jack grinned from ear to ear.

Rebekah stared into Jack's eyes passionately and said, "Jack."

"Yes, Princess."

"Don't push it." Rebekah went to her cabin, happy having Jack back.

Looking out toward the sea, Jack knew the only home he had was the *Black Rose* and the only girl he loved was Rebekah. Before retiring to his cabin, Jack made sure the men had the ship secured for the night. That night outside the cove, a bright star fell from the heavens.

PART VIII

91
Morgan's Revenge
1673

In his office, Morgan was trying to have a quiet day from the bad news and was having a sip of wine. "Ah." He sighed. "The wine is excellent today."

Morgan had been at peace the last two days not having to hear about the princess and the other villainous pirates that have been raising havoc on the high seas. Morgan rested his head back in his chair and closed his eyes and was about to drift off into a nap. Then there was a knock on his office door.

"Sir Morgan, Sir Morgan," his manservant was calling.

Morgan opened his eyes and said in a grumpy mood, "What is it, Sanderson?"

"The captain of the ship *Star Lighter* is here to see you, sir."

"All right, Sanderson, tell him to come in."

When the captain walked in, Morgan said, "You're not the captain of the *Star Lighter*. What happened to Captain Brant?"

"He gave up his captaincy to take a desk assignment."

"But why would he do that?"

"Something about the Princess Pirate raiding his ship the second time, Sir Morgan. He just couldn't deal with it, sir."

"So who are you, Captain? I never saw you before?"

"My name is Josh Gannon, sir, and I have an idea on how to stop the princess and her pirating."

Morgan laughed as he leaned back into his chair.

"I'm serious, Sir Morgan. I do have a plan, sir. Won't you hear me out before you condemn me, sir?"

"All right, Captain Gannon, fire away," Morgan said.

"I've talked with the council, and if you authorize it, they'll go along too."

"Well, let's hear it, Captain. I haven't all day. I'm a busy man." Morgan took another drink of his wine.

"My plan is to take the *Star Lighter* ship and turn it into a battleship loaded with cannons and a small army of men. I call this project *Death Ship*."

Morgan got up from his chair and went over to his winestand for some more drink and asked the captain, "Would you like some wine, Captain?"

"No, Sir Morgan, I'm on duty, but thank you, sir." Morgan, sipping his wine, said, "*Death Ship*. Very interesting, Captain."

Sitting back down at his desk, Morgan said, "I'd like to hear more about this *Death Ship*, Captain Gannon, continue on."

"We take the *Star Lighter* ship. Add forty cannons hidden behind covered flap doors. We add fifty well-trained fighting sailors and me, a well-trained naval captain. How does it sound so far, Sir Morgan?"

"I like it, Captain. Tell me more."

"When this ship is ready to sail, we'll go after these pirate ships and attack them. They won't stand a chance against the firepower this ship will carry, and when we board their ships, our sailors will do the cleanup work."

"I can say, Sir Morgan, within a year, there won't be a pirate ship left on the high seas."

Morgan sat there thinking of the princess. *And her days are numbered*, he thought.

"Yes, Captain Gannon, I like this idea. When can you get started?"

"When you sign these documents, Sir Morgan, it gives us permission to start the work and the unlimited funds we need to complete the project."

Morgan signed away on both documents. "Captain Gannon."

"Yes, Sir Morgan."

"When do you expect to have this ship in complete operation?"

"If we start tomorrow, sir, I estimate two weeks at the latest."

"Very well, Captain, the sooner the *Death Ship* is out to sea, the sooner we start sinking those pirate ships."

After Captain Gannon left Morgan's office, Morgan had a feeling of victory and sat back in his chair to finish the nap he started earlier. Drifting away in a light sleep, Morgan was saying to himself while closing his eyes, "No more, Princess Pirate, no more Pegleg Wilson or One-Eyed Jackson."

92
DEATH'S DOOR IS ALWAYS OPEN
1673

AFTER CAPTAIN GANNON left Morgan's office, another captain was waiting to see Morgan. Upon entering Morgan's office, Sanderson saw Morgan's eyes being closed and walked back out. "Captain Spencer, Sir Morgan is resting, could you come back later?"

"I'm sorry, Mr. Sanderson, but I have to see Sir Morgan. It's that important."

"Yes, sir, I'll awaken him."

Sanderson cleared his throat and said, "Sir Morgan."

Clearing his throat a second time, Sanderson said a little louder this time, "Sir Morgan."

Morgan opened his eyes and looked up at Sanderson and said, "This better be important, Sanderson, or you'll be cleaning garbage cans on the next garbage freighter sailing out to sea."

"It's very important, sir. A captain Spencer is here to see you, and he said it was urgent."

"Very well, Sanderson, send him in."

Spencer entered Morgan's office.

"What can I do for you, Captain Spencer?"

"I've just returned from Pirates Cove, Sir Morgan."

"What in the blue blazes were you doing there, Captain?"

"A Drew Wilson infiltrated the cove by getting onto the princess's ship, and we were ordered to follow the *Black Rose* back to

Pirates Cove and wait outside the cove to rescue Drew Wilson when his job of taking care of the princess was finished."

"Let me guess," Morgan intervened. "He never showed, and you presumed him to be dead, right?"

"I'm afraid so, Sir Morgan. Just days ago, my first officer and I were looking through our spyglasses and saw two pirates from the cove pushing something about the size of a man's body into the water from their small boat."

"So you thought the body might have been Drew Wilson's body, correct?"

"Yes, sir, I did, and after two more days, we decided to leave before we were attacked."

"Who gave you the authority to work with this, Drew Wilson, Captain Spencer?"

"The permission order came from the council, signed by Sir Thomas himself."

"Very well, Captain Spencer, you may leave."

"Here, Sir Morgan, this logbook tells every detail of the ship's journey and time schedule."

Spencer left, and Morgan asked himself, "What pull of authority did this Drew Wilson have with the council and Sir Thomas?" Morgan shook his head, put on his light coat, and went home to his mansion for his dinner and rest.

Out at sea, the *Black Rose* was raiding another ship. This time, Rebekah was up against a real swashbuckler, a sailor that was a fencing instructor for the navy. He was really giving Rebekah a difficult time as they were trading blade blows and blade swings against each other's swords.

"For a woman, you have very good sword skills," the sailor was telling Rebekah while taking another deadly swing with his sword.

"You're not doing badly yourself for being a sailor," Rebekah replied while blocking several of his moves.

Rebekah, with her sword blade, came close to the sailor's throat. The sailor ducked and said, "Almost but not successful, Princess."

He then thrust his sword toward Rebekah's right side and cut her. Rebekah was lucky the cut was shallow. Tired of this game and with both hands grasping her sword tightly, Rebekah turned her body completely around as her blade cut the sailor through his middle. The sailor went down but wasn't dead as the cut from Rebekah's blade just sliced the top surface of his skin. Rebekah could've killed him if she wasn't so disciplined with her sword.

This ship that Rebekah and her men took this time wasn't an easy task, but they took it anyway. Jack came over to Rebekah, looked down, and saw the blood bleeding through her blouse from her right side. Jack said to Rebekah, "Are you hurt bad, Princess? I see your right side is bleeding some."

"I'm all right, Jack. Just make sure we get what we came for." Starting to feel weak, Rebekah leaned her hand up against Jack's shoulders.

"Shall I take you to the ship, Princess?"

"I'm all right, Jack. I just felt a little dizzy."

The captain was dead after the sword fight with Sam who never shows much mercy of any kind. Thirty minutes later, after all the gold was loaded onto the *Rose*, Rebekah and her men were back out to sea. Not long after, Rebekah was feeling a little weak. She went to her cabin to rest. Later that evening, Jack knocked on her cabin door, but there was no answer. Jack knocked harder but still no answer, Jack then yelled through the door.

"Princess, you all right?" Jack didn't wait as he opened Rebekah's cabin door. "Rebekah," he said again as Rebekah lay on her bed not waking up.

Jack ran over and grabbed Rebekah, shaking her gently. "Rebekah, wake up."

Rebekah just lay there and was barely breathing.

"Micky!" Jack yelled. "Micky," he yelled again.

Micky came from the galley, asking, "What is it, Jack?"

"It's Rebekah. She's barely breathing."

Micky checked Rebekah's pulse and opened her eyelids to see her pupils. "She's very sick, Jack, and close to death."

"Didn't you take care of her side wound when she returned to the ship, Micky?"

"Yes, I did Jack, and the cut wasn't that severe."

"What's wrong with her, Micky? Why is she sick?" Jack was now frantic.

"The sword, Jack."

"What sword, Micky?"

"The sailor's sword that cut Miss Rebekah could've had a deadly poison on the blade or something else Miss Rebekah is allergic to. I just don't know for sure, Jack."

"Will she make it back to the cove, Micky?"

"No, Jack, she won't. Her pulse is weak and could get weaker. She could die in a day or two without a real doctor and the right medicines."

"What are we going to do, Micky? We can't stand here and do nothing."

"I do know of an island, Jack. It's not far from here. The natives have a lot of different medicines that might be able to help, Miss Rebekah."

"I'm not taking Rebekah to any witch doctor, Micky."

THE *DEATH SHIP* AT SEA
1673

"No, Jack, these natives don't believe in witch doctors. They've been taught different by religious teachers, and now they practice medicine from plants and things that just might help Miss Rebekah."

Jack remembered the salve Rebekah purchased from Jake that healed up some scars she received from sword fights and a pistol shot once. This salve also came from some of the natives that live on these islands.

"What's the name of this island, Micky?"

"Ardola Island, Jack. It was named after their long lost princess who was supposedly stolen away by pirates and presumed dead."

Looking at the map, Jack searched for Ardola Island. "It's not on the map, Micky."

Micky looked at the map and said, "Here it is, Jack. Between these two large volcano islands, Ardola Island."

Jack ran to the top deck, and after showing Joe the map, he ordered the ship's course chance to Ardola Island. Jack, that night, wasn't leaving Rebekah's side. He was keeping her comfortable as possible as the night wore on. Jack would cool her fever down with cloths dipped in cold water. Rebekah would awaken at times and ask Jack, "Who are you?"

Jack said, "It's me Jack, Princess, don't you remember?"

Rebekah, feverish, would say, "Father, help me please. I'm falling. I'm falling. Please catch me, Father."

Jack, trying to quiet Rebekah down, would tell her, "It's all right, Rebekah, and I'm holding onto you. You're not falling anymore."

Rebekah laid her head back, closed her eyes and fell back to sleep. The island that was only a few hours away was now in sight. Marty came down from the crow's nest to tell Jack they've arrived. Jack took Louie, Marty, and Micky so he could communicate with the natives. Carrying Rebekah on a blanket with two poles attached, they soon reached the village. When they arrived, they were greeted with acceptance as Micky communicated with the chief.

The chief ordered his people to take Rebekah into one of the huts. Jack and the men weren't allowed in the hut as their medicine people went in to help Rebekah.

"I don't know about this, Micky. I'd like to be in there with, Rebekah."

"Jack, if I wasn't sure about this, do you think I'd put Miss Rebekah's life at risk?"

"No, Micky, you wouldn't. I know how much Rebekah means to you."

Jack and the men standing there saw one of the native girls bring Rebekah's clothes from the hut and threw them into a fire that was burning.

"You were saying, Jack?" Micky said, looking up at him.

"But why burn Rebekah's clothes, Micky?"

"Not to take any chances, Jack. Her clothes might be infected with the virus or what she is allergic to."

Jack and Rebekah's men were made comfortable. They were given blankets to sleep on, good food to eat, and had a big fire burning to keep them warm.

"We may be here a few days, Jack, so we might as well get comfortable," Micky said while taking a bite of a tasty bird's wing. Jack wasn't sleeping well tonight thinking about Rebekah. This wasn't a hospital where the doctor comes and tells you something about the patient.

Back at England, the next day, Morgan got a report on the *Death Ship*. Captain Gannon, who was in charge, was talking with Morgan, "The *Death Ship* will be ready ahead of schedule, Sir Morgan."

"Ahead of schedule, you say, Captain."

"The ship already had cannon ports built in, Sir Morgan. All we had to do was add twenty more cannons on each side of the ship. Besides, sir, it was just an estimate."

"No matter, Captain Gannon, I'm glad the ship is ready and going after the princess."

"This ship, Sir Morgan, is going after other pirate ships as well, sir."

"Yes, of course, Captain Gannon, I just got ahead myself."

The next day, Morgan watched from his office window while the *Death Ship* sailed out of England's harbor and out to sea. While taking a drink of wine, Morgan stood there smiling as he thought about the princess attacking this ship now. *What a surprise she'll get!* he thought as he continued pouring more wine into his small glass.

Back on the island two days later, the chief approached Jack and his men with a smile on his face. Micky communicated with the chief, and Jack, being impatient after waiting two days, said to Micky, "Well, Micky, what's he saying?"

Micky put up his hand and told Jack, "Hang on, Jack. He's telling me now."

The chief spoke a few words and then went back into the hut. Micky said, "Good news, Jack, Rebekah is awake and doing fine."

"Can I see her, Micky?" Jack said, being impatient.

"Yes, Jack, just for a minute, you understand?"

Jack went into the hut and saw Rebekah lying in their so-called bed.

"Hi, Princess!" Jack said as he knelt down by Rebekah's bed.

Staring at Jack strangely, Rebekah asked, "Who are you?"

"I'm Jack, Princess, don't you know me?"

"I'm a princess, but I don't know you."

Jack was in total shock when Rebekah didn't know who he was. Micky nudged Jack on the shoulder, saying, "We better leave now, Jack. They want the princess to get her rest."

"But, Micky, her memory, she doesn't know me."

"Let's go, Jack, and talk about this outside."

Later, they all learned Rebekah didn't recognize any of them; the sickness affected her mind with amnesia. Jack was in total disarray about Rebekah and didn't know what to do.

I'm Princess Ardola
1673

Micky made a suggestion, saying, "Maybe if we take her back to the ship, Jack, the surroundings would snap her memory back."

Later, Marty brought Rebekah her clothes, and Jack was ready to take her back to the ship. Jack approached the hut when Rebekah came out wearing bright, shiny clothes the natives had given her to wear. Jack told Rebekah, "I'm taking you back to the ship, Rebekah, and I want you to change into these clothes Marty brought from the ship."

Staring at Jack, Rebekah ordered him, saying, "Bow down at my feet because I am Ardola the Princess."

Shaking his head, Jack said, "No, it's Rebekah. Now stop this foolishness and come with us back to the ship."

Rebekah commanded Jack and the others to bow before her while saying again, "I am Ardola the Princess, and you shall bow before me." Rebekah pointed to the ground before her feet.

"I don't think so, Rebekah," Jack said. "I don't know the game you're playing, Rebekah. It's not funny, and you're coming with us." Jack grabbed Rebekah by her arm.

The natives took this seriously as they gathered around Rebekah and held spears against Jack and the others.

"I don't think Miss Rebekah is joking, Jack," Micky said while pushing a spear away that was next to his chest. "Miss Rebekah believes she's Ardola the Princess, and the natives accept her as their princess and also believe that she is."

"One thing you were wrong about, Micky."

"Yes, what's that, Jack?"

"These natives may have given up their savage ways but still believe in princesses."

Rebekah, still waiting for them to bow before her, pointed to the ground again. "You shall bow before me or die."

Jack and the others bowed before Rebekah as she touched Jack on his forehead. The chief grabbed Jack by his arm and motioned for him to stand before the princess while the others stayed on their knees. Jack stood before Rebekah when she told him, "You will rule with me by my side."

Then she gave permission for the others to get up and leave if they wished. Rebekah and her servants went to a larger hut guarded by two natives with spears.

"Micky, what was that all about? She picked me to rule with her?"

"The princess has just picked you, Jack, to be her husband and for you to rule by her side."

"I've always wanted to marry Rebekah, Micky, but this takes all the fun out of it. She doesn't know what she's doing. I'll just have to tell Rebekah, I mean Ardola, I refuse to marry her."

Jack walked up to the large hut. The natives crossed their spears in front of Jack, making motions with their head, saying, no, he couldn't enter.

Jack said as he pointed to himself, "I want to speak with the princess."

They shook their heads no again. Having enough of this nonsense, Jack kicked the spears from their hands then slugged one native, knocking him to the ground. Then Jack, with a right cross, punched the other native, knocking him into the hut. Rebekah came out, saying, "Stop."

The natives grabbed Jack by his arms, holding him. "Princess, I must talk with you please," Jack pleaded.

Rebekah waved her hand toward the natives holding Jack. They released him and went about their working.

"You have my permission to speak."

"Princess, I'm here to tell you I can't marry you."

"Marry, what is marry?" Rebekah asked.

"Let me put it to you this way: I refuse to be your mate and rule by your side."

"No one refuses Ardola's wishes. You will stay and be by my side, or you will die."

The two native guards stuck their spears up to Jack's neck.

Jack was now in a tight spot, sort of speaking. He had to stay and hoped Rebekah's memory would return before the wedding. Jack relented and said, "I'll obey your commands, Rebekah."

"Not, Rebekah, it's Ardola."

"Yes, Ardola," Jack repeated as he bowed his head in obedience. Rebekah, or should we say Ardola, gave Jack that princess smile she always gave Jack when she got the best of him.

Jack told Micky, "That smile Rebekah gave me Micky. It looked very suspicious, and I wonder if Rebekah is having fun with us and making a joke out of all this."

"I believe Miss Rebekah thinks she's Princess Ardola, Jack."

"We've got to snap her out of this, Micky, before the wedding."

"Jack, we have to wait on her. I believe Miss Rebekah will get her memory back in time, but if she's pushed too far, it could damage her mind completely."

Jack stood by the fire rubbing his hands, thinking of the alternative.

WHY DON'T YOU SHOW NOW?
1673

THE DAYS PASSED while Jack waited to be married to Rebekah. Across the sea, the *Death Ship* was doing what it was set out to do—destroying pirate ships. The *Death Ship* had already sunk three pirate ships, and the surviving pirates were taken back to England to be hung.

During this time, Morgan had no word about the princess or her ship being sunk. Before Captain Gannon sailed out again, he was in Morgan's office.

"I have no explanation on the whereabouts of the *Black Rose*, Sir Morgan, and it's as though the princess and her ship has disappeared."

"It could also mean something else, Captain. The princess knows about the *Death Ship* and is in hiding."

"It's possible, Sir Morgan."

"Meanwhile, Captain Gannon, get back out to sea and keep up the good work."

Looking out of his office window, Morgan thought to himself, *Why don't you show now, Princess, now that I have your future destruction sailing on the high seas?*

Back on the island, Jack was getting ready to marry Rebekah in just two more days, and time was running out on her getting her memory back. Jack, still thinking Rebekah was faking all of this, would put a stop to the wedding when the day came.

That evening, Ardola came from her hut and approached Jack while he was sitting by the fire. Jack looked up and asked, "Princess, is there something I can do for you?"

"You will rise to your feet when talking to your, Princess," she said.

Taking a deep breath, Jack stood to his feet, asking, "Now what, Princess?"

"You shall not talk to me in that manner."

Jack bowed and said, "My deepest apology, My Worship."

"You mock me, I shall have your head removed!" she said.

Rebekah motioned with her hand, summoning her guards. Two nativities come running over with their spears pointed at Jack. Jack thought, *If Rebekah isn't faking this, Ardola is meaning business.* Taking Ardola seriously, Jack bowed again and said, "I meant no harm, my princess. Please forgive my rudeness."

"Very well, you have gained my mercy." Motioning with her hand, Rebekah sent her guards away. Rebekah, with great affection showing in her eyes for Jack, said, "You the one I hear called Jack?"

"Yes, my princess."

"You, from now on, will address me as Ardola."

"Yes, Ardola, your wish is my command," Jack said, bowing again in obedience.

Rebekah took Jack's hand and said, "Walk with me to the shore of the island before we are to be joined."

This was a break Jack had been waiting, for he wasn't allowed near Rebekah until now.

OH, JACK
1673

Jack and Ardola talked while walking together and nearing the shore. "I don't understand everything you have told me, Jack, but this man, Jenson, you say that killed my father isn't true. My father went to his father's many moons ago of old age, and he died in honor."

Jack and Ardola standing by the seashore and seeing the waves rolling ashore and the moonlight shining down on them gave Jack an idea. Jack leaned over and kissed Ardola in the strong moonlight. Ardola's eyes closed as she enjoyed Jack's kiss. Ardola, removing her lips from Jack's, said in a deep passionate voice with her cheek rubbing up against Jack's.

"Oh! Jack, I love you so much."

Then she opened her eyes. Jack thought Rebekah's memory had returned and said, "Rebekah, you know me. It's Jack, remember?"

Ardola shook her head and said, "No, Jack, my name is Ardola, not Rebekah."

It was as though Rebekah's inner, deep thoughts were trying to resurface but was staying submerged.

That night, Jack returned with Ardola, and he was now thinking Rebekah wasn't faking this. Jack was talking with Micky by the fire. "Micky, I have to agree with you now. Rebekah really believes she's the princess Ardola."

"What changed your mind, Jack?"

"When we were standing on the shore, I kissed Rebekah thinking it would snap her out this Ardola nonsense, but even in that passionate moment, she still claimed to be Ardola, not Rebekah."

"What are you going to do, Jack? It'll be your wedding day coming up in forty-eight hours?"

Louie, listening in, said, "Yea, Jack, what are we going to do?"

Tossing a wooden stick into the fire, Jack said, "Only one thing we can do if Rebekah hasn't snapped out of this fairy tale land she's living in, we'll just have to leave and go back to the ship without her."

Marty spoke up, "We can't do that, Jack. It wouldn't be right."

"Listen, Marty, if we don't return to the ship soon, the men will come looking for us. Then things may really bust open. There could be a little war between our men and Ardola's natives. Who do you think would win?"

Louie spoke up, "The natives will be massacred, Jack."

"Yes, Louie, because Ardola would try to prevent me from leaving."

"I think you have a plan. Am I correct, Jack?" Micky asked kneeling by the fire, getting warm.

"Yes, Micky, I do. Tomorrow night when the moon is full, we'll sneak out and head back to the ship."

"Without the princess, Jack?" Marty asked.

"We have no choice, Marty, we have to leave her. Now accept it."

Marty, with deep sadness in his heart, sat by the fire and just stared at it.

97
THE BIGGER THEY ARE
1673

At this time, the rest of Rebekah's men were back on the *Black Rose* waiting for Jack, Micky, Louie, Marty, and, hopefully, the princess to return. Back at the village, Jack and the men were eating their dinner.

Marty, putting the food away, said, "I love this meat on the stick they serve. It tastes like ham."

"It is ham, Marty," Micky said. Jack wasn't very hungry and took a drink of something they call leaf tea and handed Marty his meat on a stick to eat.

"Say, Micky."

"Yes, Jack."

"Something I just can't figure, why did the chief accept Rebekah as the princess Ardola when she was believed to be dead? What happened to them not being superstitious?"

"You know, Jack, I was curious of the same question, so I asked the chief. I found out I was wrong about these natives giving up all their superstitions. They believe that when Miss Rebekah was in a fever, Ardola's spirit and Miss Rebekah's spirit combined and they are now one."

"Come on, Micky, you expect me to believe that?"

"All that matters, Jack, they believe it."

"Rebekah didn't think of that name out of the blue, Micky. They've had to convince her she was Ardola."

"Yes, I believe that they did, Jack. These natives are always looking for a princess to protect them or rule over them."

"I've got to talk with Rebekah before we leave tomorrow night, Micky, and try and get through to her one last time."

The next evening, Jack finally got to see Rebekah again. They strolled down toward the shoreline once again. Ardola removed her sandals and walked in the water barefooted and said, "We shouldn't be seen together before the joining, Jack. It's bad luck."

"You saw me last night, Ardola, why not now?"

"I also wanted to see you again, Jack." Ardola leaned up to kiss Jack this time.

Afterward, she laid her head up against Jack's shoulder and said, "You wanted to tell me something, my future mate?"

"Look at me, Ardola."

"Yes, Jack, and what am I supposed to see?"

"Listen very carefully to my words. Your name is Rebekah, and you're in command of a ship called the *Black Rose*."

"Why do you speak these strange words to me, Jack?"

"I'll try again, Rebekah. Your name is Rebekah Martin. Your father was killed by a man named Roy Jenson, and you're out to get him and England for this misdeed against you."

Ardola put her hands over her ears, telling Jack, "Stop with these strange words. I don't understand."

"Rebekah, snap out of it." Jack grabbed her shoulders and shook her gently.

"Let me go!" Ardola yelled as she broke loose from Jack and ran back to the village.

Jack went back to the village to get the men they weren't waiting any longer; they were leaving tonight. Jack didn't want to leave Rebekah, but now she's Ardola, and maybe someday he'd return to see if she ever got her memory back. If Jack stayed, he'd eventually marry Rebekah, and she wouldn't be marrying him in her right mind.

Jack came back to the village and told Micky, "We're leaving now, Micky. Tonight, we're not waiting any longer."

"But why, Jack? One more day won't hurt."

"If I stay any longer, Micky, I might give into my desire for Rebekah and stay and marry her. I'm not taking advantage of her Micky, so get the men and our things together and let's go."

Jack and his men were sneaking out toward the jungle-like trees when they were met by the chief and his natives. With many spears pointing at them, the chief motioned with his hand "back to the hut."

"What's he saying, Micky?" Jack was asking.

"He says for us to return to our hut or die here in the jungle."

With no choice, they returned to their hut with several natives standing outside, guarding the hut. "What now, Jack?" Louie asked.

"I guess we wait for my wedding day, and we'll all attend it together."

Back at Pirates Cove, One-Eyed Jackson and Pegleg Wilson were talking about the *Death Ship* with Jake.

"This sounds serious, One-Eye," Jake was saying. "Another thing, One-Eye, I haven't seen the princess or heard anything about her or her ship in this past week. You don't think her ship was sunk by this floating death on the sea, do you?"

One Eye, taking a drink, said, "I don't know, Jake."

Pegleg walked back over to the bar with his wooden leg making the sound of *thump, thump, thump*. He stood in front of the bar, and said, "This *Death Ship* England has sent against us must be stopped before it destroys all of us."

At this time, Pete the Pirate Merchant entered through the post's door. "Jake!" Pete yelled. "When did you start letting these two darken your post?"

"If it isn't Pete the Cheating Merchant!" Peg Leg yelled back.

Pete said, laughing, "Let me buy you two old scalawags a drink for old times."

While drinking, Pete spoke up about the *Death Ship*. "Say, has anything been done about getting rid of that *Death Ship* England has sent against us?"

Jake, taking a drink, said, "That's been the discussion for the day, Pete."

One-Eye asked, "How many cannons does that ship carry has anyone heard?"

Just then one of Jake's men spoke up while approaching the bar. "Yea mate, I know," he said.

Jake told Pete, One-Eye and Peg Leg, "Meet my newest hired pirate, a man from Australia."

THE PIRATE PLAN
1673

"How are the kangaroos jumping over there?" Pete said, laughing as he took another drink.

"Better stop with the jokes, mate, if you want the information I have."

Jake said, "Listen, Tilden, the information you have just might put a stop to this *Death Ship*."

"All right, Jake, this is what I heard about it as I was sailing across the sea on a frigate to get here. These two sailors were bragging about this *Death Ship* and the forty guns she's carrying, twenty on each side."

One-Eye asked Pete, "How many cannons are on your ship?"

"I carry thirty," Pete told him.

"We carry thirty also Pete," One-Eye said.

Pegleg spoke up, "What's your plan, One-Eye?" while downing his rum.

Jake listened in as the pirates talked about their plans on destroying the *Death Ship*. The next morning, Jake watched the two ships the *Blue Scarlet* and the *Black Dawn* sail from his cove in hopes of them succeeding in their mission. Jake was already thinking the princess and the *Black Rose* had already met their fate against the *Death Ship*.

That night at Pirates Cove island, the mystery ship appeared once again behind the island. As always, a tall man walked to the cove carrying things that looked like charts, a small leather bag, plus a lantern. The tall, strange man knocked on Jake's secret door, and as always, they make an exchange. Jake took the things from the man standing in the shadow, and the man in the shadow took a large cotton sack filled with gold from Jake. Jake told the man in the shadows before he left, "We might've lost a friend."

The tall man said, "This would be tragic to our plans." He then turned, leaving to go back to the mystery ship. The mystery ship pulled up its anchor and sailed away into the darkness.

The next day, One-Eyed Jackson and Pegleg Wilson's ship, the *Blue Scarlet*, met up with the *Death Ship* and a heavy cannon battle was going on between them. The cannon fire between them was furious as men on both ships were being blown to bits.

"Where's Pete and his ship?" Pegleg yelled out to One-Eye.

"His ship was supposed to be in spyglass distance behind us."

"Pete will show Pegleg this *Death Ship* has to be destroyed, and Pete knows it."

"Yea! That's if he was following us at a distance and not getting scared and running out on us."

The fighting continued between both ships. Pete the Pirate Merchant out of the blue showed up with his cannons firing away toward the *Death Ship*. The *Death Ship* was caught between the *Blue Scarlet* and the *Black Dawn* and the gunfire coming from both ships were taking her down. Men were being blasted into the air as cannons from both ships kept firing with no letting up.

Captain Gannon ordered the *Death Ship* out of there but too late—the *Death Ship* sustained so much damage, and with the holes that were put into her, she was sinking, and sinking fast. Men were yelling, and screaming as the fire burned them beyond recognition and the blasts tore them into small pieces.

Captain Gannon ordered the men, "Abandon ship! Save yourselves."

The *Death Ship* was going down to defeat. One-Eye said to Pegleg, "The bigger they are, the deeper they sink."

They both laughed with victory. "What about the surviving sailors, One-Eye?" Peg Leg was asking.

"Let them go, Pegleg. Let them tell parliament about how we destroyed their *Death Ship* on the high seas."

Good-Bye, Rebekah
1673

Pegleg agreed as they both took survey of the damages to their ship and the loss of their men. Pete the Pirate Merchant, knowing his part in this was over, just sailed in the opposite direction.

Back on the Ardola Island, Jack was facing his wedding day. Jack and the men were standing outside the hut. Jack watched Ardola walk from her hut dressed in a beautiful white robe adorned with emeralds and rubies. Ardola was standing between two poles lighted by fire. The chief escorted Jack to where Ardola was standing and put their hands into one another's. The men had to stay by the huts until the ceremony was over.

Removing his hand from Ardola's, Jack said, "I'm not going through with this, Ardola. My men and I are leaving."

Ardola said, "You will stay, or you die."

Louie asked, "Do you think she means it, Micky?"

Micky, being afraid himself, said, "We're getting ready to find out, Louie, if Jack starts to leave."

Jack walked toward Micky and the men when Ardola yelled, "Stop them!"

The natives tried to stop Jack and the men. Jack, Louie, and Marty put up a good fight. They took several natives down when more natives came running over with their spears pointing at their throats. Ardola, standing over Jack, said, "You have a choice,

Jack: stay and be my mate, or you will stay here and die. Which do you choose?"

Jack knew they couldn't stay. With nothing to lose but their lives, Jack decided to rebel against Ardola and hoped her deep consciousness would resurface.

"I won't stay," Jack said. "Go ahead and kill me!"

Ardola said harshly. "You will stay!"

"No, I won't, Ardola," Jack said again. "Especially not against my will!"

"Yes, you will, or you will die," Ardola yelled back at Jack while tears started to flow down her cheeks. "You will. I command it," she said again. With Rebekah's inner self fighting, she fell to her knees onto the ground screaming. "You will! You will!"

Then one native pulled his spear back and was ready to run Jack through when Ardola looked up and screamed out, "No! I said no!" as she pushed the spear aside.

Ardola closed her eyes and kept saying, "You must stay. You must."

Then there was silence from Ardola. Ardola opened her eyes and looked up at Jack and said, "Jack, why are you staring at me so strangely? And who are all these people?"

Jack and the men were so relieved when Rebekah asked those questions. Jack helped Rebekah from her knees and took a walk with her down to the shore, explaining everything to her. It was hours before they both returned, and Rebekah had a hard time believing what had happened to her but knew Jack would never lie to her. Rebekah changed into her pirate clothes and was ready to go back to the ship. They said good-bye to the natives when the chief confronted Rebekah, saying something to her she didn't understand. Then the chief fell to his knees in front of Rebekah.

Micky translated: "Miss Rebekah, the chief begs for you to stay with his people. They've been so long without a princess."

Feeling sorry for the chief, Rebekah said, and Micky translated, "I am a princess to another people, and they would be lost without me. I must return to them and fulfill my being their princess."

After hearing the translation, the chief turned and went back to his people.

"Do you think he understood, Micky?"

"They aren't trying to stop you from leaving, Miss Rebekah, so I guess he understood something."

The chief watched from the mountain while the *Black Rose* sailed away and said to himself in his own language, "Ardola, you will return someday, and your people will be waiting."

It would be three days before the *Rose* would be back at the cove. It would be four days before Morgan knew of the *Death Ship* being sunk. After the sinking of the *Death Ship*, Captain Gannon and half of his crew that had survived were rescued at sea by a cargo ship the day after. On the *Black Rose*, things were trying to get back to normal. Rebekah, being curious, continued asking Jack what she was like being Princess Ardola.

One evening by the railing where Jack and Rebekah would meet after dinner, she wanted to know some more about Princess Ardola.

"I've told you just about everything, Princess."

"Jack, you're holding something back. I can feel it."

"Princess, there's nothing left to tell."

100
DID YOU LOVE HER?
1673

"One thing you didn't tell me, Jack, did you kiss me when I was Ardola?"

"Well, I..." Jack stuttered, and then Rebekah interrupted him. "You did, didn't you?"

"Yes, Princess, I did." Jack was waiting for her reaction.

"Did you love, Ardola, Jack?" Rebekah said, getting down to the brass tacks.

"How could I not, Princess? You and Ardola kissed the same, and you both are beautiful." Jack always knew the right answers to say to her. The princess reached up and kissed Jack good night before she went to her cabin.

Joe walked up and asked Jack, "Are things back to normal with you and the princess?"

"I think so, Joe. She seems to be pleased with what I told her."

"They say, Jack, that once something like this happens to a person, like loses their memory and think they're someone else, it could happen again."

Joe went to his bunk for the night. Jack stared out toward the sea and thought to himself, *Interesting!*

Days later when Captain Gannon was back at England, he had to face Morgan about the sinking of the *Death Ship*. That afternoon, Gannon reported to Morgan in his office. Gannon walked in and stood before Morgan. Morgan asked, "So what happened, Captain Gannon? I thought this ship of yours was indestructible." Morgan was ready to come down on Gannon.

"I never said or let on to you, Sir Morgan, that this ship wasn't sinkable, sir. We just were caught in a cross fire between two pirate ships, and we were outgunned, sir."

"Being a seasoned commander, Gannon, how did you allow this to happen?"

"The other pirate ship sailed out from nowhere, Sir Morgan, not the best captain on the high seas could've for seen this, sir."

Morgan was silent for a moment. Then he said, "The failed experiment will cost parliament hundreds of thousands in English pounds, and what do you have to say about that? And how are you going to explain this to the queen?"

"Look at it this way, Sir Morgan: we did take three pirate ships off the seas, and twenty pirates are waiting in England's prison to be hung. I think the *Death Ship* has paid for its use, sir."

"There's only one problem, Captain."

"What's that, sir?"

"You didn't bring in the princess or sink her ship. If her ship would've been one of the casualties, I'd be in an agreement with you. But the way it stands, you failed in your mission."

"I don't understand why the princess never attacked the *Death Ship*, Sir Morgan. In the beginning, we did our best to be an easy target for her, sir."

"You may leave, Captain. There's nothing left to discuss."

"Aye, Sir Morgan."

The way Morgan figured things, the *Death Ship's* sinking was planned by pirates after learning of her mission on the high seas, but the thing that really got to Morgan was where was the princess and her ship the *Black Rose* all this time.

John Hendrexson walked in. "Morgan, I've just heard of the sinking of the *Death Ship*."

"Yes, Sir Hendrexson, and I'm sincerely sorry you were away during this experimental project."

"Yes, Morgan, my traveling back and forth to France and being their ambassador does take up a lot of my time."

101 THE CELEBRATION 1673

"I know, Sir Hendrexson, but you were away for two weeks, sir. You're normally back in ten days. Did you have trouble on the way back?" Morgan inquired suspiciously.

"I wasn't in a hurry to return, Morgan, so I told the captain of the ship he could make stops on the way back he deemed necessary. By the way, Morgan, was the notorious Princess Pirate caught or her ship destroyed during this experiment with the *Death Ship*?"

"Sorry to say, Sir Hendrexson, the princess never showed during this time, and we made sure the *Death Ship* was an easy target. It was as though she knew about the ship, sir."

"Very well, Morgan, carry on, at least there are three pirate ships that won't do any more raiding." Hendrexson left Morgan's office having a good day.

Now that really got Morgan—Hendrexson leaving as though things were better today than they were yesterday, with the princess escaping the *Death Ship* without a scratch. Morgan sat at his desk and went back to signing more papers.

Back at the cove, Jake was having a celebration of the princess's return and of her recovery. After the celebration, Jake introduced Rebekah to Tilden who was from Australia.

"Well, blow me down," he said. "After meeting you, princess, the mates back home will never believe I met a real live princess."

"That's nice of you to say, Tilden."

"You can call me Andy Tilden, Princess."

Later at their table, Rebekah asked Jack, "Why do you have such a glum look on your face?"

"I hope this Tilden doesn't get any bright ideas in his head about you, Princess."

"Jack, are you jealous?" Rebekah said, grinning.

"Well, Princess, if I do lose you to someone else, I can always marry Ardola." Jack got up and left before Rebekah could come back with a quick answer. Rebekah set her cup of hot chocolate down on the table and said, "Later, Jack." Picking the cup back up and taking a sip, she smiled.

PART IX

ONE EVIL AND ONE LAZY
1673

A YEAR AFTER Dexter Lewis was thrown off the Princess Pirate's ship, he was from job to job in taverns. Finally, Dexter found a job he really was good at, pick pocketing.

A tavern owner who caught Dexter pickpocketing a man in his bar was very impressed with Dexter's talent and gave him a job in his tavern doing the same to drunks. The tavern owner was named Bart Davis, and he was as crooked running a bar as well as anybody. You know the kind who would stiff a man on his drink or water down his booze.

Bart and Dexter were making great partners and thieves together. This was the best job Dexter could ever have, being a lazy, good-for-nothing thief, and this title fit Dexter perfectly to a tee.

Back in France, at this time, Amber Stewart was back to her old self, well and fit as a fiddle in more ways than one. After the almost tragic death of falling over a cliff, she was now feeling her oats once again. Soon after she married Jordan, she was going to settle with Rebekah and Morgan. They still were a thorn in her side, and she wasn't resting till they both were pushing up grass.

Jordan entered into Amber's room and asked, "How are you feeling today, my love?"

"I'm feeling great, Jordan, and after we're married, I'll feel even better."

"I wish to discuss something with you, Amber, now that you're well. You see, my love, I've changed my mind about marrying you."

Totally surprised, Amber said, "You what!"

"I wanted you to get well before I broke the news to you, my dear Amber."

"I'm not in the mood for jokes, Jordan," Amber started brushing her hair.

"I'm not joking, Amber. Even though you're the most attractive woman that's ever been in my life. I'm not marrying you, and if you're planning my demise to get even, guess again, my sweet, if anything happens to me, the authorities here will never let you leave the island." Jordan grinned.

"You thought of everything, haven't you, my dearest Jordan?" Amber said, knowing she had been out foxed.

"I'll do this for you, Amber, my love. I'll give you all the money you'll need to last for one year and pay your ship fare to anywhere you want to travel too, but if you return to this island, I'll turn you over to the authorities for the murder of Franchesskah."

"You know about her, Jordan?" Amber said, thinking her tracks were covered.

"Yes, I do, and I'm very upset with you for that."

"So who told you, Jordan? And is that the reason you're not marrying me?"

"Frenchy sent me a letter on the matter. The reason I'm not marrying you is because I don't love you, Amber, and I don't think I ever could."

Amber looked into the mirror and asked, "Is there any scars on my face that I missed?" Amber looked over her face intensely.

"No, Amber, you're as beautiful as always. That's not the reason I'm not marrying you because of a scar."

"Then what is it, Jordan, your pride?"

"No, my Amber, it's that you're so unpredictable, a man never knows what to expect with you. I might look at a pretty girl one day and not wake up the next." Jordan chuckled."

"I see, Jordan. I'm a witch. Is that what you're telling me?"

"Oh no, Amber, not with your beauty, but I plan on living a long time, and it's not with you."

"Amber, when the carriage is ready, it'll take you to the docks. There's a ship sailing to England and one sailing to Sweden. It's up to you, Amber, but don't return here, or you'll be imprisoned for the murder of Franchesskah."

"You made yourself very clear, Jordan. I'll leave and not return. You can sleep without fear tonight."

"After you pack your things, Amber, and are ready to leave, I'll have a small pouch for you containing twenty gold crowns. This's for you when you leave."

103
A Woman Scorned!
1673

Coming down the stairs, Amber saw Jordan sitting with a young girl around the age of twenty. Jordan just got through kissing her when Amber told the girl, "He used to kiss me like that once before he got tired of me and cast me aside like an old shoe."

"Amber, you're bitter and shouldn't be. We had lots of good times together," Jordan said, grinning.

"Is that what you called it, Jordan? I thought you were just being nice to me for other reasons." Amber gave Jordan a sour look.

"Here's the gold I promised you, Amber, and your carriage is waiting."

"Good-bye, Jordan, and I hope your heart holds out. You aren't as young as you once were, and these young girls can be bad for an old man's heart." Amber left laughing.

Looking at the girl, Jordan said, "That Amber is one of a kind, and I'll miss her."

"I'm glad that witch is gone, Jordan. She's the most hateful woman I've ever seen."

"Yes, my little sweet, but her beauty is most uncommon. Now where were we?" Jordan asked, putting his arms around her.

Amber took the ship that was sailing back to England, and on the way, the ship would stop at a port called Sailor's Warf where she made plans on Rebekah's demise before. That would be as good of a place as any, she thought, to think of another scheme to be rid of the Princess and Henry Morgan.

When the ship Amber was sailing on docked at Sailor's Warf, Amber disembarked and then went to get a room at the Sailor's Inn. That night after her warm perfumed bath, she sat in front of the mirror brushing her hair saying to herself.

"All right, Jordan my ex-lover, you may have the upper hand on me now, but what goes around comes around."

The next day, Amber went and purchased a pistol and a knife. When she walked into a weapons shop, she told the man there, "I'd like to purchase a small pistol and a regular-size knife please. Oh yes, I'll need some gunpowder and several lead pellets."

The owner, being a little surprised, asked, "You buying this for your husband, miss?"

"No, I'm buying these items for me. You never know when a defenseless young woman like me will need a pistol or a knife."

"Yes, miss, it's getting bad for women to walk alone these days."

"Yes, and I want to be able to protect myself." Amber smiled at the shopowner. After paying, Amber left the store with an innocent look on her face.

The man's son asked, "What did she buy, Father?"

"That sweet young lady purchased a knife and pistol for self-protection."

"Does she know how to use them, Father?" his son asked.

"I didn't ask her, son, but I'm sure she knows someone who'll teach her."

"She sure was pretty, Father."

"Yes, she was, son," the owner said, letting out a deep breath.

Amber wasted no time in returning to her room and loading the pistol and hiding it inside her dress. Now she was ready to go about the little town in safety.

104 LICKING HER WOUNDS 1673

LEAVING A RESTAURANT where she had lunch, Amber decided to go to a tavern and have a drink and lick her wounds over the humiliation she suffered from Jordan. What really burned Amber was the young girl Jordan was kissing when she left.

Amber entered into a tavern that was cleaner than the one down the street. She had her dignity to think about. Amber then sat down at a table waiting to be served. She knew most taverns didn't allow women, but this one did.

Amber heard a voice say, "Miss, if you want a drink, you'll have to go to the bar and ask for one."

Amber, looking up, asked the young man, "What's your name?"

"It's Dexter Lewis, miss, and may I ask your name?"

"It's Amber Stewart, and if you get me my drink, I'll buy you one."

Dexter said, "All right, what would you like me to bring you, miss?"

"I'd like a small brandy, please."

"I'll be right back."

When Dexter returned, he and Amber had their drinks and were hitting it off like old friends. "So you sailed on some pirate ships, Dexter?"

"Yes, I have, and the last ship I sailed on—I'll never forget—they threw me off, and the man responsible was named Jack Reese, and I'll get him someday for that."

Amber set her glass down and asked, "Did you say, Jack Reese?"

"Yea, do you know him, Amber?"

"Yes, I do, and the little princess who he's so fond of."

"You mean the Princess Pirate, Rebekah Martin?"

"Yes, I do, and if I ever get my hands on her again, I'll make her beg for death."

A thought came to Amber while staring at Dexter, *He not only looked stupid*, she thought, but she could use him in a scheme on getting Rebekah.

After drinking down several drinks, Dexter felt brave and said, "I'm planning someday to get even with the princess and Jack. And you know something else, Amber? I remember one island where the princess buried two chests full of gold."

Amber poured Dexter another glass and said, "Interesting, Dexter, can you find the spot where they were buried?"

Dexter, a little drunk, said, "Forget finding that gold, Amber. She hid it so well you'd spend the rest of your life digging up the island and never find it."

Amber now had a weapon to use against the princess. "Dexter, if we go partners, we both together can get our revenge against Jack and the princess."

Taking down another drink, Dexter agreed, "It's a deal, Amber."

"Here's what I want you to do, Dexter. Tomorrow evening, meet me at my hotel at Sailor's Inn, room number 14, and I'll go over my plans with you before we leave the port."

The next evening, Dexter was in Amber's room, and she was telling him some of her plan, just enough for now. *If things work out*, Amber thought, *Dexter will be holding the bag for two murders, Rebekah and Morgan.* Standing by the window, looking out,

Amber said, "You can leave now, Dexter, and be back here in the morning so we can sail out on the next ship."

Dexter was feeling his oats around Amber. He walked up behind her, putting his hands around her waist, and then he passionately kissed her on her neck. Amber turned and slapped Dexter so hard it almost shook his brains loose. Then Amber yelled, "You rodent of a rat, you ever touch me again, I'll rip your lungs out. Now get out!"

"I don't have a place to stay, Amber. When I quit my job, I lost my place to stay," Dexter said, rubbing his jaw.

"I didn't tell you to quit your job, you fool, at least not until we were leaving."

Amber walked over to the cabinet and pulled something from the top drawer. Dexter, still rubbing his jaw, wasn't going to let Amber get away with slapping him. He wanted something in return. He approached Amber from behind again, and when he did, Amber turned holding a pistol in her hand. Cocking the hammer, Amber said, "One more step, mister, and you'll not have to worry about where you're going to sleep tonight. Now get out and be here in the morning, or I'll leave without you."

"Amber, I don't have a place to go. I must stay here tonight."

"Not on your life, Dexter. Go and sleep with your friends the rats in the cellar. Now leave before my finger tightens and pulls this trigger back."

Dexter didn't have a choice in the matter. He would sleep out in the hall tonight. Since he quit Bart, he had to leave Sailor's Warf, or Bart would get even by having his throat cut. Dexter really got himself into a fix with this Amber, but he'd get even with her too when this was all over.

That night in bed, Amber was thinking to herself, *I hope I can stand being around this Dexter until the use I have for him is over.*

The next day, Dexter was at her front door waiting. They had breakfast and then boarded a ship that was sailing to Frenchy's island. Amber's plan was to borrow Frenchy's ship one last time. While on board ship, Dexter inquired of his sleeping quarters. "Amber, do I have a cabin?"

"Yes, Dexter, you do. It's right across from mine. But if you try anything, I have this pistol, so keep your distance from me until we get to the next port."

105
Worthless Snake
1673

"Amber, how do you know this ship is going to the port you want to sail too?"

"I gave the captain some gold in payment. That's how I know," Amber said, opening her small leather pouch. "Dexter, I'm handing you several silver coins. This will pay for food while on this trip, but if you waste it and get hungry, you can go to the hold of the ship and eat cheese with your friends, the rats."

Dexter took the money from her hand, like a beggar, begging, but he felt disgusted.

"From here on, Dexter, until we reach port, don't see me or come to my cabin, understand?" Amber stared with a stern look on her face.

Dexter couldn't wait to get even with Amber for the humiliation she had been putting him through. He was now thinking of a way to dispose of Amber before the ship arrived at Frenchy's island.

After killing Amber, he would rob her cabin of any valuables and then, at night, throw her body overboard; but first, Dexter needed some kind of weapon. That night, Dexter was eating in the ship's galley, and after cutting the meat he was eating, he stopped and looked at the knife. "Of course," he said to himself as he grinned, "this will do the job very nicely and quietly."

Dexter finished eating and took the knife with him to his cabin. While in his cabin, Dexter was thinking how he was going to kill Amber. Dexter opened his cabin door staring across toward Amber's cabin door. He went across the hall and knocked on her door. Dexter knocked again, but no answer. He tried the handle, and it turned. Dexter stepped into Amber's cabin, and since she wasn't there, he searched her room for anything of value.

He closed the door behind him and started rummaging through all her cabinet drawers. Dexter was throwing her clothes and undergarments everywhere, looking for any place she'd hide money or gold. Dexter was mumbling, "The money is got to be here somewhere," as he kept searching.

As chance would have it, Amber approached her cabin door and stopped; she heard things being tossed around inside her room. Amber pulled her pistol from under her dress then opened the door and looked in cautiously. Seeing Dexter, Amber almost shot him, but with great self-control, she didn't pull the trigger. She yelled, "What are you doing in my cabin, you vermin of a worthless snake?" Dexter turned and saw the pistol in Amber's hand and knew he was in big trouble as he told her a lie: "Amber, this your cabin? I thought it was someone else's."

"You know something, Dexter? You're a terrible liar, and I ought to pull this trigger and put you out of your misery."

Dexter knew she'd be able to pull the trigger before he could stab her with his knife. Dexter hoped he could walk out of her cabin alive as he started toward the cabin door.

Amber pointed her pistol at Dexter and told him, "You try one more stupid thing like this again, Dexter, I'll put a bullet in the middle of your head to fill the empty spot where a brain should be. Got it, mister?"

Dexter nervously walked out, replying, "I'll not cross your path again until we reach the island, Amber."

"All right, you get out of my sight and stay out."

In his cabin, Dexter was thinking of the close call he had with Amber. Dexter had been with different women before. *But this Amber takes the cake*, he thought. *She's beautiful but deadly like a venomous snake.* From here on, Dexter watched his step; he loved life too much.

When the ship was anchored at Frenchy's island, Dexter and Amber disembarked and took a carriage to Frenchy's home. Amber explained to Dexter, "When we arrive at Frenchy's home, you stay silent and say nothing."

Dexter was getting real bored of Amber and her bossy ways he couldn't wait until he could cut the apron strings that tied them together.

When Amber and Dexter arrived at Frenchy's home, Amber knocked on the door. Frenchy opened the door and had a shocked look on his face. "Amber, what are you doing back here?"

"Don't look as though the world is coming to an end, Frenchy. Ask us in."

"Of course, Amber, come in, won't you?"

Amber introduced Dexter while they entered.

"Frenchy, I'd like for you to meet my associate, Dexter."

"Any friend of Amber's is a friend of mine. You two have a seat while I have my manservant get us some refreshments."

Booker now served the refreshments, and Frenchy asked, "What are you doing here, Amber?"

Taking a drink, Amber replied, "What's wrong with me being back, Frenchy?"

"Have you forgotten about Franchesskah? The authorities are still looking for you, Amber, and if they find you here, it'll implicate me into the murder as well."

"Relax, Frenchy," Amber said, taking another drink. "And don't get yourself all worked up."

"But, Amber, it's dangerous, you being here."

106
A New Plan in the Works
1673

"All I need is to borrow your ship one last time, Frenchy, and I and Dexter will be gone."

"Again, Amber, no, I can't and won't!" Frenchy said, putting his drink down. "Amber, I've paid the dept I've owed you, and if you are caught here in my house, we both will be sent to jail."

"I see, Frenchy," Amber said, setting her drink down. "You're refusing to help an old friend."

"It's not that I don't want to, Amber, but when you murdered Franchesskah, well, that changed things."

"Murder, Frenchy, isn't that a little strong?"

"What I meant was—"

"I know what you meant, Frenchy."

"Please, Amber, it isn't what you think."

"We'll be leaving, Frenchy, so don't worry. I wouldn't want you to go to jail because of me."

Frenchy, nervous a cat, wasn't only scared of going to jail but feared Amber as well.

Amber and Dexter got into their carriage and went back to the town. Closing the door, Frenchy watched them leave and knew he had to leave this island and go somewhere where Amber could never find him. Frenchy, like Jordan Peron, was now added to Amber's revenge list. Dexter asked Amber while riding in the carriage, "What do we do now, Amber?"

"Shut up, you fool, I'm trying to think," Amber said, being her pleasant self. The carriage arrived back to town and stopped in front of an inn called Rainbow Inn.

"Listen, Dexter, we'll get rooms at this Rainbow Inn, and I'll make new plans."

That night in her room, Amber wasn't only thinking of her change in plans but also filling her plate fast on the people she was going to get even with for turning their back on her.

Amber's first and second choice was Rebekah and Morgan, and then she'd get the rest later. Amber, brushing her hair, said to herself, "Nobody treats me like this and is going to get away with it."

One thing about Amber was she was patient.

The next morning, while Amber and Dexter were eating their breakfast, Dexter asked, "So where do we go from here, Amber?"

"Ask me that again, Dexter, and I'll pull the trigger on my pistol that is pointing at you under the table."

Dexter kept quiet and kept eating his eggs and bacon, hoping he'd be alive to finish them. After breakfast, Amber and Dexter went to a tavern. Amber could think more clearly after she had a little brandy. Amber sat at a table while Dexter went to the bar and got their drinks. Amber, sitting and waiting, overheard two men talking.

"All right, Phil, we'll get a load shipment to ship somewhere. I'm going to talk to the man that runs the docks here and find out if he'll hire us to deliver some cargo to another port, so keep your shirt on. I'll be back in an hour."

After the one man left, Amber ventured over to the table where the other man was sitting. Amber asked, "May I sit?"

The man named Phil said, "Where did you come from?"

"I was sitting over at the next table and overheard you two men talking and was curious about your problem."

"So you think we have a problem, miss?" Phil said, taking a drink and staring at Amber from head to toe.

"Yes, I do," Amber said. "And if you'd put your eyes back into your head and stop your drooling all over me, I might have a job for you and your friend."

"Now what makes you think we need a job, miss?"

"I overheard you and your friend talking, so let's stop the lying and get down to business." Amber sat down.

"You're right, miss. We're looking for some cargo to deliver to another port but, so far, no luck."

"When your friend returns and if you still need work come to the Rainbow Inn at the end of town and knock on door number 5, that's my room. I'll have a job for you."

Amber went back to the table where Dexter with her brandy was waiting. Amber, drinking the brandy down, said to Dexter, "I'm going back to my room, Dexter, and you to stay out of trouble."

An hour passed when there was a knock on Amber's door. Amber, with her pistol under her dress, opened the door. The man spoke, "My partner told me you had a job for us."

Amber said with a smile, "Yes, go back to the tavern and wait. I'll be there in ten minutes and give you the details."

Later that evening, Amber told the two men, Phil and Carter, what she needed them for.

"Are you crazy, Ms. Stewart? Do you think we can just sail our ship into Pirates Cove?"

"I know the code signals that'll allow your ship permission to enter, and the man, Jake, who runs the post there will think you need supplies."

"You're out of your mind, Ms. Stewart, good day!" Carter and Phil stood up and were ready to walk away.

"I'll pay you five gold crowns for your hire," Amber said.

"It could be a hundred, Ms. Stewart, and the answer still is no!"

Amber said angrily to Carter, "If you turn this offer down now and walk out, don't decide later you want the job."

Looking over at Carter, Phil said, "We've no choice, Carter. We need that gold to pay Conner's what we owe him."

"Conner's will have to wait, Phil. What good will it do us to be blown out of the waters when those cannons at Pirates Cove start firing on us?"

"She'll give us the code signals to enter, Carter. I say let's take the job."

Carter, his jaw muscles twitching, said, "This is against my better judgment, Phil, but we have to pay Conner's. We're between a rock and hard place."

Sitting back down, Phil and Carter said, "Ms. Stewart, you win. What's our job in all this?"

Amber motioned for Dexter to come to the table and bring her brandy. "This is Dexter," Amber said. Dexter sat while Amber explained all that had to be done.

The next day, the ship called the *Drake* was sailing to Pirates Cove, but before the *Drake* arrived there, the ship stopped at a small port with only three buildings on the whole island. This is where Amber was let off, and she'd wait here for the *Drake*'s return. The *Drake* would return in three days if things went according to plan. Until then, Amber would have to make do at this little port. Fortunately for Amber, she found some people who needed money and let her stay with them. Giving the old couple several pieces of silver, Amber was given a small cot in the back room. One thing about this place was that Amber was in no danger, the old man was at least a hundred years old, and the woman wasn't far behind. Amber hoped they wouldn't die on her before she left. This—being below Amber's dignity—was where she ate and slept for three days or more waiting for the *Drake*'s return.

107
THE *DRAKE* AT THE COVE
1673

Dexter's job when the *Drake* sailed into the cove was to talk with the princess and Jack and persuade them to go to the little island where Amber was waiting.

At this time, several hundred miles from the *Drake*, the *Black Rose* was locked up to a French passenger ship and Rebekah's men were having a good old sword fight with the sailors on board. The captain of the ship named Mica Sims was in a sword fight with the princess.

"I don't know who you think you are, Princess, coming aboard my ship and raiding it, but this'll be the last ship you're going to steal from." Keeping his word, Mica thrust his sword blade toward Rebekah's middle and tried to run her through.

Rebekah, using her sword blade, connected with Mica's sword blade and, with a twist of her wrist, flung Mica's sword from his hand. Mica, seeing his sword lying on the ship's floor, knew he was at Rebekah's mercy. Rebekah forced the captain backward up against a standing wall on the ship.

"Order your men to lay their swords down, Captain, if you want to see the sunrise tomorrow." The point of Rebekah's sword was within inches of the captain's throat. The captain was boxed in, and his men were losing. Captain Sims yelled to his men, "Lay down your swords, and that's an order."

Unfortunately for half of his men, the order was too late. They lay dead on the deck of the ship. The men stopped, including Rebekah's. Joe rounded the sailors up against a wall while Marty and Rex held their pistols on them. Rebekah's other men—Pete, Randy, and Brad—went below to the hold of the ship to find the gold bars.

The captain looked around his ship and saw seven of his sailors dead and others wounded. With a loud cry, he shouted out to Rebekah, "Why do you do this thing, you evil young girl?"

Pulling her knife from her boot, Rebekah walked over to the captain. Rebekah put the blade of her knife up against the captain's throat and said, "If I were the evil person you thought I was, this knife would already be sticking in you, Captain."

The captain said, "Nothing you can say will change my mind against what you and your men did here on this ship."

Rebekah said, justifying herself, "Just like England, Captain, sending a man to murder my father and take his kingdom away, and you call that defending the crown. Well, Captain, I call that evil too." Rebekah slid her knife back into her right boot.

"I know nothing of your father, Princess, but what I do know is what you've done here is wrong and the blood of these men will be on your hands."

"Wrong, Captain, the blood of these men will be on England's hands. I'll continue to raid England's ships, and as long as France and the other countries continue to be allies with England, they'll be raided as well."

The captain yelled out to Rebekah again, "You're an evil woman, and I'll live for the day when you hang from the gallows by your neck until dead."

Jack said, reporting to Rebekah, "The gold has been loaded, Princess, and we're ready to leave."

Before Rebekah jumped onto the railing of her ship to leave, she told the captain, "Captain, you just got through saying you'll live long enough to see me hang by my neck until dead."

The captain replied, "Yes, and it'll be soon, I'm sure."

"Then we're much alike, aren't we, Captain?"

"I don't know what you mean, Princess."

"I'm raiding ships in vengeance for my father's murder, and you call me an evil woman. But you, on the other hand, would like to see me hang. I call that barbaric, Captain, so who's the evil one?"

Rebekah jumped onto the railing of the *Black Rose* and waved her sword into the air as the ship sailed away.

Captain Sims stood by the railing of his ship watching the *Black Rose* sail away and knew down deep the princess was right in what she had told him. The first officer asked, "Do we fire on her, sir?"

Captain Sims hesitated for a moment then said, "Yes, fire all cannons until she goes under. We might as well live up to our evil ways and destroy her and her ship if possible."

The captain waited to hear the cannons fire, but the cannons were silent.

The first officer named Mike come running back on deck, telling Captain Sims after catching his breath, "Captain Sims, I don't know how to explain this, sir, the four cannons on the right side of the ship are no longer there."

Captain Sims said, puzzled, "What do you mean no longer there?"

"Just what I said, sir."

"Then what happened to them, Mike?"

"I think the princess's men pushed the cannons through the cannon ports and into the sea."

Captain Sims watched as the *Black Rose* sailed farther out to sea.

"Well, Captain, what do we do now?"

"Keep the ship on course, Mike, and we'll deliver the passengers to their destination, and then I'll make out a report of this incident. How are the passengers, Mike? Were there any robbed of their belongings?"

"You know something, Captain? I was just thinking about that, sir, and not one passenger was harmed or robbed by those pirates."

"That's unusual, isn't it, Mike?"

"This princess isn't the pirate. I would say she was supposed to be, Captain. Why raid a ship and only take gold that belongs to France and not take the passenger's valuables?"

"That I'm going to look into when I visit England in two weeks, Mike." Captain Sims couldn't get what Rebekah told him out of his mind. It was etched in deep, and it gave him something to think about. The *Black Rose* was sailing to an island to bury the gold and then back to Pirates Cove. At this time, the ship called the *Drake* was waiting at Pirates Cove.

Dexter had just walked through the doors at the trading post. Jake stood at the bar and said, "What are you doing back here after the princess kicked you off of her ship, Dexter?"

"I'd like to talk to her, Jake, is she around?" Dexter said with his usual sneaky looks.

"The *Black Rose* is on another raid, Dexter. I don't know when she'll be back."

"I'll wait, Jake. All I have is time." Dexter went back out the door and back to the ship.

Dexter, as he returned to the *Drake*, told Carter and Phil, "We'll have to wait. The princess is on another raid and will return soon."

On board the *Black Rose*, Rebekah was standing by the railing of the ship late that evening like always. Jack causally strolled up and asked, "How are you doing, Princess?"

"Why do you ask me that, Jack?" Rebekah said, thinking about what Captain Sims called her today.

"I was just wondering how you took the words the captain spoke to you this morning."

"About me being evil and the blood on my hands."

"Yes, Rebekah, those words."

108
THE DECISION
1673

"Yes, Jack, those words do bother me. Is that what you wanted to hear?"

"I'm not here to condemn you, Rebekah. I stand by your side and support you, and so if they accuse you, then I'm also guilty."

Rebekah spoke back boldly, "Guilty? I'll tell you who's guilty, Jack—England who sent a man to murder my father who had done no wrong to anyone, and you think I feel guilty for avenging his murder? Wrong, Jack, I'll continue to raid their ships until they've paid or have arrested Roy Jenson for my father's brutal murder!" Rebekah was upset and went to her cabin.

Jack felt Rebekah's pain, but knowing Rebekah, she would overcome her emotions and be herself in a few days. Back in her cabin, Rebekah went over to her bed and pulled her father's picture from under her pillow. Looking at it, she said, "Oh, Father, am I wrong in what I'm doing?" Rebekah knew she could never rest until this nightmare of her father's death was finally avenged.

Another day passed on the *Black Rose*, and after the gold was buried, the *Black Rose* was just a few hours from sailing into the cove. On board the *Drake*, Carter and Phil were discussing something similar to what Rebekah and Jack were discussing a day before.

"I don't know about this, Phil, setting this girl they call the princess up for the kill."

"She's just another pirate, Carter, and so are her men. Something else, Carter, England would pay us a hefty reward if they knew we helped get rid of the Princess Pirate and her crew."

"I guess, Phil, but I still think this isn't right. The princess who I've never seen should have a fighting chance and not have to die this way. I'll be glad when this is over, Phil/ I feel like a backstabber and a trader."

109
THE PRINCESS IS ON HER WAY
1673

AFTER A LONG sail and another victory, the *Black Rose* sailed into the cove. Standing on deck, Carter yelled over to Phil, "That must be the princess's ship sailing into the cove. Go and get Dexter."

The *Black Rose* settled into her anchoring position several yards from the waterfall, and her sails were raised except for the sail showing the black rose; it was never raised.

Dexter, being alerted, was in a rowboat rowing over to the post. He was going to wait inside the post for the princess and Jack to come walking in. His job was to trick Rebekah and Jack into coming to the island where Amber will have a trap waiting for them.

On deck, Jack asked Randy, "What about that ship sitting on the other side of the cove, Randy, have you ever seen it before?"

"I haven't a clue, Jack. I've never seen that ship before."

Coming from below deck, Rebekah saw the unknown ship and asked about it, "Looks like we have an unknown visitor, Jack. Do you recognize the ship?"

"Sorry, Princess, neither the men nor I have seen this ship before."

"One way to find out who it belongs to, Jack, is go over to the post and ask Jake."

Rebekah and Jack rowed over to the post, and when they entered through the door, Dexter was sitting where Jack always sits when he and Rebekah are together.

Jack said, "What are you doing back here, Dexter?"

Leaning back in the chair, Dexter said smugly, "I've missed my old friends and thought I'd come back for a visit."

A Leopard Doesn't Change His Spots
1673

Wanting to throw Dexter into the cove, Jack said, "If you arrived on that ship sitting out in the cove, Dexter, you better get back on it and be on your way if you don't want a cold bath in the cove."

"I see you haven't changed one little bit, Jack. You're untrusting and unfriendly as ever."

Jack started his move toward Dexter when Rebekah held her hand up, saying, "Before you beat Dexter to an inch of his life, Jack, let's find out what he's doing here."

"Princess, that's what I've always liked about you—your curiosity."

"You've two minutes, Dexter. Tell us why you're here and make it good," Rebekah said as she sat down waiting to hear his answer.

Playing it cool, Dexter said, "I have some information, Princess, that would be very valuable to you."

"Yes, Dexter, keep talking. I'm listening!"

"It involves some of your buried treasures you thought no one else could ever find."

Rebekah looked over at Jack. "Keep talking, Dexter. I'm listening."

Dexter had Rebekah and Jack on the ropes now, their attention. Dexter was now dealing with strength.

"Princess, there's a little island just two days' sail from here. I think you know the one, a little island with a little port called Clover Island. You do remember it, don't you?"

Rebekah remembered it all right. Every hillside was covered in clover, and everywhere you walked, there was clover. Rebekah had two chests of gold coins buried on that island. Of course, Dexter knew that too, but he couldn't find them if his life depended on it. Amber also knew. Thanks to Dexter's big mouth. That's why she chose this particular island for her trap, a small island with a few inhabitants and a great place for a murder.

"All right, Dexter, you have my attention. What about that island?"

"I was there four days ago. I was in a little tavern and overheard five men talking. They've heard of you, the Princess Pirate, being there before and put two and two together."

Jack got impatient and said, "Get on with it, Dexter, and stop beating around the bush."

Dexter knew better than to push, so he got to the point. "Princess, they've found one of the chests with gold in it, and since they found one chest full of gold, they figured why couldn't there be more chests buried somewhere on the island."

Thinking this could be true, Rebekah said, "All right, Dexter, why tell me this? What's in it for you?"

Dexter was thinking he had the upper hand and was upping the price to get something for himself. Why let Amber have it all? "Two things, Princess. I want a big reward of gold and a good commanding position on your ship."

"I already have Jack as my first mate, and Joe fills in the third position, so I don't need you for that, Dexter."

"You're the captain, Princess. Surely, you can find a place for me."

Jack said, "How about the bottom of the cove, Dexter?"

"That's not going to get my cooperation, Jack."

Rebekah said, "Aren't you forgetting something, Dexter?"

"What's that, Princess?"

"You told me everything I need to know. I don't need you for anything else. So good-bye and bad luck."

"I've heard, Princess, you'd never break a promise or your word. I guess I heard wrong," Dexter said, not giving up. "I've made no promises to you, Dexter, or given you my word on anything."

"In a way, you have, Princess. I came here in good faith to you and told you what's happening to your gold. If you leave without some kind of reward for the loyalty I've given you, you'd be breaking your loyalty for my services." Dexter was lazy but also had a sharp mind.

Jack spoke up, "Rebekah, that's nonsense, and you owe Dexter nothing."

Rebekah, still thinking like a princess, told Dexter, "When you prove to me about what you have said and identify the men who took my gold, I'll reward you, Dexter, with enough gold you'll be set for life."

Grinning from ear to ear, Dexter said, "You have a deal, Princess."

"What about the ship in the cove, Dexter, who does it belong too?"

"That ship is here for supplies and will be leaving tonight. I stowed away on board until they found me. Before they threw me over the ships railing, I told them about Pirates Cove and where they could get supplies with less gold, so they let me live, and here I am." Dexter could think up a lie faster than a rock rolling down a hill.

"Dexter."

"Yes, Princess."

"We're sailing out this evening, so be on my ship in one hour."

After taking down his drink, Dexter said, "I'll be there, Princess."

The arguing between Rebekah and Jack filled the air all the way back to the ship about Dexter. When Jack and Rebekah entered into her cabin, Jack was saying, "Rebekah, you know a leopard doesn't change its spots, and you know this is a trap of some kind."

Double Betrayal
1673

"Maybe, Jack, but what if Dexter is telling the truth? There's one million in gold bullion on that island, and there's no one taking it from me."

"Let them have it, Rebekah. It's not worth the chance you'll be taking," Jack pleaded.

"Jack, if these men get away with this and spread the news how they found our gold, it'll start a search by pirates from one end of the high seas to the other. I can't let that happen."

"It was just by accident this happened, Rebekah. It'd never happen again in a million years, not the way you had those chests buried."

"Maybe so, Jack, but I'm going to Clover Island to see for myself. The gold they found maybe someone else's gold and not ours. But I have to check where we buried the chests to make sure."

Having a hard time denying Rebekah's logic, Jack gave in, saying, "You have some valid points, Rebekah, and you have my full support."

Dexter went back to the *Drake* and gave Carter and Phil their new orders: "Sail back to Clover Island and tell Amber to have her trap ready. The princess and Jack should arrive there in two to three days."

Dexter went back to the post and waited. While drinking his rum, he thought of an idea: betray Amber for the humiliation she had put him through. Dexter knew Amber's setup plan and how she was going to kill the Princess and Jack, so right before Amber was to pull it off, he'd warn the princess and she'd be so grateful she'd reward him with all the gold he could possibly desire. Pouring himself some more rum, Dexter was thinking how he was going to have it made for life. Dexter was going to burn the candle at both ends and get even with Amber at the same time.

On deck, Jack was asking, "Where's Dexter, Joe?"

Joe said, "Who?"

"They didn't tell you, Joe?"

"Nobody told me anything, Jack. What about Dexter?"

Jack explained the details and ordered Joe to stay away from Dexter until this was all over.

"Can I stay behind, Jack?" Joe asked.

"Why, Joe, you afraid of Dexter?" "

Yes, I am, Jack. I'm afraid of running him through with my sword and upsetting the princess." Joe sent Marty to the post to get Dexter. Marty was the only man on the ship who liked Dexter and would bring him back to the ship alive.

Entering the post, Marty yelled over to Dexter, "We're ready to set sail. I was sent here to tell you, Dexter."

"So they sent you, Marty, huh?"

"Yea! Joe said something about me being the only man who would bring you back alive."

Dexter understood what Joe meant, but Marty just thought of it being a joke.

"Let's go, Marty. The princess is waiting."

Out to sea and on her way, the *Black Rose* was sailing to Clover Island. The *Drake* would be several hours ahead of the *Rose*, and that would give Amber enough time to set up her trap. A few days later, the *Drake* was docked at the little port of Clover Island.

Amber was glad to see that ship sail into the docks. Back on board, Amber went to her cabin and had hot water delivered so she could take a hot perfumed bath. The clothes she wore were smelly and dirty, and she had those burned. After her bath, she went to the galley for a decent hot meal.

Phil was there, asking, "How did things go living with that old couple, Ms. Stewart?"

After putting down some eggs and bacon, Amber said, "It was like living in a graveyard with those two."

Phil laughed.

"You may think it's funny, Phil, but I'm glad to be among the living once again."

Amber kept eating while Phil told her the princess was on her way to the island.

"How far is her ship from the island, Phil?"

"Hours, I'd say, Ms. Stewart."

"Good, when I've finished eating, we'll go up to the hill on the other side of the island. There's where the princess's men will bury her when you and Carter have done your job."

112
Ms. Stewart, We Could've Saved Him
1673

"Ms. Stewart, do you think Dexter will be able to convince the princess and her men to be where they're supposed to be when we're ready?"

"Dexter's stupid, Phil, but one thing I do know about him, when it comes to getting revenge on someone such as the princess and Jack Reese, who he blames for being tossed from her ship, he'll do his job and do it well."

Several hours later, the *Drake* was anchored on the other side of the island.

Carter said, "Phil, you go and get Ms. Stewart and tell her we're sitting on the other side of the island and we're waiting for her."

Phil knocked on Amber's cabin door. Amber said, "You may enter."

Phil said as he entered, "Ms. Stewart, the ship is anchored on the other side of the island, and we're waiting for your next orders."

Amber left with Phil and asked, "Why are you staring at me that way?"

"You're wearing a dress and high-heeled shoes, Ms. Stewart."

"Yes, I always wear dresses no matter where I go. So stop asking stupid questions and let's get going."

"Ms. Stewart, we'll be climbing a hill with rocks and loose dirt. Shouldn't you wear something more appropriate?"

"I said stop asking stupid questions and let's go!"

Not long into the climb up the hill, Amber's feet started to hurt, and they had to stop several times for her to rest. Then they would travel onward. This wasn't only a stubborn woman, Carter and Phil thought, but one with determination and an evil heart.

At this time, the *Black Rose* was docked at the port of Clover Island. Jack said, "All right, Dexter, where do we go from here?"

"When we get off of the ship, just follow me, and I'll take you to the other side of the island where those men are settled in their camp. Then the princess can take over from there."

Jack had Pete, Curt, and Brad to stay on the *Rose* and guard her until they returned. In case of a trap, Joe and the others were best with the swords and pistols if they got into a war with the men Dexter spoke of.

While on the other side of the island, Amber, Carter, Phil, and three of the ship's crew were going up a hill to lay an ambush for Rebekah and her men. When they reached the top, Amber cut her ankle on a sharp rock. She yelled out in pain when Carter reached down to grab her ankle. With Carter's hand around Amber's ankle, she shouted out, "Let go and get your filthy hands off of my ankle."

"I was just seeing how bad you were cut, Ms. Stewart. You don't want to get an infection."

"I'll take care of my ankle, Mr. Carter, you and your men get the job done I brought you here to do, understand?"

"Yes, Ms. Stewart, I do and will be glad when this is all over and we part company."

Reaching the top of the hill, Carter and his men were settling in behind some rocks. There they would wait for Rebekah and her men to walk out into the opening, and then they'd start firing their pistols and kill Rebekah and all her men.

It wouldn't be long now. Jack and Rebekah were almost to the area where Amber's ambush was waiting. Carter was looking through his spyglass and saw them walking up the side of the hill toward them. "They're almost here, Ms. Stewart."

Making sure this goes off without a hitch, Amber said, "Listen to me, Mr. Carter, and listen good. I want to get the princess first, you got that?"

"Yes, Ms. Stewart, I got it."

Jack stopped to wipe the sweat from his brow and, while observing their surroundings, asked Dexter, "How much farther do we have to go?"

"The men's camp is just right over that hill, Jack."

Looking around the hill side, Jack was thinking to himself, *What a good place to be ambushed from.* Jack continued cautiously up the hill leading the way with Rebekah and her men behind her. Dexter, knowing what awaits, was lingering farther behind.

While Carter and Phil's men waited behind the rocks, a bee was buzzing around one of the men. He tried waving the bee off, but with all that clover and honeysuckle covering the rocks, the bee was trying to get at it. The man tried to shoo the bee away, and when he did, the bee stung him.

The man cried out, and when he moved, the sun's light reflected off his pistol barrel. Marty, being at a certain place on the hillside, saw something flashing back into his face and yelled over to Jack.

Jack stopped and said, "What is it, Marty?"

"I saw something flashing at me from the top of the hill."

Jack yelled, "Get down everybody." Jack grabbed Rebekah and pulled her to the ground and sheltered her body with his. Carter saw them go down and ordered his men. "Start firing." The pistols were going off one by one. Marty got shot in his left arm, and Randy got shot in his right side.

Jack ordered, "Fire back at anything that moves up there!"

Rebekah's men were firing back, and the lead pellets were bouncing off the rocks with every ping. Dexter's plan failed, and he had to get out of there if he wanted to live. The man who would put a sword through him would be Joe, and Dexter knew it.

Dexter wasted no time; he snuck around some rocks and headed up the hill and back to where Amber and the men she hired would be. Before Dexter got there, Carter yelled over to Amber, "This ambushed has failed, Ms. Stewart, and we better get back to the ship."

Amber ordered Carter, "Stay and fight, you coward."

"We can't, Ms. Stewart. We have no more gunpowder and lead pellets."

"You fool, why didn't you bring more?"

"This was just to be an ambush, not an all-out war. You can stay if you want to, Ms. Stewart, but my men and I are leaving."

Amber was foiled again as she left with Carter and his men. Carter, with his men, and Amber were just about to the longboat when Dexter came running over the hill. He yelled, "Wait for me."

When they were all in the boat, Carter cast off. He didn't hear or see Dexter coming down the hill. About this time, Rebekah and her men were topping the hill. Jack continued down with Rebekah, and the rest of her men followed.

Dexter yelled out again as the boat was several yards out, "Wait, wait!" Dexter said, running down the hill and looking back, seeing Jack and the others coming. Dexter dove into the swirling water and started swimming toward the boat that Amber and the men were in. When Jack, Rebekah, and her men stopped at the edge of the shore, they watched as Amber got away. Rebekah recognized Amber all right, and so did Jack.

Dexter was swimming up to the boat and was out of breath. He put his hands on the edge of the boat. Looking up at Amber, Dexter stuck his one hand up, asking Amber, "Please grab my hand, Amber. I can't hold on much longer."

Looking down at Dexter, Amber said nothing. With the heel of her shoe, she ground it into Dexter's other hand. Dexter screamed with pain, he let go, and drowned in the swirling water that took him down.

Rebekah watched what Amber did and lowered her head, not believing she could be so heartless. Joe lowered his head. Even Dexter didn't deserve to die that way.

On the small boat, Carter shouted out at Amber when he said, "Ms. Stewart, we could've saved him!"

"Keep rowing, Mr. Carter. I paid you for your help, not a lesson in humanity."

"I've never struck a woman before, Ms. Stewart, but I should throw you overboard and let you drown with, Dexter."

Amber pulled her pistol from under her dress and said, "One more step towards me, Mr. Carter, and you'll join Dexter, not me, so get us back to your ship and away from here, understand?"

Carter, seeing Amber's finger tightening around the trigger, knew she wouldn't hesitate to shoot.

Carter and Phil will be glad when they dump this vicious woman off somewhere, and they hoped they'd never cross paths with her ever again.

Jack told Rebekah. "Princess, nothing more we can do here. We best get Randy and Marty back to the ship before they bleed to death."

Randy was waiting at the top of the hill as they started back. Rebekah looked at the blood that was all over Marty's arm and asked, "You think you can make it back to the ship all right, Marty?"

"It's just a small lead pellet, Princess. It doesn't weigh much, and I'll be fine."

Rebekah just grinned and followed her men back to the ship.

Several days later, Amber was back at Sailor's Warf and was getting low on money. While there, she'd have to find some way of getting money together and continue her vengeance against Rebekah.

Back at Pirates Cove, things were back to normal. Every one of Rebekah's men were fine; even Marty was arm wrestling with two of Jake's men, taking them both down.

That night on the *Black Rose*, Jack was talking to Rebekah at their usual spot by the railing.

"I don't know, Jack. This Amber must be stopped."

"This would take time away from raiding ships, Princess."

"I know, Jack, but you never know when and where she'll turn up or who she has working for her to kill me or my men."

"You're pretty concerned about your men, aren't you, Princess?"

"Yes, Jack, I am, Marty and Randy could've been killed in that ambush a few days ago just because Amber has it in for me." Rebekah kissed Jack good night and went to her cabin. She had a lot to think about.

PART X

113
Jack Returns Home
1673

Back at the cove, Rebekah's men were getting restless and fighting amongst themselves. Sam and Louie were exchanging blows when Jack ran over to break it up. During the struggle, Jack was struck in the face from a passing blow from Sam and was knocked backward. Jack, being infuriated, returned blows, knocking Sam and Louie both down to the deck of the ship.

Jack grabbed both Sam and Louie by their collars. Sam was trying to strike Louie again when Rebekah happened by and got too close to the men. Unfortunately for Rebekah, Sam's fist struck her in the lip, knocking her down. Rebekah sat on the deck floor, looking up with a bleeding lip. Jack quickly reached down and helped Rebekah back to her feet.

"You hurt, Princess?" Jack asked.

Feeling a little dizzy from being struck, Rebekah said, "Only my pride, Jack."

"Let's go and see Micky, Princess, and let him take a look at that lip."

This wasn't good as Rebekah's men stood there in shock over what had just happened.

Jake, being on board the ship, watched what happened and shook his head while standing there.

Jake, being upset, said, "You men aren't good enough to serve under the princess. And another thing, I hope she gives up pirating and let all of you numskulls serve under a pirate captain that wouldn't think twice about running you through with his sword for doing something so stupid!" Jake would see about Rebekah later; he went back to the post in disgust.

Joe turned toward Louie and the rest and said, "Let's go back to work. Jack will fill us in about the princess later."

They all mumbled amongst themselves while going back to work. Pete brought Rebekah a wet cloth to put on her lip. He knocked on her cabin door. Taking care of Rebekah, Micky said, "Come in."

Pete entered, saying, "Here, Micky, this wet cloth might help take down the swelling."

"Here, Miss Rebekah, lay this against your lip," Micky said, handing her the cloth.

Rebekah put the wet cloth up against her lip and went. "Ow! That smarts," she said.

"I'm very sorry about what happened back on deck, Princess," Jack apologized.

"Not as sorry as I am, Jack." Rebekah was saying "Ow" while applying the cloth back to her bleeding lip.

Micky said, "Better let me look at that lip again, Miss Rebekah. You might need some stitches."

Giving Micky a sad look, Rebekah said, "Well, Micky, will I need any stitches in my lip?"

"It doesn't look too bad to me, Miss Rebekah. Just keep a clean damp cloth on your lip for a while longer until the bleeding stops."

Jack left with Micky out the door and asked him secretly, "Tell me the truth, Micky. What do you really think?"

"I told Miss Rebekah the truth, Jack, about no stitches. The real problem isn't her lip—it's her pride." Micky went back to the galley.

Rebekah Regains Her Self-Confidence
1673

Jack went back to Rebekah's cabin and tapped on her door.

"Yes, who is it?" Rebekah asked.

Jack opened the door and said, "I'm going back to work, Princess. Is there anything I can do for you?"

"No, Jack, I just want to be alone for a while to think." Rebekah stood with her back toward Jack, staring out her back ship windows. Jack left, knowing Rebekah's pride was hurt.

On deck, her men were into it again, blaming one another for what happened to the princess.

"I ought to shove your brains through your skull, Sam," Randy said, threatening him.

"Go ahead and try, Randy," Sam said, pulling his knife and waving it in front of Randy's face. Jack walked up and couldn't believe this was happening all over again as he ordered Sam to put the knife away. The men stared Sam down until he put his knife back into his boot.

"You men better listen, and listen good!" Jack said with his face twitching. "I don't know what the princess is going to do now. I left her in her cabin thinking, and what she's thinking about, she wouldn't tell me. My advice to you men is this, go back to work and stop fighting. You got that? That especially means you, Sam."

Jack, standing face to face with Sam, said again. "Well, Sam, do you understand, or do I have to knock it into your head?"

Sam never messed with Jack as far as an actual fight of any kind, and he just said yeah to Jack. Jack went back to the post to talk with Jake about what happened and to get some advice.

Jake was in his office when Jack knocked.

"Come in," Jake said.

Jack opened the door and entered. "Sit, Jack, and have a drink," Jake told him. Jake was having more than one drink after what happen on the ship.

Jack sat and said. "Jake, I need some advice."

After a strong downing of some rum, Jake said to Jack. "Fire away!"

"The situation that happened on the ship with the princess has her a little jolted and disturbed."

"It does seem a little strange, Jack, now doesn't it?"

Jack, being confused, asked, "What do you mean by that, Jake?"

"Simple, Jack. The princess can cut down her opponent with a sword better than any man or pirate I've ever seen since I've run this little getaway for pirates. It's her pride, Jack, her pride."

"Yes, I see your point, Jake, and that's what Micky said also. It would put doubt into her mind about her authority over her men."

"Precisely, Jack, that's what I'm saying," Jake said, pouring himself some more rum.

"Have any suggestions, Jake?" Jack said, seeking an answer that would help Rebekah regain herself confidence.

"The princess needs a vacation, Jack, a real vacation, and go somewhere and forget about England and raiding of ships for a while."

"Yes, Jake, why didn't I think of that, and I know just the place, Regend."

"Regend, Jack? I don't think I've ever heard of Regend before, Jack. Where would that be?" Jake belched after drinking down his third mug of rum.

"My hometown, Jake. That's where I was born and also my brother, Chad. I think the peace and quiet would do the princess well, and I could see some old friends of mine also."

"Aren't you forgetting something, Jack? Like you're still wanted for killing a man in Emerson?"

"The princess is worth the risk, Jake. She needs this, and I'd like to see some people that I haven't seen in ten years, but there's only one problem, Jake."

"What's that, Jack?"

"I don't know if Rebekah will go."

"One way to find out, Jack, is to ask her," Jake said, belching again.

Jack was back on the *Black Rose* and went straight to Rebekah's cabin when he met Micky coming out of her cabin.

"How's the princess, Micky? Will she talk to anybody right now?"

"Something changed, Jack. She's eating my soup, and there's only a small bruise on her lip. She seems in a good mood, but that's towards me. I wasn't involved in the ship's brawl, if you remember."

"Wish me luck, Micky." Jack knocked on Rebekah's cabin door.

"Come in," she said.

Jack entered, saying, "Princess, I thought I would check on your condition. How are you feeling?"

"There's a small bruise on my lip and a little swelling, but I'm going to live according to what Micky told me." Rebekah smiled.

"Does your lip hurt much, Princess?"

"Only when I smile, Jack." She went "ow" again when she grinned.

"I have a great idea, Princess."

"Yes, Jack, I'm listening."

"A vacation! What do you think? A vacation for the princess. How about it? It'll do you good to get away from all of this stress for a while."

"Yes, Jack, that does sound relaxing, doesn't it?" Rebekah grinned and said, "Ow! I have something to do before we leave, Jack."

On deck of the ship, Rebekah had Joe gather all the men together while she stood before them as their captain.

"Can we say something first, Princess?" Troy asked.

"Yes, Troy, you may."

"All of us men have talked and we, well, we, ah..."

"You trying to give me an apology for what happened on the ship earlier, Troy?" Rebekah interrupted.

"Yes, Princess, and you say it so very well." Troy lowered his head.

"I accept your apology, all of you." Rebekah grinned and then went, "Ow!"

Sam turned and walked away, trying to ignore his guilt. "I'm a pirate," he kept telling himself, "and not tied to the Princess's blouse strings." Jack was going after Sam when Rebekah told him, "No!"

"But, Princess, he can't continue to disrespect you in front of the other men."

"It's all right, Jack. This hit on my lip does nothing to make me less than their captain, and I believe Sam down deep feels guilty. After all, he did save my life once."

"When do we leave, Princess?" Jack asked.

"You never told me where we're going, Jack."

"To my home, where I was born, Princess, Regend."

"Is that also where you met Angela and had your first love experience, Jack?" Rebekah was making sure Jack was over Angela, and he himself was sure that's where he wanted to take her.

"Yes, Princess, I'm sure, and you're the girl I love." Jack stared directly into Rebekah's eyes, assuring her that what he told her was true.

Staring back deep into Jack's eyes, Rebekah knew he was telling her the truth.

"How many men do we take with us to man the ship, Jack?"

"Joe, Louie, Pete, Brett, Curt, Marty, Randy, Brad, Smitty, and Micky should be enough, Princess, don't you think?"

115
NOT ALWAYS SMOOTH SAILING
1673

"You want to leave Sam, Rex, and Troy here at the cove, Jack?"

"Yes because I want this trip to be without any trouble. Besides, Troy and Rex are man enough to watch Sam and keep him out of trouble."

"I agree, Jack. Sam can keep close to his firewater and won't be complaining."

Watching the *Black Rose* sail out of the cove, Sam asked, "Troy, why aren't we leaving on the ship also?"

"The princess is going on a vacation, Sam, not a raid. Her and Jack took the only men she'd need to sail the *Black Rose* to where they are going."

Sam, with this not hitting him right, asked, "Troy, why wasn't I one of them that went?"

"Well, Sam, you're always accusing the men that they aren't real pirates, so the princess felt you'd be out of place if we weren't raiding a ship."

Sam went back to playing pirate poker, feeling that he was being left out of something.

Joe was at the helm of the ship making sure she was sailing toward the port of Regend. In the meantime, Jack was talking with Pete and Curt about the ship's sailing condition when Pete noticed smoke coming from below deck and yells, "Fire on board ship."

Jack ran below deck to see what was happening. Louie goes down after him, and so does Randy.

Smoke was coming from the galley as Jack ran in and saw Micky lying on the ships floor. Jack picked Micky up while Randy checked Rebekah's cabin to see if she was there or hurt. Rebekah was on top deck at this time. Randy, knowing Rebekah was all right, went and helped Louie put out the small fire on the cook stove. Jack laid Micky down on the ship's deck when Rebekah came running over to see what was happening.

Jack was tapping Micky on his cheek to bring him around. Louie and Randy successfully put the fire out and opened every window below deck, including the back windows in Rebekah's cabin, to let the rest of the smoke out.

Micky was coming around and coughing when he opened his eyes.

"You all right, Micky?" Jack was asking as Micky continued to cough.

"Yes," Micky said while rubbing his face and eyes, trying to get himself together.

Louie and Randy were back on deck when Jack asked Micky what happened. Micky said, still coughing, "I don't know exactly, Jack. All I did was put some wood into the stove and lit it. After five minutes, there was all of this smoke coming from the stove as I tried to stop it. I was overcome by the smoke, and I guess I passed out."

Curt went down to the galley to check on the damage and look into the stove. The smell was terrible, but Curt did notice that the flue pipe, which released the burning smoke into the air, was stopped up. Later, when the stove cooled, Curt removed the clog, and things were back to normal. The bad part out of all this was Rebekah's cabin smelled of smoke and she had to sleep in the small cabin in the rear of the ship until Pete and Curt cleaned her cabin. Jack's cabin wasn't too bad, and he slept just fine.

The next day, Jack offered Rebekah his cabin. She refused, telling him, "The little cabin in the back is fine, Jack, and I'm very comfortable sleeping in there."

That night by the railing, Rebekah and Jack were talking.

"Jack, it's been a long time since you've been home and visited Angela's grave?"

"I'll be fine, Princess." Jack then kissed her good night.

Several days later, the *Black Rose* was anchored three miles from Regend Port. The *Black Rose* was flying an English flag, and her sails were also showing English.

Jack was in Rebekah's cabin, helping her to get ready. "Princess, before we get to the town of Regend. You need to buy some new dresses? And since this is a vacation, you should leave your sword here on the ship."

Rebekah, putting her hands on her hips, said, "Anything else, Jack?"

"Yes, Princess, leave your pistol and knife. You won't be needing those either."

Rebekah stared at Jack and said, "I can go with you to Regend, can't I?"

Jack grinned, saying, "I'm sorry, Princess. I haven't been here in so long. I'm a little nervous."

Rebekah reached up and kissed Jack, gently saying, "I understand, Jack, and I'll be wearing my yellow dress to the port, and once there, I'll buy new dresses before we arrive in the town."

Jack remembered his hometown of Regend the way it was when he left ten years ago, but during that time, things have changed and not for the best.

116
STEALING, KILLING, AND BREAKING THE LAW
1673

BEFORE REBEKAH AND Jack left, Rebekah asked Bret and Brad, "Would you two like to go to Regend with Jack and me?"

Joe spoke up, "That's a great idea, Princess. Having them along would be adding safety for you and Jack."

A half hour later, Rebekah and her men were in the port of Regend, and while there, Rebekah went into a shop to buy some new dresses. Brad, while he and the others waited outside, was complaining about Rebekah taking so long. "Brett, I don't know why it takes women so long to buy a dress or two. It seems like they have to try on every dress in the store first."

Then Rebekah walked out wearing a purple dress. Bret and Brad stared at Rebekah, speechless. Jack spoke up, "You were saying, gentlemen?"

Clearing his throat, Brad said, "We better get to the town of Regend before it gets dark."

When the carriage Rebekah and her men were riding arrived into Regend, there was a public hanging going on in the town square. Stepping out of the carriage, they were listening to the constable telling the man sitting on a horse under a tree with a rope around his neck the charges: "Mr. Homes, you've been found guilty of stealing five pistols from the general store, and by my authority of constable, I pronounce you to be hung by the neck until dead."

The wife of the man to be hung pleaded for her husband's life and cried out, "I told you, Constable Madison, my husband was with me that night. He couldn't have stolen those pistols."

"My assistant and the men with him searched your premises, Mrs. Homes, and found one of the pistols hid out in the barn. That's all the proof I need." Constable Madison was now ready to have the man hung.

Rebekah told Jack, "One pistol isn't enough evidence to hang a man, Jack."

Rebekah and her men watched as Constable Madison gave the order for the man's hanging. The hangman slapped the horse on the rear, and when the horse ran, the man sitting on the horse was left hanging from the tree with his legs kicking in the air while the rope around his neck choked him to death.

Rebekah couldn't believe what she was witnessing while yelling out to the constable, "You hung a man on one piece of evidence being proof of his guilt?"

Jack tried to calm Rebekah down, saying, "This isn't the time or the place, Rebekah."

"But, Jack, they just hung a man not knowing for sure he was guilty."

The constable with two men holding pistols walked over and confronted Rebekah. "Who do you think you are trying to interfere with the law?"

"I think you should've had more evidence than just one pistol to hang a man," Rebekah said, standing boldly up to the constable.

The constable responded, "That was enough evidence for me. My law is easy and quick. You get convicted of stealing, killing, and breaking the law, you get hung!"

Squinting her eyes, Rebekah said, "What happened to spitting on the wooden walk, Constable?"

"Listen, miss, whoever you are, if you don't leave, I'll arrest you and put you in jail and hold you for contempt, understand?"

Jack grabbed Rebekah by her arm, gave it a tug, and said, "Rebekah, we don't have any weapons to fight with, and his men are holding pistols. We better leave."

Mrs. Homes, who lost her husband, was kneeling down under the tree crying as Rebekah came over and tried to console her. She kept saying over and over, "He was innocent—he didn't do it!" Rebekah knelt down on the dirty ground by Mrs. Homes wearing her new purple dress trying to console her. "There's nothing left you can do. You must go home and rest."

Two town's men cut her husband down from the tree and took him to be buried. Rebekah helped Mrs. Homes to her feet. She asked, "Why are you so concerned about me who you don't even know?"

Rebekah held Mrs. Homes by her hand and said, "I think there was an injustice done here today, and my men and I would like to be of some help to you." While Rebekah and her men took Mrs. Homes to her home, the constable was in his office talking with his assistant.

"I wonder who that young woman with those three men were, Constable Madison."

"I don't know Miller, but if she interferes with another hanging or my law, there's plenty of rope in the general store to hang her, and I don't care how young or pretty she is."

Around midnight in a clearing just outside of town, a wagon covered by a canvas and pulled by two horses pulled up under a tree and stopped. A man stepped down from the wagon and stood by the wagon looking around. The air was chilly that night, and he could see his breath in the night air. He just stood there like he was waiting for someone. Not long after, there was another wagon pulling up, but it was empty. A taller man stepped down off the wagon, and the two men started talking. The second man walked behind the first wagon and pulled up the canvas. "Very good," he said while handing the first man an envelope.

The first man opened the envelope, pulled out a large sum of money, and then counted it. "It's all here," the first man said as they shook hands. Then the second man got into the wagon with the canvas covering it and drove the wagon away. The first man got into the second wagon that was empty and went back into the town of Regend.

The following morning, Jack went to visit Angela's grave. Standing over her grave, Jack said, "I've returned, Angela. It's been a long time, and I've missed you. I've found a new love. Her name is Rebekah. I believe you would approve of her. She and you were alike in many ways. Rest in peace, my love." Jack then laid her favorite colored roses—red, purple, and yellow—down on top of her grave.

Jack turned away with tears in his eyes and then went on from there to Angela's parents' house. Jack walked up to the door and knocked. When the door opened, Angela's mother, with a surprised look on her face, said, "Jack, it is really you?"

"Yes, Mrs. Harris, it is, and how are you and Mr. Harris doing these days?"

"Come in, Jack. It has been what, nine years or ten, I just can't remember."

"It has been ten years, Mrs. Harris," Jack said, entering their house with memories coming back as though it was yesterday.

"It's been that long since we lost Angela." She lowered her head and was about to cry.

Mr. Harris entered the room and said, "I thought I heard your voice Jack, but I had to come in here to make sure. Where have you been all of these years, Jack? You know we wanted you to stay. You were like a son to me and Margret."

"I just couldn't stay after Angela died. I sailed with my brother, Chad, for five years, and now I'm, well, let's just say, I'm a first mate on a ship."

"A naval ship, Jack?" Mr. Harris was asking.

"Not quite, Mr. Harris, but it's a job if you know what I mean."

"Yes, of course, Jack, and what brings you back to Regend?"

"I brought some friends who you'll meet later for a vacation."

"You can bring your friends anytime, Jack. They're welcome just as you are," Mrs. Harris said.

"Do you still have that dress shop, Mrs. Harris?"

"No, no, Jack, I sold that dress shop not too long after Angela died. Without her there helping me, it wasn't the same."

"Something wrong, Jack?" Mr. Harris asked.

"I do have a question."

"Yes, what is it, Jack?"

"I notice things have changed, not just a little, but a lot."

Mr. Harris motioned with his hand, saying, "Let's sit, Jack. Two years after you left, Jack, the town which was very peaceful started to turn violent. Men from the outside brought in gambling and other not-so-desirable things, which I won't go into. We needed someone with guts and authority to put this town back the way it was. We, the townspeople sent someone to represent us and to find someone with those qualities."

Jack said, "Let me guess, the town constable we met coming into town?"

"He's not perfect, Jack, but things are better than they were," Mr. Harris told him.

"I saw how things are better, Mr. Harris. Soon as we got here, they had a town hanging. Do you call that better?" Jack said, sitting there with a discoursing look.

"You don't know how things were, Jack. You weren't living here at the time when women were being harmed and molested, people killed just walking down the street. It wasn't safe anymore living here, and we had to do something."

"This constable of yours just hung a man for one item that wasn't proven he stole."

"He's tough with his justice, Jack, but we can walk down the street at night without fear, don't you understand?"

"Yes, I understand, Mr. Harris. You're safe until you're the one being hung for just one piece of evidence."

"It's not perfect, Jack, but that's all we have." Mr. Harris lowered his head.

Jack stood up and said, "I must be leaving now. My friends must be looking for me. I'll come back tomorrow and introduce you to my friends. I know you'll like them." Jack smiled as he went out the door.

At the same time, Jack was at Angela's parents' house, Rebekah was visiting Mrs. Homes, the widow of the man who was hung in the square the day before. Mrs. Homes was speaking, "My husband was home all day and night with me when the general store was broken into. I testified to that under oath, but Constable Madison wouldn't accept my word by itself and sentenced my husband to hang."

Rebekah stared at Mrs. Homes with a puzzling look on her face, saying, "That makes no sense at all—hanging a man with no further proof than that is what I would call murder."

Mrs. Homes started weeping again. Rebekah hugged Mrs. Homes and said, "I have to leave now, Mrs. Homes. If you need anything while my men and I are here, just let me know before we leave."

Mrs. Homes took Rebekah by her hand and said softly, "Thank you for all that you have done, Rebekah. You and your men are welcome in my home anytime."

Later that evening, Rebekah, Jack, Bret, and Brad were in a restaurant eating and talking about this Constable Madison and his way of judgments.

"I don't like the way things turned out here either, Princess, but we come here for a vacation, and that's what we're going to have," Jack said.

"But, Jack, aren't you concerned about what has happened here? You told me of the wonderful life you had here growing up with Angela, and this doesn't bother you?"

"Of course, it bothers me, Princess, but that's the law here, and we're not here to interfere and get hung ourselves."

Bret poured more wine into his glass and said, "After I have finished my meal, Brad and I are heading down to the fencing school where Jack used to teach fencing. You want to come along, Princess?"

Rebekah, having other things on her mind, said, "You two go ahead. Jack and I might later."

Jack, knowing Rebekah and her stubbornness, said, "Princess, let's go down to my old fencing school. I'd like to show it to you, and I'd like to see how the new students are doing."

"All right, Jack, I'd like to see where you trained to fence, and later, you can show me around this town of Regend."

That evening, Constable Dirk Madison was at home waiting for his son to be back from the next town he was visiting. Just then, the door opened, and in walked his son, Corey.

"Son, how did things go in James Town with the job you were seeking?"

"It went great, Father. I'll be going back and forth once a week for training until I have the experience to take on a full-time job on my own."

"That's great, Corey. I knew persistence would eventually pay off."

"I'm tired, Father, from all the traveling back and forth. I'm going to bed now."

"What about dinner, son?"

"I've eaten already, Father. Good night."

117
TWO HANGINGS TOO MANY
1673

JACK CONVINCED REBEKAH to let things be and to enjoy herself and have the vacation she came there to have. Things were quiet there in Regend for a couple of days until fifty sacks of grain were missing from the warehouse.

"I don't know what happened to those fifty grain sacks, Constable Madison. When I took inventory last night, it was though they disappeared."

"You wouldn't be selling some grain sacks on the side now, would you, Mr. Michaels?"

"Constable Madison, I take an offence to that accusation."

"Just checking all the possibilities, Mr. Michaels. That's my job."

"What about those new people in town, Constable Madison?"

Mr. Michaels asked. "I'm having Judd Miller, my assistant, keep an eye on those four. You can bet your life on that."

That night, Madison's son was at home and his father was late getting home from the office, so he went to town searching for him. Corey went to his father's office, and Miller was there but not his father. Corey walked through the door, and Miller said, "Hi, Corey, your father said you were back. How is the new job coming along?"

"It's coming along fine, Mr. Miller. Do you know where my father is?"

"He left here three hours ago, Corey, and I thought he was going home."

Corey looked at Miller suspiciously while leaving out the door. Corey decided to go back home and wait for his father. Soon as Corey arrived back home, his father just returned.

"Father, where've you been, sir? I've been looking all over for you?"

"I took a walk, son. I was looking around town and went down the road a ways, trying to figure how those grain sacks were stolen from the warehouse."

"Have you any suspects, Father?"

"Nothing as of yet I can put my finger on, but sooner or later, the thief or thieves will make a mistake, and I'll bring them to trial."

Madison said, yawning, "Good night, Corey. I'm tired and have to get up early tomorrow morning."

Corey, with a hesitant speech, said, "You get your sleep, Father, and I'll see you in the morning for breakfast."

The next day, Rebekah was feeling insecure without her sword. She met with Bret and Brad early, giving them some orders. "I need you two to go back to the ship and bring back my sword and sheath and a pistol for each of us."

"What's wrong, Princess?" Bret asked.

"I don't feel comfortable without my sword, Brett. And when you two return, bring everything to my cabin where I'll hide them."

"We'll be back as soon as we can, Princess."

"One more thing, you two."

"Yes, Princess."

"Don't tell Jack."

"Why not, Princess?" Brad asked.

"I'll explain later, but for now, just follow my orders."

Later when Jack and Rebekah were having lunch, Jack inquired about Bret and Brad and their whereabouts.

"They don't have to be with us all the time, Jack. I came here to spend time with you, not them."

Jack grinned. "Yeah." He continued eating his sandwich. That night, Bret and Brad returned to Rebekah's room and brought her sword and some pistols.

"Where do we store the pistols and Jack's sword, Princess?"

Rebekah opened her closet door. "Put them up on the upper ledge, Brad, where they should be safe."

"Jack won't like this, Princess, if he finds out," Brad told her while putting the pistols and swords on the top ledge.

"What Jack doesn't know won't harm him, Brad," Rebekah said, smiling. Brad and Bret left. Brett said, "If Jack finds out what the princess had us do, Brad, they'll be arguing about it all the way back to Pirates Cove."

In the constable's office the next day, the man who owned the general store was telling Constable Madison about discovering all the store stock that was missing. Constable Madison went over the list asked, "When did you discover these items were out of stock, Marsh? Or did you sell these items and forgot to mark them down?"

"I was taking inventory last night as I always do every three months, and that's when I found out these items were missing, and I didn't sell them and forgot to mark them down."

"First, the pistols. That was easy to figure because the back door lock was broken, but how did these items get taken and there was no sign of entry?" Madison was talking out loud to himself.

"Who else has a key to your store, March?" Madison asked.

"Besides you, Constable? No one else," the storeowner said, now giving a suspicious look toward Constable Madison.

"I'll do some more investigating on this, Marsh. For now, you'll have to put this down as a loss to your store."

"Yeah," Marsh said, leaving and going back to his store.

That day, Corey went to his father's office to get some money for supplies they needed at home. Jack just happened to be walking by and noticed Madison walking out of the office with his son. Jack, always curious about somebody new, asked a town's person who the young man was.

"That's Constable Madison's son, Corey. He arrived back in town several days ago," the man said.

"Several days ago, huh," Jack answered.

"Yea, and you better mind your own business, mister, if you don't want any trouble from Constable Madison."

Jack went about his business.

That evening, Jack took Rebekah to meet Angela's parents, and when they arrived at the house, Jack knocked on the door. Mrs. Harris opened the door and said to Jack, "Jack, come in, and who's this lovely young lady you have with you?"

"This is Rebekah Martin. I, ah, we work on the same ship together."

Mrs. Harris inquired, "What possible work could a pretty young girl like you do on a ship, Rebekah?" Of course, Mrs. Harris was suspicious of this whole thing between Jack and Rebekah.

Rebekah was already getting nauseated by Mrs. Harris's suspicious question, but she answered nicely: "I do book work for the captain, Mrs. Harris."

"Oh, that's nice Rebekah, and I guess it gets kind of lonely being the only woman aboard a ship full of men."

Seeing Rebekah's right eyebrow raised, Jack intervened with, "Her father who's captain of the cargo ship who we work for really enjoys his daughter being there keeping up the paperwork. Right, Rebekah?" Jack said, trying to keep the peace.

"Why, yes, Jack, I love working with Father and all of his men," Rebekah responded back with a smile.

Mr. Harris entered the room and said, "Mrs. Harris just finished baking some cookies, Jack. Would you and your lovely friend, Rebekah, join us for some?"

While seated at the table eating some freshly baked cookies, Mr. Harris and Jack talked about Constable Madison most of the evening. Mrs. Harris and Rebekah just had "woman talk."

"Well, we better go, Jack. It's getting late!" Rebekah said, standing and ready to leave.

"Thank you for your hospitality, Mrs. Harris," Rebekah said kindly. "You're quite welcome, Rebekah."

Mrs. Harris was still curious about Rebekah and wasn't satisfied with the answers she got.

Before she left, Rebekah noticed Angela's painted picture hanging on the living room wall. Rebekah asked Jack, "Is this Angela's picture, Jack?"

"Yes, Prin...I mean Rebekah."

Rebekah stared at the picture of Angela and now knew why Jack loved her so much.

"She was very beautiful, Jack, like a morning in spring," Rebekah told him as they both were leaving out the front door.

After Jack and Rebekah were out of hearing distance, Mrs. Harris told Mr. Harris, "You know, dear, there's something strange about this Rebekah. It was like she was royalty."

"It was more like she was a sword fighter to me," Mr. Harris said, taking a bite of a cookie."

"A what?" Mrs. Harris asked.

"You didn't see the palm of her hands and how rough they were, my dear?"

"Her hands looked soft to me, Joel."

"She didn't get those rough palms from pen writing, Margret," Mr. Harris said, drinking some coffee and washing down his cookie.

The next few days, Rebekah was enjoying herself more, knowing that her trusty sword wasn't far away. Jack was telling her, "Well, Princess, I'm glad you've settled down and now enjoying your vacation." Jack was also having a good time being with Rebekah.

"Yes, Jack. I said to myself, 'I'm here, and that's what I'm supposed to do is have a good time,'" Rebekah said, giving Jack that great big beautiful princess smile. Jack gave Rebekah a second look because she only gives that certain smile when she's holding all the aces and very sure of things and herself.

That night, Jack took Rebekah back to her room and to say good night. Jack leaned over to kiss her. Rebekah whispered something into Jack's ear. "They do have a preacher here, Princess, and we can go back to the cove as husband and wife." Jack kissed her again.

"Oh, Jack, if only my job was finished, I would." Rebekah sighed when she went into her room and closed the door behind her.

The next day, things broke loose again as one of the farmers was accused of theft. The farmer known as Tom Bender was brought into town by Madison's assistant and two more other men. Miller had a sack full of some of the things the storeowner Marsh was missing from his store. Farmer Bender confronted Madison, saying. "I don't know where those things came from that I'm accused of stealing, Constable."

"They were found in your barn, Bender, by my men, and I know they didn't put them there."

"I didn't steal those things, Constable Madison, honest I didn't." He cried.

"I'll still have to lock you up, Bender until the trial. There's nothing I can do." Madison's trial start the day after a person had been brought in. He doesn't like to waste time on convicting someone and hanging them.

At the trial, Rebekah and her men were there, also watching this travesty happening again. During the trial, the farmer Bender couldn't prove his innocence, so they took him back to his cell for him to wait and to be hung the next day. After the trial, Rebekah stormed into the constable's office and asked,

"Why didn't you give Bender more time to prove his innocence, Constable Madison?"

"Miss, I don't know who you are or where you come from, but that's the way things are done here, and if you or your men interfere, I'll see to it the next hanging will be yours, understand?" He pulled a pistol from his desk drawer and pointed it at Rebekah.

"Yes, I understand, Constable Madison," Rebekah said but making plans of her own.

That evening, Rebekah told Bret and Brad what they were doing tomorrow—stopping a hanging. Jack passed by Rebekah's room and noticed she was talking to Bret and Brad and decided to listen in.

"Are you going to tell Jack, Princess, of what we're going to do?" Brad was asking.

Jack walked in and said, "Yes, Princess, you going to let me in on this little secret or whatever you're planning?"

"Brett, Brad, and I are stopping another useless hanging tomorrow. And don't try and interfere, Jack, and that's an order!"

Not letting Rebekah down, Jack said, "I don't like the way things are going on here either, Princess, so count me in."

"Brad."

"Yes, Princess."

"Bring down the swords and pistols from the closet."

"I knew you were holding some aces, Princess," Jack said upon seeing the weapons.

"Yes, Jack, if we don't stop this hanging tomorrow, it'll be two hangings too many!"

"All right, Princess, I'll meet you three in the square before the hanging, and we'll try and put a stop to it."

Jack couldn't sleep well that night, so he took a walk down the dirt road he and his brother would walk when they were little. Jack took a lantern and a pistol in case of a wolf or something that might attack him. Staring up at the moonlight, Jack was thinking, *It sure would be nice having Rebekah with me walking in this moonlight shining so bright.*

Jack walked down the dirt road and heard a horse and wagon coming down the road his way. He stepped behind a tree so as not to be seen. The wagon passed by, and with the bright moon shining, Jack saw who was driving the wagon. *I wonder where he's going this late at night with a wagon and a canvas over it,* Jack was thinking. Jack followed the wagon and hoped he could keep up. After a ten-minute run, Jack came upon two men talking under a tree, and now there were two wagons. Jack recognized one of the men but never saw the other man before. Jack blew the light out in his lantern, got closer, and listened to what they were saying.

118
THE BOOT ON THE OTHER FOOT
1673

"We better stop for a while, Jade. The people in town are getting suspicious, and we're running out of people to put the theft blame on."

"Yes, I understand," the other man said as he gave the man Jack recognized an envelope full of money. The man Jack didn't recognize got into the wagon with the canvas and drove away. The other man Jack recognized got into the empty wagon and went back to town. Jack took his time getting back to town thinking of a plan on the way and would tell Rebekah in the morning before the hanging.

The following morning before the hanging of the farmer Bender, Jack and Rebekah were having a little talk.

"Are you sure about this Jack?" Rebekah was asking.

"I'm very sure, Princess, of who I saw last night, and these two men have to be the ones doing the thefts and framing innocent people to get the law off their trail."

Rebekah stood there in amazement and couldn't believe what Jack had told her, but it all made sense to her now.

"Where's Bret, Jack? I see Brad standing across the square with his pistol ready."

"I sent Bret on a little errand, Princess. He should be back before the hanging starts."

Rebekah was wearing her sword fighting outfit this morning, and her sword was waiting for her in a big sack that Brad was holding while standing on the other side of the hanging tree.

As noon grew near, the townspeople gather for this big event, so does Rebekah and Jack. Miller brought out the farmer Bender with his hands tied behind him as he walked him over to the hanging tree. Madison ordered Bender to be put on a horse and the rope hanging from the tree to be put around his neck. Rebekah was getting restless. She asked Jack, "Where's Bret?"

Constable Madison opened up a rolled-up paper and began to read the charges against Bender. Bender cried out, "Madison, you've known me for seven years, and I was one of the men who voted you in for this job. How can you believe I stole the things your men found in my barn?"

"I have to go by the evidence, Bender, not friendship. Now let me continue reading the charges against you, or I'll just give the order now."

During the reading of charges, Bret returned with two envelopes in his hand and gave them to Jack. Soon as Madison was finished reading the charges against Bender, Rebekah got the nod from Jack to let her know everything was ready.

Madison, ready to tell the hangmen to do his job, was interrupted when Rebekah spoke up.

"Listen, all you people of Regend, Madison's son, Corey, has been doing the thefts in Regend and pinning the crimes on innocent townspeople."

The people standing around started murmuring about what Rebekah had told them.

Madison got furious and spoke out against Rebekah, "I told you if you and your men interfered with the law, I'd put a rope around your neck as well!"

"I don't think so, Constable Madison," Rebekah said. Jack, Brad, and Bret pulled their pistols and pointed them at Madison and his men.

"Brad."

"Yes, Princess."

"Remove that devilish rope from around Bender's neck."

"Yes, Princess, right away." Brad removed the rope and helped Bender from off the horse.

"I'll see to it you'll be the next one to swing from that tree, woman," Madison shouted out to Rebekah.

Rebekah confronted Madison, telling him again, "Your son and another man who doesn't live in this town have been doing the stealing and planting some of the stolen goods on people's property knowing you would hang them fast before they could prove their innocence."

"That's a lie!" Madison shouted back.

Rebekah motioned for Jack to come over with the two envelopes he was holding in his hand. Jack handed the envelopes to Madison and said, "Open the envelopes, Constable, and see for yourself."

Madison was opening the envelopes when his son came walking up, asking, "I thought you were hanging Farmer Bender today, Father?"

Madison, with his mind on what was inside the envelopes, didn't answer Corey's question. Then Corey noticed the envelopes his father was opening.

Madison stared at Rebekah and asked, "Where did you get these envelopes full of money?"

"Bret, my man over there, found them in your son's bedroom hidden in a desk drawer."

"That's a lie! He wouldn't steal from anybody, and I taught him better than that."

Corey spoke out in fear, "They're trying to frame me, Father, so Farmer Bender will go free for stealing, and you know that."

"I know that, son, and when this is over, they'll hang for this outrage, I promise you." After Madison said that, one of his men knocked the pistol from Bret's hand and pulled his sword.

Rebekah walked toward Bret and said, "Brett, hand me my sword." Rebekah approached the man holding her sword, ordering him, "Put your sword down, mister."

He laughed and said, "You have a choice, miss, die from my sword or hang from that tree." Rebekah raised her sword in a defensive move, and then the swords were in action as the man tried to cut Rebekah down.

"You haven't a chance, mister," Rebekah told him while backing him farther and farther. The man started to make a stand against Rebekah when she ran her sword through his right side. He let out a scream while falling to the ground. Rebekah went back over to where Constable Madison was standing. "He's not dead, Constable, but he could've been if I wished it."

Madison watched some of the townspeople take the man Rebekah almost killed to the doctor's office, thinking it could've been his son.

"I'm getting tired of playing your games, woman. What is it you want here?" Madison asked.

"The name is Rebekah, and I want nothing but the law to be done fairly."

"Your accusing my son of stealing will get you and your men hung, Rebekah, and I'm not holding a trial next time."

"What if my man, Jack, can prove what we're saying is true? Would you believe it then, Constable?"

Corey, close to running in fear of his life, shouted out, "They're lying, Father. It's a trick. Don't believe them,"

Jack spoke up in front of the townspeople, "I guess Madison's son is exempted from Madison's law and justice here in Regend. What do you think, Rebekah?" Jack said, trying to temp Madison into proving him wrong.

"My son is innocent," Madison exclaimed again. "Then you won't mind taking a short walk down a dusty road, will you, Madison?" Jack had Madison in a corner.

"I don't know what you have in mind, but I'll go with you to prove you're lying about my son."

Corey said, "Father, it's a trick. Don't let them do this."

"It's all right, son. They have no proof, and I'll go just to prove them wrong." He then put his hand on Corey's shoulder for support.

"Which way?" Madison said.

Corey started to go the other way when Bret pointed his pistol toward him and said, "You're going too." Brett stuck his pistol in Corey's side, motioning him to get going.

Madison, not liking the treatment his son was getting, cried out, "You vermin will pay for this humiliation you're giving me and my son when I prove his innocence."

Jack took everybody down the dirt road where he followed the wagon last night. When they all came to a clearing under a tree, Madison spoke up, "Why are you bringing us here? There's nothing to show us but these old trees."

"Yes, there is Madison," Jack said, bending down and pointing to the ground. "All I see is some dirt and some footprints," Madison told Jack.

"Yes, and some of them are your son's footprints," Jack replied.

"So my son was here. That proves nothing," Madison exclaimed.

"Tell me, Constable, what would your son be doing with a wagon full of supplies meeting someone here at night under this tree?" Jack then pointed at the wagon wheel tracks in the soft dirt.

Madison bent down to get a closer look at the two sets of footprints and the two sets of wagon tracks. He then looked back at Corey.

"They're lying, Father. They did all of this, the wagon tracks and the footprints." Corey was now ready to run.

Now having his doubts, Madison said, "Come over here, son, and let me see if your boot prints matches these on the ground."

"Their lying, Father."

"If they are, son, then your boot prints won't match and this will all be over."

"No, Father, I won't, and if you love me, you won't make me."

"I said walk over here, son!"

"All right, I will. I've nothing to hide."

"All right, son, if your boot prints don't match up to these prints, we'll go home and forget this nightmare." Corey set his boot next to the first print; it wasn't as big. Corey hesitated setting his foot next to the other boot print.

"Well, son, go ahead. Set your foot next to the other print."

Knowing it was his, Corey took off running. Jack tripped him as he went by. Corey fell to the ground, saying, "All right, I'm guilty. I did the stealing!" Corey lay on the ground, crying in the dust.

Madison stood over his son and said, "Stop that sniffling and stand up like a man and face me." Corey stood to his feet and stared at his father with rebellion in his eyes. Madison was emotional. He asked, "Why did you do it, son?"

"You, Father, that's why. You made it so easy with your quick to hang ways. That's why."

Looking down on Corey, Madison said, "I've hung several innocent men who were never guilty, and you stand there with a smirk on your face."

"What are you going to do now, Father, hang me?" Corey said in bitterness.

Madison drew back his fist and hit Corey so hard he knocked him to the ground. Corey sat back up, rubbing the blood from his face. Madison turned his back and said, "You're no longer my son, and you'll face the same law and justice I gave out to others."

Jack told Corey, "Get to your feet." They took Corey back to Regend to face justice.

The next day, Madison was leaving Regend and turning himself into parliament for disciplinary actions for hanging one man he now knew was innocent, but he wasn't sure about the other men. Jack and Rebekah were in his office asking about his son, Corey.

"I'm taking Corey with me, Rebekah. He'll face the same charges that I'll face plus theft."

"I'm truly sorry, Madison, and I wished this would've turned out different."

"You did me a great service, Rebekah. If you and your men wouldn't have intervened, I would've kept hanging innocent men and continued to add more innocent blood to my hands and my son would've kept being a thief."

Rebekah and Jack left Madison's office. Rebekah spoke up, "Jack, I've had enough vacation time. Let's get back to the ship and sail home."

Before Jack left, Angela's parents came to town to wish Jack a safe trip to where he was going. When Rebekah, Jack, Brett, and Brad left, Mrs. Harris looked at Mr. Harris and said, "Am I seeing things today different, or was the girl Jack introduced us to wearing a dress when we first met her?"

"Yes, I think she was, but now she's wearing what looks like pirate clothes and carrying a sword."

Mrs. Harris looked at her husband and said, "You're right, dear. She must be a sword fighter."

They watched Jack leave and wondered what Jack got himself into now.

Back on the *Black Rose*, Jack and Rebekah were back by the railing that evening after dinner.

"Jack, I was wondering, how did you know which boot prints were Corey's?"

"Well, Princess, that morning, I went back to that clearing and was hoping the wagon tracks and boot prints would still be there, or Madison would never believe my story. Corey getting scared and panicking helped as I figured he would. You didn't realize you had such a smart first mate, did you, Princess?" Jack said, grinning from ear to ear.

"Yes, Jack, luck was on your side too."

Jack asked, puzzled, "How do you figure, Princess?"

"What if it had rained, Jack, and washed the boot and wagon tracks away? How could you prove Corey was guilty then?" Rebekah leaned up, kissed Jack, and told him good night.

Author's Note

I hope the journey with the princess has been an exciting one thus far. More adventures to come with death and intrigue around the corner. Will her pirates stay loyal and continue to stand by the princess's side? Will Henry Morgan finally have his victory and hang the princess? The following books will have the answers to these questions and other mysteries that are yet to be solved.